Mo,

This book is meant to help pick up your spirit, during this important Rehab period.

Best of Luck our prayers & hope have been with you since day 1.

Betty & El

Coyote

Coyote

A NOVEL

PETER GADOL

CROWN PUBLISHERS, INC.
NEW YORK

Author's Note: Thanks to my parents, Charles Gadol, Paula Roy, and Rusty Gutwillig. Special thanks to David Groff and his expert blue pencil. I owe a great deal to Mary Evans, and words cannot adequately express my gratitude.—P.G.

Copyright © 1990 by Peter Gadol

Published by Crown Publishers, Inc., 201 East 50th Street, New York, New York 10022

CROWN is a trademark of Crown Publishers, Inc.

Manufactured in the United States of America

Library of Congress Cataloging-in-Publication Data

Gadol, Peter.
Coyote / by Peter Gadol.
p. cm.
I. Title.
PS3557.A285S7   1990

813'.54—dc20

89-38608
CIP

ISBN 0-517-57549-3

Design by Jake Victor Thomas

10 9 8 7 6 5 4 3 2 1

First Edition

For Stephen

ONE

*P*erhaps she had heard the story before. Madeleine had been sitting in the sparse but luxurious shade of the Great Tree with her knees tucked into her arms, but when I started to tell the myth of Arbol Magnifico, she fell back onto her elbows and stared at the sky. Something in the way she scanned the branches, not with her mouth agape in awe but rather with a placid grin of familiarity, led me to believe that she had indeed been here before, that she had on some other occasion taken refuge from the same June sun, white and empty. Maybe she did not interrupt me because she was afraid we would have had nothing to talk about while we waited for the guru to drive past. I hesitated but plunged forward anyway and told the story of Arbol Magnifico, which was fine, because I enjoyed telling it.

The Great Tree stood on a ridge at the edge of a savanna, what most referred to as grassland. If you drove down from the mountains, it appeared to you as a slow stripping away of green, a bleaching that left even the sky seeming meek and barely present. Trees disappeared and were replaced by low and pale shrubs. By the time you got to the village of Frescura, the mountains and hills appeared as a purple line, a dream to the north and west. Rivers became arroyos only occasionally engendered by rain. Then, you drove another ten miles to the ridge and beyond it you saw a desolate dryness, an endless desert. But above the desert, high on the ridge, stood an anomaly, the Great Tree. From a distance, it looked like the silhouette of a giant splayed hand sitting on the horizon. No one knew how it got there, and no one knew how it survived. It had endured so long: a stubby but massive trunk supporting a hemisphere of long branches, thick to the tips. Its plumage was perfectly verdant with a bluish tint against the pallid, cloudless sky. It leaned somewhat, listed toward the desert it presided over, toward the immense landscape of clay and cactus.

The tree became a celebrated monument throughout the Southwest, though few actually traveled here to pay it homage. It had been here before people, and when the Spanish settled Frescura over four hundred years ago, they broke off a low and particularly bluish branch of the Great Tree to use as a reliquary for their new church. While the Great Tree fit into a new religious iconography, it lasted as an empty symbol, one that accepted the meanings you imposed upon it: hope or last resort, genesis or the end of the world.

I thought the tree looked sad, despite the myths that it spawned. To me, anyway, it seemed that it had grown and reigned as much as it was going to, that the bark was turning flaky and dark. However, one childhood perspective never changed. When I was little, I would hike up here and climb into the first low intersection of the trunk and branches so that I could look down at the desert and count the cactus plants as far as I could see. Then I counted yellow blossoms. I thought that I sat perched at the center of the universe, that everything else in the world radiated from this point.

Ultimately a road was built alongside the Great Tree, but it was a minor highway that no one ever used and that was constructed in the days when things were built mostly to combat unemployment. The road had never been finished, although a small crew continued to pave the futile line of gravel across the plain. Few wanted to drive across the desert, an awesome and possibly dangerous journey.

Now the legend was, I told her, that once upon a time the air around here was so completely listless—it still was as lifeless as an abandoned house, the furniture covered in sheets—that the leaves of the tree never stirred and went undisturbed for weeks. When the leaves of the tree did ruffle, when its limbs perhaps swayed, when possibly the tip of the squat tower bowed (and assuming someone was here to witness this odd moment), it was considered an omen.

Then five years ago an ashram was established ten miles beyond the tree, and now the leaves were ruffled at least once a day at three in the afternoon when the guru zoomed past in his limousine, accompanied by a caravan of jeeps.

As I started to tell the story of Arbol Magnifico, I couldn't see Madeleine's eyes behind dark sunglasses, and I couldn't tell whether she listened. In fact, she probably wasn't listening at all. Pilgrims about to step into the other world of the desert usually had only one thing on their mind, their new life, and at that point I still thought she was a pilgrim. I didn't care though, because I was used to dealing with strangers, I was used to babbling and playing the enthusiastic, faithful tour guide to my native terrain.

Once upon a time, a long time ago—when it was exactly does not matter—there was a lonely woman in Frescura who had tried to bear a child for fifty years. For fifty years she had failed. She was miserable. Finally she deemed that her life was not worth living if she couldn't produce a baby. She decided to bury herself alive, far away where no one would see her. She would once and for all put an end to her relentless suffering. So she went to the Great Tree, thinking that in its patch of shade she would find some kind of final peace. With her bare hands she carved out a grave in the cool soil at its roots. It took a whole day and night and another day. When she was done, she climbed into the shallow trench. She began to shovel the loose dirt over her body. And then, all of a sudden, with her legs already covered in soil, she felt an unmistakable warmth in her belly. The fecund earth around the tree had nourished her body. And sure enough, nine months later, she gave birth to a healthy son, who without a moment's thought was named Arbol. He grew up and became a prominent Frescuran, and by the time he was sheriff he was called Arbol Magnifico.

Under Arbol Magnifico's leadership, Frescura fared quite well. This was when the town, as small as it was, emerged as a trading post, when the river still flowed. People were content. And then disaster struck. Around here, the sun was very white, just as it was colorless today, and the light had a cleansing effect. In a place where there were so few plants, the sun became the principal form of life. When disaster struck the happy town of Frescura, a kind of eclipse took place.

Disaster took the form of a bandit, who became known as El Moreno, the dark one. About once a month, with no warning, El Moreno galloped into town on a fantastically quick stallion, and he raided Frescura. He robbed the bank, the general store, and he even stole the coins left in the church collection plate. He swooped down upon Frescura during the long siestas, and he fled so quickly that Arbol Magnifico and his deputies could never overtake him. El Moreno kept looting Frescura, and each time he descended so swiftly out of the sleepy heat of midday that he was never caught. Arbol Magnifico began to make it his mission in life to seize the bandit. He was practically attached to the saddle of his horse, ready to pounce upon him.

And Arbol did chase El Moreno. The whole town chased the bandit, as far as the Great Tree. But it seemed as if the bandit simply dashed over the ridge into the vast valley of the desert and disappeared. From the perch by the Great Tree, you should be able to see a galloping horse. But Arbol only saw the cacti, which occasionally cast shadows, murky mirages of El Moreno and his stallion, but only mirages. What was the secret?

"What was the secret?" I asked her.

She sat up. "Uh, what? Oh, the secret. I don't know. Something to do with the tree?"

"Exactly," I said.

What happened was that as soon as El Moreno reached the meager bit of shade the Great Tree provided, he came to a halt. He dismounted and waited for the sheriff and townspeople to arrive. In the shade of the Great Tree, the bandit found that he could make himself invisible. After one of his raids, he had come to the Great Tree and on the verge of being captured, he closed his eyes and prayed for some kind of shield. The lone tree heard a desperate plea, because it listened without prejudice to the whispers of every distraught soul. When Arbol and his friends arrived, they could not even hear the bandit snicker.

In time, the sheriff Arbol Magnifico went mad. The town was slowly drained of its livelihood—no one wanted to trade anything there, no one had any money. The bank's empty vault possessed a chilling echo. El Moreno continued his raids and he always got away. The town became poor, unhappy, dismal. The spirit of poverty was more defeating than the actual hardship itself. Arbol went mad and one hot day, he pressed a gun against his temple and pulled the trigger. Frescura mourned. They buried their defeated hero in the cool soil of the Great Tree where according to legend he had been conceived.

The day Arbol Magnifico was buried, El Moreno had the audacity to strike once more. He rode into town, robbed the bank, and sped away into his magical shade. This time all the people of Frescura, men, women, and children, chased the bandit. They all followed him to the Great Tree. They all pursued the ruthless bandit. And under the tree, he snickered, They'll never catch me, never. Well, lo and behold, the bandit El Moreno found that he was being grabbed by the shoulder and thrown to the ground and kicked in the back. The Frescurans all roared and cheered. They'd caught him. What had happened? As soon as Arbol Magnifico was returned to the soil of the Great Tree, the shade that had cloaked the bandit ceased to hide him. To his chagrin, he was nabbed. The Frescurans immediately hanged him from a branch of the tree.

Oh, if only Arbol Magnifico had lived to see this, to catch him, someone cried. Well, he can, someone else said. How? Of course. So they buried the bandit there, at the roots of the Great Tree, right where they had laid Arbol to rest. And so, for all eternity, the sheriff would finally catch the bandit. Over and over, every instant, the sheriff would achieve certain victory.

When you think about it, though, the townspeople were assuming that they had endowed the legacy of the sheriff with a happy ending. But what they did was to plant two men's corpses together in the shade of the strange tree. And over time, what could happen, but the remains of good would mix with the remains of evil. They said that when the limbs of the tree rocked, it was an omen. The Frescurans were too busy to notice that when the noose of the hanged man was cut, when the rope was severed after the bandit's neck had snapped and the body fell to the spot where they'd bury it, the branches of the Great Tree swung up and down.

"Where did you pick up that story?" Madeleine asked me in the way you might say, Where did you get those boots? so you could buy some for yourself. She walked over to her car, reached in, and pulled out a plastic container full of lemonade. She handed it to me.

"When I was little," I said between gulps, "I used to visit an old man on a pueblo, and he'd put me on his knee and tell me stories."

"Great." She seemed unimpressed.

As she should have. I made that up. When you lived around here, you knew everything, you were born with the stories in your blood. I didn't know where I had heard it. In fact, I knew that I had added some details to what I had been told, but I couldn't remember what they were. However, something about this lady inspired sincerity.

"Actually, I didn't spend a lot of time listening to old men. I don't know where I heard the story."

This woman who had picked me up hitchhiking twenty miles south of the Great Tree, outside Frescura, was strange indeed. I rarely told the truth, except to Frog and not even to him sometimes, yet she brought the truth out of me. She just was not your average pilgrim about to devote her life to the guru and his cult in the desert.

"You're not your average pilgrim," I admitted.

"Who said I'm a pilgrim? I never said that."

"But you said you wanted me to take you to Rancho Flora."

"Does that mean I'm a pilgrim?"

"Well, you're not from around here," I said. She wasn't, or she would have been darker. As it was, her pale skin was getting a little pink. She would wake up tomorrow with a sunburn.

"I'm not a pilgrim," she repeated.

"Then why are we waiting for the guru to drive past?"

"I want to see the parade," she said, and then finished drinking the lemonade. Defensively she added, "You said you could set your watch by when the guru went to get his ice cream cone each day."

"You can."

"Three o'clock."

"So?"

"Well, I want to see it." Her hair was very short, long in front, and parted on one side, but she managed to tuck her gray-blond bang behind one ear. And we waited for the guru.

"If you're not a pilgrim"—I tried to sound polite but not too intrigued—"then why are you interested in Rancho Flora?"

"None of your business," she said flatly. She was getting anxious and started pacing the stretch of road by the tree. I gathered that she did not like to wait for anything.

"Okay." I nodded.

"What flavor?" she asked. She walked over to her car and pulled out a slim pad of paper. A stenographer's notebook.

"What flavor?" I repeated. It sounded logical to her, but I was lost.

"Is everyone this slow around here? Is it the heat? What flavor ice cream?" She looked exasperated.

"Ah. The guru always has two scoops in a sugar cone dipped in chocolate sauce. Uh, let's see. . . . Mint chocolate chip and peach."

She wrote down what I said. Then she looked at me, rolled her eyes, and threw her pad back in the car. "You're making it up."

Right she was. "How can you be sure?"

She didn't answer. She strolled over to the ridge and looked out over the desert. "Damn," she muttered to herself. "It's been a long time."

"What has?"

"Since I played in that." She waved to the desert.

"You've been here before?" Another unanswered question.

Even though we did not have an audience, I felt as if I were being upstaged. Usually when I led pilgrims to Rancho Flora, they were quietly puzzled by me. Who was this young, dark fellow who knew so much about life on the edge of the desert? They asked all sorts of questions about my past, which licensed me to fabricate elaborate fictions, my favorite being about how I was in reality a brilliant young rancher gone bankrupt who now survived by feasting on rotting cattle by the roadside and by selling the bones to still-life painters. I tried to be mysterious, and when people stopped asking questions, I usually resented them. I had started to answer her questions with unfamiliar honesty. I had the opportunity to lie with every breath, but I did not feel the need.

"Look." She pointed out at what appeared to be a cactus. "Look, he's coming."

And sure enough, the afternoon was nearing three o'clock, and due east a glint appeared on the horizon. At first it was a silver flash, intermittent and possibly a figment. Then the pulse evolved into a constant beam of light becoming more intense with each second. Then it was a slow train moving toward us that seemed as if it would eventually creep up to our feet and pass beneath us.

I felt as if she were going to cheer it on, she seemed so suddenly elated, nodding in amazement. Then something I had seen many times before, but not really looked at very closely, whizzed past. It was a long silver car, a stretch limousine, with impenetrable tinted glass, and with three jeeps driving behind it. In the jeeps were members of the ashram. They wore their usual garb, a uniform, a red-purplish jumpsuit. "Mauve people," she said. That was what they were called by the outside world, though they referred to themselves as pilgrims. The men and women in the jeeps appeared entirely normal. They looked young and fit, tanned by the desert sun.

Though I had ushered many into the desert, I knew very little about the pilgrims. I had only dealt with them (after they had entered Rancho Flora) on one occasion, three weeks earlier, when a gang of them stole Frog's meteorite right out from under us. They crept into the desert in the middle of the night and nonchalantly snatched our astronomical find.

When the limousine passed, we gazed into the rear windows. I had never seen the guru who had become the villainous king in the new mythologies of Frescura, the Great Tree, and its dry environs. And we didn't get much of a glimpse of him now. Through the smoky glass we saw an instant of white: beard, hat, and cloth. There was something at once godly and ghostly about the image.

"He's licking his lips," she said to me.

I couldn't verify this because the limousine and jeeps had passed in a breath, leaving a trail of exhaust that made the hot pavement ripple. I looked up at the branches of the Great Tree and watched the leaves try to gain control, the broad and pointy leaves flapping against one another and fluttering in the man-made breeze. They rustled for a long while and settled as the stuporous heat squelched the last trace of the parade. And then we got in her car and were on our way, to the ashram in the desert, and the tree quivered one more time.

*E*arlier in the day, a small blue car had pulled over to the shoulder of the highway. That was when I met her.

"Okay," she said in a voice of concession, "where do you want to go?"

"Toward Frescura," was all I said.

"Get in." She opened the door. She sighed, and I could tell that as a rule she usually did not pick up hitchhikers. She said nothing for the first couple of minutes despite my questions: "Where are you headed?" and so on. She was older than most pilgrims, not elderly at all but middle-aged and graying. Most pilgrims were in their thirties.

I could tell a great deal about the driver who picked me up in the middle of nowhere, because when I first examined the stranger, I was drawn to two telling traits: how the person's hands gripped the steering wheel, and the manner in which these hands drove. Madeleine's hands were long and skinny. Beneath pale, freckled skin I could almost see the bones as she grasped the wheel. Veins sturdy and green. She was pale, yes, but there was something completely rugged about her, and I got that from her driving. She sped along the road with one thin eyebrow raised above the metal frame of her sunglasses. She looked suspicious of what lay ahead. She seemed not to be watching the road, but rather to be surveying the region in disbelief. How could it be so barren?

"Well, what's your name and what the hell are you doing standing in the middle of the highway in the middle of nowhere, trying to get killed?" she asked—laughed to herself—in one breath.

"Well, I was just walking." I smiled. I tried to be cute and charming.

"No, no, no, that's what people hitching always say. I never understand it. I mean, how did you get where you were, if you didn't have a car? Did you spontaneously generate out of a shrub, or did you just walk down the road and say, okay, now I'll turn around, except I don't feel like walking back?"

"Okay," I nodded. Strange lady, I thought.

"And?"

"And what?" I couldn't tell why she seemed so belligerent. Had she been driving for too long?

"And what's your name, stranger?"

"Coyote," I answered.

"Your name is Coyote? What kind of name is Coyote, Coyote?"

"I'm not sure, but it's *my* name."

"Just Coyote?"

It is the one thing I never lie about.

"No," I said. "Coyote is my first name, Gato is my last name."

"Gato? That's Spanish. For cat, isn't it?"

"Yes."

"So, you're name is Coyote Gato—wild-dog cat?"

"Why not?"

"It's great," she said. She glanced at a trailer parked on the side of the highway. A sign announced weekly bingo at a nearby pueblo.

"And you?" I asked. "What's your name?"

She ignored the question and only muttered my name to herself in private amusement. I had to ask her three more times before she answered me.

We soon came to a fork in the highway, and Madeleine quickly noted that there were no signs, only the posts where signs had once stood beside the road. She shook her head. "Now where?"

Luckily she did not see—and only one person I had played this trick on ever had—the thin sheets of metal lying off the road under some brush. I hid the signs so that I, the hitchhiker, would have to be tapped for a lesson in local geography. And then soon after that, I would have sifted the pilgrims from the passersby. I would be able to secure my position as a paid guide to the gates of Rancho Flora. I would have guaranteed my fee as the Sherpa at the edge of the desert.

"Well, hell," Madeleine groaned. "Now where?"

"Are you going to Rancho Flora?" I asked innocently.

"Maybe."

"Are you going to Rancho Flora?" I asked again, making it clear that I could identify her as a pilgrim, she could not disguise herself. There was no hiding it.

"Yes, sure, okay. Which road do I take?"

"That one," I pointed to the right. "But you'll have to pass through Frescura. And if they find out in Frescura that you're on the way to the ashram, they'll arrest you for speeding or something, anything to detain you for hours. Then they'll force you into the church to make a confession instead of continuing on to the cult. They nab pilgrims twice a day." An exaggeration for effect. "But I could get you through safely." I sounded confident.

"Where?" She wasn't even paying attention to me, she was busy maneuvering the car down the correct path.

"To where you want to go."

"For a price, no doubt," she snorted. "All right, all right, Mr. Coyote Gato, you just get me to Rancho Flora."

So my plan had worked once again, I was enlisted. This introduction was more abrupt than usual, but that didn't matter. I figured she would be good for ten dollars, and I would get to tell my stories. However, if anyone was being led somewhere, it was not her but me.

I had woken up this morning in my trailer—alone, as had been the case for the last year—with a dull ache in the small of my skull. The day before I had ushered a station wagon carrying four pilgrims to Rancho Flora and squeezed fifty dollars out of them. Now normally I would have blown that all at the café, but they were getting tired of me there. Everyone was increasingly hostile, and recently, I also simply did not enjoy anyone else's company. I really didn't want to be alone so much, but I didn't have much choice. You either liked everyone or you were a hermit like Frog, the meteorite-chasing ex-physicist. When I was in my teens, I used to hang out with Frog at his ranch—he was my mentor, and for a long time I wanted to live my life the way Frog lived his. But he was in his fifties, and with only a score and a year to my name, I was too young to follow his model just yet.

I admit that I had never tried very hard to fit in. I had a speech I gave to the lizards who lived underneath my trailer: I'm in a rut. I've been sad for a year, maybe longer, I'm tired of feeling this way. I feel incomplete. What should I do? But lizards are useless psychiatrists, and I just want to terrorize the little dragons. So with the fifty dollars I bought some beer and lemonade, and I went home to my trailer, and I sat outside and drank until it seemed as if the stars were moving around in an infinitely slow waltz.

I woke up with a hangover and drank some leftover lemonade and found my boots, which were lying on the ground somewhere, the least torn of my torn jeans, also outside, and a fresh T-shirt. Then, looking as dandy as I could in this groggy state, I hiked up to a nearby pueblo and hitched a ride to where the signs were still scattered from the previous day.

I had been doing this for a year. I had perfected my routine. But I was bored. I hitched rides with pilgrims and got them to Rancho

Flora, on the way describing as much local history as I could cram in twenty or thirty miles. I felt urgent about the stories, I really did, because inside the ashram I was sure the perspective was very different. I lived on what money they gave me at the gate to the ashram. It was lucrative, because in the last year, at least one hundred people came to Rancho Flora, and they somehow had to find the oasis in the desert. They knew that they would travel for days in circles if they couldn't find the place, and they knew that they would die of dehydration out there. What no one ever realized was that the entrance to the ashram was really quite visible from the road, and there was only one road to take, and anyone could find Rancho Flora. I wasn't needed at all, but that didn't matter because I was entertaining. I made enough money doing this. I had only the cult to thank, the cult that everyone in the area passionately despised.

"Have you lived here long?" Madeleine asked me.

"All my life."

"Your parents from these parts, too?"

"My mother was a member of a pueblo," I explained. A pretty, tan woman, I had been told. "I never knew her."

"She named you Coyote?"

"After her cat, which she had also named Coyote, because Coyote was her favorite character in the stories her grandfather would tell her when she was young."

"And Gato?"

I didn't want to get into it. "Oh, it's complicated." I hesitated. A few fibs, used and thrice-told each, came to mind. Unintentionally, the truth spilled out.

"One day my mother was in Frescura with her cat, and the cat jumped out of the front seat of her pickup truck, and the animal dashed down the road toward the desert."

"Why?"

"No one knows. My mother was dumbfounded. Anyway, she could have hopped in the truck and driven after it, but for some reason, she chased it on foot."

"Why?"

"No one knows. So my mother ran after her cat for ten miles."

"That's far."

"It got to the point where she couldn't turn around to get the truck because she might have lost the cat forever. So they just kept running, all the way to the Great Tree. Another thing I don't know"—I anticipated her question—"was why the cat stayed on the road, why it didn't stray off toward some fun shrub to hide in. And just when my mother, ten yards back from the galloping creature, thought she would catch up to him, the cat climbed the Great Tree."

"What kind of cat?" This woman had a penchant for detail.

"A big fluffy orange one with green eyes." So I had been told. "And Coyote the cat looked down at my mother with these green eyes, and he meowed when she reached up to him and meowed when he realized that he couldn't get down and that she couldn't grab him."

"Silly cat," Madeleine said.

"Well, it had been a quiet day in Frescura," I continued, "and when my mother chased after the cat, it had been noon, at the beginning of the siesta. And no one saw her run down the highway toward the Great Tree, except for one man." He would through an act of violence become my father and destroy my mother. "This man—I never found out his name—saw my mother with her flowing black hair run after the cat. The man got in the abandoned pickup truck and drove behind my mother, but far enough behind so that she could not hear the engine."

"Uh-oh." Madeleine frowned.

"When the man got to the tree, it was clear what the problem was. And he said, 'You could climb the tree and get down the *gato.*'"

"What did your mother do?"

"She said nothing and began to reach toward the lowest branches. The strange man grabbed her waist as if he would give her a boost, but instead he held her firmly. 'Okay,' my mother said, indicating that she was ready for a lift."

"A bad move," Madeleine murmured.

"'Okay,' the man repeated, and he pulled my mother to the ground, and soon she was screaming for all the world to hear, for the entire desert as far as it stretched. But no one was around. So he ripped her dress, and he ignored her scratches, her punches, and my father raped my mother."

"Oh, hell," Madeleine said. She seemed bothered.

"Then the cat acted. It dropped from the tree onto the man, landed on his shoulder, clawed him, and bit his neck. I don't think it meant to go for his jugular, it just meant to scare him off. But it did nip some vital cord, and the man jumped into the truck and drove away."

"Wow."

"My mother somehow picked herself up"—I sat up straight in the car seat—"and slowly she walked back to Frescura. The cat followed quietly, head low." I imitated the animal.

"My mother got back to town. It was dark. She saw her truck on the edge of the road. She wondered why no one had seen it. Maybe they had and they didn't want to deal with its contents. Because there was my father"—to call him my father stung—"slumped against the steering wheel, all cold and stiff. He had bled to death."

"What happened to your mother?"

"Well, there was some kind of investigation, but my mother ran away as soon as possible and took the cat with her. She was afraid it would be put to sleep for having murdered the man."

"A capital offense."

"But the cat wasn't a murderer, he was a hero. And my mother was a fugitive in her own mind, whether or not the sheriff pursued her, and she gave birth to me under the stars out in the desert. She named me Coyote, after her cat, whom she preferred to think of as my father. And she named me Gato, because in some way she wanted to acknowledge my horrible birth, and the fact of the matter was that the man who raped her had spoken Spanish. I was born and my mother disappeared." I repeated the basic facts. "I grew up here and there with this name, for the longest time truly believing I had been fathered by a cat. After all, look, I have the cat's green eyes."

Madeleine didn't say much after all this. She continued to stare at the road and at the town we were about to enter. I felt somewhat empty, as I did whenever the story of my birth was revealed or told. Frog had taught me to be proud of my name. He knew all the Native stories about Coyote, and he said he'd rather have my name than his any day. He'd rather be feline than reptilian. To be a wild-dog cat—that would throw people off, he said, make them wonder.

I was a celebrity as a child. Everyone was predisposed to believe that since I was conceived amidst the combined forces of good and evil in the cool soil beneath the Great Tree, I had to possess a certain mystical potential. I convinced myself of this, too, because one day when I was young, I sat in a field, looked in the distance, and I decided I wanted it to rain. Not just rain, but thunder. So I willed an electrical storm, and lo and behold I saw clouds gathering far away. Soon enough it rained in the distance, and heat lightning flashed all around like a white river gorging through the sky. I sat in the field and watched the full duration of the storm miles off, but it never came overhead of me. I was in control.

When I told an old man named Carl who worked in the gas station about this the next day, he said that all little boys believed that they contained such magnificence, and I was no different. He laughed and laughed and told his saloon buddies, and I vowed then and there never to tell anyone about my secret powers, should I discover any others. Which I did. I also learned early on that I did possess a certain feline self. I'm half cat. *I can turn myself into a cat.*

That is to say, I can be alone wandering the edge of the desert, and without any fuss or bother I can become a cat with green eyes. I only divulged this once. I told James after he'd lived with me for a while—he believed anything anyone said. He did ask me to show him, but I had to say no, because I can only become a cat when I am alone. Actually, I remember that I did once try to turn into a cat for him. I guess I failed, and he simply asked me why I was lying facedown in the dirt. Maybe someone has spotted me among the low shrubs at dusk, the silhouette of haunches and a skinny tail running along against the pink sky. No one could see me undergo the transformation, but someone could have seen me after I had become the cat. That was possible. Maybe others have seen what James saw—a man crawling around the earth like a drunkard. I have never looked in a mirror after becoming a cat, I never will.

With Madeleine, I stopped just short of my cat confession. She was someone to follow, this woman who had to be twenty-five, thirty years older than me. I knew from the start this woman couldn't be lied to. She was the sort of person you learned things from just by tagging along.

When we drove into Frescura, she asked me, "Do you know a good place to get a bite to eat?"

"Do I know a place?" I said. "The Sunflower Lives Café, over there." I pointed to the diner toward the middle of the main drag.

Frescura was a tiny town of maybe ten streets, which all folded into a skewed grid. The streets here lacked signs (no fault of mine), and a dry river cut diagonally past the whitewashed adobe church in the center of town. That church had an empty belfry and a white cross that reached into the sky, taller than any other point in the basin. Every building was adobe, including the general store, the school, the post office with its long porch. Most people did not live in the town, but rather on ranches or pueblos that were positioned on skimpy extensions of the roads that converged in the downtown. Frescura was a small village, yet it was a key town. Everyone was proud that while on the county map it should have been represented with only a tiny dot to signify a small population, it actually won a dot with a circle around it, which meant that it was the oldest community in the county (though not the seat, signified by a star). Proximity to a onetime river and to the Great Tree made it a magnet as well. And though a Frescuran would never admit it, the town did benefit to some degree from the presence of the cult.

Each small table in the Sunflower Lives Café was painted with a giant sunflower. Madeleine and I both ordered a Sunflower Burrito. She asked for a tall glass of Sunflower Iced Tea, and I had a Sunflower Beer and some Sunflower Lemonade. The owner of the place, Virginia Martinez, a stout woman who I was sure had feet beneath a great sweeping blue apron, served us herself.

"Coyote," Virginia said, nodding. "You up to no good?" She could have said this in a maternal way, because I had spent a month or so at different times in my childhood living above the restaurant, but she said it more with a hostile drawl.

"That depends." I smiled. She really was the only one in town who talked to me without having to.

Madeleine pulled a large watch out of her jeans. "What time is it? My watch stopped." She tapped it on the table and it seemed to start again.

"Almost time for the parade." Virginia frowned and buried her hands in her apron.

"The parade?" the woman asked.

"Almost three. You from out of town? Of course," and Virginia explained the daily ritual. Then, cautiously, "You going up there, to Rancho Flora?" Virginia asked Madeleine.

"I smell the burritos," I interrupted.

"Well, are you?" Virginia persisted.

"Yes." Madeleine grinned.

"Coyote, they have their place, why didn't you take her there?" Virginia huffed, then reluctantly disappeared to get the food.

"They only serve ice cream. Besides, I like it here," I said to her back. I did. I thought that if I was going to do anything one day, I should open a restaurant, a diner like this one, where people came and ate and just hung out and told stories.

Contemptuously, Virginia spun the customary bowl of blue corn chips into the slight well in the center of the painted sunflower. A few chips bounced out. Madeleine responded to the hostility with a smile. She seemed to be writing something down in her mind, absorbing and not reacting. Maybe she was tired, but it was while she was silent in the café that I began to suspect a whole system of motives which were unusual and unique.

After we had gobbled our burritos, after Virginia grunted good-bye, we stepped out into the street and Madeleine spotted the other café. I was not sure if she actually saw the people inside, pilgrims clad in mauve attire. I know she read the sign, THE SUN-FLOWER CAFÉ, and I know she was confused. Why would a town this small have a diner called the Sunflower Lives, and then also maintain The Sunflower Café on the same street?

"I'll explain later," I said. And that way I did not have to get into the messy narrative of the political scene. I was sure she would either hear about it at the ashram or once inside never suspect that there was a problem in the world.

We drove into the gas station on the edge of town where the old attendant Carl smiled briefly and then looked at the woman with disdain.

"Fill 'er up," Madeleine said.

"Going to Rancho Flora?" Carl wiped the windshield and wore a toothless gape.

"Perhaps," I intervened.

"If you're going to the cult, that'll be a buck fifty extra." Carl rubbed his hands. I don't know why he tried to pull this, what with me in the car, too.

"He's full of shit," I said to Madeleine. "He makes this up, and pilgrims actually believe him."

"Buck fifty extra." Carl looked at me. "It's a toll."

I never liked him after he made fun of me for thinking I could control lightning.

"Nine dollars, plus a buck fifty extra makes ten fifty," Carl calculated. He removed the gas hose from the car.

Madeleine handed him only nine dollars, and I waved as we sped out of the station.

Once we were headed toward the Great Tree, we saw all the signs of protest, at least one hundred along the ten-mile stretch. The hand-painted warnings were sprayed onto planks of plywood nailed to two-by-fours and planted alongside the road.

"Wow," Madeleine said.

"Don't worry," I tried to reassure her. After all, I still believed she was a pilgrim.

"I'm not worried. But will you look at this?"

Some of the signs were completely faded. They had been posted over five years ago, when only a rumor was circulating that a cult would arise in the desert. Some whitewashed panels boasted fresh red lettering—they could have been positioned yesterday. The signs faced both lanes, so that the town's defiance could assault the guru as he both came and went into Frescura for his daily ice cream cone.

"Wow," Madeleine repeated as we drove toward the Great Tree. The most daunting was a sign painted black with fluorescent green lettering that dripped like blood down the panel. The sign succinctly said, GURU GO FISH. But around here there are no significant bodies of water.

*B*etween the Great Tree and Rancho Flora there were no more signs of protest. Few people actually journeyed that far into the desert unless they absolutely had to. Even the most ardent opponents to the cult did not want to endure the savage heat. Once we dropped over the ridge, we had no sense of the world we had just left. Each time I came here it seemed that the memory of what I'd passed through just moments ago evaporated in the persistent thirst of the new depth.

Each lonely cactus looked eager to befriend us. The prickly plants stood like banished tree trunks determined to turn despair into happy defiance with twisting bifurcations and juicy stalks. I always believed that the plants wanted to get closer. The huge-fence-post kind hoped to inch toward the many-headed-snake variety. But they had to remain apart. If the cacti bunched up too much, they would strangle one another.

We boated along the endless paved river toward the ashram. For the most part it was desperately flat, yet we found ourselves almost climbing in and out of wide basins bordered and divided by unexpected groups of small hills. These beige and ruddy mounds were barren and without plant life, yet they seemed oddly animated. They exuded a peculiar warmth. The small hills in the distance looked like animal limbs, like haunches belonging to great drowsy cats, barely alive, unaware of our visit. We were in the presence of sleeping beasts, and when we watched closely, we saw the gentle rise and fall of life, we saw them breathe. That breath was somehow soothing, as if to remind us that no matter how far off these hills were, and we never seemed quite able to roam among them, we were not alone. Some other living thing was crazy enough to journey here with us.

"Do you know anyone inside the cult?" she asked.

"No," I said flatly. Yes, I probably did, though I wasn't sure. I didn't want to be sure.

"Have you ever even gone inside?"

"No." I never had. I had not gone in for the simple excuse that I could not go in if I wanted. First of all, you could not just enter and say you were looking for someone because they guarded against relatives, families seeking lost members, and so on, and they preserved their privacy with tight security. I could have gotten around that, I suppose. I knew James had gone there when he left my place, and I knew he was there all of last year. I was lazy about trying to work things out with people. And I had, to be frank, thrived on the pain of his departure.

"Is that a rainbow?" Madeleine pointed to something in the distance.

"That's it," I said.

"It looks like a rainbow."

"It is a rainbow."

On the horizon the arch sat, looking as fragile and temporary as a prismatic arc of dew. As we neared the rainbow, turning off the highway at an unmarked exit and driving downward and east, it became apparent that this rainbow was a gate. Over the rainbow there seemed to be a small gold coin, a disc as we neared, and then a dome.

We finally reached the ashram entrance and confronted a twenty-foot-high adobe semicircle, which had been painted in the colors of the spectrum. It enclosed an enormous pair of wrought-iron barred doors. And on either side of the rainbow, there was a twenty-foot-high potted palm tree.

"How the hell do they water it?" she asked.

"Good question," I said.

Beyond the palm trees, it appeared as if a tall wire fence ran on forever in either direction. And through the gate, it seemed as if paradise had been set up.

She looked at me as if she should now pay me for my services and let me find my way back to civilization.

"I'll go in with you," I said.

I don't know where this impulse came from. My heart pounded fiercely. But I was able to think of at least one reason for going in: if I went through the gate, I might be able to find out what the pilgrims had done with Frog's meteorite. After they sped away that night, they must have taken it here. . . . But how could I legitimize my presence? I did not want to pose as a prospective pilgrim. And then I wondered, what was she doing? She said she was not a pilgrim, so why would they let her inside? Perhaps she had a son or a daughter in there.

A guard in a mauve jumpsuit was examining a letter she showed him. He smiled and opened the doors of the rainbow. "Welcome to Rancho Flora," he said with a trace of a foreign accent.

I had come up to the ashram gate dozens of times before and never entered. Why now? It was more than curiosity, more than tracking down a stolen meteorite. What was I getting myself into? I'd have to look for James, and I didn't want to find him. But I passed under the rainbow, and once through the gate I looked at Madeleine. Suddenly she wasn't tired, she had perked up with enthusiasm, and she didn't seem to care that I was tagging along. She pushed her sunglasses up on her forehead. There were crow's-feet by her eyes, wrinkles in her brow, and her cheeks were rough from too many years in the sun. Although now she was pale, and that meant that she had not been on an adventure in a while. I knew she had traveled places, there was something of a nomad in her face. More than anything else, I wanted to travel with her.

A couple of bulldozers crossed the road, and then we had a clear view of the ashram. Laid out before us was an oasis made by man, a slowly rising, stepped hill, a small city of adobe structures climbing up toward a pristine white building overlooking everything, the dome of that structure sparkling in gilt. Everywhere, it seemed, mauve-clad pilgrims bustled about with something to do, a task, a mission. We were amidst an ecological and engineering wonder. Later we would learn about how the earth was dug up and shoveled in place, how water supplies were discovered miles away and piped here, how the elevation above the rest of the desert created a lofty coolness. I imagined soaring above the ashram and looking down, and how it would have appeared to be an Edenic anthill, complete with red ants, each with some vital, important purpose. But I was not above, I was within, and as far as I could see, the hill rose and the oasis spread and there were mud-brick structures melting into the landscape.

Another guard waved his mauve arm at a parking lot where we stowed the woman's car. "We have our own transportation here." We were ushered into a small building at the base of the oasis, a visitors' center, which also served as a security command post. It was just one large room with two desks. Over each desk was a map of the ashram, and in the center was a portrait of Guru B, as he was commonly referred to.

Guru B had a long, dark face and a fine white beard, long, which met up with long, white hair, most of which was tucked into a braided white cap. He was wearing a silky white robe with lacy gold trim. His round, liquid eyes, a deep, deep brown, at once seemed glossy with wisdom and dry with distance. His eyes followed me. The portrait that appeared everywhere we went was also a tad larger than life, not too much, but enough to make you feel ever so slightly small.

The two women who sat behind the desks at the visitors' center stood up and smiled. They each wore wide, royal-blue sashes wound around their waists. One with long flowing red hair said her name was Lulu, and the other, owl-faced woman said her name was Cassandra. They shook our hands and then pressed their palms together, thumbs pushed against their breasts, fingers pointing toward their chins.

"And you're Madeleine Nash," Cassandra said to the woman. "I'm the one you talked to on the phone. We're honored you're finally here."

"I'm happy to be here, too," the woman said.

"And you are . . . ?" Lulu looked at me.

"Coyote," Madeleine said. "He helped me find the place."

"Coyote Nash." I shook Lulu's hand and imitated her gesture with pressed hands against my chest. Madeleine glared at me. She was mad, but luckily she said nothing. "I'm the husband," I announced.

Cassandra replied, "Well, we weren't expecting you, but that's groovy."

Madeleine continued to stare at me. She sighed, rolled her eyes, and seemed to mutter, I thee wed, but just for the time being. Lulu and Cassandra did not notice this interchange because they were busy setting up our tour of Rancho Flora.

Lulu took us outside to a jeep, and I climbed into the backseat. Lulu donned a pair of sunglasses, tucked her red ponytail into her jumpsuit, and revved the engine. She looked kind of chic—all the pilgrims did.

Our first stop on the tour was the administration building, which was still at the base of the hill, and at the foot of the main drag, which circled through the ashram. The main drive was called Walt Whitman Way, which I learned from Lulu was named after Guru B's favorite saint, and which intersected Krishna Road, Christ Boulevard, and Susan B. Anthony Street.

Madeleine had to meet Vanessa, who was, after the guru, the most important person at Rancho Flora. I knew who she was even before Lulu described her, and I knew of her reputation long before I set eyes on her. Vanessa was slender and had shoulder-length black hair, which she let fall over one side of her narrow face. She wore a blue sash like Lulu's. She offered a bony hand and an icy smile. Thin sienna lips fit around words precisely. When she folded her hands into the welcome gesture, it was with dramatic austerity.

"I'm Vanessa." She knew she did not need to identify herself, but she knew the act was ingratiating. She had a succinct British accent. This was the person, more than any other, responsible for landing the guru and his ashram ten miles into the desert beyond the Great Tree. She had imported the guru from India, first to the East Coast and then to the Southwest. "So have you made any important assessments yet?" Vanessa inquired as she led us down a hall. "We're anxiously waiting. And excited, I might add."

We entered a large room, the exposed rafters of which were two floors high. Everywhere there were rugs, Native American rugs, which combined into one mad pattern of shapes and dyes. There were two fireplaces (which were probably only used for ceremonial purposes), crowned of course by the haunting portrait of Guru B. In the center of the room was an enormous glass table where two women sat, two women with blue sashes, both of whom nodded hello, but both of whom were busily engaged in phone conversations, the contents of which were impossible to ascertain.

"Elise and Jakarta." Vanessa introduced them as she assumed a middle chair at the table. She addressed us loudly. "This is where the special council meets." She pointed to her blue sash. "Anyone wearing a blue obi"—she called it an obi—"is a member of the council. The council sets policy and sees that Guru B's wishes are fulfilled."

"Are all the pilgrims wearing blue obis women?" Madeleine asked, having swiftly adopted the correct vocabulary of the place.

"Yes," Vanessa said. "The guru thinks women make better managers than men."

"Interesting," Madeleine said. I thought she was a bit intimidated by Vanessa. Or maybe she was just pretending to be intimidated.

"Well, I hope you find many interesting things to say for your magazine," Vanessa said with no time for subtlety.

"I will," Madeleine said, and she smiled.

"I hope it will help our current program," Vanessa continued. "We hope that tourists will realize that Rancho Flora can offer more than just a sunny holiday, but become for them a spiritual spa, which I think you'll find during your stay. A spiritual spa." Vanessa was trying out the phrase for the first time. She liked it and found a pocket tape recorder. She pressed record, then once again uttered, "Spiritual spa."

"How long is our stay?" I whispered to Madeleine, thinking she would say a day or two.

"The rest of the summer, maybe," Madeleine whispered back. "As long as it takes."

Vanessa was acutely aware of our every whisper, so she bent her head forward to indicate that she wondered what we uttered privately.

"Lulu will take you on a tour and show you to your rooms." Then without further ado Vanessa picked up a phone and began talking louder than her colleagues.

Back in the jeep, Lulu told us that new pilgrims took names that defined their new life. In some ashrams a guru assigned a name with spiritual uniqueness, but here, you simply picked the name you had always wanted, a name your parents had not chosen for you. The new life at the ashram was all about fulfilling pent-up desires, getting past them to reach higher planes. Lulu steered us up Walt Whitman Way, past Mohammed Lane. She asked a few questions about Madeleine's project, which was good, because then I didn't have to pretend anymore and wait for a private moment to pursue all of the pertinent issues. So Madeleine was a writer. She was going to issue a series of features that Vanessa and the blue obis all hoped would raise the profile of the cult, invite tourists.

We continued up the hill, leveled off at a plateau, crossed Albert Schweitzer Road and Simone Weil Drive, and glided past a series of adobe dwellings. Normally you painted any wooden frames on your adobe turquoise, doorways and window frames, because this is what both the Spanish and the Natives did. But at Rancho Flora, all of the frames were painted with a ruddy color that I assumed was supposed to approximate the mauve shade of the jumpsuit.

"Why mauve?" Madeleine asked.

And Lulu, who it turned out had also been with the guru in India along with Vanessa and who had helped find this place in the desert, knew all the responses. Eight hundred people now lived at Rancho Flora and subscribed to the teachings of Guru B. The ashram covered nine square miles of land. There were fifty-five blue obis.

"Mauve"—Lulu said everything with abundant pride and ebullience—"because it is the color of the clay we live upon and the color of our blood when it is filled with oxygen."

We passed some more houses, stacked on top of each other into the hill in the way that the ancient cultures of the region built communities along cliffs over a thousand years ago. And everywhere, the mauve jumpsuits rushed about with an importance not appointed by the self, but by the fantastic setting, the sheer success of having built a mountain in the desert and having declared it paradise.

"More precisely," Lulu corrected Madeleine's terming Rancho Flora as a kind of heaven-on-earth, "what we have stumbled into here is a Buddhafield. Guru B declared that it was. If there is a nuclear Armageddon, which Guru B is sure there will be, the Buddhafield will be spared."

"How nice to know this." Madeleine smiled politely.

As we drove higher up the hill, climbing toward the gold-domed structure, I inspected the faces we passed and half-expected one of them to belong to James. I looked among the crews of laboring pilgrims, but the thought of James working was laughable (I should have been looking among the jumpsuits to see if anyone was sunbathing). Now and then, in addition to street signs, there were other signs, each one addressing its reader as "cherished." Over a garbage can: CHERISHED, PLEASE THROW YOUR TRASH HERE. By a well: CHERISHED, KINDLY DO NOT WASTE PRECIOUS WATER. And little reminders that punctuated the roads and paths: CHERISHED, SMILE. Or: CHERISHED, HAVE YOU HUGGED SOMEONE YET TODAY? I tried to imagine James saying, "Cherished, please pass the salt." I don't think *cherished* was a word that would come naturally to him, or anyone for that matter.

Everyone in Frescura believed that Rancho Flora was a nonstop orgy. They said in Frescura that you could feel the breeze of sweat wafting in from the desert. But that was simply not the case this afternoon. Sweat, yes, but from apparent work in a greenhouse or on new buildings, people everywhere busy with their hands. I knew most outsiders would be shocked to find that the pilgrims simply did not look any different from anyone anywhere else. I looked at every face and I measured a certain placidness, a peace, I thought, as they went about their chores. But something was wrong in this man-made oasis, something was mysterious and spooky about the place. It was too early to tell what. It was cooler here, the sky completely azure, a much more brilliant hue than elsewhere in the desert. And despite the white sun there was a light that cast everything in opaque mist—like that of an old adobe church with narrow clerestories and the ever pungent, dewy smell of ancient mud. Madeleine seemed to sense the strangeness. She had one eyebrow raised as she listened to Lulu point at houses with mauve-framed windows and doors and say this or that about the tonnage of earth and mud that went into this place. Madeleine had one eyebrow raised the way she did when she drove us here. I knew she knew things beyond what Lulu said. I wanted to see what Madeleine saw.

Our jeep reached a broad plateau, and soon we were amid a series of relatively larger buildings. One, Lulu informed us, was a hospital, another a new hotel (not yet complete) for visitors and, they hoped, tourists (we were not staying in a hotel—we were to be treated as regular pilgrims, which Madeleine had requested). There was also a disco, apparently, next to the hotel. Just down Gandhi Street was the refectory, a long adobe with many skinny windows, rows and rows of long tables, a massive kitchen, walls of shiny white tiles and counters of glistening metal pots, a kitchen where pilgrims were baking bread, chopping bright vegetables, preparing the daily feast. Behind the refectory was a greenhouse twice as long.

Lulu took this opportunity to wind her long red ponytail into a bun and clip it with a barrette. I wasn't paying attention, but I think she was propounding something about the spirit of community here, about how everyone lived in similar quarters, had hands-on jobs, and dressed alike, and how this communalism was cleansing. We drove farther down Gandhi Street to find the library, which was filled with books about the lives of the saints, books by and about this holy lot, and a school. The school was in session,

Lulu said, which was why we hadn't seen too many children running about.

"Can anyone have a kid if they want?" Madeleine asked.

"Yes," Lulu said. "But the child does not belong to one father or mother. The child becomes everybody's responsibility. Everyone adult is responsible for every child. And children are circulated among the various compounds of dwellings." Lulu said this with a self-satisfied, breezy logic. To an orphan, I have to admit, this was an awesome prospect.

The jeep turned back up Walt Whitman Way and ascended to the highest point, from which the entire ashram could be surveyed. At the top was the temple, what turned out to be a whitewashed adobe octagon, three stories high, with a round dome that was difficult to look directly at due to the strong reflection. Here the pilgrims listened to a daily lecture that was composed by the guru but delivered by Vanessa on his behalf. Here all important teaching occurred. Here, in short, was the heart of the ashram. And looking down, I finally felt as if I saw the anthill I had mounted, filled with red ants.

The temple interior was bright. The mosquelike structure was arranged so that the altar was a stage in the round. There was red carpeting and a series of gilt chairs on the stage. Wooden benches formed concentric circles until they reached the walls of the temple. From the dome hung a broad white banner, on two sides boasting the largest version of the portrait of Guru B. Now his eyes were no longer vaguely aloof. His glance seemed entirely omniscient. He was watching everyone. Or maybe he was not watching anyone, but he was simply seeing something important, the future. All around the circumference of the octagon, high up where the dome began, words had been painted, words in tall gold letters.

Madeleine immediately identified the text. "'Song of Myself,'" she said. "The opening lines."

"Saint Walt," Lulu said, nodding.

As we exited the temple, I noticed that there was a tall fence with a gate. Some shrubs made it impossible to look through the fence, and the slant of the hill prevented me from peering over it. "What's back there?"

"Oh, that's restricted," Lulu said, and started up the jeep.

"Restricted?" Madeleine wondered.

"Well, that's where Guru B lives," Lulu conceded, "and some of the blue obis. Behind there are just a few buildings but nothing really that you need to worry about."

And it was quite clear that there was something indeed to wonder about. There was a fence and some shrubs that had been planted in front of the metal wall. From this vantage, it was virtually impossible to assay the depth of these buildings, how far they continued down the other side of the hill. One puzzling fact emerged: the ashram was supposed to cover nine square miles. Yet we saw maybe half of that. And in those four miles, the population and structures easily fit into two or three miles of the oasis. What was beyond the temple?

I wondered, too, about the meteorite. I thought that by now I would have seen it displayed prominently in one of the larger structures I had visited—in the refectory or temple. However, it could have been stowed in any number of buildings I passed. Now and then, I saw a beehive-shaped room, a tiny adobe structure modeled after ancient kilns. Any one of these ovens might be perfect for storing a meteorite. I had a long list of places to inspect.

We journeyed down the side of the hill we had come up. We had one more stop on the tour before being deposited in our rooms. The museum was another long building, as long as the greenhouse, if not longer, with what seemed to be a gas station next to it. The museum, it turned out, was made up of one squat adobe dedicated to the life of Guru B—and a garage, which deceptively consumed most of the space.

I had never in my life seen so many cars. A troop of mauve people attended to them, repairing them, polishing the chassis of sports cars and limousines, luxury cars all, dozens of shiny, sleek cars, each with subtle lines and bold curves, a fleet of spectacular vehicles, some vintage, with spokes and convertible tops, some looking as if they belonged to an automotive future, low and aerodynamically grooved. This was the guru's personal collection of automobiles. And there were, Lulu boasted, seventy-three cars.

"When he makes his daily trip to Frescura," Lulu said, "he likes to drive the armor-plated limo over there." She pointed to the car that had passed us not too long ago. The guru must have come back already. I soon learned that Guru B spent a large part of his day driving around in different specimens from his collection of international cars—though I had never seen anything but that limo on the highway.

Inside the museum proper—what wasn't the vast garage—a display of photographs documented the guru's life until he emigrated here. Two other rooms were devoted to his two other collections. The guru collected gold watches, cases and cases of gold watches, from which he wore from two to seven at once on any given day. It was a treasure trove. Madeleine shook her head when Lulu bragged that there were at least five hundred gold watches now. We met a mauve pilgrim named Chuck, who grinned. Lulu said that the guru was very proud of Chuck because he managed to keep all of the watches running at the exact same time, to the second.

"Were you a watchmaker before you came to Rancho Flora?" Madeleine was cordial.

"No," Chuck said. "I was a high school French teacher."

Then there was the last collection, what Guru B had been amassing since he was a child. Not as glamorous as five hundred gold watches, not as spectacular as seventy-three luxury cars. There were three thousand stones, rocks the size of your hand. The guru, Chuck said, used to go to the rivers of India and collect the rocks. Guru B's mother used to sew extra pockets in her little son's pants so that he could carry home all of his finds. The stones were striated, speckled, sparkling, spotted, solid, smooth. Rough, porous, crystalline, in all colors, pastel, black. In fascinating combinations of metals and silicons, an elemental zoo, a history of the earth, all arranged chronologically by when the Guru had acquired them. One big rock not on display, I quickly noted, was the meteorite.

"Guru B's greatest passion," Lulu said, "is collecting things. It's how he reached the highest attainable plane."

Madeleine, I could tell, was about to comment on the paradox, so obvious, between the pilgrims' uniform equality and the guru's excessive hobbies. But Lulu would probably just dismiss this observation. Madeleine instead said, "I hope the guru will grant me an audience."

To which Lulu smiled and shrugged. That was Vanessa's domain.

We drove halfway down the hill, past many more newer dwellings, and finally Lulu let us off outside a small house, an apartment really, joined by three others. Outside, a few pilgrims were waiting to greet us. I was tired and would need another introduction to our housemates before I could associate names with faces.

"I hope you have time to find what you're looking for," Lulu said, as if Madeleine and I were new pilgrims.

As soon as we walked into our rooms and were alone, Madeleine began shooting questions at me. "Well, what are you doing, Mr. Coyote Gato, just what the hell are you doing here?"

"I'm taking off my boots."

"You are not my husband," she said. "I don't have or want a husband."

We were in the living room, which had a couch and an armchair, a bookcase complete with best-sellers, novels of all kinds, and a radio—and a poster of the guru, of course. In the next room sat just one four-posted, queen-sized bed.

Madeleine looked at the single bedroom and said, "I need this space. I have to work. Hell, I'm going to dinner, and you'd best be out of here when I get back." She left, slammed the door, and went over to some pilgrim's house and then probably to the refectory. I was exhausted and as soon as Madeleine left, I headed for bed, dropping my jeans and T-shirt as I went.

The next thing I knew, it was dark outside, and someone had whipped the blanket off my body. The lamps in the bedroom came on and Madeleine was looking at me. I was naked, but that didn't seem to bother her. She started laughing.

"What's so funny?"

"I can't remember the last time I couldn't get a guy out of my place."

"Do I have to go?" I was groggy. I felt like a child being told to go to school.

"Yes, you have to go." Madeleine stopped laughing. She picked up my clothes and threw them at me.

"Why?"

"You have to ask why? Because you're in my way."

"I can help you." I slipped into my jeans.

"You don't even know what it is that I do. How can you help me?"

"I'll just, you know, help." I really didn't know what to say. My first concern was that I did not want to get out of this bed. It was cozy and comfortable, and I thought, if I could just stay here a little longer, I could stay for good.

"Coyote, you're a swell person, but you can't pretend to be my husband."

"No one believed that, did they?"

"No," Madeleine said, "especially not after I explained that you were actually my nephew."

"Ah, see." I sat up. "You've already started to make a place for me."

"No, I was saving myself from embarrassment." Madeleine paced the room.

"Madeleine," I pleaded, "I'll help you research your articles." I paused. "If you don't let me hang out, I'm just going to sign up as a pilgrim, which I don't want to do, but I will, and then I'll still be here to follow you around."

"Well . . ." She hesitated. "Look, I really do like you, I don't know why."

A long pause. I begged with my eyes. I thought to myself, what will I do if she says no? There isn't anything else I want to do.

Finally Madeleine sighed. "You can stay, if you promise not to bother me."

"I promise."

"You remind me of someone," she said. And now she looked grave, in a flash almost ashen.

"Who?" I suddenly became aware of sounds, bodies moving it seemed, on the other side of the wall in the next suite of rooms.

"I found these." Madeleine produced two six-packs of bottled beer she had taken from the refectory kitchen. "There's quite a stash."

Growing up, I had heard about local nomads who would band together and cross the desert. I was not sure exactly why they did this—the desert was barren of riches. If you were near the desert, looking over it from the edge, you could see fires at night where the nomads camped. There in the reprieve of sunless night, they told each other the stories of their lives. Something about the still desert ushered in, demanded, this honesty.

Now Madeleine sat at the edge of the bed and drank one beer after the next. She handed me one bottle as she took two for herself. I pulled a blanket over my body, and I was soothed by the cool malt. If only there were some lemonade.

"There's going to be a lot to write about here," Madeleine said after a while.

"It's a bigger place than I thought it was," I replied.

"I want to be the first reporter to describe this place," Madeleine confessed. "Get at the heart."

"What kind of articles have you written before? Have you been to other places like Rancho Flora?" I wanted to know.

"I suppose." Madeleine shrugged.

"You've been all over," I decided.

"Yes," Madeleine admitted.

"You've traveled. You're a travel writer." I drank my beer.

Madeleine shrugged. "Okay."

I had never met a travel writer before, never read travel writing, but there was something odd about the way Madeleine was describing her assignment. She opened her mouth and seemed to be on the brink of telling me something important. I could feel it in the air. But then she laughed instead. There was something slightly silly about her as she became intoxicated. I became woozy at a fast pace, so that the whole situation became dizzy and surreal for me.

"Should we wear jumpsuits like everyone else?" I asked.

"I hate those getups. No, I want to maintain, you know, some kind of distance."

"All travel writers have to," I said for some reason. Drunken arrogance. "Have you been all over the world?"

"Oh, sure." Madeleine smiled. "You name it, I've been there."

I tried to come up with some exotic, far-out place, but geography escaped me with the last swig.

Another beer, and I wanted to tell her my life story. I was staring at the ceiling. "I had a friend."

"Oh?"

"His name was James."

"James?" she inhaled. "Great," she breathed out.

"I think he became a pilgrim."

"He did? Is he here now?"

"Possibly."

"We'll have to look him up."

"I guess so." I shrugged.

And another beer, until the bed was spinning. Then I was dancing about the room, around and around, and I felt so gleeful for the first time in so long. And Madeleine stayed seated, in one place. Around and around, as if she were a maypole. I was so dizzy. And I looked at her, and she was solemn, grave.

"What's wrong?" I fell to a rug on the floor.

"I've met a lot of young men in the last ten or fifteen years."

"Have you?" I thought she was going to say something about her sex life. But she didn't.

"A lot of young men," she repeated mournfully.

"How many?" I was drunk. And then sobered.

The day's sunburn made her cheeks pink. A tear was about to slip out, though it never quite made it. She wasn't the type to cry.

"But none has reminded me so much of my son as you do," she said.

"I'm sorry." I frowned.

"Oh, it's all right. You just remind me of him somehow."

*O*ne night three weeks before I ended up at the ashram, I was lying on my back, staring at the sky. The evening's drama was a ballet of falling stars, a splendid meteor shower. Minute bright dancers attempted to leap inconspicuously through the night and return unnoticed into black obscurity. They dared you, these deviant, errant cosmic animals, they teased you into sighting then following them. They lured you into a chase, if they strayed, if they stumbled down to the distant desert planet. That was what Frog Reading did professionally. He tracked meteorites. He was an astronomical big-game hunter, and I missed him. It had been so long since I'd been on safari with him, though for a time, for five years when I was a teenager, I went over to his ranch every night. But in the last five years, in the time since Frog's son was struck dead by a meteorite, I'd had only a handful of conversations with him. We'd drifted, or more correctly, I'd drifted. Frog had lapsed into an even more desperate isolation at his ranch, and I was busy wandering around the Southwest and then entertaining James. Then there was the last year alone, and lately I had felt burdened by this solitude, by too much introspection. That evening three weeks ago I was filled with the desire to travel back in time, to simple, lazy evenings in Frog's observatory. And so I decided that the next day, I'd go over to the Rancho Fantasy Eccle.

When I arrived in the midafternoon, I found Frog raking a rectangular plot of clay into a garden. It was tricky to find any topsoil worth risking plants' lives in. Frog looked up and said, as if he had spoken to me just the day before, "I thought I might try leeks here."

"Leeks are nice," I said. "Will they grow? Isn't it too hot?"

"Probably." Frog leaned on his rake and lit a cigarette. "But I like leek soup."

"Did you ever make that for me?" I tried to remember.

"No." Frog puffed. "I never had any leeks."

I scanned Rancho Fantasy Eccle quickly, and it looked the same as it always had, the long and flat adobe blending into the landscape, the distant observatory overlooking the desert. Frog had bought this large chunk of land with some money he received for some prestigious physics prize. He had decided to leave the science world while he was at his peak, while, in his words, he was still an *enfant terrible* and not a doddering old fool, and he retreated to the land where he was born. Since he was raised on the desert's edge, he had grown up with a clear view of the sphere of constellations. Their timetable, when they came and went, where to look for them, was in his blood. Astronomy had seemed a natural course when he was a student of physics, but at some point as a college undergraduate he chose to enter the more fashionable arena of subatomic particles. He had to prove that he was brilliant, able to conquer avant-garde science. It wasn't until he left the labs that he could return to the stars. He bought the ranch from the relatives of a man named Ecclesiastes Eccle, who also had built a reputation as a hermit. Frog named the place Fantasy Eccle after muttering a phrase over and over in a fit of silliness (or drunkenness). *Fin de siècle*, the end of the century, impending apocalypse, the end of the world as we know it. Frog constructed an observatory on his ranch so he could devote his life to chasing meteors. This would be a nice change from the labs and accelerators, the universities and global conferences that had torn him from the desert, the only place, he once told me, where he truly believed "the Earth is real."

Although long periods would pass when I wouldn't see Frog, though he must have slid further into middle age, he always looked the same. His shoulder-length hair, usually banded in a ponytail, had turned completely white. But there was the same perfect posture. The same round gold glasses. The same cigarette constantly emerging between the third and fourth fingers of his right hand. The same tattersall shirt with a frayed button-down collar. The same slender image, since he ran ten miles every day out into the breathless desert, and the same deadpan raspy voice, quick but legato. I imagined that in another five, ten years he would look much the same, as if it weren't the description of a proton's innards that had made him famous, but rather some wonder drug that defied the aging process.

Before I was thirteen, I lived with various Frescurans for stints as long as eight months, as short as a fortnight. And then when I was thirteen, the Frescurans all pitched in to fix up an abandoned trailer for me. I was no longer anyone's responsibility. But this was at the same time that I started going to Rancho Fantasy Eccle several nights a week. Though I didn't actually live there, Frog's ranch was my home for five years, the only place where I felt completely comfortable, more at home than in my trailer. Frog and I would sit in his observatory and talk about everything from astronomical matters to the plots of novels I borrowed from him. I learned how to spice enchiladas. I learned all the desert myths. I actually stopped going to Frog's ranch before his son died, but that was because I had found my own life. Those evenings with him have been dyed in nostalgia—enough time has not passed (and I'm not sure it ever will) for me to be objective about those years.

Frog's ranch overlooked the desert. It was about twenty miles southeast of the Great Tree, near the Mexican border. Frog's routine was simple. He got up in the morning, fed his cat Tycho, and either went on his run in the desert or made some repairs here and there on the ranch. He made the day's celestial calculations, got drunk on a bottle of tequila (having long ago abandoned the beer and lemonade concoction he picked up in Europe). He slept some, sobered up, fed the cat again, and just after dusk, hurried to his observatory, where he worked all night.

Tycho stepped out of the house to greet me, but I didn't notice him until he was careening into my calf and meowing hello. Hi, Tycho, long time no see. He was a small cat, mostly white with a tinge of beige here and there that made him look dirty under certain light. Tycho had short legs, the hind ones black as if he wore pantaloons. He also wore a black ascot, sported a black spot on one side and black fur over one eye and the back of his head. The latter half of his tail was black, too, as if Tycho had dipped it in an inkwell. But his truly distinguishing feature was his nose. It was gray, almost silver, which was why he was named after Tycho Brahe, the sixteenth-century Danish astronomer who, among other things, was known for having lost his nose in a duel and having had a silver prosthesis fitted in its place. Tycho the Gato's nose was real, and it did not feel shiny and metallic, but rather like a wet rubber eraser.

"I had an odd dream"—Frog pointed at the cat—"during my siesta today."

"About what?"

Frog said that he dreamed that Tycho was standing at the foot of his bed. "The cat was dancing on his hind legs, waving his front paws back and forth. And then I noticed something I'd never seen before, not in all these years with him."

"What?"

"Tycho had a zipper running down his belly. I could actually see where the fur parted into a line, and if I reached over and was gentle, I could unzip the cat."

Tycho looked up at Frog while he told the story. He glanced at me and said, Sometimes I think he's just weird.

"It occurred to me then," Frog declared with gravity and import, "that Tycho wasn't a cat at all. Tycho was a little person trapped in a furry suit, and what seemed to be a dance was actually this desperate little man inside asking me to unzip his costume. 'Unzip me, unzip me.'"

Either out of embarrassment or out of boredom, as if he'd heard this story before, the cat bolted around to the other side of the house.

"Well," Frog said, laughing, "I sat up and reached over to his belly to gently pull the zipper down, free the little person. But that wasn't popular." This was the end of the dream.

"Tycho must have thought you were insane," I gathered.

Frog nodded. Poor Tycho. Little men in cats, little cats in men, nothing was what it seemed. Frog continued to hoe his leek plot, and when the cat returned, I could tell Frog was looking for the zipper, not convinced that his dream was completely untrue. The cat cleaned himself, he squinted and licked a paw, and then he wiped the moistened paw over his black brow and silver nose. Tycho decided to nap next to me, and he had a habit of sleeping on his back, his hind legs projected like plough handles. This gave me an opportunity to look for a zipper. In Frog's mind, I was sure, the cat could never be treated the same, just in case there was a little person trapped inside.

Frog never asked me too many questions about what was going on in my life. He waited for me to supply him with pertinent details. But I hardly wanted to discuss me, I was trying to avoid me for the moment. So we talked about meteors. Tonight Frog had calculated that there was going to be a massive shower. At this point in the summer the earth was enduring the end of the Ophiuchids meteor showers, the beginning of the Capricornids. A careful nocturnal observer might find twenty shooting stars per hour at this cusp. I couldn't wait—it was as if we were about to see a favorite, epic movie, which despite any tragic content was soothing to watch. It was just pleasant to be hanging out with Frog.

In the waning afternoon, a few gray birds lost the refuge of shadows cast by fence posts. Rancho Fantasy Eccle under the ownership of Ecclesiastes Eccle had actually contained cattle. I couldn't picture the beasts roaming about the drought-ridden plain. Frog said the smartest men in the world had been the people who had learned to grow things and raise livestock on this land. The Indians, for example, who could make corn grow in desert dust. This was something, for all of his mathematical prowess, Frog could never do. It was a major struggle just to get a nice tomato.

To kill some time, Frog picked up an open can of paint and proceeded to finish repainting his back doorframe. He dipped the thin brush in the turquoise liquid and applied the paint. It was a cathartic act, painting the even turquoise color over and over again, so this was something Frog did: he painted door and window frames whether or not the wood needed a new coat. Sometimes he applied new mud plaster to his adobe walls. But when he ran out of turquoise paint, and when he couldn't spackle any more mud, he became unhappy. If he ran out of catfood, too, then he had to make one of his rare trips into town. He tried not to deal with anyone for as long as possible. For a little while, I had been the exception.

Frog had purchased the Rancho Fantasy Eccle not only because it was conveniently located in the region of the country he loved, but also because it was situated smack in the middle of the so-called Iron Belt. He wanted to be a meteorite hunter, and the Iron Belt was where the most number of meteorites (of the large and metallic order) landed in the world. Frog developed a unique way to determine relationships between sightings of shooting stars in the sky and actual finds on earth. Most people, most scientists, could see the tumbling meteors, but they could not then easily relate the falls with finds. Frog's method was infallible, or so he boasted. He built an observatory on the highest ground at Rancho Fantasy Eccle. In a white-painted dome, a helmet-shaped adobe, a powerful telescope was mounted on a stand that could be swiveled and tilted in any direction.

Given trajectories and probabilities, atmospheric conditions and gravitational forces, Frog would locate meteorites that should have landed in the great desert, and he would drive his jeep to the hypothetical site and find the stones, sometimes crater-forming and massive, sometimes the size of your fist. He carted the meteorites home. In a one-room lab adjacent to his observatory, he used his special knives and saws made of tungsten carbide to cut the asteroid pieces, which were harder than diamond. He made analyses, kept some samples, and then called various institutions and universities. He sold the meteorites and thereby supported himself. One pound of a meteorite could go for five hundred to a thousand dollars. Finds were rare, but he only needed to trap one now and then to get by.

Night fell, and in the evening sky the eagle constellation flew prominently—Aquila, the stars of which formed a breast, wings, and a tail, a bird flying eastward. The night was particularly black and clear, the perfect weather for viewing a shower. Frog sat at his telescope, and I sat next to him, using a stack of old notebooks as a wobbly stool. Soon specks began to appear high in the sky. Sparks shot out of an unseen cannon. They were white, bright, then orange, and fading into effervescent zaffer. Some flashed. Some left a trail. It was just the spectacle Frog had predicted.

We followed the shower for a while, Frog letting me sit before the telescope for a bit. I could see where the meteorites were plunging with my naked eye, and then I could use the telescope to focus on that piece of the sky. At one point, I thought I heard something, a whiz overhead, just for a split second, a pesky insect buzzing past my ear.

Before I could say anything, Frog blurted out, "Did you hear that, Coyote? Did you hear that?" He pulled away from the telescope.

"Yes." I was astonished.

"I think it was one of the little devils." Frog shook his head. "I thought I saw it, too. You know how rare it is to hear them?"

"I don't think I ever have," I realized.

"You just did." Frog was certain. He stepped outside the observatory, looked briefly at the sky, then made some calculations in a lined notebook. His formulae made awkward predictions about where a meteorite might land at the heart of the Iron Belt, but they were not as accurate as empirical clues. We had heard a distinct yet faint hum, the sound that defied statistics: you weren't supposed to be able to hear what you could see of falling stars. It was true that the iron meteorites fell as far away from civilization as they could, and therefore liked the desert, and the whiz indicated a clear vector into the open space north of Frog's observatory. And it had to be heavy to make a noise. Could it have been one of the one hundred million meteors that crashed against the atmosphere daily? Only five hundred survived and landed on Earth, since most broke apart when they hit the atmosphere, and even then, most of the fragments that made it through were smaller than a pebble. And then only one hundred fifty or so meteorites a year were planted on terra firma. There was a one in a billion chance that a meteor would land and earn the distinction of *meteorite*.

Frog scribbled with a red pencil over pages of a graph-paper notebook. He figured out where exactly the meteorite should be, given the volume of the noise, the direction, what we had been seeing earlier, the quality of the air tonight. Frog calculated that the meteorite should be ten to fifteen miles north of Rancho Fantasy Eccle, in the desert, and near . . . near the crater where his son had been found dead five years ago.

"I have a hunch," was all Frog said to me. That meant, Get in the jeep and let's go. So we drove toward an area where Frog's approximations and instinct lead him. The jeep was equipped with a small but adequate searchlight and a trailer. We drove silently, rapidly, through the unpaved terrain, over the bumpy cracks in the clay, swerving madly, and smashing through brush and tumbleweed. I had to hold on to the dashboard with both hands, and with one sudden turn I almost bounced out. Frog raced after the meteorite as if it were alive, galloping away. Had I fallen out of the jeep, I don't think Frog would have stopped to retrieve me.

In the darkness, I thought I saw a large round body just to the left of where our jeep zoomed by. "Go back." I reached over to the steering wheel to direct Frog. He shook his head as he leaned into the turn, saying I didn't see anything. And to my dismay, he hadn't, because when we arrived back at the spot I'd picked out, nothing was there. "Sorry," I apologized. Even at night the desert could conjure mirages. Frog continued back along the course he should have stuck to. One truth seemed to be that meteorites tended to land near previous finds, and so we had that to go on, too. Frog knew this landscape so well, he knew every inch of the desert, and when I once again pointed to where I thought I saw something in the night, Frog smiled politely but pressed ahead.

We drove a while longer, and after ten miles of scanning the hot sand lit by the searchlight, lit by the brilliant eagle constellation in the sky, I was afraid we'd find nothing tonight. But then I did spot something, this time an object more suspicious. This time I pointed at what appeared to be a nocturnal animal rummaging about, an enormous possum, disoriented and completely lost. A creature that seemed to take a few small steps in a futile effort to escape. Then it stood still, frozen in terror. But as we neared, as I aimed the searchlight at the dome of the beast, it glittered. Head-lights illuminated a steamy sphere. Closer, I yelped a cheer and Frog grinned.

The stranger from outer space, this alien craft still recovering from its long voyage, lay in a slight well of dirt, a depression cast in the soft clay. The meteorite must have weighed three hundred pounds. If I had tried to hug it, I would not have been able to stretch my arms all the way around the globe (a globe, I noted, with a large indentation on one side). It was full of holes from the friction of its fall. It glimmered. Heat still emanated from it. Even the seasoned Frog, versed in all forms of cosmic matter, marveled at the extraterrestrial boulder. Its shimmer and glow seemed less haunting than it did magical and knowing. It had somersaulted so far and traveled past planets and frontiers of space that we knew so little about firsthand. It was a pioneer dispatched from the asteroid belt, sent here to explore. It was an adventuresome expa-triate, curious about the new world.

An unwritten rule among nomads of the desert was finders/keep-ers, first come/first serve, which guaranteed that since we had found the meteorite before anyone else, even though the land was technically not no-man's but owned by the state, we would have the right to claim the rock as ours. Frog would pay a tax—that was how the state got some money out of what it conceivably may never have known existed—but the meteorite was Frog's. It was worth a fortune monetarily and scientifically. Green specks sparkled. The meteorite oozed with unknown power—it glowed with living-breathing beauty. It was ours: Frog's for the science, and the money, sure, and mine in spirit. I don't know why I felt this way, but I thought, this is my meteorite, it has my name on it.

And then the mauve people descended. They appeared out of nowhere, scavenger birds dropping down on the corpse, thankless ravens fufilling a final link in the cycle of nature. We had maybe ten minutes at the most with the spectacular boulder, and then we both saw a jeep race toward us, toward the meteorite.

We watched in amazement, and before we knew it, four men in purplish jumpsuits and one woman with a blue sash had hopped out of their jeep and had loudly started assessing how they would lift the stone into a trailer rigged to their jeep. The trailer had affixed to it a small crane that was used in construction. The mauve people came prepared. I don't think they even noticed that we were standing there.

"What the hell do you think you're doing?" Frog nudged me to say something, but no words came to mind. I think I was fascinated more by the pilgrims' cool indifference than by the coincidence of our nocturnal quests.

"Oh, we're taking this stone back to Rancho Flora," one man said.

"To where?" Frog shook his head.

"Rancho Flora."

"Hey, we were here a long time ago. Not to be greedy, but the meteorite is ours."

"Yes," I managed to say.

"You can come see the stone in Guru B's museum," the woman with the blue sash reasoned, "anytime you like. Just contact a woman named Lulu. . . ."

"Lulu?" Frog said. "No, no, no."

In all my time with Frog, he had never once raised his voice with such volume. He never once displayed any kind of violent behavior, anything beyond passive wisdom. And when he tried to pull one of the jumpsuited men to the ground, I was beyond speechlessness, I was immobile, unable to help him out. My timid reasoning was that there were five of them, two of us. This was our meteorite, but I avoided action at all costs. Frog cast me an annoyed look when a second pilgrim grabbed him and threw him toward the jeep.

"Don't play around, old guy," one of the men said.

"He's not old." I managed to offer some defense.

"It's not yours!" Frog dove at another man and was thrown toward the woman, who elbowed Frog in the ribs.

"It's ours," she said quietly. "We were here first."

"What? How did you know how to find it anyway?" Frog knew that his skills were rare.

"We saw it," the woman said.

"You saw it?" Frog found it impossible that anyone else could have spotted his meteor.

For the next twenty minutes, Frog several times tried to tackle the mauve people as they carefully used the crane to grasp the meteorite, lift it, and lower it into their trailer. Each time Frog was pushed back toward me. I tried to hold him back, almost as if I were abetting the criminals.

"C'mon," he rallied me, and wiggled out of my arm. When he was tossed back, he said, "It belongs to us, you know."

"I know, I know." I tried to be supportive but at the same time move back from the pilgrims at work.

"It's an incredible find, and it's ours."

"They won," I sighed, "we're just outnumbered." I knew that I should act. I did feel disappointed, frustrated, as if I were losing something, not a possession but a memento, an important memory. I felt all that, yet I almost preferred defeat. It was easier to do nothing.

"You're not going to get away with this," Frog shouted loudly. "This is outrageous," he added more softly. To me he whispered, "We could follow them. . . ." Then Frog winced. "No, I don't want to do that, I guess."

Soon the ferric wonder was secure in the trailer, and the pilgrims sped away fast, ignoring us as they left, pretending we'd never been there. We had lost the meteorite to the mauve people. Frog definitely had not been too aware of their existence before this scuffle. I was more annoyed with myself than I was with the pilgrims because deep down, in some perverse way, I had enjoyed losing. Frog looked at the eagle, still flying east in the night, then at me, and I knew that he was already planning how he would win the meteorite back.

B could stand for brown eyes, those glossy round puddles that followed you as you moved about in any room at Rancho Flora.

"I hear he likes backgammon," Madeleine said.

B could stand for backgammon. A few days after we had arrived at the ashram, Madeleine and I were trying to figure out what the initial tacked on to the reverential term *guru* could signify.

"Of course *B* might be for Benares, which is where he's from."

"*B* for Benares," I said.

"When he was in India," Madeleine reminded me, "he was known as Shree Barnhi Dar."

"Right." I nodded.

"When he went to Oxford"—Madeleine tried to remember—"didn't he take an Anglo name?"

"Bernard," I suggested.

"He read philosophy. Maybe he liked Martin Buber."

"Maybe it's a word . . . an adjective to describe him."

"Benevolent?"

"Bearded."

"Business minded."

"Benefactor," I said.

"That's a noun, not an adjective."

"So?"

"You know"—Madeleine nodded as if, yes, she had found the answer—"*bhagwan* means 'blessed one.'"

"Have we mentioned Buddha?" I asked. We were hastily missing the obvious.

"Buddha." Madeleine now liked that. "When he got back to India, he taught religion. Then the lecture circuit. Then the first ashram."

"Maybe the first car he acquired after he founded the first ashram was a Mercedes-*B*enz. . . ." I was stretching things. Then I thought, "Benares was where his first ashram was, right?"

"Yes," Madeleine said. "It *b*oomed. People came from all over to *b*ow"—she was silly—"*b*eautify their *b*eings, *b*e *b*orn again."

"Or maybe," I truly thought, "the *B* is for 'be quiet.'"

"Why 'be quiet'?"

"Because the guru went into silence when he left India and came here."

"I heard some pilgrims talking about this," Madeleine said, moving on.

"No, it's forbidden. We shouldn't be discussing it too loudly."

The guru was called Guru B, but there was a rule that pilgrims at Rancho Flora were not supposed to discuss what the B stood for, because to speculate about such a thing would demonstrate a lack of blind acceptance in the holiest man on earth. The letter was there, dangling, unidentified, ambiguous, for all the world to wonder about. But those inside the ashram were required to take the letter at face value, accept it as a secret, as the thing they would never know for sure, because after all you weren't supposed to know the true name of your god. Madeleine and I participated in the goings-on of the cult, but as distanced observers we could safely *b*laspheme.

"Who the hell cares if we figure it out?" I was learning that Madeleine possessed an irreverent strain. "Can you imagine if we ran up and down the hill chanting '*B* stands for this, *B* stands for that?'"

"We'd be gunned down," I said. "*B*attered *by b*ullets."

"Yes. Anyway, I did hear two pilgrims indicate that they thought the *B* stood for biology."

"Guru Biology."

"As if all knowledge of life were possessed by this man, as if he even knew what was beyond life."

"*B*eyond," I said.

"Let's face it," Madeleine said, "the *B* is a tease."

"It doesn't stand for anything?"

"I mean it's a tease—not to *b*elittle, but it's just meant to *b*affle."

"Nothing more?"

"Nope."

Madeleine and I were in our adobe apartment during the first glimpse of dawn, which was supposed to be reserved for morning prayer, the first segment of a pilgrim's structured day. We had practically slept through the first rite, and now we were drowning the solemn moment in silliness.

Guru B's spiritual program was supposed to lead the pilgrim to a higher plane of existence. A lofty freeway to things unimaginable. The highest plane was a place where truth was pure, everything clear and calm, a place where your own inner harmony finally coincided with the larger harmony of the universe. It was available to anyone, on or off the ashram, but the gradual enlightenment that would finally permit the perfect, keen vision could only successfully proceed with the kind of program and guidance offered by a guru like Rancho Flora's own bona fide old sage.

We had talked a lot in the last three days to various pilgrims—that was all we did after our arrival, gregariously plunge ourselves into introductions and interviews—and Madeleine always asked what I thought was a rather personal question, but what the pilgrims all answered with delight. What does the highest plane look like? Their dreams of absolute paradise were often attached to rather mundane images, ordinary in the sense that they described something that might be found in any inconspicuous corner of the globe. It was just a matter of finding the secluded spot. Sameness and totality were common motifs. So a former labor lawyer named Eldredge with bushy blond hair always wet with sweat claimed that the absolute harmony resembled an urban diner after the lunch hour had subsided, and the restaurant had cleared out, and you could order your lunch and eat in relative quiet. Margot, an ex-chorus-line dancer who had long limbs and a long nose, believed that the highest plane looked like a movie theater, lights out, film in progress, with everyone alertly watching the same screen, the same action, the same old film. Delmar, who gave up a life as a tax accountant with a major medical-supplies manufacturer proposed a more surreal vision. He saw an endless tent outdoors, a kind of carnival, in which there were thousands of potter's wheels and everyone there was seated at a wheel and threw pots. Each lump of clay was being fashioned according to the exact same design. Martha, who had been quite successful selling homes to the rich and famous on Florida beaches, liked to stroke a skinny, punkish braid emerging from her head of short-cropped hair as she described her heaven: an enormous tree house in the middle of dense woods, a tree house that could actually travel like a helicopter from one large tree to the next, ultimately hovering over and landing on every tree in the world, an endless journey.

So far I had followed Madeleine around like an apprentice learning a trade, and she didn't seem to mind. We met a lot of people quickly, who blurred together. Madeleine, however, could say hi to whomever she saw, and say hi so-and-so. The pilgrims liked the fact that Madeleine was doing a series of articles and were willing to answer any questions, pleasantly surprised at how fascinated Madeleine seemed to be, for her probe went far beyond issues of accommodations and sight-seeing. I wondered what they thought I was doing tagging along, like a photographer without a camera. But as it turned out, no one was really worried about why I was silently observing and why I wasn't wearing a jumpsuit. No one remembered that I had claimed to be Madeleine's spouse, that she said I was her nephew. The pilgrims liked Madeleine, they liked me, they liked anyone.

Today we tried to compose ourselves before the sun had a chance to climb the sky. Each pilgrim was still going through his self-styled prayer. We sat still, and if we strained, we could hear the faintest hum, a purr that seemed to be the mauve meditation. Then, as if some silent gong had sounded, the calm morning was overtaken by bustle. The pilgrims went to whatever jobs were as-signed. Vanessa's office created the work schedules, and people more or less did what they wanted to do, given the possibilities. Some operated the bulldozers, some made the mixture of cement and mud to build new adobes, some taught the children, and some baked bread. Some aided the blue obis in administrative tasks. Many pilgrims had performed different jobs in their pre-ashram lives. They had been doctors and lawyers and brokers and academ-ics—all in all, they had entertained professions entirely unlike what they now found themselves doing. So a doctor made bricks, a lawyer laundered bedsheets. Except for a few, who did do what they had always done, because every utopia needed its doctors and electricians.

We stepped outside into a glorious day and encountered Regi-nald on his way to the refectory.

"'Lo!" Reginald said. Three years ago he gave up tennis instruc-tion to come here and be a baker. We walked with him a bit.

"Nice day," Madeleine said.

"Indeed," Reginald piped.

"Do you miss teaching tennis?" Madeleine asked. She always got to the point quickly.

"Hell, no." Reginald grinned. He had a smooth, lazy way of talk-ing. "I mean there's technique in whatever you do. I got tired of whacking those silly rubber balls, you know? I sort of feel renewed here. Know what I mean? With each loaf of zucchini bread—it's a baby." I imagined him cradling a warm pan just out of the oven. We let him hop on a jeep with some other pilgrims and drive down Walt Whitman Way.

We spent the morning wandering the hill, checking in on pilgrims busy at their daily labors. A woman painting signs for the roads, a man watering eggplant in the greenhouse. A crew of mauve people raking tar over a new road, tar that seemed to emit no heat, no noxious odor, a glistening asphalt of some magical formula.

I looked for James among the workers. I wanted to ask someone about him, but if he had really bought into the pilgrims' routine, he might have changed his name. I also inspected faces to see if anyone resembled the thieves Frog and I encountered that night, but I frankly had trouble remembering what they looked like. I dashed into a few houses for the meteorite when no one was looking, while Madeleine was busy interviewing. I searched quickly but found no clues.

We strolled over to where some new buildings were going up. Sandra, a onetime big-city advertising executive, now a plumber, gripped a foot-long piece of terra-cotta piping.

"Did you end up winning that gin game the other night?" Madeleine inquired, remembering the last time she saw Sandra.

"No, I always choke," Sandra sighed.

"The plumbing world must be very different from the ad world." Madeleine picked up a wrench that had slipped out of Sandra's utility belt.

Sandra rolled her eyes and nodded. "I know it's weird," she said, "but the truth is, I didn't ask for it. I was just told, here do this. And okay, at first I was pissed. But then, I got to like it. I mean, think about water. Are you thinking about it? Okay, now: water in a desert. Right? I mean, that's far-out." She had a point. Her hands gripped the terra-cotta pipe more firmly. Sandra was soon going to be honored with a blue obi after only a year at the ashram, and she confided it was because she had been fortunate enough to receive this assignment.

The sun reached its peak height, and the pilgrims at Rancho Flora suspended all temporal activity and appropriated the hot part of the day for purely spiritual pursuits. In this region, siestas were not unusual, but for the mauve person, this was not a time to fall asleep.

After lunch in the refectory, they trekked up to the white temple and took seats on the benches. Chatter subsided. Then the guru entered, supported on either side by a woman with a blue obi. Vanessa followed him. The guru looked frail, much older and smaller than he appeared in his portrait. It was hard to tell how he shuffled along, because when he walked, gold sandals were hidden by the gold-embroidered white robes. His skin was darker than in the pictures. His complexion was like a glazed oil painting, darkening and darkening with the years, until someday, it would crack and flake.

The guru sat in his throne and donned a glassy gaze—looking nobly at the future—and Vanessa stood at a podium and read the day's lecture. Vanessa always read the guru's sermon. The guru, in fact, never spoke in public, and he only directly addressed pilgrims wearing obis. When he left India, he had gone into silence, as was the fashion for holy men of a certain age. Vanessa pronounced his texts as smoothly as if they were her own, managing to seem less unctuous now than she did when we met her.

It occurred to me that the guru might have had little more than final approval of the scripts, and that the daily lectures could have been written by a blue obi at the glass table. But the pilgrims did not look at Vanessa, they watched Guru B, whose eyes occasionally drifted down to someone in the audience to offer an approving glance that at once said, You are my child, and, I am on top of the world. The design of the temple, we were told, followed the guru's plan for the original synagogue in the first ashram. The pilgrims sitting on the benches around the bema of the temple were supposed to compose a flower (and thus the name of the ashram). The guru was at the center, the pollinating force, and all around were the mauve petals. I supposed that this made Vanessa a kind of queen bee. (I had trouble restraining myself from the constant comparison of the ashram with insect colonies. It had looked like an anthill at first, and now it seemed more like a beehive. Here we were sharing our honey in the hive, the temple, even shaped a bit like a hive.) All of the mauve uniforms compacted into one area did look kind of pretty, and only at lectures did I feel a little conspicuous in my normal duds.

The lectures were usually highlighted by tales of exemplary pilgrims who had progressed toward the mystical higher plane. The brief accounts led into some restatement—though I'd only heard a few lectures now, I knew that they were restatements—of the same philosophy that the guru had been peddling for years now. Today it was David, the neurosurgeon turned sous-chef who lived in the same compound we were staying in. David had become a vital member of the ashram, finding peace in chopping vegetables, and so the guru's lecture focused on the Buddhafield's absorbing the sins of the city. Not sins really, aggravations, inhibitors along the path toward spiritual purity.

"David understands," Vanessa read the guru's words, "that in the bold slicing of squash, he erases the tension of crowded subways. Now he dices onions instead of attending tedious conferences and meetings. David is spiritually centered when he cubes a tomato." Vanessa crescendoed. "Do you think he even remembers the pile of memos reminding him to return phone calls? Not with eggplant to slice and chop up for the ratatouille."

Madeleine claimed that the guru probably enjoyed the hazy image he offered outsiders of what actually happened inside his ashram. After all, the mystery lured people to him. What the guru advocated was transcendence, transcendence any which way you can: if you had to get beyond the material world through means of violent expression, that was legitimate (although the guru had played this down upon entering the States). If you wanted to fulfill your sexual desires in order to reach salvation, that was sanctioned. You could climb a mountain, raft down rapids, learn to be a bartender, become expert at the violin—whatever it took. You could transcend the material world by becoming the utmost collector—that was ordained. Here was a strange logic: you could reach the immaterial plane by claiming all that was in fact material, because if you possessed everything you could want, if you had all that there was to have of a certain thing, you wouldn't be bothered by leftover urges for what you didn't have, and you would be free to grasp the higher truths. This was the method of transcendence, after all, exemplified by the guru's odd museum of watches, rocks, and cars.

When the lecture was over, the guru, Vanessa, and the attendant obis departed, then the pilgrims filed out of the temple. I watched the river of uniforms spill out. As we left, I whispered to Madeleine, "How can this place be so communal while the guru collects anything he wants?"

She explained softly, "The guru's acquisitions have to do with his transcendence, but the design of the utopia is another thing. It's a model universe." Madeleine nodded while she explained this to me, as if she had to convince herself of what she said as she said it. "The guru believes that the spirit of the masses reinforces the providence of the individual. An individual can collect, amass, acquire . . . but as a member of a larger system, he has to fit into an overall harmony."

Peer support and group involvement were expressed in the truly mesmerizing part of the pilgrim's day that followed the lecture each hot afternoon. Group dynamic it was called, or dynamic meditation. In Frescura they used the words *orgy* and *group sex*, and before I came here, I was sure they were exaggerating. But the tolerant community's slurs were after all born from rumors, and those rumors had a base in reports from ex-pilgrims, those who had left (there were a few). Frescurans, it turned out, weren't really too far off in categorizing the ritualized free sex.

After leaving the domed temple, the mauve people retreated without much conversation to their compounds, their homes. Madeleine and I fell into the pack of our own neighbors. The group gathered in one apartment of the larger adobe complex, usually the same one day to day. So for the last few afternoons, Madeleine and I had found ourselves in the corner of David's place. We didn't participate. Madeleine sat and took notes, and I sat and wondered what she was taking notes about. Madeleine put on her dark sunglasses, which she often wore at the oddest moments. I felt exposed.

These six or seven mauve people would try to conjure up what it was that clouded their inner harmony today. They sat in a circle. They held hands. And more or less, they moaned. The pilgrims attempted to bring all the pain buried in the deepest trenches of their gut to the surface. The moans became more rhythmic. The circle swayed somewhat. Quiet sounds were emitted, low and guttural. And after ten minutes or so, the pilgrims choked and coughed as the pain passed. One man slapped his chest with clenched fists. I put my ear to the window, and I heard a low rumble coming from other dwellings. But it was not timed, it happened organically, all at once, by sympathetic consensus. And then, out of the blue, the mauve-clad pilgrims were flailing about the beige room. They were somersaulting and hitting each other gently, pushing themselves into walls and flipping over furniture. Madeleine and I sank into the corner, not really sure whether at this point the others in David's apartment were even still aware of our presence. David dashed from wall to wall and rammed the cream-colored surface with his shoulder.

This small bit of violence, the pain fomenting to a head, was minor in the amount of time it took up. Maybe a minute. In India, reportedly, it lasted longer, but this was the chunk of the dynamic that had been trimmed by the guru five years ago, when he had probably decided that if anyone found out about this portion of the therapy, they would be outraged and claim that criminal battery was ordained. The sex that followed would pass, but not the violence.

Finally, the various pilgrims in the room started to undress. It happened unexpectedly, but on cue. They slowly, erotically, tenderly pulled off each other's jumpsuits. Most people here didn't wear underwear, a curious delight. And it was only a matter of stepping out of the one-piece frock before the pilgrim was nude. Clothes were pushed to the edges of the room.

We became total voyeurs, and Madeleine stopped taking copious notes. Throughout it all, she maintained a straight-lipped expression beneath the sunglasses. I swallowed a lot. There was a burning in my groin, and I crossed my legs.

The seven pilgrims, four men and three women, had peaked in collective angst, stripped quickly, and now quelled their violent urges with petting and a gentle collapse to the rugs on the floor. A futon lay in the center of the room, and some rolled onto that. There were pillows everywhere. There was a brief period of mutual soothing and caressing. It was easy enough to adjust to this somehow. Naked men and women, okay. Now they're touching each other, sure, fine. Then David, I observed, made the first real move. The seven pilgrims lay on the floor in one sort of mass, and he rolled out of the heap with Illyanna, a thin, blond woman, and in a matter of moments he was into heavy stuff with her.

Pure pornography. I'd never witnessed or dreamed of anything like this. The frenzy spread and everyone had grouped into lumps of foreplay and intercourse. I took note of how they paired off. (And the day before, they had stayed in the same compound, but permutations in the partnering occurred, and the day before that it was different, too. There was a limited number of combinations, but the pilgrims explored them all and made an effort not to duplicate a pattern from one afternoon to the next). Today David the neurosurgeon-turned-sous-chef went with Illyanna. Ingrid went with Marguerita and Henry. And Marcus and Reginald tumbled into a satellite heap that seemed to orbit the futon. At times, the groups bumped into one another, but they maintained the subdivisions. Their frolic was oddly quiet, the sighs of ecstasy surprisingly subdued. The overall sound reminded me of a child's making noises as he happily, quickly gulped his cereal.

I couldn't help but get aroused. I wanted to jump in, but a very sober Madeleine prevented me, not physically, but with a glance that I interpreted to mean that she would be uncomfortable if I left her as the sole voyeur. Meanwhile, bodies seemed undefined as they folded and crossed and wove. There was a shimmer to it all, a kind of oil in the cogs, the sweat of the romp.

It was incredible. I could smell this sweat, human exhaust, and it was overwhelming. I became bleary eyed, dry mouthed. I watched buttocks flex and breasts flop and hair and limbs fly everywhere. The motion of bodies moving up and down became mechanical, engineered. There was even a moment choreographed into the dynamic when condoms were slipped on with great enthusiasm. Practices of safer sex had become necessary additions to precautions already in place for birth control, but the act of taking time out for such matters was in no way clumsy or awkward—it was a joyful component of the ritual. After a half-hour (maybe less) of glorious frolicking, climax evolved separately, bodies rolling off bodies at different moments. A series of gleeful, rewarding yelps. The cluster of flesh unpeeled like a flower.

As the pilgrims in our house started to pull on their jumpsuits and comb their hair with their fingers, Madeleine stood up and proceeded to interview them, scientifically, unabashedly, candidly. I was a mess of an aroused and unfulfilled person.

Marguerita, married twice to the same man, testified, "At first I had problems doing it with a woman. I was hung up on doing things the way I had always done them. But once you realize that any combination is okayed by the group—I mean once you actually see that anything goes—you feel incredibly liberated." During the dynamic tomorrow, the partners would switch off, everyone was eager and willing to participate in any kind of arrangement, so a universal sexuality existed (at least during the midday dynamic).

Madeleine turned to Ingrid. "So how does the dynamic affect your day?"

Ingrid replied quickly, "Afterwards I feel centered. Like someday, yes, I will reach that higher plane."

I managed to stand up and whisper an uncomfortable hello to Marcus. "Did it bother you that we were sitting there watching?" I asked apologetically.

He replied, "No way. It was a turn-on."

Unwittingly, I had joined the group. I wondered if James was into this routine.

So the frenzy had subsided, and the pilgrims, now dressed, all chatted happily as they walked out of the adobe into the remaining afternoon. They did this every day after lunch. Prayer, violence, and sex. A nice purge. They returned to their jobs replenished. Madeleine was going to watch David cut up vegetables in the kitchen, and I told her I would catch up with her later. As soon as she was gone, I retreated to our rooms next door, and I stripped and masturbated. I was left feeling hollow and self-conscious.

At the end of the day, when the sun went down, everyone piled into the refectory and ate dinner. We sat at long tables, and since I had fallen asleep for most of the afternoon, I was groggy. I tasted sesame in everything, and peanuts in the whole-wheat linguine with carrots and scallions. Not in the spinach soup. But yes, peanuts even in the twelve-grain bread. I felt somewhat overwhelmed in the company of so many strangers. But tonight, the pilgrims seemed less like strangers, more like a village of people I'd lived among for a long time. At one point, I stood on a bench and surveyed the dining pilgrims. I scanned all of the heads bowed over plates of linguine. No James. I was sure now he was not at the ashram, he was gone for good. I didn't have to worry about running into him accidentally. In a way I felt relieved.

In the evening, the pilgrims did whatever they wanted to do.

They took walks, some even went to Frescura, some went to other's houses and spent the night. The disco was open a few nights a week. There wasn't rampant promiscuity, that was clear. People interacted within their small puddle of pilgrims during daily rites, and in the evenings, rather monogamous mating and dating was the norm. What I heard on the other side of the wall at night was a more private version of the dynamic, that was all. Nights offered time for solitude, if one wanted it. So you might see people sitting alone, musing, examining constellations. Finally, everyone went to sleep, cleansed for the time being. The next day: the same routine.

That night I strolled up and down the hill, not really paying any attention to where I was headed, and before long, I found myself wandering away from the developed part of the ashram and into an unused quarter. I was all set to turn around when I noticed a pilgrim, a woman, who was marching at a quick pace into the same darkness. There was less and less light over here, and the light from dwellings became dimmer as people went to sleep. Yet I could see that this woman, whom I now followed at a safe distance, was carrying a flashlight. She was prepared for this hike, and she seemed to know exactly where she was going. What was over here? Why would anyone be here this late at night?

I kept my distance and pursued the woman, who seemed to be on a direct path toward the other side of the hill, toward the fence dividing the ashram. I was going to move in a little closer, maybe even shout howdy, when suddenly the flashlight blinded me.

"Who are you?" the woman whispered, hissed. "I thought I was being followed." She approached me, and since she kept the flashlight pointed like a pistol at my nose, I couldn't see a thing.

"Could you maybe not point that at me?" I tried to sound friendly.

"Could you maybe tell me why you're following me?" Yet she did point the flashlight at my feet. My eyes adjusted to the darkness again, and I could see her ponytail and her deep-set eyes. In this light, it was hard to tell how she looked at me, with curiosity or disdain.

"I'm sorry," I apologized. "I didn't mean to follow you, but I noticed that you were wandering into a part of the ashram I didn't know had anything important." I stumbled through an explanation. "I mean any buildings or anything."

"It doesn't." the woman was curt.

"I'm Coyote," I introduced myself.

"I'm sure you are," the woman said. "I have to go somewhere," she added, "and I'd really, really like it"—she was nasty—"if you got lost."

"You aren't by any chance looking for a meteorite?" It was just a stab.

"A what? No, I'm not."

"I am sorry to bother you," I said. I turned around to indicate that I was following orders, but I couldn't resist asking, "So where are you going anyway?"

The flashlight was off my face, and the woman turned around and marched away. "Good night," she shouted insincerely.

I didn't want to let her get away. So I turned into a cat. I scampered behind the woman, at a safe distance. And she did turn around to see if I was still following her, but I anticipated and dodged her beam of light: I slithered beneath it, stayed low to the ground. Cautiously I followed her all the way to the fence. And though I couldn't be certain, I thought I saw her climb the fence and disappear into further darkness, to the other side of the hill, the forbidden other world. She was a strange pilgrim with a secret mission, but that's all I learned. I went home.

"Damn," Madeleine muttered from the bedroom as I walked in the house. "Oh, screw it." She was working as she did every night, typing out her notes, the day's discoveries, transcribing interviews, shaping what would become her articles. "Look at you." She shot me a glance when I stepped into her room and took a seat on the end of her bed.

"What?"

"You're filthy," she said, laughing. Indeed the knees of my jeans were covered in clay. Then Madeleine looked serious. "You know, it's not entirely safe for young men to wander around the desert at night."

"I didn't leave the ashram," I said.

"Well, I'm just saying, the desert at night is not always safe. Okay?"

"Okay." I shrugged. I had spent my life roaming the desert at night, and Madeleine knew that. I had no idea where this admonishment came from.

Madeleine sat on the bed with her small typewriter on her lap. Her sunglasses rested on her forehead. "I hate writing," she said. "It's so fucking hard. But what's really getting me mad is that we haven't seen the whole place."

"We haven't?"

"What's beyond the temple?"

"Just the guru's house, Vanessa's, where the blue obis live." I recited the official list. We knew that there might be more than we had seen, but for an instant, I didn't want this world to be complicated, I didn't want to think that there were any secrets. But there were secrets, that was the truth. Things to figure out.

"No, there's more there than meets the eye," Madeleine sighed.

"B is for beyond the temple," I decided.

"Bewildering," she replied.

I wanted, then, to kiss Madeleine. I thought she was pretty. Yes, she could have been my mother. But I wanted to climb into bed with her, not for sex—though sex all around made me crave pressing someone's cool flesh against mine—but for solace, and so I sat closer to her on her bed.

Madeleine started to examine something she'd already typed. "I do have to work now," she said abruptly.

I got up, pecked her on the cheek, and she flashed an uncomfortable smile. I said, "B is for 'Bye now.'"

"Bye now."

I fell asleep on the couch to the soft patter of the typewriter and the writerly grumbles coming from the next room.

*W*hat on earth did you think you were going to get out of it?" Madeleine scolded me. I had never seen her get mad, and when encountering someone's temper for the first time, I tended to shrink and offer no defense. I was too amazed by the new costume of anger. I thought, however, that she exaggerated, as if I had committed an irreparable act.

"You're the one who takes all the notes," I finally countered. "You tell me, what did I think I would get out of it?"

"I'm the one who takes all the notes, great. Get in the jeep."

I obeyed and climbed in the ashram vehicle, which Madeleine preferred over her own jalopy. The jeep could handle the terrain better. She was now going to Frescura to make a phone call. I didn't want to continue this ridiculous tiff, but I plopped down into the passenger's seat anyway. We said nothing to each other until we had passed through the rainbow arch and waved good-bye to the security guard, who was watering the palm trees with a hose that seemed to emerge magically from the soil. Once in the desert, I was on fire, mad, and hot. I had forgotten how cool it was back at the elevated oasis.

I had not been outside of the ashram since we entered one long week ago, but that didn't occur to me until we zoomed past the Great Tree. For the first stretch of the journey I was reliving what I had just been through, what Madeleine was scolding me for, what rightly I should have been consoled about. She was mad at me because she learned that during the group dynamic (which she had been observing in various parts of the ashram on different days so that she could determine if it was the same from house to house), I had gone by myself back to David's apartment in our block. And I had participated.

"Participated" was a misleading term, and I tried to convey that. I remained as apart and as much an observer as I had before I entered the fray.

"I had no choice," I explained.

"No choice—oh, you're full of shit," she said. "Were you raped? No."

"No." I unintentionally mimicked her voice.

It had not been rape. David had simply looked up at me when things were starting to brew. "David touched my wrist," I tried to tell her. And then I fell rather naturally into the heap of bodies, the sex machine on the floor, on the rugs, pillows.

"What did you think you were going to get out of it?" Madeleine repeated herself. "Tell me." It wasn't that she disapproved of the group sex—she was no prude—and I realized that in fact, she wasn't even really very mad. My ordeal made her nervous, and her insecurity made her nasty. When she was uncomfortable, she was just unpleasant.

"I don't really know," I said.

"No, you don't. We've been here a week, Mr. Coyote Gato, and maybe you have had enough time to answer this question?"

"What?"

"Tell me why the hell you're getting in my way. Well? No answer. I could just leave you in Frescura."

"No," I protested.

"I'll leave you at the café."

Maybe she actually believed that I would be fickle enough to be drawn into the ashram, into the daily routines. And I got mad at her.

"You don't know shit," I said.

"Oh, I know shit," she shot back. Unfortunately, I believed she did.

Then I thought: I had only been here a week, and I *had* been drawn into the sex. That was where involvement in the cult began. Maybe there was some truth lurking in her concern. Sex was a way of life at the ashram, a way of conversing, transcending, but a way, too, of finding new members and making them conform. It was the guru's strategy: pleasure could expunge pain, desire displace despair. Sex to initiate, sex to prove membership, sex to keep pilgrims devoted to the man who gave them all a message after lunch and then sent them off for more sex.

In the jeep I tried to trivialize the experience. I told her David had touched my hand, that he was very gentle, and it was refreshing to feel flesh, have physical contact. I did not go into how Illyanna joined the scene and how I felt rather supplementary after she dropped down on David and me. I just remembered stroking a lot of forearms and thighs at that point, and now and then, when the three of us rolled, feeling a bit uncomfortable if I was on the bottom of the heap. I remembered wearing an ear-to-ear grin, all the while unable to erase this foolish expression. I found myself then strategizing like a wrestler: what would be my next hold? I ended up determining that David was too hairy, and that Illyanna too lumpy for my liking. Somehow, I found myself floating above the scene, wishing indeed I weren't here. I squeezed a calf or an ankle, for I seemed to be left with feet, and then I felt like a physician clinically examining pieces of anatomy as if they were found objects. I appointed myself as today's condom dispenser, it was something to occupy myself with, and I distributed packets as if I had fetched everyone coffee. Extraneous to the intercourse, I had to fabricate my own high, because in the air there was an insipid pressure to conform and be happy and exhibit your glee. At one point, I tried to escape, realizing before the grand finale that I'd made a mistake. But when I stood up, I tripped over someone's foot and fell back into the romp.

"It was all rather gentle," I told Madeleine. Of course, when everyone exploded, it was not gentle at all, in fact it was very athletic. In my own moment of ecstasy, I made a point of holding nothing back—I was going to get something out of it. Yet whatever I felt, I knew it was muted. There was a false triumph. We were a team. We had won some match, some game for which I didn't even know the rules. I was detached. We had all climbed some craggy mountain together, but I wanted to be alone, and I resented company. When it was all over, I watched pilgrims get dressed, and they seemed more satisfied with their complex acrobatics, thrilled with their extraordinary dexterity, than with the ritual itself.

Maybe if I fell into an orgy every day, I'd feel differently, less coaxed, less betrayed. But I didn't want to participate in the dynamic again. Too much of a letdown this time. More than a letdown—it wasn't me to try to fit in. I wanted sex, I needed sex, big deal. But now I was mad at myself, too, for succumbing to the pressures of conformity and community, which as a teen I had proudly, defiantly grown beyond.

"I'm annoyed," was all Madeleine said when she dropped me off at the gas station, where Carl gave us both a dirty look. She zoomed off, indicating that our little adventure had ended.

I shuffled along the dusty main drag, kicking up dirt. Then, like one of those wind storms that can without warning rush across the desert and engulf you in an instant, I realized why Madeleine was mad. I could only be flattered, and I could only want to be her best friend in the world. The mere suggestion that I might become a part of the cult, the simple fact that the dynamic was the means by which new pilgrims were signed on, bothered her because it meant that I might stray from her side. I might become a regular mauve person. She didn't know me very well yet. I would always be on the outside looking in, like her, with her.

I found Madeleine's car parked by the Sunflower Lives, and inside, she was talking on the pay phone. She could have used a phone at Rancho Flora, but clearly she thought she would not have privacy there. However, at the café, Virginia Martinez in her immense apron was quite nosy. She stood a yard away from Madeleine and watched her make her phone call. When I walked into the café, Madeleine looked relieved, because Virginia stopped staring at her and turned to me.

"Well, Coyote?" Virginia said, hands on hips.

"Well, what?"

"Do they have orgies all day and night up at that place?"

"I don't know what you mean, Virginia." I was glad that Madeleine was too busy talking to hear our exchange.

"You used to be a good boy." She turned away from me.

"Virginia, how about a beer?"

"Read the sign," she yelled from the kitchen.

A sign over the counter read WE DON'T SERVE MAUVE PEOPLE.

"Virginia, I'm not really *living* there." I found her in the kitchen. "It's not like what you imagine. It's not. And I'm just there on assignment with Madeleine"—I pointed to the phone—"so how about a beer?"

She handed me a bottle and rattled, "Get. Go drink it in there."

Madeleine hung up the phone and glared at me.

"Who was that?" I asked.

"None of your business," Madeleine snapped. Then she sighed, realizing she was being too mean, and said, "My editor, and don't ask any more questions."

"Okay," I said, nodding. "I'm sorry about before," I was quick to say. "I didn't much like the dynamic anyway."

"Fine. Look, just don't get in my way." Madeleine stepped outside and I followed. "I have a job to do." She started walking away from the café, away from her jeep. "And I don't have time to rescue you from the undertow."

"Okay," I chimed.

She looked at her watch and picked up the pace. I had to jog to catch up. We walked up the wide boulevard quickly.

"Where are we going?"

"I want to be at the Sunflower Café when he gets here."

"Who? Guru B?"

"Yes, for his snack."

So we hurried up the main drag, because it was almost three.

"Why do you need to see him *here*?" I wondered.

"Because I want to make sure he really sees me."

"Why?"

Madeleine didn't answer. The interior of the Sunflower Café had been decorated by the cult with mirrors everywhere, glossy mauve wainscoting, and a sparkling, pink marble counter. The glass case of ice cream tubs was crystal clear. A hum of refrigeration filled the large room. The ashram had bought this place out from under Virginia Martinez, and she ended up opening the café down the street, finding a defiant new title to paint over the entrance.

We approached the counter and examined all of the flavors. "I'll have a double scoop of mocha peach in a dish," Madeleine decided. The woman behind the counter scooped out the ice cream.

"I'll have just one scoop of banana mint," I said.

The pilgrim stared at me as if I'd told a dirty joke. "That's not really very funny," she said once she determined that I was serious.

"I didn't mean it to be," I said. I pointed to a tub in the center of the array of pastel flavors. "That is banana mint, isn't it?"

"Don't you know the rule?" the attendant wondered.

"What rule?" I shook my head.

"Well, that flavor, banana mint," she explained, "is the guru's personal and unique flavor. It's sacred. Only he eats it."

"Fascinating," Madeleine inserted between spoonfuls of beige ice cream.

"And he eats it every day?" I asked.

"Every day without fail," the pilgrim confirmed. "It's his favorite flavor. He doesn't eat anything else." Somehow this seemed in keeping with Guru B's outlook. "Vanessa sends over a gallon each week just for the guru," the parlor worker explained, "and it's the only rule at the Sunflower Café: the guru has his private flavor."

"I'll have what she had." I pointed to Madeleine's dish. I was sort of mad. I could smell the banana mint so clearly among the other fresh scents in the parlor. The banana had an overriding aroma. But I sniffed the cocoa bouquet of the dish I was handed, and once I tasted the mocha peach, all-natural and tart, I was happy enough.

Madeleine and I sat at a small table in the corner. There were two other pilgrims, a man and woman, at another table nearby. They seemed to be having a frustrated-lovers' quarrel. No one fought or entered disputes at Rancho Flora because the Buddha-field was supposed to be a place of perfect harmony, and when pilgrims wanted to argue, they had to do so in town, here, in public.

"So while you were busy flopping around," Madeleine said, "I met up with Elise."

"Who is Elise?" I tried to remember if I'd met her.

"You saw her at the glass table. She's one of the guru's closest companions. A blue obi who was with him in India, before Vanessa even. It's hard to imagine, but the guru, according to Elise, was quite a ladies' man back in India."

"No way. Do you think he still has sex?" I asked innocently. I was a little timid to be back on the subject of sex again, but Madeleine didn't care. She did shush me, though, because I was talking too loudly. We were in the Sunflower Café after all, a cult establishment, and we couldn't talk so freely.

Madeleine lowered her voice and addressed my question. "Yes, in a way. Elise told me that he takes two blue obis with him to bed every night."

"Vanessa?"

"Are you kidding." Madeleine laughed. "No one of import, except maybe Elise. He takes two from the same lot of five or so. Not to do anything really, just for the company."

"Why did Elise tell you all this?" I wondered.

"I guess because I asked." Madeleine shrugged. But I knew why: people simply trusted Madeleine and told her everything.

I watched the pilgrim behind the counter polish the glass case, in preparation for the guru's visit, a braid of hair wagging as she scrubbed. I wondered if she had ever had pinched a taste of the banana mint. Probably not. Pilgrims obeyed the few prescribed rules: Don't go beyond the temple, and don't eat the banana mint ice cream.

Finally Guru B's limousine and the accompanying jeeps pulled up to the café. Madeleine pointed out with her pinky that two or three of the pilgrims wore pistols in hip holsters. I was sure no one would take a shot at the guru, not in Frescura, because people here didn't shoot unless you had stolen something. Maybe the guns were supposed to flatter the guru in a way. He was so important he needed this protection. The pilgrims who had been quarreling stopped fighting—in fact they stopped talking altogether and smiled at the sight of the guru.

I had finished my ice cream and was going to the counter to get seconds when Madeleine tugged my T-shirt and ordered, "Sit."

The guru teetered in on the arms of the blue obis. One of them was Lulu. The other, Elise. The guru was unsteady. I could barely see much more than the beard and the general whiteness, since mauve people filled the café and surrounded him.

Guru B was seated at a center table and handed his usual double-scoop cone. He slowly rounded his mouth and fit it over the yellowish dome of ice cream. A large drip trickled down his beard, but he didn't notice and no one said anything. Elise extended her jumpsuit sleeve. The guru giggled and wiped his chin on the blue obi's uniform. It was as if he were the mad grandparent out on furlough from the nursing home. At one point, the wall of mauve people inadvertently parted, and Madeleine and I faced the guru directly. He looked first at me and I was haunted. His face was totally blank, as if he saw right through me. More likely he was bored. And then I saw tired eyes focus and he nodded his head. I smiled politely. Then he saw Madeleine, and it was as if she had sent a spark to the old holy man, because faint eyebrows against dark skin rose, and he nodded and even waved a hand (the one not dropping the ice cream cone on Elise's lap).

I wish I could have registered Madeleine's reaction, but her back was to me. She hadn't said anything to the guru, but she had communicated a message, a friendly gesture that no matter how it was construed would have said, remember me. Soon the guru was scooped up and escorted back to his limousine. The jeeps and limousine zoomed off toward the Great Tree.

"Well," Madeleine chirped. She was satisfied with her subtle entrée into the imagination of the guru. "Shall we?" She stood up.

We strolled back toward the Sunflower Lives. A bunch of Frescurans had gathered around a table.

"Who are they?" Madeleine asked me.

I looked at the group of men and women busy eating Virginia's burritos, drinking an afternoon beer, and gesticulating madly.

"Oh," I explained, "they're what's known as the Coalition."

Before I could explain what the Coalition was, Madeleine had entered the Sunflower Lives and pulled up a chair at a table far enough away from the center group to be only a minor distraction, yet close enough to hear their banter. Visitors to these informal Coalition meetings were welcome, so we didn't have to pretend that we weren't listening. In fact, if we didn't eavesdrop we'd be deemed intruders. Virginia approached our table. She looked annoyed.

"In, out, in and out," she said. "Make up your mind."

"Two beers, please." I was polite.

She slammed down two orange bottles and did not give us glasses. Then she returned to the Coalition. They were the Frescuran town leaders who abandoned their local jobs each afternoon for an hour or so to gather and discuss the latest manipulations and political maneuvers of the cult.

On a napkin Madeleine discreetly penned a diagram of the chairs around the table. She would point to a chair with her pen, and I would whisper the identity of the Frescuran occupying it.

Virginia paced in front of the group. I whispered to Madeleine that she was the one in charge, really, that everyone listened to her first and foremost. She was a celebrity not only because of her famous burritos but also because of her alleged skills as an alchemist. She was known countywide for citrus-based potions that were supposed to possess medicinal powers.

"I don't think we should be talking about a rally now"—Virginia paced—"not just yet. If we call attention to it too early before the election, people might have time to change their minds and vote with them."

"I agree with Virginia," one man said. "People who don't normally vote will come out and vote for the Proposition, because they'll feel sorry for the cult. Civil liberties and all."

Madeleine put her finger on her napkin. She pointed to the chair belonging to the man who had just spoken, a slender gray-haired man with broad shoulders. His jaw was always agape and he panted like an old dog. That was Sam Burns, the mayor, though the title meant little these days. Sam was known for being slow and cautious, but he spoke with such leisure that often it seemed as if he would never finish a sentence. There was no sheriff per se in Frescura anymore (he resided in Chiaroscuro), and Sam was the closest thing to the law in the town. His authority had been greatly diminished when the cult's population surpassed the town's, when the ashram ran a woman named Jakarta to run the town council and she won. (She had been a local named Mary Louise, who thought Frescura was provincial, and who now never left the ashram except for minimal campaigning.) Rumor had it that Sam Burns had once been in a shoot-out, an old-fashioned duel at noon, which was hard to imagine, given Sam's nearly breathless state. Some hooligan had tried to set Sam's general store on fire by substituting a bag of gunpowder for a bag of cornmeal. Everyone claimed the terrorist was a descendant of the notorious El Moreno. By luck, Sam caught the delinquent, forced the man to put out the cigarette he would have used to ignite a fuse, handed him a pistol, and said, "Outside, pardner," or something he got from the movie he had seen the day before. It was all a bluff—the guns weren't actually loaded—but when the young man saw the pistol pointed at him from down the main street, he must have remembered the ultimate fate of his ancestor. He turned, ran, and was never seen again.

Madeleine scratched out some notes on her pad.

"As usual I disagree," Padre Christopho said. "You're all too worried about what to say and when to say it. The time for a rally is now, before Proposition Eight is law, not after. Now is the time to get the people who don't vote to vote, now is the time to get them to vote on our side."

The clergyman looked over at us as he spoke. He knew me, of course, but wondered who the new face was. He also noticed that Madeleine was conspicuously scribbling. Padre Christopho, who led his parish in the ancient church around the corner, believed that he was a man of action and didn't subscribe to the theory that Frescurans should passively wait for events to unfold. He wore the same Frescuran uniform of jeans and cowboy boots, except he added a black shirt and collar. He had spent one night in the Chiaroscuro jail when he ripped down an ashram sign after the cult had tried to rename the streets (which was a real trick, since the streets never had names to begin with). When the holy man was arrested, the Coalition was formed to seek his release, which would have happened the next day anyway. But the rallying together was nice for the padre: he got to experience brief martyrdom without having to suffer much.

"Oh, sometimes you are as thick as beans." Virginia stood over the padre and slapped his shoulder. "People around here don't vote unless they want something to happen."

"Right," Sam backed her up. "No Frescuran bothers to vote against anything. You get off your behind and vote something *in*. The concept of voting something *out* doesn't exist."

Isabelle Burns, Sam's wife, snapped, "But Proposition Eight isn't in yet, so it can't be voted out, it has to be voted *down*." Isabelle ran the post office. She tended to side with Padre Christopho, with whom she shared an interest in the theater, and with whom she once tried to mount a musical, which no one auditioned for. Isabelle and the padre ended up performing a revue themselves in the musty church, but no one attended. Her retort didn't much make sense to me, but then again, neither did this entire conversation. The issue was when to hold a rally, not whether a rally should happen, and in a typically Frescuran fashion, there were more opinions than people.

There were others present, and as Madeleine pointed to their chairs on her diagram, I whispered their names. José Rey, the real estate broker, for one, who had seen some hard times lately but always wore a neatly pressed suit and a bolo tie. He deeply regretted having sold the initial land in the desert to the guru. It was a mistake others had forgiven or forgotten, yet he never stopped atoning.

Padre Christopho finally looked over at our table and raised his eyebrows. Madeleine missed this because she was jotting something down, and I had to put my hand over hers so that she could meet the padre's glare.

"Hello, Coyote," he acknowledged me. Everyone looked, except Virginia, who pretended we weren't here and continued to make some point. "Hello . . . ?" Padre Christopho tried to greet Madeleine and indicated that he didn't know her name.

"I'm Madeleine," she said.

Now all attention was paid to us.

"I see you're taking notes." The padre tapped his fingers slowly on the table. He tried to seem casual. "Why are you taking notes?" he asked.

This was something I'd like to have heard an honest answer to myself. Why was Madeleine indeed recording a proceeding that only typified the way Frescurans talk around issues, and that could have very little bearing on the average tourist's agenda?

Madeleine didn't miss a beat. "I don't know much about Proposition Eight, and I'd like to know more."

I could detect a note of pretended naïveté in her voice. It suddenly occurred to me that Madeleine probably knew more about Proposition Eight than I did. What was she up to?

Sam countered what seemed like unwarranted paranoia on the part of the padre. "Well, let us tell you about it," he huffed.

Proposition Eight was a new term to describe Frescura's worst nightmare. It all came down to the fact that Rancho Flora owned and controlled Frescura now. The town property was leased from a new landlord in the desert. It seemed as if the cult had manifested itself in a single day, and now it was trying to gain control over the county. The cult had grown rapidly and in its first year was larger by fifty people than Frescura. In fact, the ashram with its eight hundred citizens almost, but not quite, surpassed the number of people in the county. Chiaroscuro tipped the balance— it was as urban as a town gets around here.

"Proposition Eight is the devil's trick," Virginia said flatly.

To that, there was general accord in the room.

"It would move the county charter to Frescura." Isabelle Burns sounded as if she were warning a bunch of second graders about drugs. "They already run the town council, and this—"

José Rey interrupted, "They would have control over not just the town's zoning board, but the zoning regulations for the whole county, and they could build wherever they wanted to. It's immoral."

The ashram had not declared itself a town with a charter all its own because it had always claimed that it wanted to work with the Frescurans, not against them. But the cult bought property in Frescura slowly, until it owned the diners, stores, much of the downtown. No one had any choice but to sell to the guru. With control of a zoning board, as José explained, the cult could rip up a restaurateur's or merchant's license if it so chose. You couldn't really run a business without cult approval. Virginia was ready for the day when the cult tried to take over her new café, vowing, "This time I'll beat 'em in court." Now a public question was petitioned onto the ballot of the general election, and that election was going to take place at the end of the summer.

"But what I don't understand," Madeleine said, "is what the cult could really do if they had the charter. Besides the zoning board," she added.

"It would mean," Sam Burns panted, "that the county's entire government would be controlled by the mauve people."

"The police," José Rey said, "the highway construction workers, all maintenance vehicles . . ."

"The bureau of tourism," Virginia added.

"The courthouse could be moved to the desert, and the school," Isabelle said.

"And the jail," Padre Christopho added.

"They'll set up a new county legislature," Sam Burns explained slowly, "and hand down all sorts of crazy laws."

Padre Christopho rarely spoke to me since the time when I was ten and I told him that I had seen God impaled on a cactus and as a result I had lost all faith. Now, however, he seemed to address not only Madeleine, but me as well, and he spoke to us with great passion. He hoped to sign on two more activists to the cause.

"Can you imagine"—the clergyman raised his index finger—"if all the county's constituents were required to wear those ridiculous uniforms?" It got worse, and he whispered, "Can you imagine if the indecent behavior that goes on in that place were legalized?"

"Is it illegal now?" Madeleine asked.

"It's immoral." José Rey tugged shirt cuffs over his wrists.

"But will they really move to enact these laws?" Madeleine prodded. "Will that much really change?"

"Maybe." Virginia hovered above everyone, her breast at one point brushing against my shoulder. She looked at Madeleine for a moment rather suspiciously. "Maybe not. But why wait and find out?"

"And so we have to act, quell unrest now, and once and for all." Padre Christopho raised his eyebrows, satisfied with pulpit eloquence.

Madeleine looked at him. "What does that mean? 'Once and for all'?"

"Just talk," Sam muttered.

"A rally," Padre Christopho improvised. "And take note"—Padre Christopho pointed to Madeleine's napkin with all of her scribbling—"there are questions being investigated by county officials now, about the legal status of the cult and that wicked daughter of Lucifer, that dark-haired bandit." I assumed he meant Vanessa. "Questions of fraud."

"Fraud?" Madeleine asked.

"Fraud," Isabelle Burns said nodding. She shook her head. "What if they decide to actually send their children to public schools? And what if they don't want to bus their kids out of the desert?"

"What if?" Virginia stood above everyone, towering. "What if? We simply won't let it happen. That's all. *Finito.*" She disappeared into the kitchen.

"Can we at least agree," Padre Christopho begged, "that wherever we stand, we must come together to defeat Proposition Eight?"

"Oh, of course," Sam Burns said. "We all are for that."

"Of course," said everyone in the Sunflower Lives.

Madeleine and I stood up to leave as the Coalition meeting disbanded, with nothing accomplished as usual, just a lot of grumbling.

Virginia emerged from the kitchen abruptly and loudly asked Madeleine, "Who are you anyway?"

There was silence. Someone new had taken interest, and even Padre Christopho had let it go at that. She took notes, so what?

"You've been here before, haven't you? I don't mean the other day, but before that. . . . You're a reporter, aren't you?" Virginia could be nosy in a mean way.

"Perhaps." Madeleine smiled and tried to seem friendly. She turned to leave.

Virginia said to her back, "I know who you are," but we were out the door before anything more was said.

I was baffled. "Why would Virginia know you?" I asked.

"I wouldn't worry about it." Madeleine smiled. She was not fazed. I was.

Madeleine let me drive the jeep back to Rancho Flora. As we dipped into the desert, she ran her fingers through her hair and slumped in her seat. She had been wearing her large watch, with its enormous white face and large Arabic numerals printed in red.

Sometimes it worked, but often it stopped and had to be banged a bit and reset. She noticed now that it had stopped again. She held it to her ear.

"I know where you can get it repaired," I said.

But she didn't hear me. Or maybe she did. In any event, she said, "I can hit that thing," and pointed to a cactus near the road about three yards ahead. She flung the watch at the cactus. I saw the glint of metal disappear. I slowed the jeep so she could retrieve the watch, but she waved me on. She looked at me, shrugged, and looked ahead.

*J*rog once told me, when I was fifteen, about the one time he had an affair with a man. We were drinking lemonade and beer underneath the H-shaped constellation of Hercules in the early May sky.

"Were you married to your wife at the time?"

"I never married." Frog did not like to talk about her. I didn't even know her name. "Not officially anyway."

"You know what I meant, were you *with* her?"

"I was *with* her, yes," Frog made fun of me. "But it hadn't been that long. And this was really before her, actually, if you're going to insist on a chronology."

"What was his name?" I wanted all the details.

"Can I tell the story?"

So his name was Frank—or Hank, I don't remember which—and though he was a graduate student, he was older than Frog. Frog was the star doctorate, having earned his degree in record time. He was a wunderkind who dazzled everyone with formulae that seemed to be drawn from thin air. Scientific legerdemain. He could take the proverbial café napkin, crumple it in his palm, and unfold it—it would be covered with significant equations. He was called Frog because he could leapfrog steps in tangled processes and reach a final concept far before anyone else. (Actually, Frog said, his ex-wife had named him Frog for no real reason, and Frog spent the rest of his life meeting people who would define his nickname for him.)

Well, one awkward night in the lab, when Frog as professor was trying to unfold some mathematical formula for Frank/Hank, Frog wondered why he felt so silly when he should have been serious. Frank/Hank was simply not grasping the twists and turns of the equations, ignoring the secret corners of the algebra, and he became in Frog's eyes an attractive dumb hunk. Frog started noticing how Frank/Hank was constructed, how pretty his eyes were as he stared at the chalkboard. Long lashes.

"Let's say screw it," Frog said to him.

"What?" Frank/Hank was confused.

"Let's go for a walk."

This happened at some West Coast college on a cool spring night. So Frog and Frank/Hank took a stroll around the part of the campus where the science buildings were located, on the edge of the university where new structures went up, where there weren't too many people this late at night. And somehow Frog asked if he could kiss Frank/Hank. The man was shocked.

"In those days, you weren't supposed to know," Frog explained. "I mean I wasn't supposed to know he was gay, and he couldn't have expected that I was interested in him."

"Why not?" I asked.

"Because I had a reputation."

Leapfrogging beds, I decided. Leapfrogging the tartan skirts.

So Frog and Frank/Hank ended up fooling around in the dark space at the edge of the campus. I pictured lab coats used as blankets or rolled up into pillows. I imagined pens and pencils falling out of breast pockets, and security badges getting tangled. Then the course of the affair, weeks according to Frog, was altered when Frog had to go work in a lab near the desert, and when things with his soon-to-be girlfriend were picking up.

"Weeks?" I was astonished.

"Let's make it a month."

"What happened?" No one had ever told me about this sort of thing. Not a personal account. I was thrilled to know other people felt the way I felt then, that night, pouring my heart out to Frog.

Frog was generous with details: how he became Frank/Hank's tutor in math and student in lust, and how it was a grand sort of experiment, very physical. But Frog became detached after a while, which his graduate student could detect.

"I was straight, that was the sum of it," Frog said. "I could have gone on, I was still curious, but I was straight."

I was disappointed, but then I remembered that indeed this had been a revelation in the first place about Frog. I would not have guessed it.

"I think everyone has to fool around, perform these acts. . . ."

"Experiments," I said.

"Yes. Until they find what they want."

"I know what I want. I want blond," I said.

"Well, that's great. Go find blond," Frog said to me.

"Where?"

I had come over to Rancho Fantasy Eccle as I was doing most nights of the week that year, but on this night I was extraordinarily depressed. I had driven to Chiaroscuro where there was a movie house that one night a week showed gay porn, and after the movies, I had watched two drunken lovers have a shoot-out right in the middle of the street. I didn't know exactly what they were arguing about, but they each had a gun, and driven by some cinematic notion of how to once and for all settle a dispute, they paced to separate ends of the street and turned to gun each other down. They were so drunk that when they fired, one bullet hit a weather vane on top of a bank, and the other bullet ricocheted off the cinema marquee. No one was hurt, but all around a circle of people was clapping and hooting and supporting the debacle. Would the lovers survive this? Love seemed impossible, and I was so angry at the mindless, cheering crowd. I went over to Frog's thinking that he would tell me how to conduct my life, how to bury whatever I felt and become a monk.

"I'm bisexual," I said to Frog. "I think."

Frog handed me a beer. "I know that."

"You what?" I had never felt more transparent in my life.

"It's something I suspected."

I worried that now he judged me by how devoted I was to him, an older man even—all these thoughts rushed through my head. I worried he would think I lusted after him, and then I realized, well, yes, maybe this was why I had been so happy in the last two years visiting Rancho Fantasy Eccle. I worried, I was speechless, so Frog did all the talking.

"A long time ago, there was a man named Frank."

And there was something so entirely lofty, carefree, innocent, about the story Frog told, full of tenderness and fun. Different from the porn in the dark theater with its sticky floor, and no drunken shoot-out at the end. Frog's story did not wind down with a couple driving off into a sunset, but it was happy somehow. But where was I going to find anyone in this empty part of the globe, this big, hot, vapid sphere?

"Around," Frog tried to reassure me. "People have a way of bumping into one another."

I had downed a lot of beer and lemonade, so I was dizzy and words came slowly. "But you," I started to say.

"Me?"

"But you, you're alone. You didn't bump into anyone."

"I did. For a while." Frog disappeared into the darkness and then returned with more beer.

We must have slept out under the H-shaped constellation, because I remembered waking up at dawn and brushing the soil from the back of my head. At one point, it occurred to me that Frog could have made up the entire story about Hank/Frank simply to make me feel better about myself. I had no reason to doubt the sincerity in Frog's reminiscence, but I almost preferred to think that the affair hadn't happened, that it existed only for my benefit.

Before we fell asleep under the stars that night Frog said, "You can't really be happy until you know how to be happy alone, by yourself. It took me a while to realize this." It was a simple philosophy, not one he was proud of. Yet I found myself silently dissenting. I wanted to believe his credo, it seemed like noble dogma, but it was an idea for someone older. Frog just never realized that.

"Are you happy?" I asked Frog.

He didn't answer.

"Are you happy?" I asked on more than one night.

Once Frog shrugged, but usually his response was to disappear for a moment and then return with more beer.

There were nights spent with Frog in that five-year stretch that weren't focused on my life, and fewer spent on his past. In fact, most nights revolved around the celestial events of the evening. Frog was my teacher, and he loaned me every book he owned—there were thousands lining the shelves in his living room. Frog's house was more of a school than the one I attended in body but not in spirit. I picked up a habit from Frog. Whenever Frog wanted to learn something about some area of knowledge, he became determined that he would know everything there was to know through obsessive, compulsive reading. He acquired whatever books he had to, and with great speed he inhaled, absorbed, ate up their contents until he was cerebrally satiated, spent. Then he'd move on to entertain some other curiosity. So if I asked how a computer worked, Frog would point to a shelf in his living room. Shelves and shelves to answer a question about how Native nations rose and fell. An exhaustive habit, but one that made me alive in a way I never expected to be alive. Frog never told you what a word meant, he handed you a tattered dictionary and instructed, While you're looking that word up, why don't you skim the whole page. Frog taught me how to think, he ritualized acts of discovery.

Most nights we hunted meteorites. Frog taught me how to track a shower. We looked at other things, too, such as the occasional comet. Once we even spotted a supernova, a star explosion, or implosion as Frog put it. I was told how lucky I was to witness something many veteran astronomers had never seen. And I was full of awe and respect, which is probably why Frog didn't mind having me around, even though he said he couldn't stand people. I took everything he said for granted, I guess. I can still feel the impressions the bifocal eyepiece would make against my cheekbones after long hours of peering into the heavens. I also remember a certain dizziness to these evenings in the observatory. Dizzy conversation over lemonade and beer and a zigzag-patterned bowl of blue-corn chips. I was sorry that I had stopped hanging out with Frog, but he understood. I had to deal with the world he no longer wanted to be a part of.

I stopped visiting around the time Frog's son died because I wanted to go off and wander, but I had first ended up at Rancho Fantasy Eccle by pure chance when I was thirteen. When I was thirteen, I was depressed, even though I had just been outfitted with the abandoned trailer the Frescurans had found for me. I was lonely. I decided on a whim to walk across the desert, not really for any reason, just a notion that whatever was beyond it had to be less dismal than what I lived in. I walked and walked until I felt my feet dragging with each step, and my T-shirt sticking to my skin, and I walked until I lost feeling in my boots, until I collapsed. The next thing I knew I was staring into the round glasses of Frog Reading, lying in his bed, buried in wool blankets. Frog had been out on a run, and he had found me not too far from his ranch (which meant I hadn't penetrated very far into the desert). Frog gave me some lemonade, scolded me, and told me lots of Coyote stories. Later that night, I made my first visit to his observatory.

I got to know Frog, I learned why he left the world of physics and returned to the desert. Everyone said that the crazy hermit had exiled himself, but that was ridiculous, he had come home. The warm hand of the sun pulled him here, the same paw that pressed down on my shoulder and forbade me to leave. I slowly gleaned facts about Frog's childhood. He grew up on a ranch with siblings and horses. He came from a house that spread low over the grassland—beamed ceilings, and hearths you could camp out in. In the summers he went up to the purple lines of the mountains, and under aspens he read and read so that his curiosity could not be contained within the dry plateau. He was given a telescope, and when he was ten, he ran away with it and nothing else. A small child's weak telescope, like a child's violin: miniature for little fingers, but still capable of richness. Frog camped under the stars and studied the blue heavens. He was found, punished, but his telescope was not taken away. That was the beginning. He would lie on his back on the dirt and look up and watch, count stars, say to himself, this is the only place to be.

Toward the end of my time with Frog, I was only stopping by maybe one night a week, and the other days, I was buying dope in the dimly lit alleys of Chiaroscuro and filling my trailer with fetid fumes. I got picked up for possession in Chiaroscuro, and I had to call Frog to bail me out. He had to drive a long way in the middle of the night. He paid my fine, signed some kind of papers saying he would keep track of me, and then drove me back to my trailer. He was so mad because there had been a magnificent sky that he had wanted to stay up all night and watch.

"I almost didn't come," he told me.

"I'm sorry."

"Well, don't get caught again."

"Okay."

"Why don't you wander around a little more, don't just sit in one place and be prey. Hunt for things."

Frog babbled more. He was drunk, he drank so much alone. He was my hero, my guru, he taught me so much. But on that night, he seemed so completely alone, and I didn't want to be like that. I was confused, because if you didn't live as Frog did, then how did you cope on the desert planet? The next day I got in a car and drove away.

The one and only time I ever used a map was the day after Frog had paid my fine. I went to a gas station and purchased one. I climbed into my car and ultimately drove to every point on this map of the Southwest. And that was what I did for a couple of years, what filled an undefinable span of time during which I roamed the larger region, not just my native turf, but the entire stretch between the desert and mountains. I drove for the sake of driving. The simple act was fatiguing in a purging way. I wanted to visit every faint dot on the map. Past every salmon-colored reef in the desert sea, past every striated mesa as plateaux stepped toward mountains. I pushed up to the edge of the expanse, though I never went over the northern and western snow-capped peaks. I preferred to stand in the dusty realm, with a lizard at my boot, a lizard chasing shadows cast by breeze-rustled juniper branches, and simply look at the white, surreal pinnacles in the distance. I drove everywhere in the clay tundra. Two events punctuated my wistful sojourn: a siren named Yvonne seduced me into a tea-leaves reading, and my car blew up.

One day I had rented a raft and decided to paddle my way down a white-rapid river that ran northeast of the desert. The water was high and tempestuous after a month of storms had drenched the region. During one rush of rapids, the current parted over a sharp rock. I didn't see the rock, and it ripped the rubber of my already patched craft. The jolt threw me from the sinking boat and I tumbled out. I was lucky because I drifted to a riverbank and was swallowed up by muck. A woman found me during her daily rounds, and she dragged me out of the mud. She pulled me by my legs into her trailer.

I didn't remember much more than the groggy slosh through the mud of the riverbank. I didn't remember what came next. But I woke up sitting in her bed, in her trailer by the river, and she was spooning hot and spicy black bean soup into my mouth. I wore a T-shirt that wasn't mine, but was naked under the sheets. And I already felt as if I had not only endured the crash of my raft, but also intercourse. I was tired all over. And I learned I had indeed made love with the woman. Sex with any woman was revelatory, I discovered. Later with men it would be glorious, but with women I learned something. And I was proud of myself and my sexual ambidexterity, because on the one hand I suspected and believed something about my proclivities, but on the other hand, I was once again hiding in versatility. I'd actually been with a few women before, but oddly I had held off from seeking male love. I didn't think of myself as a virgin in this regard. I just conceded to what I considered an all-embracing understanding of humanity—I could enact love with anyone.

When I woke up, Yvonne, who I didn't learn was named Yvonne until a week had passed, pulled open her bathrobe and revealed her dark nudity. She put down my soup bowl. She massaged the inside of my thighs, and before I knew it, she was lying on top of me, her chest totally engulfing my own. Later I looked down at her. Her knees and legs formed an arc, an archer's bow.

For days she spoon-fed me thick bean soup, I wore only a borrowed T-shirt, and Yvonne left occasionally. All of this without telling me her name. After the first night, I realized that I was indeed not dreaming, and I tried to figure out where I was exactly. I walked around the trailer looking for my own T-shirt, jeans perhaps, my boots, but I could not find anything.

After a week I said, "I'm Coyote," which I had tried to say before, but had always met a hand of long fingers placed over my lips. I never had been able to utter my name.

"Hush." Yvonne tried to cover my mouth. Then, "Well, that's that."

"What's what?"

"I'm Yvonne," she sighed.

She looked disappointed. She climbed off me and put on her robe. "I drive the van for the rafters," she explained. When a rafting group would drop off their van or bus at the starting point of an expedition, Yvonne greeted them and then drove their vehicles to where their trip down the rapids would end. Yvonne put a kettle on the stove.

Sex after introductions were made proceeded awkwardly. I was clinical at best, still proud of my agility, but aware that something dishonest passed between us. We drank a few cups of tea between the stilted acts, and finally Yvonne said, "You have to move on."

"Why?" I said. I liked how casual everything was in this world.

"Why?" Yvonne mimicked me. "How long can you be a stranger?"

"I don't want to be a stranger. I love you." I thought I loved her. I wanted romance, and why not romance entered without pretension, haphazardly, without chase? I wouldn't be in love for a long while, not even with James. But stupidly, I always believed that I had ripened as much as I was going to, that there was nothing more to learn. But in Yvonne's trailer, I said again, "I love you," and denied the subsequent hollowness. I truly believed that I would never have to step out of this trailer again, that I would never don another article of clothing, that this T-shirt was enough.

Yvonne was sage. She ignored me. She handed me a final mug

of strong tea, and after I had gulped down the hot liquid, she said, "I will read the leaves for you, and then you can go."

"Is this how it works with you?"

"This is how it works with me." I hoped that at least most men had their leaves read after one or two nights, and that I was special, having lasted a week.

Yvonne emptied the last drops of tea onto a napkin. She held the empty mug with her thumb and forefinger of one hand, and with the fingers of her other hand, she gently felt the arrangement of spent dregs along the wall of the mug. Slowly, a forecast: "Someday there will be a man with hollow eyes. A smooth complexion the color of the moon. There will be adventures. And . . ."

"And what?"

"And you're a cat?" Yvonne had never read this before in her men's leaves.

"Sure," I said.

"Well, as a cat you've got many lives."

I was embarrassed to find out that there was going to be a man with hollow eyes in my future, because I had confessed my undying love to this woman, Yvonne, and she had seen through it.

Yvonne stood on a stool and reached to the top of a closet, where my boots were, and where my jeans and T-shirt were rolled into a ball and stuffed into a hat box. I dressed, and she sat on the edge of the bed without saying a word, watching me. I realized that dressing in front of someone who was still naked (or naked underneath a robe) was the same as undressing in front of someone who remained clothed. I occupied myself with this thought to avoid the plain fact that I was going away and felt rather relieved.

I forgot fairly quickly what the content of my fortune predicted, and when I met James, it didn't occur to me that his eyes were not hollow (whatever "hollow" meant). They were lackluster blue, like sapphire all scratched and dull. He was perpetually tan and without any planetary aura.

My nomadic life ended near where it began, in Chiaroscuro. I was playing strangers in a pool hall there. In the late evening, I picked up a cue and joined a game with two men who were twice my size. I had never played pool much before. It had not been my idea to bet—it was the idea of one of the two men—but I bet five dollars. And then I won again. The men said I couldn't leave until

I bet some more, and they said that if I were a hustler, they would kill me. I won a third time, purely by accident, and the men were furious. I said I really had to go and left the pool hall. I was terrified they would come after me, and I when I stepped outside, I ran to my car, my reliable jalopy.

I drove madly through the streets of Chiaroscuro, constantly looking over my shoulder, taking back alleys when I could. And as I turned onto one dark side street, I saw a frightened blond man standing in the shadows. I was anxious to get out of town, but I stopped. He was my age, or a little less, yet he seemed so young. He ran up to my car and said, "Could you give me a lift somewhere?"

I opened my car door, which could only be done from the interior on that side. He hopped in and looked tenuous.

"Where do you want to go?" I asked.

"I don't know. I'm lost."

"Where were you headed?"

"I don't know."

I pointed out that he couldn't be lost if he didn't know where he wanted to be in the first place. A bit of logic Frog had taught me. He seemed stunned by this revelation. And then one of those waves rushed through me as I looked at this blond stranger, one of those rare moments when you have to decide something quickly, answer a question not posed, choose a path not visible, and some powerful instinct beneath your skin makes you all hot and red and you say what I said to James Theroux upon first glance: "Come with me."

So James drove with me until we were about one mile from my trailer, and all the while I had known my car was going to collapse beyond repair at any minute but ignored this fact because James was rendering his life story. He came from a prominent family in the Southwest. The Therouxes had bought land at some point, lots of land in the pioneering days. The Theroux I had found had been enrolled at the college his family had endowed, and he decided to drop out. He wanted to see the world, and he drove off in a little sports car into the hot desert. He drove to Chiaroscuro and soon enough, found himself lost. Then while he was using a pay phone, his car was stolen.

One mile short of my trailer, my car chugged to a halt. I said we could walk it and we got out of the car. When we were a hundred yards away from the car, it blew up. Flames rose hundreds of feet, but it was a flash fire, and soon there was just a low tent of flames and the smell of burning rubber spreading across the highway.

"We could have been in it." James stated the obvious.

"We're meant for each other," I said, but I don't think James heard me.

Sex unwound slowly in my trailer. I did not tell him that in these matters I was a virgin, because I knew if I revealed the truth, I would have pulled back and sent him away. I had to jump in as if I knew what I were doing, and surprisingly, I did. The sex was exuberant, exhilarating, and I was so happy, released, indebted. There was pain, but I contained the physical hurt in silence, because it was part of my pretense to seem like a veteran. James stayed for a year in my trailer. A trailer: he must have adored me to give up the ranches he knew (and may have owned). He wanted the obscurity of this place most of all, I suppose. He had to figure out who he was, and our discussions centered on this. What he wanted to do in life. A career, a dream, the whole package.

One day James just disappeared. He talked to no end in his final months about the ashram. That was why I knew deep down that he went there.

*I*t occurred to me that the pilgrims who stole the meteorite from Frog and me may not have been acting on the part of Rancho Flora at all. Perhaps they were actually fleeing the cult, and they needed money. And after they grabbed the loot, they had not returned to the ashram but instead had run away. That would explain why I had not found it anywhere, and that also would mean that I would probably never recover the stone. I had hoped to return the meteorite to Frog and make up for not having adequately come to his defense, but I had just about given up in my quest. I was frustrated about all this, but at the same time, I had grown rather content living at the ashram, and I was not about to venture elsewhere in the desert in search of the bandits.

Weeks passed quickly, like a dream, busy weeks in which Madeleine and I were completely thrown into Rancho Flora routines and rituals (observed with a certain distance). During the day Madeleine conducted countless interviews and explored every inch of the ashram. She became closer to the obi Elise and spent a good deal of time following her around. At night, she tapped away at her typewriter and organized the day's revelations. For the most part, I followed Madeleine wherever she went. We did not buy into the program of spiritual enlightenment, but nevertheless, Rancho Flora became home. When Madeleine announced one day that the time had come to venture into uncharted land, to go off the map, to finally explore the other side of the hill, I felt a little lost. As if I had misplaced a reliable, smooth, old worry stone, as if it had fallen out of my pocket and been picked up by someone else. Madeleine insisted we sneak beyond the temple—she was saying, don't get settled, there's always something else to get up and discover.

Madeleine made me feel like a fellow explorer. I didn't just set up the tripod for her, she also let me peer through the telescope to measure boundaries. I inspected anything she surveyed. Although some days I did feel there were certain things she knew and didn't tell me, and I couldn't get past this notion that some true and secret mission was veiled. She didn't tell me everything she thought, and we had little arguments. I admit that I was probably a bastard now and then—I was the nasty one—and I just had to go off by myself and be alone. I'd find an opening under the ashram fence through which I could crawl (you weren't supposed to venture off without permission). I'd scamper into the dirt and dash from cactus shade to cactus shade. I had to get away whenever I spent so much time with one person. I hated this need to escape humans, but it felt so good to run on four legs over the sand, tail tacking me left, right. A white sun washed me clean. After a while I'd return through the hole in the fence.

An odd desire, too, alien since childhood, crept up in the weeks with Madeleine. I wanted parents. I wanted the stories parents told you about their common past, the lore of their early years. I wanted to know how it worked. I wanted an example, even if the marriage had later failed.

For several days Madeleine would discuss how we would sneak over to the other side of the hill. She'd say, "We'll make our move during the lecture."

"Maybe we should wait another week," I'd reply. "Have you really finished looking into everything on this side of the hill? I mean, do you know everything about accommodations and sight-seeing—"

"Hey," Madeleine said to me, "you don't have to come. I can go over alone."

"No, I'll go with you." I was determined to see everything Madeleine saw.

"Maybe you shouldn't come." Madeleine was irritated, I could tell.

"No, I'll come," I insisted meekly. The thing was, I was afraid I might run into James, and I had grown comfortable with the suspended state of not knowing where he was. But then again, I thought, if he wasn't among the pilgrims, why would he be on the other side of the hill?

"Why don't you tell me what the big deal is?" Madeleine made it seem as if I kept things from her, not the other way around.

"There is no big deal. Look, why are you so hot to go over there anyway?" I asked point-blank.

"Because it's there." Madeleine tossed her head back.

"Let's just do it, let's stop talking about it and go," I said finally. Curiosity, after all, is like smelly bait, and yes, there was something I was keeping from Madeleine. Maybe I thought she'd think I was silly if I told her that this was of major importance to me. There was one more possible place where the meteorite just might be, in the guru's house. This was my last guess.

A road wound around the temple to a gate in the fence cutting off the other side of the hill. Whatever lay over there was a complete mystery partly because of the way the hill was positioned relative to the distant highway. You really had no idea of what the slope looked like since the ashram was angled in such a way that its front always faced the road. The gate behind the temple was only paces away from a rear tunnel entrance to the synagogue, a tunnel running up to the stage. This was the route Vanessa and the guru and attendant obis took each day to the lecture, appearing rather spontaneously, magically on the pulpit. The gate was left shut, but not locked. A sentry stood guard. Madeleine and I had noticed that every day, no matter which pilgrim was assigned to patrol the gate, the guard would stroll over to the entrance to the tunnel and stick his head in to hear the sermon, his back turned.

The sun climbed its midday ladder, pilgrims rolled up from the refectory to the temple, children were led up from the school, and from a distance, we watched a limousine pull through the gate. The long car deposited the guru right by the basement tunnel, and in a matter of minutes, the lecture was under way. The guard looked briefly around, but did not notice us sitting against an adjacent face of the whitewashed octagon, and he turned his back. Swiftly, Madeleine and I slipped through the gate.

We stepped down the hill only a few paces before we encountered a series of factorylike windowless buildings. Off to the left, there was a maze of poles and coils beyond a wire fence. A power plant glimmered in the midday light. You looked into the metal complex and it appeared as if you could actually see the electricity. Another building allowed a series of wide and silver pipes to run in and out, and yet another building sprouted a spindly television antenna from its flat roof.

"The guts," I whispered to Madeleine.

"I'll say," she replied.

Later, on the way back up the hill, I'd see that on the other side of the power station lay a series of hundred-foot-long glass windows, solar panels aimed to gather maximum rays.

"I knew that the hardware of the ashram had to be up here," Madeleine said, "because it wasn't back there." She pointed toward the temple. I assumed that it was hidden to preserve a certain mystery about the ashram (indeed I was a little let down to discover the mundane system of utilities). The guts of the ashram were kept secret so that everyone would be amazed and dazzled by the utopia, in awe of the Buddhafield. For most pilgrims, the vital resources, water, power, radio reception, were all plentiful but mystical, miraculous in origin.

"C'mon." Madeleine pulled my elbow. We walked downhill, past the power plant, and we found ourselves looking at an entire other city. Speechless, we stared at Shangri-la. The hill beneath us was covered in a spill of adobe villas, complete with splashes of blue pools and flashes of plush green shrubs. That was the most amazing detail at first glance, that there was flora on this secret side of Rancho Flora. A few small trees, even, popping out of terraced houses. And around one distant pool, it seemed, a lawn. The stubby palms swayed in a vague breeze. On this side of Rancho Flora, it was even cooler, and in the faintest way the air carried a saltiness from some distant sea.

"I don't believe it," was all I could say. The cornucopia of villas seemed unreal, a fabulous plot of land about which there was something dangerous. I had never seen the palette of the landscape out here become so creamy and glazed blue.

"I can," Madeleine answered me, as awestruck as I was, but less surprised.

The first structure in front of us now stretched endlessly down the sharp slope—a palatial spread of building blocks that, given the cars parked outside, had to be the guru's digs. This mansion presided over everything else. It was supported by endless tiers of smaller squares terraced into the hill, adobes tumbling downward with an interconnecting series of staircases. Stairs led from one roof to the next rooftop balcony.

It was easy to slip into the guru's palace. There was only one apparent entrance. We passed swiftly through large rooms, all sharing a common view of the desert, the kind of panorama that glorified the landscape, made you feel indeed above it, proprietary over the expanse. The rooms were sparsely decorated, which was not what I would have expected. There was an ample amount of square furniture carved in the Spanish style, clever rosettes at every juncture, each chair like a church pew in miniature, but there were no signs of excess. The red tile floor was polished, in no way scuffed. Rooms and rooms, each with rugs and some furniture, but rooms and rooms that lacked human breath and dust. An empty museum, without art or decoration. Definitely without a meteorite. Finally we came up to an atrium with a square pool, which I imagined the guru getting his white beard wet in. A pool in the desert—I couldn't get over it. It was obscene.

Madeleine and I dashed over to the other side of the atrium, and here we found a bedroom. The bed in the center was immense, more than enough for the old man and his two attendants. There was a vast spread of silk sheets and cylindrical pillows, a few cottony blankets. The room had the cloudy smell of an infant's de-humidified chamber. Curtains of a heavy white fabric gently answered the breeze. Lying on a pewter plate on a night table were five or six gold watches. On a matching table was a large glass vase filled with red and white tulips. Tulips, fully opened and crying oxygen into the room. Tulips: where did they come from? There were more questions posed, I thought, by an empty bedroom than by any other place you could go. The mere patterns impressed into the sheets were oddly titillating.

We passed through a short, dark hall to make our exit beneath an unlit poster of the guru, the ubiquitous portrait. Next to the portrait were several Polaroids tacked up, pictures of luxury cars that I'm sure the guru could just point to and have waiting parked outside. Then we nearly tripped over knee-high metal canisters right in the hall. Plastic masks were attached. There must have been a dozen tanks in all.

"Ouch." I slammed my knee against metal.

"Oxygen tanks," Madeleine said, reading a label on one of the dozen or so tanks.

"For the guru?" I guessed. "He's old, but is he sick?"

"It seems unlikely," Madeleine whispered, "that anyone would need oxygen in the desert. Unless . . ."

"Unless what?" I wondered.

"I don't know." she shrugged. Madeleine pulled my elbow and we walked across the atrium again. We found a flight of warped, often-trodden stairs that led out of the guru's spread and down to the next level. We ended up in a hallway that had many rooms off it, like a hotel. It was a kind of dormitory, and you could walk up and down, across and out, to stairs and down to a balcony, down to another level. All along these corridors, grim and monastic, were not-so-monastic, spacious studios. Doors were open, and we could tell that these apartments housed the obis. Closets contained spare jumpsuits and spare blue sashes. Each room had a solid bed and night table. On the table was a vase, and in each vase in each obi's room was a red or white tulip like the ones the guru had in his bedroom. Then there were the accoutrements, too, of an individual's choosing: books, pottery. Room adjoined room, now and then interrupted by a hallway or stairwell down to the next tier. A vase holding a tulip was the unifying touch.

The compound of the blue obis' quarters fit like a house of cards underneath the guru's palace, necessarily supporting the guru's mud mansion. Madeleine and I split up, rather accidentally choosing different paths through the seraglio. I found myself moving down through the harem of blue sashes, trying to find Madeleine again. I saw her at the other end of one hallway, but I didn't want to shout. No one was here, everyone was at the lecture, but I still didn't want to call attention to myself. I went down another flight—each new stretch of clay jutted out a little farther beneath the structure above it. I saw Madeleine again. I cut across the red tiled passageway, down another staircase. Madeleine stood outside on a balcony.

"Hi," she said. I was breathless and could only nod. "So that's where the obis live," Madeleine surmised, "and I'd guess that underneath us now is where Vanessa hangs out." We went down yet another staircase before I had a chance to rest.

We entered a series of larger rooms, much like the guru's place. We walked through here rather quickly, not stopping to really examine a rather pretty room with white couches and glass coffee tables. We entered what must have been Vanessa's bedroom, but more intriguing than a bed that matched the guru's was a glass door at the opposite end. We tried the door, expecting to find it locked, and to our great surprise, it was unlocked. We entered.

"Wow," Madeleine said. Now she was really impressed, now she had found something, I think, which neither one of us imagined possible. The room was a greenhouse, much smaller than the one by the refectory, but a luxurious space, humid, with a glass ceiling and with a wet floor. What was amazing was that everywhere there were tables and tables of potted plants, the same variety of flowers growing in each. Rows and rows of tables with tulip plants to be exact—the red and white tulips that ended up in the obis' vases, by the guru's bed. The room was warm enough to keep the tulips happy and silky.

"Why would Vanessa maintain a special greenhouse of tulips?" Madeleine asked. "The funny thing is you don't see these tulips on the other side of the hill at all. Only over here so far."

"Look." I pointed to a metal door at the farthest end of the greenhouse. "Maybe it leads out."

We quickly discovered that this door was not an exit but rather a closet. I located a light switch and we found ourselves first looking at some sacks of plant food and tulip fertilizer. And then we saw a rifle, black and shiny, leaning against one corner.

Madeleine examined it. "Well, some of the guru's guards have pistols, so this isn't too surprising."

"What's Vanessa doing with a greenhouse of tulips and a rifle tucked away? I think it's weird," I said.

"Maybe," Madeleine conceded. "But then again, lots of people in Frescura, I'm sure, have shotguns in their houses. Right?"

"Who is this Vanessa lady, anyway?" The tulips were pretty, yet the hothouse air they breathed was dense with something invisible and sinister.

"You tell me," Madeleine sighed. Then, "Let's get out of here. The lecture will be over soon, if it isn't already. We'd better head back."

We found the street and looked back up at what we had descended. Madeleine pointed toward the road. "It would probably be fastest to walk back up this way."

Like the other side of Rancho Flora, once you were midway up or down the hill, you had no sense of the total depth and range of the city. The secret side of the hill, however, was sharper in slope, and I could see that beneath us, the spill of adobe houses continued. "There's more," I said.

Madeleine's back was already to me, and she had ascended a few yards before realizing I wasn't following. She turned around. "Obviously there's more, but we don't want to get caught when the lecture is over."

"But there's more." I wanted to see everything beneath us. You could look down and see a different sort of arrangement than the villa we had just burrowed through. Mud mansions were spread out. We were closer to the one with the lawn. From our current vantage you could see maybe twenty houses, and there even seemed to be people in the pools, tiny and far away. Maybe the meteorite was sitting in somebody's living room.

"Some other time," Madeleine insisted. "I know what I'm doing."

"I'm sure you do," I snapped back. "Do you know who lives in those houses?"

"I can guess," Madeleine said.

"Please do," I begged.

"We have to get back."

"Who lives here?" I pointed to the stretch of homes spread out like an enormous picnic blanket.

Madeleine hesitated. "This must be a whole other ashram, a smaller one, or not even an ashram at all."

"What then?"

"Well, I'm not sure," Madeleine confessed.

"We're here, so why don't we find out?"

"Later." Madeleine started walking up the hill again.

"I'll go and tell you what I find," I decided. I was being persistent for no reason. I couldn't resist gravity. I was drawn downhill.

"Don't get snagged," Madeleine issued one last warning.

"I won't." I watched Madeleine disappear in a turn of the road. Then I scanned the secret cascade of quiet mansions below me. Cautiously, I continued prowling.

The houses on the secret side of Rancho Flora, past the guru's palace and the obi dormitory, looked so pristine that I wondered if they were occupied. Each seemed angled toward the desert in such a way as to guarantee a unique vista. The adobe compounds of the ashram proper were bunched up like barrios compared with the spread-out splendor of the secret side. The only indication that these homes had anything to do with Rancho Flora at all was that all door and window frames were painted red.

Down the road a way, I saw a house that looked interesting. The entrance opened onto a pool area. As I stepped tentatively through the gate and slipped over to a potted palm I could hide behind, I came across a series of men in mauve jumpsuits, slender men, beautiful and tan, only a few yards away, who were bustling about, each with a task. Some of them attended a man and woman who were reading a newspaper in matching poolside chaises. One mauve-jumpsuited man pulled the zipper down the front of his costume and stepped out of the outfit. Wearing only a black bikini, he jumped into the pool and swam a few laps before getting out and walking into the towel held by another mauve person. It was hard to tell who was serving and who was being served. Music emanated from the house, through sliding glass doors, a concerto rolling over the whole scene. In one corner of the walled-in area, three pilgrims were talking as they arranged sandwiches and drinks on trays. Two men and a woman. They looked as if they had just stepped out of an ad in a glamour magazine.

A woman was saying to a man, "Did you see what Marla Washman was wearing at Chad Ashford's party?"

On this side of the hill, last names apparently were used, and in the ashram proper, they were not.

A man: "No, what?"

"I'm too embarrassed to say."

"What?"

The woman answered, "Saran Wrap."

Another man, unrelated: "I am *so* bored. Mrs. Chapman wanted to play canasta all night."

One man saw me and smiled politely, as if I were a friend of the served, even though I was hiding behind a plant.

"Hello," I said. "I'm not from around here." This seemed to be the logical thing to add.

The woman disappeared with one tray and started circulating among certain pilgrims around the pool.

"I'm not sure who lives here," I said.

One man said bluntly, "The Chapmans, silly." His chin pointed to the couple sunbathing at the other end of the pool. He had a particularly freckled face. Tan filled in the space between brown specks.

I nodded as if I knew who the Chapmans were. I stared at the quiet blue ripple of the pool. Then the freckled man disappeared, leaving me with the other man, whom I noticed was smiling at me with a forlorn pout that was supposed to be seductive.

"Where you from, then?" he asked with a smooth timber.

I didn't answer.

The zipper of the man's jumpsuit was nearly open to his belly button. He leaned on one hip so that the jumpsuit gaped open. These mauve uniforms were very sexy. It was the zipper up the front. During the group dynamic, no one had trouble quickly slipping out of their clothes. And the jump suit, in this warm weather, provided a vent that was on most pilgrims open to some degree, a tease, a suggestion.

"Do you want a beer?" the man asked.

"Sure."

"Come with me. We can sit, chat, find out where you're from."

Was he a servant or someone who was served? I couldn't tell. I had more than a vague feeling that I was being picked up.

The more mundane aspect of the mauve jumpsuit, but one that certainly provided ample discussion and comparison of observations with Madeleine, was how everyone wore the same attire but everyone maintained some feature, some way of wearing the clothing, that individualized the garment. So Vanessa, for example, wore a long-sleeved version (despite the temperature), and she had her cuffs crisply folded three times on each arm, exact and even from one arm to the other. Some men and women rolled up the more common short sleeves over their shoulder, some cut off the sleeves entirely. Some people tied charms to their zippers. Some wore their pants tucked into the usual ankle-high boot. Some let the pants cover most of the shoe. (Many wore sandals.) Patch pockets might be buttoned or not. The narrow collar could be open, or closed with a single button. The collar down or turned up. Some wore belts, and some belts were tied instead of buckled. Of course the blue obis could be worn a thousand different ways: wrapped with a certain tautness, folded over so many times, positioned in such a place on the waist, and so on. The hair of the person in this uniform world became all the more important. Complexion, too, though most had a rough tan. They all filled their mauve jumpsuits differently. I had always been stuck on the tease of the open chest.

The man led me to some rather small room on the side of this hacienda, beyond the pool, beyond where it seemed the Chapmans lived. His jumpsuit was tight, showing off muscles, and it appeared as if the reason his zipper was almost completely undone was because the outfit didn't fit him well enough to close up.

"Where you from?" the man repeated.

What was he going to say next, Do you come here often? I had never been good in these situations. I am wonderful with strangers, I was reared among strangers, but I am lousy with people who pursue me in any way. A cat bolts away when chased by someone larger.

"Do you work for the Chapmans?" I said nervously. I wanted information.

"Sort of."

"Do the pilgrims down here ever go to the other side of the hill?"

"Oh, sure, for lectures and stuff. When we want. It's real open." He tried to sound sweet and sincere. He handed me a bottle from a small refrigerator in the corner. "Here."

"So how many of you are there?"

"Of what?"

"Of your type of person." I didn't know what I was trying to say. He was good-looking. The room had a small bed and a refrigerator, that was it.

"My type?"

"No, no, no." I fumbled for words. "Servants, or whatever you are." I hated this sort of miscommunication. I didn't want to lead him on. Finally, I explained my mission. "I'm sorry, I am just trying to find something."

"Oh," he said, and sat on the bed. "Who?" He wanted to be helpful to prove he wasn't fazed by being turned down.

"Not who," I corrected him. "Not a someone, a something."

"What?"

"A meteorite," I said. I thought for sure the man would laugh, but instead his face lit up.

"It's fun to look at, isn't it?" the man was excited. "It will make a nice present."

"Present?"

"You know," the man said, "for the guru. Everyone on this side of the hill is always giving the guru presents."

"They are?"

"The meteorite is for his birthday," the man announced proudly.

"Right." I nodded as if I knew what he was talking about. The stolen meteorite was a present not yet awarded to the old man, and that was why I had failed to find it. "I forget when his birthday is," I bluffed.

"Me, too." The man giggled. "I never remember birthdays, but I think it's soon. Where are you from anyway?" the man asked.

"Here," I finally said. "Not *here*, but . . . here."

The man nodded.

"So you people"—I wanted to figure this place out—"work for these other pilgrims."

"When they're even around," the man said, laughing.

"They're not around often?"

"No," the man explained. "A lot of them work on the Coast and just fly out here for weekends and stuff. You know what I mean?"

"Sure. What kind of work do you do—"

"What are you asking?" The man wanted this pleasure. He wanted me to say it.

"Are you here as servants . . . sexual servants?"

"Sometimes," the man said. A different sort of dynamic meditation, I gathered. He was oddly proud.

"How many would you say work down here?"

"Twenty, fifty, I don't know."

"And how many people are there actually who live in these houses?" I felt like Madeleine.

"Twenty, thirty, tops. But I don't know. Why so many questions?"

"Curiosity."

"Curiosity killed the cat," the man said. I must have looked rather startled, since that's no mere cliché to me.

I had to pose a question I really didn't want to ask. I'd run this one by quickly, then move on. Nervously, I stuttered, "So did you ever meet a guy named James?"

The man grinned. "James Theroux?"

I gulped.

"Sure," he chuckled. "He lives with this guy Chad Ashford in a house down the road. Do you know James well?"

"I didn't say I knew him," I was quick to insert. "One more question. How did they end up here, these people who own these houses? Do you know?"

"It's no secret." The man smiled. "They gave Guru B some money at some point. Or a car."

The man was wrong—it was a secret, at least from the perspective of the other side of the hill. So that was it: the secret side of the ashram was a private resort for the rich, for major donors. I wondered how much you had to give. And now the donors had acquired a cosmic stone as a present, a stone for the guru's collection.

"I'd like to take a peek at the meteorite," I said. "I love meteorites," I explained.

"I'm not even supposed to know about it." The man hesitated. "Someone showed it to me, and I suppose you could say you stumbled on it, but you can't say that I said it was there, okay?" The man took me out to the road and pointed me toward a house down the path a turn. "And see that place over there?" The man pointed to a house closer to us.

"Yes." I was afraid of the wry look the man was giving me.

"That's where James lives, if you care." The man smiled, as if he was getting even with me.

I thanked him and he rushed away, clearly interested in going back to the pool. I found myself dragging my boots as I continued downhill. I saw the place where James was supposed to be living and I reminded myself that I was on a mission of reconnaissance. I should proceed directly to the meteorite without distractions. I decided that I would stroll past the house, but as I neared it, I changed my mind. My heart pounded, and I thought, I'll just try the door, it will be locked, no one will be home, I'll press on.

No such luck. Why were all the doors always open in this world? I stepped inside the house and said hello. No answer, good. There were some photos on the wall, a table covered with brass animal sculptures. I noticed a bedroom. There were suitcases on the floor and a stack of polo shirts all folded, ready to be packed. Still no James, great. But through the glass door I saw one blond head, the rear of a familiar coif, one blond head resting on a plastic chair by a pool. Damn.

I pushed aside the doors and there he was, startled that anyone had come out from the house—he was alone—and startled that it was I. He was tan, a deeper tan than I had ever seen on him. The same beautiful James. And he wore only blue-and-white-striped swim trunks as if he had known I was coming and wanted to tease me.

"Coyote?"

"Hi, James." Without explanation I sat down in an unoccupied chaise. He stood above me, astonished. For some reason, maybe the angle, I noticed his belly, or nonbelly, and I noticed him breathe in and out rapidly. Then more slowly as he realized he wasn't dreaming.

"'Hi, James'?" He mimicked my casual tone.

"Hi, James," I said more assertively. He was different, more hair on his chest. Taller, maybe.

He was speechless. Then a series of phrases spilled out. "Long time . . ." "How did you find . . . ?" "Well, gee . . ." "I've missed you." The one complete sentence sounded fragile and shallow.

"Me, too," I said, except I knew that I didn't mean it. "So you live with this Chad guy?"

"Ah, yes." James nodded slowly. "He's not here. Actually, I'm in the process of leaving. Tomorrow." He let out a short, contrived laugh. "You just caught me."

"So do you like it here, at Rancho Flora?"

"It's weird." James sat down.

"Why?"

"Well, when you're here first, it's kind of like . . . you're just crazy over the place. . . ." James couldn't think of the right words. "It's wild, you have fun for a while, a lot of fun. Then things get kind of day-to-day." James looked at me as if to apologize. "I hate day-to-day routines."

"I hate day-to-day routines, too," I said. "I always said—"

"Whatever." James did not want to dwell on, even consider, unfinished business. "Anyway," he continued, "then you begin to see that so much is messed up. Like they're all into this guru guy, and I don't see what the big deal is anymore. At least you get to choose a new name. I chose Walton. I think I'll keep it. Call me Walton, but not Wally."

"Do you go over to the other side of the hill often?"

"I haven't recently. It's a real pain. You have to put on your jumpsuit and all."

I asked, "Now what?"

"You mean, where am I headed?"

James was so slow.

"I thought I'd take some acting classes somewhere. Chad thinks I should."

Finally I couldn't stand it. I had to blurt out, "Why did you walk out without saying good-bye?" I said this as if only a day, a week at most, had passed, and not a year.

"The trailer was too small." James sat down on the bed.

"I know that." He was so dumb, I don't know how I stood it. "We all knew why you were going to leave, but you could have said good-bye."

James probably knew that someday we would encounter each other once again, and he must have waited for this confrontation the way a petty thief always wonders if the authorities will bother to catch up with him. I couldn't maintain this preposterous cool any longer. I grabbed him, I buried my head in his stomach, flesh hot from a sunbath, and I sobbed. I cried because I had anticipated, avoided, and imagined this reunion for so long, but I was let down by how inexplicably urbane the whole scene was.

I was imagining what I would say to Madeleine, how I would convey my instant disappointment. "So it's great you found him?" Madeleine would say.

"No." I'd shake my head.

"He wasn't excited to see you?"

"No."

"Are you bothered?"

"No, I knew it was over. I knew that when I didn't try to find him sooner."

But then on the patio chair a bizarre thing happened. I looked up and stared at James, he stared back, and we looked at each other without saying a word, I with my tear-streaked face, him with his beautiful tan. Without actually speaking aloud, we endured, I thought, the best conversation we'd ever had.

And then James stood up from the chaise and took me into the house, pulling my fingers. I don't think he understood why I was pensive. He wasn't that astute, and his impulse was to console me, to be stronger. Nevertheless, we soon were in the bedroom, with half-packed luggage all around, and James sat me down on the edge of the bed. Like old times, he pulled off my boots, one in each hand, both at the same time, and I wiggled my ankles to facilitate the rusty maneuver. At the same time I pulled my T-shirt over my head. James was out of his swim trunks, I could feel him pressed against my leg. Then he soothed me the way he used to soothe me. We went through the old routine, slowly, sharing a familiar warmth that I had forgotten. But the old routine was painful, because while it lasted, I knew it was a fleeting thing. I wanted it to be a fleeting thing.

So when this thin breeze of passion had passed, and James was lying in a beautiful pose on the bed, James the Adonis, I was left only with my anger. I became mad at the first thing to become mad at, and that was how easy it had been, how seamless our gestures were. Without texture. That was how it had always been. Then the air in the room was stifling, I felt claustrophobic. I dressed while I was still untensed, feeling a little wobbly, and James sat up. He watched and talked about his life. I don't think he noticed that I was annoyed with him, with myself. He just prattled away.

"You know, I've always wanted to take acting classes," he said. "I must have mentioned it to you. Chad's been pushing it for a while." It suddenly occurred to me that perhaps Chad was dumping James and acting classes provided a means to accomplish this end. I wasn't sure if James had caught on yet.

"Has he? Well, good luck." That was the last thing I said once I'd dressed. I just waved good-bye and left James looking rather befuddled. This had been sex as a last act, nothing more. And this time I had to be the one to commit the juvenile act, the one who got to slam the screen door and walk away.

"Bye?" I heard him call after me, more question than statement.

I stepped outside and followed the road as it twisted farther downhill. Then in a fury, I started to run. I had to get to the meteorite, I had to see it—nothing else seemed as remotely immediate or vital as my finding the stone right now. Faster and faster toward the building that had been pointed out to me. Faster yet. My heart throbbed and my shins ached. Faster, as if every fiber of iron in that meteorite had lined up, magnetized itself, as it reeled me in with great force.

I was out of breath when I reached the adobe, an apparently unused garage. And in the garage, unattended, quietly hidden from the guru, waiting patiently for its debut, glimmering even in the dank, darkened room, a slight trace of petroleum in the air, was the same meteorite Frog and I had tracked, hunted, trapped, the splendid rock kidnapped in front of our very eyes. The meteorite breathed the slow, drugged breaths of a great jungle animal in zoo captivity. In a way, its edges had softened, its grooves and holes smoothed out somewhat, but its green flecks still sparkled. The meteorite seemed lonely to me, glad that someone was paying it a visit.

So are they treating you well? I asked the meteorite.

Oh, fine, it answered. I am a little bored, though.

Well, I'm glad I found you, I said.

But you, the meteorite said, you don't want to hear me talk about me. You're crying. You came to tell me what's on your mind.

So true. I had to laugh. This was a wise, well-traveled stone. What's on my mind is James, I confessed. He reminded me of how I still feel incomplete.

The meteorite heard me, and like a kind psychiatrist, hummed sympathetically. What do you mean, incomplete?

It's hard to explain.

Try.

Well, the problem with James, I started, was that there was a seed of dishonesty planted from the start. I never told him that he was my first male lover. I didn't share that with him for the simple reason that I wanted an edge. But it was a burden to carry this thrill inside and not share it. I always thought, tomorrow I will tell him, and he will be surprised, impressed, love me more. I don't know why—pride, maybe—but the day of revelations never arrived.

Why not? the meteorite asked me.

I don't know. I kept coming up against waning passion and a person whom I liked less and less—not someone I could admire or even be straightforward with. Our conversations became like the teeth in the pavement of bridges: they fit together in cold weather, but during great heat they pulled apart, and you know how hot it is here most of the time. When he left, I felt relieved for a while. And then bitter. Then as if I were still missing the vital component I thought I had found. As if my body and mind were still not welded together.

In the garage with the meteorite, I told the rock, I rambled, I preserved in my mind only the fun times with James. I made him out to be noble and kind. Then, just now when I saw him, I remembered what he was like. His mere presence reminded me. Sex brought back all the old sentiments, happy, physical, sad, incomplete.

The meteorite buzzed, But now you clearly have distance you didn't have before.

This is true. I guess that not many people are fortunate enough to reach such a resolution, to say: this phase of my life is over, the next is just beginning.

Exactly, the meteorite replied quickly. So now get on with life. If you're incomplete, go complete yourself. I dove through the night very far and for a long time, and look, I survived. So will you, you won't break up in the atmosphere.

Yes. My head felt cleared, like a smoky morning filtered of its fog. The ashram suddenly seemed like the perfect place to begin whatever it was I was beginning. I didn't want to leave the company of the meteorite, but I promised to come back. I had to find Frog and tell him where the creature was caged. A stone so smart should not be imprisoned. It should reign someplace where other people could come and talk to it, listen.

I had kept so much hidden, bottled up. I had fooled myself so easily. Despite my disbelief in caffeinic auguries, I knew what the tea leaves had predicted. I climbed the secret side of the hill and sneaked past the temple without being noticed. The sun was setting over the side of Rancho Flora to the west, the side most of the eight hundred pilgrims believed to be the whole and complete utopia. A peachy wash settled over the desert beyond.

*T*ycho the cat blinked hello at me through the screen door of the Sunflower Lives. I was surprised to see him looking over Frog's shoulder, more astonished that Frog was indeed inside the café. I was actually on my way to his ranch to tell him about the meteorite when I noticed his jeep parked on the main street. I guessed that he had come into town to pick up turquoise paint and catfood (I saw boxes packed into the backseat of his jeep), but I wondered how he managed to wander into the café where it looked like a town meeting was under way. I stepped inside. A roomful of fifty Frescurans turned around and then looked again at the padre, who was preaching. Frog nodded hello. The circles under his eyes meant that he had probably stayed up the night before worrying about the journey. When he saw Frescurans, he no doubt was sure that they muttered under their breaths, Oh, there's that hermit physicist, he's a bit crazy—which in all likelihood was what people indeed whispered. But the townspeople did not, contrary to what he believed, mutter, Oh, there's that hermit physicist, he's the one who would not tell his wife when his son died where he buried the body. They did not talk about that too much anymore.

The Sunflower Lives was full, every seat taken. People stood against the walls, and I leaned against the screen door with Frog. I watched Sam Burns, Virginia, and Padre Christopho run the emergency town meeting that had apparently been called by the Coalition to finally organize the long-awaited rally at the Great Tree.

"They were talking about it in the general store," Frog whispered, "so I thought I'd drop by." The cat in his arms yawned. "Tycho hopped into the jeep without my knowing it," he explained. The cat looked all around, sniffed the air, curious, unused to strange faces. "I haven't seen you around," Frog said.

"I've been up at the ashram," I admitted.

"You've what?" Frog said loudly. Everyone turned around and shushed us. Frog shot me a look of disapproval.

"Later," I whispered.

"The election"—Padre Christopho spoke with greater volume to insure he had everyone's attention—"will not be the end—it is only the first battleground from which we must march on to the next until all our land is free of the enemy."

The crowd responded with a lazy cheer.

Sam Burns puffed, "With all due respect, Father, you're blowing things way out of proportion."

A woman stood up from the crowd and waved her fist. "But we can't back off, or they'll think we gave up." More applause.

"I'm not saying give up." Sam was angry. "I'm saying calm down."

The crowd stirred and the volume of irked chatter rose until only Virginia Martinez could bellow louder than anyone else.

"We aren't going to lose the election. They will. We'll have this rally, and we'll win. And when they lose, that'll be it. They'll have their lot, we'll have ours, and they won't dare to bother us."

There were some disgruntled dissenters who lightly banged beer bottles on tables.

"Then we become rich again"—Virginia continued her scenario—"we buy back our property, and we make sure no one threatens Frescura ever again."

All were silent, until the padre hummed. "That's sweet," he smirked, "with sugary idealism."

A rustle, the air dense with tobacco fumes. Padre Christopho extended his arms as if to unite his parishioners in prayer. "The reality is that our war is already under way. Justice will be ours only if we fight until the end." Virginia and Sam just wanted to organize a rally. The padre wanted to incite a riot. Already, every day, a group of townspeople took turns trotting up and down the stretch of highway between the town and the Great Tree, wearing sandwich boards lettered with outrage. The guru would see these, and the protest, Frescurans hoped, would overwhelm and intimidate the cult.

I noticed that Frog was looking at the room and petting his cat nervously. I'm sure he was anxious about having left his hermitage, unsteady in the company of so many people. Virginia saw Frog standing in the back and smiled her broad grin at him. Frog blushed. A few people turned around. They all noticed the cat in Frog's arms and smiled, as if it were a baby he held. Tycho's eyes were wide and golden, a taupe stare.

Padre Christopho had been trying to assay the general sentiment of the crowd, sensing that the gathering was being converted to his stance. He raised black-clothed arms. He'd thought of something poetic to say. "We must burn a flame all day and night, until we nip the jugular of the evil beast, that monster which lurks in its unnaturally carved labyrinth in the desert."

"Them's fighting words," someone shouted.

Virginia saw the crowd breaking up after a long breath of silent prayer, and she raised her voice. "Anyone for another beer?" Controversy had to be good for business.

"All right then." The padre rubbed his hands. "Folks, stay tuned because we're going to wage this big march some night soon and we'll show them who runs this town." The meeting was adjourned. Returning to their jobs and houses, the townspeople poured out of the café. The padre walked out, too, a triumphant grin making his eyes small and beady.

Frog sat down at a table with me. "I can't believe you went there, Coyote, I thought you'd be above wearing mauve jumpsuits and—"

"Frog"—I sat down beside him and interrupted—"am I wearing a jumpsuit? Calm down. The ashram isn't such an awful place."

Tycho perched sphinxlike in the center of the sunflower painted on the café table and went to sleep. Tycho could nap anywhere—he was the most adaptable of his species.

"How can you stand it there when they stole the meteorite?"

"Well, actually," I was happy to announce, "I found the stone, and I think I know how it could be rescued, if you're interested."

Frog was startled by a hand laid on his shoulder. "Long time, no see," a jovial voice said.

"Hello, Virginia."

She handed him a beer. Without saying hello, Virginia also handed me a beer, but she didn't want to be too pleasant. I smiled a thank-you. She hovered behind me, her breast brushing against my shoulder. She shook her head. "You been up at that godforsaken place?" she asked me without really wanting an answer.

I shrugged.

"Hello, Frog," Sam panted. He was on his way out of the café.

"Hello, Sam."

"Frog, you don't know what's been going on." Virginia shook her head. "They want the county, and sometimes it seems they want the whole universe."

"Well, to tell you the truth"—Frog adjusted his glasses—"we ran into some of them not too long ago, in the desert."

I nodded. Tycho at this point turned onto his back and slept in his usual upside-down position.

"What happened?" Sam asked.

"Well, you know how I hunt meteorites," Frog started. Sam and Virginia nodded and smiled politely. "Coyote and I found quite a marvelous meteorite one night in the desert, what looked to be a truly large and rare specimen, and all of a sudden, out of the night, they descended."

"How many?" Sam wanted to know.

"Four—no, five," Frog said. "Enough to take the meteorite from us."

"Horrible," Virginia lamented.

"And you know the rule of the desert," Frog added, thinking that they may not know it.

But Sam huffed, "First come, first serve when it comes to meteors."

Tycho, still on his back, licked his paw and washed one side of his face.

"They probably worship it," Virginia said.

"Do you think so?" Sam was amazed.

"Oh, sure," Virginia said.

"They don't," I tried to chime in.

Virginia turned to me. "Where's your friend?"

"Who? Madeleine?" I asked.

"Madeleine?" Frog raised his eyebrows. He took a long swig of beer. Tycho rolled onto his stomach, then sat up.

"She was here," Virginia said to Frog. "That reporter person," she added. "First time, I didn't recognize her. Second time, I knew she was the reporter."

"Madeleine's great," I said defensively. "She's the person I've been hanging out with lately," I told Frog. "You'd like her, she's very smart. She's writing some travel articles on the ashram."

"She is?" Frog wiped his eyes.

"She interviewed us," Sam inserted.

"She did? Here?" Frog seemed oddly pale.

I thought he must have been feeling tired, what with his trip and all. "Get Frog some tequila," I said to Virginia. Frog probably was missing his siesta ration.

"No, that's okay. I have to be going," Frog said quietly.

Tycho cocked his head at his friend: We just got here, why are we leaving?

Virginia detected Frog's mood swing, too. She put her hand on his shoulder. "I can get you something else to drink, some iced tea . . ."

"Oh, no, that's okay," Frog managed to say. I couldn't figure out what was bothering him. "Excuse me." Frog stood up and picked up his cat. You could see the vein in his neck pulsing with a quick rhythm. He was flush.

"Well, don't be a stranger," Sam said to be polite, not that he expected any kind of turnaround in the hermit physicist.

"Maybe you'd like to join our march, when we get it organized," Virginia suggested.

"Yes," Frog said.

I followed Frog out. He seemed to have forgotten that we were having a conversation about the meteorite before we were interrupted. "Frog?" I yelled after him. "You okay?"

"So are you going back to that cult?" Frog was suddenly curt.

"Yes, actually."

"Why?"

"I don't know why." I hated to have anyone mad at me. But his sudden nasty mood was contagious. "Look," I finally said, "I am going to try to get your meteorite back." I knew I was promising something I wasn't sure I could achieve. "I will."

"Sure," Frog snorted. I don't think he heard me. He made sure the cat was secure in the passenger's seat, and the two of them zoomed away.

Frog left me in a bad mood, which at night had blossomed into a terror I was eager to share with anyone I encountered. Madeleine fell victim. I had dutifully reported to Madeleine everything I'd learned after she had left me alone on the other side of the hill, including information about the meteorite—though I didn't tell her about my conversation with the rock, and I didn't tell her that I had met the stone before, indeed welcomed it to earth, I made it seem as if this were my first encounter. I had also gushed to Madeleine about James, about whom she seemed more disappointed than I did.

Madeleine was working as always, and when I tried to talk to her, not about the politics of the ashram, not about our voyage to the other side of the hill, she had nothing to say. I sat on the edge of Madeleine's bed and asked innocently enough, "Would you like to go on a walk, pick out the constellations?"

Madeleine didn't even answer me, she just looked up from her typewriter and asked, "If you had to guess how many people were over on the other side, how many . . ."

I didn't hear the rest of what she asked. Something was bothering me about her, something in the way she hammered away at the cold statistics of the secret side. The revenue, the benefits of supporting elite sponsors. . . . I suppose this was her job, to figure it all out. But was it? Madeleine was always indirect with me, and she never indicated in any way how any of this had anything to do with tourism. Fascinating as the machinations of the cult might be, what did they really have to do with travel?

Madeleine lit a cigarette with a quick flick of a lighter. "Did you notice any key obis over at the bottom of the hill?"

I shook my head. Suddenly, I had to know what her game was. I was mad that she could pretend to go on an expedition with me, yet not tell me what she was hunting. We had seen so much in a short time, I felt as if I had been through something with this odd woman—but whatever closeness I felt seemed unrequited, unreciprocated. "What are you up to?" I had to know now. "What are you really up to?"

Madeleine smiled, puffed, and shrugged. She got up from the bed and walked into the living room, plopped down on the couch, hugged a throw pillow. I had asked similar questions before—such as why Virginia thought she knew her, or why she was so keen on uncovering all the ashram's secrets and flaws—and this is what I usually met, a quick evasion, a puff of cigarette smoke. But Madeleine surprised me with the blunt truth tonight.

"I'm not a travel writer," Madeleine confessed.

"You're not?" Of course, I thought, I knew that deep down, but she said she was, so I bought it. "You said you were."

"No." Madeleine grinned. "You said I was. I never said that, you did, and I never actually said yes. Oh, don't frown, I could be a travel writer, it's conceivable"—she waved a hand—"that I could be writing travel pieces as a change of pace."

"What pace are you changing?" I asked. I tried not to sound angry, because I had the vague feeling I was not the only one who had been misled, but I did hear something hostile in my voice.

"Well, if you read *The Friscan* you'd know," she replied defensively.

Frog subscribed to the celebrated national weekly, but I had never read it. "I read a lot of books," I answered.

"I've written books, too," she said.

"Are you famous?" I felt stupid asking this, but I wanted to know.

"Hell, yes." She didn't worry about modesty. "I've won all the awards. This is probably the only place in the world I could go and be quasi-undercover."

"Do other people here think you're a travel writer?" I wondered.

"Oh, sure, some do. Most just think that I'm going to put out a series of fluff features, probably." Madeleine laughed.

"You're not," I gathered.

"I don't write fluff." Madeleine was almost offended by the notion.

"So what are you doing here?" I asked. "I don't mean to be naïve, but you seem to be masking your intentions."

Madeleine stood up and started pacing the room, speaking with a kind of fluid ardor I hadn't heard from her before, zeal for her mission, passion. "I want to be the first one to really get at the heart of this place," and I heard echoes of earlier chats we'd had when I had thought, yes, she was after something and wondered what it was. "I can't snoop around if Vanessa thinks I'm an investigative reporter eager to churn out an exposé. I have to be doing something that might benefit the ashram, and they're bent on attracting tourists."

"Why not just pose as a pilgrim?" I wondered.

"Two reasons." Madeleine had considered all the angles. "One is that if you're a reporter of any kind, you get to go places the average Joe, in this case Joe Pilgrim, doesn't get to go. Talk to people you wouldn't normally talk to. And then because I might not be able to get out, if I were Joe Pilgrim, when things got messy."

"Will things get messy?"

"They always do." Madeleine had a glint in her eye. She combed her hair with her fingers. It was fine and straight and always fell neatly into place.

"I need a beer." I moved toward the small refrigerator in the corner of the room, but Madeleine got up first and opened one for me. It was a subtle gesture, the beginning of an apology.

"I'm sorry," Madeleine said, "if I wasn't completely honest with you."

I nodded. How about just plain dishonest. But I accepted her coming out to me now.

"I thought," Madeleine added, "that you would figure all this out anyway. You're smart."

"Well, I didn't know for sure," I snapped. I was still angry. Then I became worried for Madeleine. "Wait." I stood up and paced. "Everyone thinks you're writing fluff, that you're putting the ashram's name in the paper, that tourists will come. But Vanessa . . . my God, she's a with-it person."

"I know." Madeleine rubbed her hands together.

"She reads magazines," I said. "Doesn't she know what you usually write?" I did not know myself what she normally wrote, but I feared the sparkle in Madeleine's eye.

"Oh, Vanessa knows who I am," Madeleine stated confidently. "Until now she hasn't permitted any journalist access to the ashram, she hasn't given anyone a free run of the place. Local reporters, state reporters, would just paint a bizarre picture, outsiders wouldn't get it. But she needs some publicity, and she wants to raise the profile of Rancho Flora to a national level. She wants to time this with a successful election campaign. She's got it all figured out, she's very crafty. Vanessa chose me because I have the national stature and magazine affiliation she wants to take advantage of. Even if what I publish isn't entirely positive, mind you, this little desert oasis will be put on the map. New pilgrims will arrive here, too, with their fat purses. From Vanessa's perspective, as long as there isn't too much that's unflattering," Madeleine reasoned, "it's a great public relations maneuver to give me my scoop. And you know I'm famous for something."

"What?"

"Well"—Madeleine puffed her cigarette without modesty—"I'm known for making even the most unattractive rulers look human."

"Do you want to talk to the guru?"

"Of course." Madeleine clapped her hands. "Do you realize that no one has interviewed him since he left India? Vanessa doesn't want that though, she wants to be the voice. I asked her today, and she said no. The thing I don't think Vanessa counted on was that we would sneak over to the other side of the hill."

"Secrets won't be secrets much longer," I predicted. "Why did you choose Rancho Flora? What had you heard about before you came here?"

"The few reports of orgies, that sort of thing," Madeleine said. "But I'd also met an ex-pilgrim, one of the two dozen or so there are, who mentioned that there was a woman who was in charge who really ran the city. Then I heard that she read the guru's lectures for him. That's all I needed."

"So what will you end up writing?"

"A series of articles, a book, who knows."

"No, I mean, will it be flattering or unflattering?"

"It will be fair."

Fair: somehow that sounded hollow.

As the night was the time for absolute honesty, for stepping into the past, I heard about Madeleine's voyages to Cambodia, Haiti, the Philippines, Uganda. El Salvador, Burundi, Chile, Angola, Poland, Northern Ireland. She'd covered insurrections, coups d'état, revolutions, assassinations, student protests, strikes, and just plain everyday elections with unexpected returns that boosted the opposition party. And she'd covered her share of scandals, mostly abroad, a few in the States. She'd done most of her work overseas, but now she wanted to explore her own homeland.

Madeleine and I talked for hours, and we both fell asleep at opposite ends of the living room couch. At about three or four that morning, I was woken up by a loud cheer coming down from the temple. Madeleine was startled, and she looked at me as if I had made the noise, ruined her sleep. I shrugged and she shuffled into the bedroom. Some pilgrims partying late at night, I assumed, gallivanting around Rancho Flora—they were the culprits.

The next day at the lecture, when Madeleine and I entered the temple, there was an addition to the stage, a massive stone.

"Oh, no, the meteorite," I whispered to Madeleine.

She nodded. "The guru's birthday. I meant to tell you that Elise told me that Vanessa had decided the birthday would be today."

"Vanessa decides when the guru has his birthday?"

"Apparently the guru has more than one a year. They're feast days. Morale boosters. Last year there were two, and this one is the third this year."

The pilgrims last night had been cheering because they were finally getting to add a grand new stone to the guru's collection. The meteorite cast a mild sheen, a bluish glow over the entire white interior of the temple.

After everyone had assembled, the guru emerged from an opening at the rear of the stage, and he smiled. This was rare. One never saw the guru smile this wide. He touched his bony fingers to his lips and then held his palms outstretched to the petals of pilgrims laid out around him. The audience clapped, clearly exuberant that the guru enjoyed his present. He assumed his throne and placed one hand on the meteorite beside him, patting it throughout the lecture. He was clearly pleased. However, when Vanessa stepped up toward the podium and started reading the sermon, her visage was solemn, her words very serious for a birthday celebration.

Thank-yous were not extended to the finders of the meteorite, which was not unusual—the deed was something to be taken for granted at best. At one point, Madeleine whispered to me, "I think she must feel upstaged," and that explained why Vanessa turned the speech into one of remorse. I wondered if the pilgrims had intended to give the guru the meteorite right away when they had stolen it, and Vanessa had made them wait. I certainly was devastated to see my meteorite, Frog's meteorite, now in the guru's possession, part of his collection, his eternal transcendence, but I became more frustrated, I think, with the way Vanessa twisted the whole scene. The guru patted his rock, and he barely (if at all) paid attention to what were allegedly his prophecies. Vanessa, however, spoke today with greater histrionics than usual.

Vanessa began by saying that the guru knew a rock would fall, but no one should panic because all who resided on the Buddhafield were safe, the one place free from nuclear war and viruses sweeping the world, because here there would be eternal harmonious peace. Only here at Rancho Flora.

"This stone that fell from the sky," Vanessa read, "represents the dawn of Armageddon, of the universe falling to pieces, of the world crumbling, of worlds far off where the destruction has already begun."

The meteorite, glowing, stately, austere, was baptized as a symbol of doom. Vanessa read from the saddest piece in Saint Walt's opus:

O powerful western fallen star!
O shades of night—O moody, tearful night!
O great star disappear'd—O the black murk that hides the star!

By this point, the mauve people had been robbed of their glee. Vanessa indicated to some of the blue obis in front that they should bow their heads, and as they did, the rest of the pilgrims bowed, too. Vanessa read:

O cruel hands that hold me powerless—O helpless soul of me!
O harsh surrounding cloud that will not free my soul.

"Hollow, hollow," Vanessa said, and most pilgrims probably thought the guru was still quoting Whitman, "hollow is our world. Except here at Rancho Flora, where we taste purity and where we see truth."

Now Vanessa was chipping at the boulder with a sharp tool. She was truly conniving. Madeleine had come to Rancho Flora because she had heard about a woman who intrigued her, but had she expected to find someone so plotting, so sinister? When I first saw the meteorite I was determined to win it back, but now the game involved another goal. Sure, I wanted the meteorite back, but what irked me now was the way the pilgrims had endowed the stone with glory and the way Vanessa drained all that energy until she was in complete control of the mood. The cult was her horse, and she clutched the reins, and she could gallop at her desired pace. The pilgrims had listened to what Vanessa said, and now they felt renewed. They kept their heads bowed in prolonged reverence, and looking down, they could not see Vanessa's victorious turned-down smile. They did not notice that the guru's hand rested on the stone, that his chin pressed against his chest, and that he dozed.

uring the lecture, staring at the meteorite, I began to
have visions of rescue and escape. I tried to imagine
myself somehow stealing the rock out of the temple. In
my daydream, I skipped the part when I actually had
to remove the meteorite from the temple, and I sped ahead to my
moment of triumph. I was steering a forklift cradling the meteorite in its two metal arms, steering the truck right through the
rainbow gate, past the pair of palm trees and into the desert. I was
driving madly toward the purple mountains in the distance when
I heard a boom, and it felt as if someone had thrown a brick into
my back. Boom: I turned around and saw Vanessa aiming her rifle
right at me. . . .

"What?" I woke up out of my daydream.

"Are you coming or are you going to sit here until tomorrow?"
Madeleine pulled my shoulder. I hadn't realized the lecture was
over. Most pilgrims had already emptied out of the temple.

As we walked out of the octagon, Madeleine said hello to a fa-
miliar-looking woman leaving at the same time. "Coyote," Madeleine said, "meet Amy de la Lune. She works in the school. I interviewed her while you were in Frescura yesterday."

Amy nodded hello. It occurred to me that of course I'd met her
before, but it had been dark, and she was wandering off into an
unused precinct of the ashram. "I think we met late one night," I
said.

"I can remember everyone I've met in the last five years, and I
know that I never met you." Amy turned her back to me.

Madeleine had a jeep parked outside the temple. To me she said,
"I want to go into town and make a phone call. Want to come?"
She turned to Amy: "Want a ride down the hill?"

Amy shook her head no, yet at the same time, she hopped into
the backseat.

"I'm fairly sure we ran into each other that night—" I tried again
as we reached the bottom of the hill.

"Sure, why not?" Amy replied this time. "Look over there," Amy
said to Madeleine.

"What's going on, a new project?" Madeleine asked.

Just beyond the administration building, in front of us, off the
road a bit, a group of pilgrims were greeting a pickup truck full of
building supplies. Then a squadron of jumpsuits unloaded what

looked like broad, corrugated pieces of sheet metal. They seemed ready to construct something. A bulldozer was smoothing out an area, and I wasn't sure why Madeleine was so interested, since construction was going in a dozen places ashram-wide. But then a jeep arrived carrying blankets and pillows.

"What's up?" Madeleine asked Amy, thinking Amy might know.

"I don't know," she said. "But I'm sure Vanessa's about to pull something out of her sleeve."

I looked at Amy, baffled. This was the first time I had heard any pilgrim say something negative about Vanessa.

"You'll find," she said to Madeleine, "that all kinds of strange things are probably going on at this ashram." Without explaining her cynicism, Amy left us with, "Thanks for the ride."

Instead of pulling away into the desert, Madeleine made us watch from our jeep a while longer. Soon a van pulled through the rainbow gate. A couple of fatigued-looking obis hopped out the front, and then they proceeded to help two or three rather wan-looking men climb out the back of the van. I couldn't really get a good look at these people, clad in tattered clothing, but they looked like refugees. The obis slowly ushered them toward the administration building. One man wandered quickly in the opposite direction. An obi chased after him, hooked his elbow, and turned him around.

"I don't know what it all means, but it means something," Madeleine said. Cassandra passed by, and Madeleine asked, "Who are those guys?"

"Oh, them? They're new pilgrims." That was all she would say except, "Groovy, huh?"

That night I was feeling restless. During the day, you could observe everything around you, throw yourself into the rhythms of the cult. But at night, there was so much time to think, and even while in Madeleine's company, perhaps because she was often working, I felt rather lonely. Even with other pilgrims, I felt alone, as if there was something I couldn't share with them. So I decided to visit Amy. She was mysterious and different, she intrigued me. Madeleine told me where to find her.

I suppose I've always been attracted to honesty, to people who could simply and unabashedly express what they thought and felt. Maybe it had to do with my own dishonesties. I was attracted to other things, too, but when honesty was a trait, it seemed most important. Amy was half-honest, it seemed, freewheeling with her opinions, but guarded about some secret—it had to do with the other side of the hill, I knew that much. I needed an excuse to visit her, so I decided to teach her about the virtues of beer and lemonade. After collecting the ingredients in the refectory, I went down to her house, low on the hill.

Amy lived in one of the first compounds of dwellings built at Rancho Flora, and these structures had a coziness that the newer adobes lacked. The walls were darker and the house looked more solid, since it had baked for the last five years and now seemed to be a natural part of the landscape. Its round corners and doorframe, which could have used a new coat of paint, provided a lived-in quality that the place Madeleine and I stayed in simply did not possess. Our accommodations had an air of hotellike transience.

Amy had told Madeleine that her name before she came to Rancho Flora was simply Amy Lune, and she had always wanted to add the preceding little words. For two weeks sometime in the last decade she had visited the ashram in India, and when she needed an escape five years ago and the ashram was being founded in her own backyard, she decided to join early on. I had wondered why she wasn't a blue obi by now, but I found out later that she had turned down the honor because she thought at one point she was actually going to leave. She had been an archaeologist in South America and then in the States, Madeleine had learned, and now she taught in the school, which seemed to be one of the ashram's more logical career progressions. In fact, she had started the school, and were she a blue obi now, she would be the principal.

Amy had long, elegant fingers. When I knocked on her door and opened after her "Come in," she was in the process of eating an orange. She tore apart the sections with steady grace, delicately stripping the layers of white fibers, and I thought that these must be the fingers that had excavated relentlessly in the desert sun. It hadn't occurred to me that it was actually rather late, approaching midnight. But when I arrived, it was as if she had been waiting for me. Her body filled the doorframe. Amber-colored hair was parted on one side and bounced off her shoulders. A thin gray streak cascaded out from the part.

"I hope it's not too late," I said.

"I was expecting you." Amy sat down on a couch, finished her expert peeling, and offered me a piece of her orange.

"You were?" I was surprised.

"Not now, but sometime."

"Well, that's good. Do you like beer and lemonade?"

"And lemonade?"

I had found a student. Inside Amy's house I saw a lot of rugs and pottery. Amy's place was instantly comfortable, more so than anywhere else I'd been on the ashram. The portrait of the guru was noticeably absent (Amy, I learned, made a point of ignoring the imposed ubiquity of the bearded man). And all around the house was a unique array of small bronze and clay sculptures. Madeleine hadn't mentioned the sculpture. The pieces were little, but they sat on tables everywhere in the two bedrooms and living room. The bronze figures were abstract. Not a polished bronze, but oxidized and antique looking by virtue of its pale green patina. Corrosion lent the shapes a fragile quality. I liked one bronze best among the dozen or so works, and that was what appeared to be a foot-high cactus. It was planted on a base etched with the words DESERT NIGHTMARE. The arms of the plant coiled and reached toward the ceiling with a prickly grasp. These bronze and the one or two clay sculptures were clearly efforts by the same artist. There was a distinct eeriness carried from piece to piece.

"They're studies." Amy saw me looking at the figures. "For larger things."

"Oh."

Amy found a pitcher and mixed up the lemonade. Then she found some glasses in her makeshift kitchen. Obviously she had taken to stealing things from the refectory and eating alone. There was a hot plate with two burners and a small refrigerator in one corner of the living room.

Without thinking, I ran my fingers along a piece of green wire that connected two arms of one of the bronze abstractions. The wire looked like rigging and the sculpture a piece of a shipwreck.

"Matthew would be mad if he saw you touching the art," Amy said in a nice way. I was afraid she might be abrupt with me, she had been before, but she was surprisingly warm.

"Sorry. Who's Matthew?"

"My brother," Amy said. "They're his. I mean, he made them." She seemed a little nervous.

Amy pulled my elbow as if I were more interested now in the art than the beer and lemonade, and she directed me outside. We climbed up an uneven wooden ladder resting against her house, and we sat on the flat roof. The sky was full of stars. With one sip, Amy was sold on the concoction. In the dark, Amy's eyes looked deeper. They were already set back deep. They were a brooding brown. And she had this way of smiling that was incredibly cute.

"Matthew went to Frescura," Amy told me. "Actually, he snuck out through a hole in the fence and went to his studio for a few days. Maybe he'll be back later."

"Does he do this often?" Pilgrims, after all, were only allowed to take ashram vehicles to the Sunflower Café, and the unofficial vow you took when you came here was not to wander into the desert (not that there was anywhere to go really).

"Well, he's not a very serious pilgrim," Amy explained. "He's just here because I'm here. He was having some problems and he came last year to visit. He stayed. I had this other roommate, Paul-René, and he was awful. So Matthew came when Paul-René moved up the hill, and that way I didn't have to live with a stranger."

That seemed like a funny statement given the fact that all anyone did at Rancho Flora was deal with strangers and make them intimates as quickly as possible.

"Siblings are rare at Rancho Flora," I said. It was something Madeleine pointed out early on. Most of the people, interviews revealed, were familyless or by choice cut off from their relatives.

"We didn't grow up together," Amy said. Then she asked questions about me, and I was straightforward. Most of the questions evolved into a query into Madeleine, however, and I forgot whether I was supposed to pretend that Madeleine was a travel writer or if I was supposed to give the impression that she was writing fluff.

"I once read an article she wrote about a deposed sultan," Amy said. "I used to get *The Friscan*." I had to chuckle. Madeleine may not have been as anonymous as she thought she was. That would be nice for her ego, not that it needed petting. "I hope she writes something ghastly about this place."

"You don't like it here?"

"No, but I keep finding reasons to stay."

"Such as?"

"Such as sex. That was the thing at first. I mean the sex, let's face it, was great. I was coming out of bad sex, so lots of sex was a nice change."

"And now?" I said this as if it were a come-on, which I didn't intend. I tried to cover my tone with a laugh. That made things worse.

"And now what?"

"Sex," I managed to say soberly.

"Oh, no, it's just not what it used to be. I miss having just one true love. During the dynamic, Matthew and I come in here"—she pointed down, at the house beneath us—"and we take a nap together. It's nice. Everyone in the compound thinks we have some kind of incestuous affair going on, and where else could we carry on but at Rancho Flora? But we don't. I try to tell them that, but Matthew makes it worse, because when we're with them, he hugs me and kisses me on the cheek and whispers things which they think are lewd."

"Why, what does he whisper?"

"Oh, he whispers gibberish, and that makes me giggle."

"I see." The beer and lemonade was making me dizzy. Soon we were on our backs, not bothered by the roughness of the roof, looking up at the stars.

"Have you been to Europe?" Amy asked.

"Me? No. Why?"

"Because of this." Amy raised her glass.

"Oh, no, a friend taught it to me. He had been in Europe a lot when he was younger."

"*Une bière panachée* in Paris," Amy said, her voice slurring over the French. "A shandy in London." She affected a bad cockney brogue. "I've never been to Venice. Have you been to Venice?"

"No, I've never been to Europe," I reminded her.

I had brought a six-pack, and we went through all the bottles. After a while we went inside, and once on her living room couch, where she had peeled an orange so delicately, Amy now smoked cigarettes rather clumsily, ashes everywhere. She tapped ashes onto my boots and jeans.

Inside her house Amy ranted. She complained about Vanessa, said she was manipulative. She was aware of the other side of the hill, and she claimed that many of the original pilgrims at Rancho Flora were there. They just figured it was a necessity of finance and a matter of privacy for the guru, and they made an effort not to tell those who were new and naïve about it. Why complicate matters? That wasn't what the guru would want.

"Why do you stay now, if not for sex and all?" I wondered. I fingered a sculpture.

"Hands off the art."

"Sorry."

"The school was it for me for a while. But not anymore. I'm sick of teaching those rambling poems."

"Saint Walt."

"And I walk on one side of you"—Amy feigned ministerial haughtiness—"and I am there on the other side of you, and there is someone else between us, and everything is contained in the ant, who eats grass on the one side of you. . . ."

The way Amy's eyes widened and the way she shook her shoulders as she teased the poet made me laugh so hard my ribs hurt.

"Guru B tries to be like Whitman, you know."

"How?"

"The beard and all." A pause. "I was hoping you'd visit me."

"Well, here I am."

"Here you are." Amy giggled. She found an elastic band for her hair and pulled it into a ponytail. I noticed she had small ears. "Well, then Matthew came to visit and stayed on." Amy abruptly picked up where she'd left off minutes ago.

"Of course," I inserted.

"And then I found something. I discovered something."

"What?"

"It's a secret."

"Does Matthew know?"

"Matthew's great," she said. "I really love him. You'd like him, too."

"What's the secret? Is that why you were going over to the other side of the hill?"

"You shouldn't follow people." It was a mild reprimand.

"I wasn't really following you," I protested. "I sort of ran into you."

Amy hesitated. "Well, it's a secret," she said again.

"You can tell me." I tried to sound trustworthy.

"I'd like to tell you, but I'm afraid I can't."

"Why?"

"Maybe you'd tell Madeleine," Amy said.

"No, I won't." I desperately wanted to know her secret.

"Well—" Amy stood up to tell me her secret, but collapsed back into the couch, and we couldn't do anything but laugh at the slapstick for a while.

"What?"

"No. Some other time."

"But this thing, whatever it is," I said, "is what keeps you here?"

"Yes."

I found myself grinning widely. I think we were seducing each other. I didn't mean to, but I couldn't help it. "Well, I need something to keep me here, too." I didn't know why I was saying this.

"I can't tell you, Coyote." Amy laughed. Everything seemed silly.

"Well, if you don't tell me," I lied, "I'm going to have no reason to stay." I was bluffing about leaving Rancho Flora, but Amy misunderstood. She thought I was talking about leaving her house.

"Don't go, I like you." Amy tugged at my elbow.

"So tell me your secret." I started giggling and couldn't stop.

"No." Amy smiled.

"Yes."

We had each downed three beers and a sizable amount of lemonade. Consequently, we started to spend a great deal of time in the bathroom, which adjoined Amy's bedroom. And I don't remember who pulled the blanket off the bed, or who pulled whom onto the bed. I didn't seduce her, and she didn't seduce me. Somehow we mutually fell into the foreplay and undressing. But the problem was that the evening shifted momentum when we started making love. We stopped talking.

Movement became awkward. I felt her touching me with either too much or too little meaning, and I found myself unable to read what gestures pleased her, which had no impact. And so, aroused but frustrated, we lay on our backs and started laughing.

"I'm sorry—" I started to say.

"No," Amy said, "I'm the one who is sorry."

"No, I am sorry," I reiterated.

"Shut up. You're sorry, I'm sorry, fine. The truth is, I'm depressed." Amy sighed.

"I'm sorry," I said by accident. I started to give her a back rub. "I know you're not going to tell me everything," I said, "but why don't you just leave the place?"

"Well, I don't want to. That feels good." The back rub I gave her, and the one she would give me, while we talked, sobered somewhat, was so much better than sex.

"Coyote," Amy said, "just give me a little time and maybe I can tell you what's what, all right?"

"Okay," I said. "Look"—I made a pledge—"if I can help you at all, you let me know."

"Really?"

"Sure," I said without any idea of what I was talking about.

I rolled over and Amy climbed on my back. My turn to be massaged. Amy's fingers were incredibly strong.

"I know it will sound clichéd," Amy said, "but I don't usually jump in the sack with the first new john to come along."

"Me neither."

"I was lonesome, you know?"

"Me, too. Oh, don't apologize," I said.

"I'm not apologizing." Amy laughed. "I'm just talking."

"You know, Amy . . ." I started to say.

"You don't have to come out to me," Amy said.

"I don't?"

"Like I said, I was lonesome." Sarcastically: "And this is Rancho Flora after all."

I blushed. "I feel a little transparent."

"Oh, don't. Besides, we're better friends now."

"We are." Amy was not Madeleine—you could talk to Amy so easily.

"You should meet my little brother. You'd like him."

"Why?"

"You'll see." Amy raised an eyebrow.

There was something peaceful about just being naked in her bedroom, exchanging the sorts of things it might take years and years of living with someone to bring out. Amy told me that she had broken up with a man before she came to Rancho Flora, someone she was so in love with, a man with whom she was going to have a child. And when they had broken up, Amy had an abortion. And then Amy tried to conceive again, with other people, and failed. Then she went back to the man and it was horrible. So she came here. Five years later, all of this still devastated Amy. We talked for hours more—a lot about politics. I don't know why, but Amy got onto causes and peace movements and things she did earlier in life, which to me seemed like the history of a much older generation. The thought of college campuses and student protests was for me exotic, for Amy sadly nostalgic.

Then we heard noises in the living room. It must have been about four in the morning now, or later. A light flicked on and someone stood in the doorway to the bedroom. "It's me," a man's voice said sweetly. Amy turned on a lamp by her bed.

There stood a man who was pulling a gray T-shirt over his head and revealing a slender and beautiful body, a sculpture in its own right.

"Matthew?" Amy said.

"I decided to come back early," Matthew Lune said, still with his T-shirt over his head. Then I saw his face, and I groped for a sheet to cover my nudity, but it was too late. I think Matthew was more embarrassed than I was, or than Amy was, because he had walked in on us, even though we were lying rather innocently in bed. He had walked in and just pulled off his shirt. He covered his chest with the shirt. His features were her features, the same thin eyebrows, thin lips, perfect nose, the same pale complexion, except his hair was short, now tousled, and browner. His eyes were deep set, too, and brooding brown. I could almost smell the soapy scent of tea in the air and see the pattern of dregs in a cup, shriveled leaves arranged like a new continent of islands.

"I'm sorry," he apologized. But he stood still, staring at his sister, staring at me.

"Isn't he gorgeous?" Amy whispered to me proudly, loud enough so her brother could hear.

*T*he summer became so sultry, even at Rancho Flora with its cooler air. On dog days anywhere, cats like me can become rather unpleasant company, a sluggish breed. This was the hottest summer I remembered, but no one else at the ashram seemed to notice. If anything, the pilgrims only labored harder and longer as if the higher temperatures had been levied as a greater challenge to their spiritual pursuits. But the sun had become its whitest, the air its driest, and it was hard not to feel dizzy at times. The best thing to do was to take sanctuary in the shower, where I found myself several times a day. It was where I was during the midday dynamic (through the shower wall I heard the romp next door), and where I was when Elise came over to see Madeleine.

Madeleine had noticed something about the way that Elise seemed to watch Vanessa, with a certain amount of disdain. Elise was close to the top—she sat next to Vanessa at the glass table. But Elise became increasingly candid with Madeleine about how she was being cut off, her responsibilities taken away, about how Vanessa was consolidating power. Elise liked Madeleine, everyone did, and Madeleine tried to make herself available so Elise could vent her frustration.

Elise was a round woman, with a round face out of which shot a thin nose like the blade of a sundial. She had shoulder-length blond hair and a gruff voice. When she whispered, she was barely audible. She'd come to the ashram in India via French schooling and British publishing. Her perspective was bitter, and as far as I could tell, only her devotion to Guru B and her steadfast belief in his teachings sustained her. In the last week I'd spent time with Elise when Madeleine did, which was why, though Elise was a little shy at first to have me on hand, I ultimately got to hear the revelations she blasted forth.

I wasn't aware that Elise was in the living room talking to Madeleine, and when I stepped out of the shower, I only heard the low tones of her whispering. I couldn't hear clearly what she said, but I did know that her scratchy ranting was full of anger. I wrapped myself in a towel and still dripping, quietly wandered into the room.

"And now"—Elise was shaking her head—"and now she"—she,

I gathered, referred to Vanessa—"has arranged the guru's schedule in such a way that only certain obis can talk to him."

"How'd she manage that?" Madeleine asked.

"Well, there are rules about visitation which Vanessa's set up, because she claims the guru's getting too tired out."

"Is he?"

"Well, yes," Elise snorted. "But it's still completely unnecessary. That's what I'm worried about. That I'll be next, that she'll figure out a way to cut *me* off from Guru B." This was what had probably sent Elise over today.

"Guru B wouldn't let that happen." Madeleine tried to be reassuring.

Elise caught my eye and I nodded.

"I guess not," Elise sighed. "I think Vanessa's handling this whole Prop Eight thing all wrong. I've told you before, she's making more of a mess out of it than she needs to. It's so goddamned frivolous." Elise didn't usually swear, not that I had heard.

"I have to ask you something." Madeleine shifted her position on the couch so that she sat closer to Elise. Madeleine whispered, "Coyote and I stumbled on a greenhouse full of tulips a little while back."

"You did?" Elise seemed surprised.

"Well, yes." Madeleine for a moment was disappointed that perhaps she knew something Elise didn't.

"That means you've been over to the other side." Elise smiled. "Very sly." Elise looked at me. "Oh, you're sly, too."

"I know we shouldn't have sneaked over, but we did," Madeleine said.

"It's strange that the other side of the hill is closed off," I said.

Elise ignored my comment, indicating that she did not think the segregation of pilgrims was strange at all. She whispered, "So you saw Vanessa's digs?"

"Yes, greenhouse and all," Madeleine said.

"Well," Elise whispered, "only a few obis even know that it exists. It's another one of Vanessa's brilliant gimmicks." Elise dolloped sarcasm on the word "brilliant."

"We saw tulips in every obi's vase—" I started to say.

"Well," Elise said, "your exploration was thorough." I detected a minor note of resentment. I had to be more careful. We couldn't be sure which rules we had broken, Vanessa's or the guru's. Elise might look with disapproval on an act violating Guru B's word. I wondered how much Elise knew about Madeleine's true project—she'd probably gathered everything.

Madeleine tried to diffuse any paranoia Elise might harbor. "We just want to know what's what. We are interested in Rancho Flora's welfare."

"The tulips are Vanessa's hold over the obis," Elise explained. "You have to realize that she's got her own subcult of pilgrims with the obis. Vanessa holds daily meetings and almost all of them—of us—take whatever she says as gospel. Vanessa, after all, is the one writing the guru's lectures. Oh, yes, she writes them. She's revered. And if I say anything to anyone, they all just say, 'Oh, Elise is bitter 'cause Vanessa's closer to the guru. . . .' You know what I mean? Infighting does no one any good. It hurts the ashram."

I got the feeling that Elise cowered from confrontation, that her only means to strike back and steer the ashram on its correct course was through Madeleine, through whatever Madeleine was going to write.

"The obis don't know about the greenhouse," Elise continued, "yet each day, a tulip magically appears in the vase by their night tables. The average pilgrim, I'm sure you've noticed by now, doesn't know where the water comes from. The obis, most of them, don't know where the tulip comes from, but they do know that Vanessa delivers them while they sleep. It's Vanessa's trick, it makes her more . . . I don't know, larger than life. You know what I mean?"

"Sure," Madeleine said.

"And I'll tell you something," Elise snorted. "Handing out those little flowers has made Vanessa very popular, so much so that she can do whatever she wants."

"Like what?" I asked.

"Like Vanessa has total control of financial matters, because she's trusted by the obis. I used to see the books, and now I don't even know where Vanessa's got them tucked away."

"I'd like to get an audience with the guru," Madeleine announced. This was not the first time she'd brought it up with Elise. "But Vanessa said no."

"Well, it's virtually impossible. I mean I could try to arrange it, but it'll take a while. Do you think it would help tame Vanessa?"

"Sure." Madeleine shrugged. I felt a little uneasy about this, because I knew that Madeleine's main interest was not in helping Elise, but in getting the scoop interview. I couldn't help but feel that Madeleine was using Elise to some degree. But then again, an interview was a fascinating prospect.

"I'll tell you something else." Madeleine looked Elise in the eye. "We were in the guru's chambers, too."

"Oh, that's—well, that's—" Elise was bothered. We could invade Vanessa's privacy, but not Guru B's. That was sacrilegious.

"I know we should have talked to you first"—Madeleine improvised an apology—"but we just sort of stumbled upon it." That was true. "We also stumbled upon a series of oxygen tanks."

Elise looked at me as if she wanted me to leave the room. I even started to tighten the towel around my waist so I could stand up and go. But Elise didn't say anything. Her lips became pale. A tear even slipped out.

"The guru has acute asthma, which even the desert climate cannot always suppress," she said. "That's why we have oxygen on hand."

"I'm sorry," Madeleine said, since Elise was disturbed.

"Oh, he's had it for years," Elise said. "All his life. But you know, it's a secret." She looked at me for a silent nod to promise secrecy. "There shouldn't be disease on a Buddhafield."

"No." Madeleine nodded.

"It's not really disease. If anything, the asthma's under control." Elise's voice went higher—I think because she might have been fibbing. "Actually, the guru's been tired in the last year more because, well, he's older. He gets a few headaches now and then, too, but not too many coughing fits, you know?"

"Sure." Madeleine sounded consoling.

"Well, the dynamic will be over soon, and I have to go back to my desk. Thanks for letting me complain." Elise stood up.

"Oh, anytime," I said cheerfully. I caught a glimpse of Madeleine's posed austerity. "We're glad we could listen," I said more solemnly.

After Elise had left, Madeleine just slumped down into the couch. She clapped her hands and whispered through a wide smile, "Bingo." Then she looked at me. "We always knew Vanessa was the one to watch, but now we really know." She lit a cigarette and let her sunglasses drop down from her brow. "We know that she's the one we've got to figure out." Madeleine found her type-writer and started tapping madly. I watched her work for a few minutes, and when Madeleine stopped, I thought it was to tell me to get lost. But Madeleine looked stumped, and she said, "What's her game? I mean what the hell is she dreaming up?"

Dusk provided relief from the sun. I had always been a night person, and now more than ever I found myself napping away the hot part of the day to trade it in for darkness. I decided to drop in on Amy at the school. We'd been having fun just hanging out at her place. Amy was intent upon really introducing me to her brother, but he was always absent, off in the desert somewhere.

The children were finishing up their day when I strolled through the building. I was overwhelmed by the breeze of high voices, all glee and curiosity. The school was like a school anywhere. When the children were inside, it bustled with the chatter of geography, grammar, and games. Yet from the outside, during the day, the building seemed vacant, uninhabited. You rarely saw the sixty-odd children at Rancho Flora, or if you did, they appeared to be little adults in scaled-down jumpsuits. In several rooms there seemed to be as many mauve grown-ups as there were mauve children. The kids studied and played as one would expect, but I was sur-prised by how conventional their lives seemed. The things they learned, the books they used, the games they invented. The only differences between them and the rest of the young world were that they wore these mod uniforms, that they called all the adult pilgrims by their first names, and that they had a rather scant sense of history or American legends like Washington or Lincoln. But they did know when and where Walt Whitman lived, and they knew all about the various editions of *Leaves of Grass*. The revision dates composed a time line. They also knew that he was a male nurse and that he loved men, and they thought this was nifty.

At the same time, they all knew the history of Guru B, all the key facts, and as far as they were concerned, he was the greatest man who had ever roamed the world. They were encouraged to imitate him. When I peered into the classrooms, I saw that on each pupil's desk there were two boxes. In one box, the student was supposed to place small stones, which he or she had found around the ashram. Some of the children were quite entrepreneurial and had more than one box of stones. Stones of all sizes, the vast majority smaller than a child's palm. The second box, though, was for whatever that student wanted to collect personally. Stones ultimately perpetuated the myth of the guru, but a student had to begin to reach up to his own higher plane of pure truth. So there were boxes of whatever could be collected in the fantastic oasis in the desert. Pieces of glass, cactus petals, pieces of clay bowls. One girl kept a lizard, another a jar of lightning bugs, which she refilled whenever she could.

At night the children could watch as much television as they wanted. This was the guru's wish, that these little people learn early that you can have what you want in this world. They were allowed to change their names as often as they wanted, which confused the younger children, not to mention the teachers, but they all were sure of one thing. When they sang the poem that one teacher had set to music, they knew that the words referred to them and every child. *"I celebrate myself, and sing myself . . ."* They felt special. I envied them in a way.

Just as I approached Amy's classroom I was pressed against the wall by a river of children flowing out of the school to go play before supper. I survived the flood and found Amy sitting at her desk, staring at a shard of clay in her hand. She held the fragment as if it were an ancient gold coin, and she dusted the faint ruddy pattern with a free pinky. She looked pensive, lost in speculation about this bit of pottery.

"One girl in my class"—Amy didn't even say hello—"a while ago started collecting clay fragments. That was her thing to pick up."

"She probably can find a lot."

"And I started to look at them," Amy said, "and I'd ask, 'Becky, where did you get these?' and she wouldn't tell me. Which led me to believe that she was going someplace she shouldn't to gather her broken pots and whatnot."

"Like to the other side of the hill," I said.

"Right," Amy said. She put down the piece of pottery. "You're a quick student."

I smiled.

"Well, I may have found where Becky was picking up these little bits, like this one."

I noticed that on the chalkboard the word "ecosystem" was scrawled in bold capitals.

"So you've been snooping," I said. "But what's the big deal about a piece of a pot?"

"Oh, I'm quite an expert about fragments of clay, you know."

"Of course."

I walked around the classroom among a series of aquarium tanks on various tables. Each was labeled with some kind of geological tag: rain forest, desert, savanna, coral reef, mountain. And in each tank were things cut out in construction paper to depict in diorama scale the type of terrain studied. In the tank marked DESERT, there was a real lizard. He blinked at me and gulped timidly.

"Well, I'll tell you something," Amy said quietly. "These bits of clay that little Becky collects like a good pilgrim—they're ancient."

"Really?" I had the feeling that I was being let in on Amy's big secret. "What does it mean?"

Amy stood up. "I have to show you something." She walked out of the room ahead of me, switched off the light before I had exited, and led me to a spot behind the long schoolhouse. The sun was setting and washing the rounded corners of the adobe.

Amy crouched down to the ground and began to scoop up the salmon-colored dirt and clay with her hand. Then she opened her fingers enough to sift out most of the clump of earth. What was left was a particularly pinkish soil.

"What do you see?" Amy asked.

"Soil?"

"What color is it?"

"It's rather light." I searched for the response she wanted. "Pink."

"And is it as pink as it usually gets in this area?"

"It's pinker."

"Right." She rewarded me with a smile. Her amber hair also seemed pinker in the meek light of dusk.

"Where does the earth come from?" she asked.

"It was bulldozed here. So it's from somewhere else." I was thinking about how the oasis was built up.

"Great." I got an A. "And what does that tell us about anything we find with this dirt, like a piece of clay?"

"That it, too, came from somewhere else?"

"Right. So"—Amy breathed in—"what would soil look like if it hadn't been bulldozed?"

"It would be darker."

"And pieces of clay found there would not have been bulldozed there," Amy said.

"So?" I was lost.

"You don't see?" Amy asked.

I thought about these bits of clay she was keen on, and I thought about this soil business, but I still couldn't get what she was driving at. "No."

"Okay," Amy said. "You will later."

"Later?" I may have seemed a bit exasperated, but then again, I was used to the way Amy let me in on things slowly. I used to be different, impatient with people. But this summer I was learning to cherish mystery, and I guess Madeleine was to blame for that. I still was impatient, though, but I was better. I dug my fingers into the earth and tried to end up with the same salmon silt Amy had sifted, but I was not as delicate. Her long fingers had a special practiced bounce as she filtered the sand.

"No. Grab, like this, and sift lightly." Amy corrected me. "You only want to gather a small clump from the ground just beneath the surface. It's tricky."

"Hello." Matthew approached us.

The light at dusk made him glow even more than the previous time I had seen him. He seemed taller. He hugged his sister and shot me a quick wave. "So?" Matthew looked at the pile of dirt at our feet. "You guys building a sand castle?"

Matthew wore only the bottom of the mauve jumpsuit. He had cut off the top part with a pair of scissors. The pants on him looked more maroon. He had belted the frayed waistline with a thin white sash tied into a knot. He wore a gray T-shirt on top, black boots on his feet, and a green bracelet made from dyed corn kernels. In all the variations I had seen in how to wear the uniform, Matthew was the first pilgrim to think of cutting off the top.

We walked down the hill toward Amy and Matthew's house and listened to Matthew's stories about the Native road workers he had spent the day talking to. They were part of the crew that continued to pave a highway in the desert, a road that no one would ever take. I found myself amazingly silent, able only to listen to Matthew's lilt. I didn't hear Madeleine call me from behind. Finally she tugged my elbow.

"Oh, hi," I said.

"I was on the way to the refectory," Madeleine said.

"Oh, come with us," Matthew said, smiling, "and have a beer."

"This is my brother," Amy explained.

"Well, I've heard a lot about you," Madeleine said, not really meaning anything by it. So we marched down the hill. We kept having to stop on the way because Madeleine, like some candidate out handshaking, greeted every pilgrim who was wandering uphill to dinner.

Matthew, once inside the house, became the host. He offered me a beer and added, "Oh, Amy says you like a little lemonade. . . ." So he produced a pitcher of the light yellow liquid, a particularly pulpy batch, which led me to believe he had squeezed the lemons himself. I was embarrassed by the way he said "Amy says you like," and I assumed he had a received a full account of my escapade with his sister. But then I noticed something funny: Matthew tried not to look me in the eye, instead glancing bashfully at my boots.

"How are the ecosystems?" Madeleine asked Amy.

"The rain forest is particularly popular," Amy said.

"I bet." Madeleine nodded. "Thank you," she said as she accepted a drink from Matthew. "I've always liked this combo."

"For the kids," Amy continued, "it's like some fantasy world. The beach is popular, too."

The small talk lapsed. Matthew still couldn't look at me for some reason.

"So you're the sculptor." Madeleine turned to Matthew.

"That's me."

"Well, I'd like to see your work. These studies"—Madeleine waved her arm around the room—"are intriguing."

"Thank you." Matthew stood up and smoothed the wrinkles out of his pants, and I thought he was going to get more beer, but he passed behind the couch where I was sitting. "I have to tell you about my new thing," he said.

"What new thing?" Amy asked.

All of a sudden I felt Matthew's palms pressing down on my shoulders. I sat up, startled. He began massaging my shoulders with hands used to kneading clay. He talked about his "new thing," and while I felt conspicuous, confused, I realized that no one was paying attention to me. Madeleine and Amy both listened attentively to Matthew.

"It's a bronze cow skull," Matthew explained. He described the source of inspiration for his new work of art. I didn't hear what he said. I was being sculpted by expert hands. I caught only a word here and there: something about a rotting cow in a field, and how he sat and sketched the putrid corpse.

Amy kept inserting, "Ooh," "Ick," "Gross," and "Please stop," as Matthew's description of the decaying beast became more graphic, and as he talked about how he tried to match the horror of the gruesome sight in bronze.

"It keeps coming out looking too handsome, though," Matthew complained. My shoulders prickled.

Madeleine ate all of this up. She knew all the right questions, and ever the inquisitor, she asked Matthew about what he wanted to take from the rotting cow and put into the sculpture. A decaying animal never seemed so lovely to me as when Matthew described it. My neck felt so loose and free, as if I could have turned it all the way around like an owl. Finally Matthew ended the massage, and I chirped, "Thanks."

Matthew nodded. Then he stood behind Madeleine's chair and proceeded, unsolicited, to give her a massage, too. So I wasn't special: this bothered me at first, but then it didn't matter because my whole back felt limber. "Oh, that's wonderful," Madeleine said.

Amy looked pale. "Matthew," she said, "next time just tell us about your art."

"Sure." He smiled. Maybe he was only interested in teasing his older sister.

I was happy Madeleine was here with us, because as usual, she wound her way through a series of questions, and as Amy and Matthew answered, I learned more about them. They hadn't grown up together. Part of this was because she was ten years older and left home when he was only seven, and part of this was because in the four or so years before her departure, Amy lived with her father out in the desert, their parents having separated the day after Matthew was born. Their father ultimately became a Chiaroscuro bum. He died when his liver failed. Matthew spent the rest of his childhood with his mother on the coast. She was not around much of the time, since she worked as a fisher"man" on a trawler in the bay. Ultimately she was lost at sea—her shipwreck was not found for a month. Orphans came together. Matthew was old enough to leave home, and he tried to get to know his sister, which was hard because she hopped around the world on various digs. But he followed her to the Fertile Crescent and to the Amazon basin. Her specialty became Native American culture, and she came to a university near the desert. He found a studio and began sculpting. They saw each other often, but then they drifted apart again. Then Amy moved here, Matthew arrived at the ashram, and they were reunited.

I was a cat-child of the desert, and it occurred to me that Matthew was unquestionably a child of the moon. If you looked at the night sky over the desert when there was a full moon, you saw the dependent planet as a strange sight. All the stars twinkled with brilliance and charm, but the moon cast the most looming, dominating glow. It was aloof at times, seemingly unaware that it was even being looked at. Or it noticed you, and if you stared at it long enough, it appeared to crash down with an angry velocity that only blinking could bring to a halt. The moon sped toward you, you blinked, it stopped, but then it hurled itself toward you again when you opened your eyes. However, the next time it happened you realized that the moon was a great teaser, and all of this was a silly game.

After dinner, Madeleine went off to work, and Amy said to me again, "I have to show you something." Matthew came with us, too. Amy led us away from the road and dwellings into darkness, away from any building. She wouldn't say where we were going, and Matthew—who I gathered knew the destination—followed silently alongside me. I realized we walked all the way to the edge of the ashram, flashlights illuminating only a few yards at a time. We were taking the same route that I had followed Amy down once before. We kept walking, and when we reached the fence separating the ashram proper and the secret side, Amy ordered, "Climb over."

"Climb over?" I said. "What if someone sees us?"

"No one will see us. No one comes down here, there's nothing here yet." We were in an unused quarter of the ashram. "Climb," Amy ordered again, and so we did. The fence was high, but we had no problem dropping over to the forbidden area. We took turns climbing over, helping each other with footing and jumps. A chill ran up my spine as Matthew clutched my ankle in his hand and then threw me up and over. I thought for sure we'd be nabbed. But the pilgrims obeyed the law of the guru: they respected the fence, so there was no reason to patrol the border. We were safe.

The three of us rounded a corner of the estate, to a section of the ashram you couldn't see from the road, and we found ourselves directly downhill from the massive glass panels that trapped the sun and supplied the ashram with energy. We were at the bottom of the slope. The panels seemed to stretch hundreds of feet up the hill. At night they appeared useless, cold, impotent. Nonetheless, I was awed. I had seen the solar panel complex from above, and it had seemed like nothing more than a series of large silver windows. But now I could see the massive machinery and structure that lay beneath. Below the rectangles of millions and millions of solar cells, I felt for the first time so much smaller than the ashram. A massive machine churned and kept this oasis alive, this hill breathing, and the ashram itself was larger than life, larger than the eight hundred lives combined.

"Wow," I said. I continued to shine my flashlight up the hill.

"Wow." Matthew hadn't been to this part of the ashram either.

"Wow is right," Amy said, pointing her flashlight down, not up. She had knelt down to use her grab and sift method to dig into the soil. She lit her hand with her flashlight, and I saw what I was supposed to see, having been trained just today in soil analysis. The dirt lit in her hand was a deeper beige color than any we had sifted earlier. Here was a fairly flat spot in the ashram with a sharp slope above and a gentle slope beneath it. Here at the base of the expansive solar panels, we had been taken to a relatively undisturbed patch of earth.

"Okay, Coyote," Amy said. "Dark soil. What does it mean?"

"That this part of town wasn't bulldozed." I had figured that much out.

"Oh." Matthew seemed to understand something. "This is where Becky's shards of clay come from?"

"You got it," Amy said.

"I don't get it," I confessed.

"Coyote, you can't tell Madeleine any of this, okay?"

"Any of what?"

"My secret," Amy said.

I beamed. "Sure."

"I told you that those clay fragments were ancient. They're almost like Anasazi pots, very rare, very old. And they come from here."

"I'm surprised this is the spot," Matthew interrupted. I shushed him so Amy could continue.

"There's a legend which only a few people in the field have heard about—and fewer believe it—a legend of a lost, outcast tribe who built up a little city out here somewhere."

"Outcasts?" I asked.

"Made up of a bunch of intertribal marriages and whatnot. And legend has it that they mined and traded turquoise out here, somewhere. It wasn't always desert, you know, it was a little grassier. But even so, no one has been able to find or uncover this city."

I jumped ahead. "You think it's here? This lost city?"

"Lost city," Amy murmured. "That sounds romantic."

"Is it here?" I pointed down.

"Maybe," Amy said.

"I keep telling her there's only one way to find out," Matthew said. "Dig."

"It's going on a lot of speculation and not a lot of scientific data." Amy was hesitant to make any definite claims.

"There's only one way to find out," Matthew repeated himself. To me: "She doesn't listen to me."

Amy crouched low to the ground. She almost put her ear to the dirt, and then she did press her cheek to the soil, the darker age-old soil. Not nouveau-pink soil, but rich and unturned old world clay.

"Usually, I feel something there," Amy said. "Like a kick." Like the anxious baby in the womb. "I have this knack for feeling when ruins are buried somewhere."

"She's usually right," Matthew added.

"But I don't feel anything here," Amy said.

"Well, maybe you will." I had picked up Matthew's attitude without even thinking.

"You think so? Look, I can't be sure, but I do think this Lost City is around here somewhere." She looked at Matthew, then at me. "I haven't dug in years," Amy protested.

"We can help," I said.

"You guys would be into an excavation?" Amy smiled.

"Sure," Matthew said.

"If it is down there," Amy said, "I can just imagine how it would be spread out." She started to pace. "Along here, there might be houses, like cliff dwellings pressed against the hill." Amy started walking away from us. "Down there, some kind of meeting house. And over here"—Amy walked almost out of view—"a kiva, perhaps, a sacrificial pit. Over here they might have weaved baskets, tanned hides, roasted beans . . ." Her voice trailed off and she disappeared.

"This is what she likes to do," Matthew explained. "I wish she did more of it."

Amy returned into view, still lecturing. "If they did mine in these parts, chances are the mines were out there." She pointed toward the open desert. "But of course, the stripped-out hills are probably buried, too. Matthew?" She walked toward us. "I'll need my tools. Could you go to your studio and get them?"

"Sure," Matthew said.

"I'm not promising anything." Amy was skeptical.

But clearly she had brought us here to get us interested. An excavation sounded romantic to me. I gazed uphill at the solar panels. The only way to get beyond the machine of the ashram was to dig at its base, to find something underneath it, underground, and to bring to the surface the long-smothered hill, the hidden city.

Amy looked at me, but said to Matthew, "And take Coyote with you, okay? He'll help you get what you need."

"Sure." Matthew shrugged.

"Oh, gosh." Amy put her hand to her forehead as if she had forgotten to do something essential.

"What?" Matthew asked.

"I don't know. Doubts." She pointed to the ground. For me the prospect of excavation was charming, but for her, it was terrifying.

"I'm sure something is under there," I said. I was not sure, I had no idea how far we would have to dig. "In any event, let's go home and have some beer and lemonade." That was a popular idea. What was left of the night would be spent in happy orbit with the Lunes.

*E*ach day men from pueblos as far away as Chiaroscuro rode down the highway in the desert to the point at which it stopped, and each day these men added a little more onto the aimless route. It was a state road no one would ever use, but since it was their project, their livelihood, they diligently paved under the tormenting sun. Matthew knew these men by name. While he was at the ashram, he parked his car near their work site and they kept an eye on it for him. Matthew would leave the car to melt into the desert for as much as a week, but he was always able to start it right up without even a hesitant gurgle.

We snuck out of Rancho Flora just after midnight the day after Amy sent us on our mission. We climbed through a hole in the fence he used often and that I, too, had discovered. We then hiked under the stars up the road until it ceased, and there was Matthew's car, reflecting green in the moonlight. It was a little car, and surprisingly, its torn seats were chilly. In one sweeping turn, Matthew drove his car up onto the road and we zoomed away, setting a few balls of tumbleweed in motion.

We were going to drive for the rest of the night on a road northwest, through canyons and higher ground, and by dawn reach Matthew's studio. Matthew made me feel comfortable, indeed invited, although he himself looked uneasy at times.

Matthew steered over the ridge where the Great Tree stood. We raced through Frescura and connected to another highway at the fork where I used to dismantle the signs (no one had put them back up), then proceeded up the long road that became lighter as the earth turned and the night slipped away. I watched him surreptitiously as he drove, face forward, both hands on the steering wheel. The way the car glided so smoothly and quickly, the way he pushed back in his seat and at the same time pushed forward on the wheel made me feel that he was in control, a confidence that somehow soothed me. His arms and hands were strong, yet his feet rather delicately tapped the gas pedal. Floating. He was like a part of the car, part of the machine.

When the sun was up, we found ourselves in a different-looking place, a variation on a theme, still the Southwest, but not what I was used to. I had been up here thousands of times before, yet the turf seemed new, as if this were my first encounter with this landscape, a projection of the person I had followed here. The terrain was prettier in many respects. There were more colors, the air was cooler and more bubbly, and the contours of the land were more dramatic. Much more complicated than the Frescuran environs, where there was the pallid sky, the beige earth, and the all-encompassing heat. Here, near Matthew's studio, it was cooler in the morning, and so I was actually cold in my T-shirt. Matthew had a sweatshirt on the backseat and I borrowed that. It was large on him, like a poncho on me.

We drove along a hilly, winding road. Mountains slept in the distance. We wound around mesas that had been sculpted through the centuries by the wind's erosive chisel. They were flat on top and their steep sides were rough. The mesas looked like chunks of cake because of the way they were striated, distinct layers of geological history revealed in a virtual pageant of yellows and beiges and ruddy colors (including mauve), a very specific pattern repeated from hill to hill.

Matthew asked if I was hungry.

"Not really," I said.

"We can stop," he added as if he thought I was being polite.

"No, I'm fine."

"Let's stop," Matthew said. *He* was hungry. As we neared a town, he pulled into a parking lot outside a dingy coffee shop appropriately called Mesa Morning. "I come here often," Matthew explained.

It was early, but the place bustled with aprons and Spanish chatter, jovial and bouncy, as people on their way to work, mostly road work or jobs at the state forests to the north, chugged wide-brimmed and sturdy cups of coffee. I expected Matthew to know everyone, but this was not the case. Still many people did nod howdy, and several waitresses smiled as we plopped down in a booth on the side. Each booth had a jukebox, but none was in use. Several people passed our table and nodded at Matthew as if he were a local politician. Matthew made a point of smiling back at everyone. There were unfriendly faces, too, people mad at the world, but when they saw Matthew, they couldn't hold back a polite nod.

"Hullo, there," a waitress said, wiping our table. "What can I get you boys?"

I was surprised when Matthew ordered eggs, bacon, and toast. "I never thought you'd eat greasy food like that."

"Oh"—Matthew smiled with guilt—"I have a craving for this food all the time. Now and then?" he seemed to ask permission.

"Oh, me, too," I reassured him. "Got a quarter for the jukebox?"

"That wouldn't be cool, Coyote. You don't play music in the morning here. It makes people nervous."

We listened to two men at the counter gently argue about some kind of wage dispute they were both involved in. They drank their coffee and talked about the weather conditions for work today, and work today led to what a bastard the foreman was, which led to this discussion about the employer, and then one man whacked his spoon against the countertop, sending a few drops of coffee flying. The men agreed not to discuss this issue anymore, and they returned to the weather.

We were sopping our eggs up with toast when I had an uncontrollable urge to share my deepest secret with Matthew, right here in the Mesa Morning diner. Cautiously, I started slowly, and then it came out.

"I can become a cat." The simplest phrase, yet in my mind I couldn't confess this without automatically becoming defensive.

Matthew looked dazed, but he nodded his head. "I thought so," he said.

"You did?"

"I mean, I didn't know it was cat, but I knew you could do something extraordinary. That's incredible, though, amazing." In front of all these people, though none paid attention, he placed his hand on top of my hand on the table. "I think that's incredible," he repeated. No questions, no suspicious smiles to check to see if I was joking, no giggles, just an acceptance.

"I don't usually tell people," I said. I wasn't entirely sure why I was telling him.

Matthew smiled to indicate that he was honored. He crunched on a piece of bacon.

"I mean, I can just be alone and think of myself as a cat, and I am one."

Matthew nodded and swallowed his food. "Oh, you don't need to explain it. I understand completely."

The strange thing was, he did. People who just think you're

crazy don't ask questions, and the same goes for those who whole-heartedly trust you. He was the latter. Why, I don't know. His hollow eyes looked at me with an added twinkle.

"*Why* do you believe me?"

"Because," Matthew said, "people can do strange things. I believe that. And I think you must just be very cute as a cat."

I couldn't curb my ear-to-ear grin.

"Let's get to my house," Matthew said. Soon we were in the car winding around the mesas, past a few other roads leading to ranches, and then we came to a place that was clearly his. The gate by the highway had a bronze fish, wafer thin, about a foot long, solidly attached to a pole, which twirled around in the softest breeze like a weather vane. Matthew had bought the land, a lot of land since it was cheap, with money he inherited from his mother, money derived from the sale of a trawler. Not much, but enough.

The land had been owned by a movie studio, and the square ranch house was once a set. It sat at the base of a rather expansive plateau that boasted unusually brilliant striations. Matthew had never seen the movie that was made at this location, and he couldn't remember its name. The adobe structure existed before the movie. It was more than just a façade erected for two brief months of shooting. But Matthew did not know who had sold the place to the studio. As we drove down a slight slope off the road, we coasted through a field of squat shrubs and what from a distance looked like cacti. But they glimmered in the sun with unnatural shine. As we veered toward one of the alleged plants, I saw that these were not real at all, but sculptures in bronze allowed to oxidize green, like much of Matthew's work. I had seen the study for this work in Amy's living room. The bronze cacti were spread out among the brush, and each looked to be the same five feet in height with the same branching and turns. They did not, however, look to be prickly. There was something classically ancient about them.

"I wanted a few cactus plants here and there," Matthew said. "I kept the cast. I can add more, if you think I should."

"Seems fine for now. But you may want one over there"—I pointed arbitrarily—"sometime later on."

The house lay low with a rhombus-shaped mesa as a backdrop. It had a square courtyard and a red tiled roof like a hacienda. As we came closer to the house, the sun rose higher, and there were sculptures all of a sudden planted everywhere, a garden of bronze. Did Matthew ever sell any of his work? Either he didn't, or he was very prolific, which turned out to be the case. The sculptures on the plain around the house were very large. Most of them looked like totem poles, which they were in a way, a series of abstractions mounted one on top of another and connected on a pole. There were a few faces, a few shapes that could have signified animals, but on the whole, the totems were not representative of anything. Just shapes, wire, and planes soldered and industrially bolted and welded together in a style half-haunting, half-humorous. Each totem in the abstract column was clearly delineated in mood and components from its abutting neighbors. There were maybe six or seven of the separate abstractions, each at most two feet in height, so that the whole totem pole was quite tall.

We passed through a large, unstained wood door and into a hall that seemed to divide the house, then straight through to the courtyard. "Half of the house I use as my studio and foundry and bedroom, and half I give to them."

"Who?" I asked.

In the Spanish style, the courtyard had a porch with posts and lintels. The dusty courtyard sported shrubs, a cottonwood tree, and a fountain in the middle, a movie prop left behind but made of cement. Matthew had fixed on top of it a smaller, leaner version of one of his totem poles.

"Who?" I asked again, but then I didn't have to wait for an answer.

Sitting all around the courtyard were groggy men and women, most of them apparently over sixty, maybe fifteen in all, most if not all of them with distinguished Native faces. They sat on blankets in the shade of the porch all around the courtyard, and though they waved at Matthew, they altogether ignored me and returned to what they were doing.

"Hello, everyone," Matthew said. "This is Coyote."

I waved shyly. A few nods. "They live here?" I whispered.

"They come and go. Most of them have been here awhile."

"Do they pay rent?"

"No." Matthew was matter-of-fact. "They take care of the place. Look after my things." This sounded logical. Then he beamed. "And they like my sculpture."

The old men and women sitting on blankets on the porch all had baskets in front of them containing corn kernels. One or two of them were actually busy dying the dried plant. They dipped the kernels in powders and liquid and laid them out to dry along the edge of the porch. Most, however, slowly reached into the basket and picked a kernel and then sewed it to a string of leather. They made necklaces and bracelets out of the dyed corn and sold them at a stand not too far away on the highway, Matthew said. The bracelet Matthew wore was clearly fabricated at this atelier on his courtyard porch.

Inside the house, one could turn left or right, and Matthew never turned right: those rooms he left to the old men and women. We toured his half of the hacienda, however, and most of it was devoted to his studio. Inside, there was a lot of open space, a series of long rooms filled with totem poles in progress. In one room, the largest, I saw a potter's wheel and vat-sized kilns that I learned were where Matthew made his casts. A few blocks of stone, too, stacked in corners, waited to be chiseled. On every wall, there were large sheets of paper tacked up, broad strokes of charcoal filling the pages. The sheets of drawings covered cracked plaster walls. I kept thinking how impossible it would have been for someone like James to craft anything so beautiful or mysterious. Matthew's abstract totem poles were puzzles, in a way, enigmatic like him.

Matthew was not a child of the desert, although he might well have been—he made it his home. Nevertheless, he did not take for granted the things I don't think about, the cactus for example, and so he tried to ponder it in bronze. The skulls he was now tinkering with were the latest proof that he had grown up outside and was still assimilating the ingredients here. So he etched sheets of metal and he soldered on certain features, and he attached horns in most cases. Eerie bronze cow skulls. Several lay on the floor, each one more gruesome than the previous attempt.

"So you like living in this part of the world?" I asked.

"I never want to leave," Matthew said very seriously.

"Never?"

"Never."

Finally, we entered what was the only room (besides a narrow kitchen) in Matthew's self-allotted quarters not devoted to his art. It was his bedroom, a large chamber occupied centrally by a bulky bed. There were books and a closet filled mostly with Amy's belongings. There was a dresser pushed against one wall, and over it was a mirror framed in antique wood. Two snapshots were tucked into the frame, one of Amy, and one of their mother, who looked like neither of her children but had a round and full, almost fat, face. Over the bulky bed, the latest version of the cow skull hung low above the headboard.

"Just not horrific enough," Matthew said.

I lay on the bed and felt oddly comfortable in his most intimate space. I pretended not to watch him as he peeled off one gray T-shirt and put on an identical one. Then he began to sort through the things in the closet.

"Not a lot of people have been to my studio," Matthew confessed. "Just Amy and the people in the courtyard." He probably felt on display, like his art.

"I'm honored."

Matthew knew exactly where to find what Amy wanted. When Matthew set a backpack down on the bedroom floor, it clinked with metal. It was filled with all kinds of instruments, from trowels to special metal combs and brushes, tweezers, and picks. A compass, a canteen—a few implements necessary for dry, remote places. And in a series of three shoe boxes were some vials and rags and booklets that had to do with dating processes, I think, although Matthew wasn't sure. He pulled out a large machine for chemical analyses and another backpack that contained some books and a small, thin telescope for surveying. A ball of green twine rolled out onto the floor.

"Here it all is." Matthew looked at me prone on his bed. I don't think I looked seductive, but he sat down next to me and gently and innocently patted my knee. "Amy's great," he said.

"I like her a lot."

"She's not happy." Matthew shook his head. "She's been through a lot in the last few years."

"She broke up with her lover," I said. "And then she couldn't have a baby." I proved what I knew.

"She tried to find someone to donate sperm," Matthew said. "The whole thing was so impersonal, it killed me. And when things didn't work out again, Amy went back to that creep." Matthew sighed. "He was mean to Amy, and she knew I didn't like him, so she didn't tell me. She knew I'd flip."

"Did you flip?"

"And how. I was mad at her. That was wrong. It's her life, I should have been sympathetic."

"You made up."

"We did," Matthew said. "It took a while, I don't know why. Amy broke up with the creep again and then went to Rancho Flora." Matthew gathered together his sister's equipment.

I didn't want to leave this room. "Wait," I said.

"What?"

I shrugged.

"Here." Matthew handed me the backpacks.

We loaded the gear into Matthew's car and he climbed into the driver's seat.

I was not ready to go. "Do we have to leave yet?"

"Why?" Matthew said. "What else is there to do?"

I didn't have an answer, but I was staring right at the mesa, striped and omnipresent. "That," I said.

Soon we were walking along a narrow path along the side of a small cliff. It took about an hour, not because of distance, but because of the incline, to reach the top of the plateau. We sat on the edge of the rock formation and looked down over the highway cutting through ranches and through the salmon-colored hills as far as the eye could see. At sunset in these parts, the landscape looked reddish, as if it were covered in watery blood. It wasn't an ugly sight though, it gave the earth a sense of vitality. Now, it was going on midmorning, and we lay on our backs and breathed an air noticeably cooler than in the basin below. The world was spread out beneath me, and on this dais of clay, I exhaled a sigh. I heard an unidentifiable echo in some distant canyon. I was acutely aware of Matthew lying beside me, aware of his every twitch. He was quiet: he had taken me to his studio, his private hideout, and now he had let me in on something else, this perch, which I imagined he must have climbed many times to survey the landscape. Up here, you could let your emotions, glee or sadness, slip out of you and then watch them float away, flip over several times and waft down to the plain below.

Climbing down was trickier than getting up, and we took turns plunging down from one level to the next, the person in front reaching for the one still descending. We got back in the car and were set to drive away, but Matthew remembered something he'd forgotten. So I eagerly followed him back into his house, through the long studio rooms, and to his bedroom. He searched for something in his bottom dresser drawer. I hovered above him, and finally I couldn't stand it anymore.

I pounced. I leapt toward him, swooping him onto the bed, and we fell onto the bouncy mattress.

"No." Matthew pulled himself up. He combed his hair with his fingers.

"What?"

Matthew hopped off the bed and proceeded out through the long rooms, out of the studio, outside to the car, not answering me as I followed, yelling, "Wait," frantically, "wait, wait." It all happened so quickly. Matthew didn't even stop for whatever he'd come back inside for. I felt so completely clumsy.

I jumped back in the car to talk, not to drive, but Matthew, already poised with two hands on the steering wheel, turned on the ignition and quickly steered toward the highway. He didn't drive quickly, but to me it seemed as if we hurried away from his house, out past the totem poles, past the thin fish on the gate, and onto the highway back the way we had come.

A thousand apologies came to mind, and I couldn't choose one. We drove for a while in silence.

"I'm sorry," Matthew finally said, looking straight ahead. Pause. "It's not that I didn't want to fool around. I did, maybe." His voice vibrated. His earlobes were red.

"Then why did you run away?"

"Because I didn't feel comfortable."

"Why?"

"You can turn into a cat, and that's special, but other people can do things, too."

"Like what?" That sounded harsher than I intended.

"Things," Matthew said.

"I know. You're a great sculptor," I said.

"People can do all sorts of things, if you give them a chance."

"Okay."

"If you don't know someone well, all sorts of horrible things can happen. Really horrible."

"Okay," I said.

"You don't know me very well, and you're asking for so much. Not just fooling around, but everything else."

"I am?" Yes, I was. I'd spent two nights and a day with him, but he was on target—I wanted everything else.

"You need to ask me questions."

"What questions?"

Now I was desperate. I knew when we were climbing up and down the mesa that I could spend the rest of my life with this Lune, and that he knew that—what was he scared of now? I was frantic. What questions?

"You're it." I tried to convey my devotion.

"It's not that I wasn't into doing stuff back there," Matthew began again. "There are things you need to know about me."

"I want to travel around the world with you," I said. It was the largest thing that came to mind.

"Me, too." Matthew even smiled faintly. He hesitated. "But we're just not there yet."

"Where are we?" I looked out the window.

"Not far from there." Matthew tried to sound hopeful. "Wherever that is."

Back along the highway, back to the fork in the road, back through Frescura. Why were return trips always faster? I wanted the space of the journey to work things out, and I was frustrated by how quickly we flew back to the desert. Back to the ashram. I felt as if I were risking more than I had risked before, that everything counted now, and he knew it. He hadn't rejected me really—he hadn't been repulsed or anything. I worried that I would be too impatient to ask the right questions.

I tried not to be glum the next day at lunch, but I couldn't help it. Madeleine and I got to the refectory late and were still munching on our food when most of the pilgrims had already gone up to the temple for the lecture. Madeleine did nothing to bolster my mood. She wore her sunglasses, which she often did when we were alone, and which she often did when inside, if she didn't want to talk. The opaque walls of lenses irked me. She concentrated on slowly eating her salad, a piece of whole-wheat toast, and coffee, her standard diet. She had an odd way of attacking the salads she improvised at the salad bar. She would pull apart the lettuce with her fingers and then assemble forkfuls of vegetable combinations. The prongs became a single skewer on which she jammed the torn lettuce, a piece of cucumber, a morsel of pickled beet, a slice of cucumber, a crouton, a single bean or chick-pea. Then she swirled the kebob in a bed of pepper, which she substituted for dressing. She pulled the bite off in one gulp, and proceeded to arrange another forkful.

I watched her for a while, stewing and infuriated at her easy withdrawal, at how she shared mysteries at the ashram but never really told me what she thought about what we discovered. I had a sudden desire to see her eyes, and so I reached over the long refectory table and pulled the sunglasses off her face.

She squinted at me. "Oh, now why'd you do that?"

"I'm here, too."

"Hi," Madeleine said shyly, and went on eating in silence.

"Madeleine," I started.

"What?"

"You never tell me what you think."

"I always tell you what I think." She didn't look up.

"What do you think about this place?"

"What, the refectory?" Madeleine looked around at the emptied dining hall. "It has its charm." She was well aware of what I meant.

"I mean the ashram."

Madeleine shrugged. I finished my lentil soup and Madeleine her salad without further discussion.

"Why don't you tell me about your son?" I burst out. "You never tell me anything that's at all—"

"Why dwell on the past?" She looked longingly at her dark glasses. Madeleine Nash: a journalist whose livelihood and world view were set in the present tense. She rarely entered the past, and if she did, it was by way of history, the larger scope of things, never on the level of her own biography. Her past, what I knew of it, consisted of interviews with deposed rulers. The only other person who so stubbornly, systematically, effectively blocked out the past was Frog, whose former life, recorded in a few photos and some papers, was crammed into a cedar trunk at the foot of his bed.

"Because I want to know," I said to her. Dwell on it a little for me, I begged.

"What's eating you?" Madeleine said.

A pause. I told her about my trip to Matthew's studio, including the awkwardness that followed.

I expected Madeleine to laugh, utter some patronizing, flimsy adage, and then move on to something else. But surprisingly, she was sympathetic. "You know, a desert romance is a hard thing to pull off, although it can be wonderful."

"You're talking from experience?" I said sarcastically.

"Yes, actually." A small smile and a sigh. And then, slowly: "I know what it's like to have an affair here, sure. Around thirty years ago I loved this guy and we romped around this place."

"Really?"

"My boyfriend told me all about Arbol Magnifico in the shade beneath the Great Tree. Things fell apart here with him, too. Though mind you, there was a point when it was happy, that's what I'm trying to tell you—don't worry. But well, it was ugly when it was over."

"I'm sorry."

"It was a while ago," Madeleine said, which was how she distanced herself from anything too unpleasant to bring to the surface: it was a while ago, so it can't be too important now. "So believe me, I know that you can still be lonely in the desert, even when you're with someone. I know that."

It was hard to imagine rough and tough Madeleine involved with anyone, but it had to have happened.

"It's a cruel world out there."

"I'm sorry," I apologized for the desert.

Madeleine's revelation was a lean confession, but nevertheless rich, soulful, a bit of dull gold panned from a deep brook. Madeleine looked uneasy. "Let's go, we have to find Elise."

As we drove a jeep downhill, Madeleine told me more. Since she drove, she didn't have to look at me while she spoke. "When you said your friend's name was James, I was hoping that your James would be my James."

"Is your son's name James?"

"He died," Madeleine said flatly.

"My god, I'm sorry."

"The dumb thing is," Madeleine chuckled, "that I was terribly disappointed when you and James didn't get along perfectly. It's like all the Jameses are gone now."

"I'm sorry," I apologized.

"Don't be silly."

There was this whole part of Madeleine I didn't know. Her son had died, and I realized now that this was a loss I could not fathom. I'd grown up without people, I'd had my tragedies I suppose, but I had never lost anyone. . . . I imagined Madeleine and some blond boy playing tennis—I don't know why this came to mind—but I saw them hitting a ball back and forth on a summer morning. Back and forth, I could hear the lazy rhythm of the bounces and racket swats. Then the boy was gone, and Madeleine was left alone: no more game, no more sound. I wanted to ask her more about all this, but Madeleine had timed this last confession so that there would be no time to continue the discussion. Elise was in sight.

Elise waited for us down by the administration building. Between the first buildings of Rancho Flora and the rainbow gate now, a series of metal shacks had been set up. The men I had seen wandering around down here were now evident in greater number—women, too. They looked like tramps, wearing rags, toting bottles in brown paper bags.

"Elise, what's happening here?" Madeleine asked as we walked over to a jeep.

"When we're out of earshot." Elise indicated we should drive away. Once the three of us were beyond the ashram, Elise said, "It's the next step in Vanessa's program to ruin Rancho Flora."

"Who are all those people?" I asked.

"They're your average bums, indigents, homeless people." Elise was frank. "We've been getting them from all over."

"Why?" I asked.

"I know why." Madeleine shook her head in disbelief. "I saw this once somewhere else."

"Vanessa has now thrown all her energy into winning Prop Eight," Elise explained to me, "and she's busing in these bums to improve our chances. She's having them register to vote before the cutoff date."

"You want to win the election, Elise," Madeleine asked. "Don't you?"

"Oh, sure," Elise replied quickly. She drove the jeep with her hands high on the steering wheel, and as she talked, her hands clenched the grip in frustration. "But not this way. This way just gets people angry."

We were driving to the Great Tree on a specific mission, and as we neared it, you could see what we had come to observe. The Frescurans were planning a big rally there for the following week. In fact, a platform for speakers was being set up. But townspeople were already protesting in large numbers. Vanessa, Elise explained, was planning on staging a counterdemonstration, but in the meantime, she did not want to let these minor protests go unmatched. We parked our jeep off the road a safe distance and watched the circle of sandwich boards and angry signs move around the innocent tree. Vanessa's newest ploy was to dispatch a group of pilgrims each day before the guru and his caravan passed on the way for ice cream. The pilgrims would arrive early, and when the guru came past, they'd sing loudly, loud enough to drown out the protesting mob. The guru didn't have to hear any of the violent slogans aimed at him. The mauve chorus then waited until the guru came back down the same road to go home, and they sang a different song.

"All it's done is exacerbate matters," Elise said. "You'll notice that there are more protesters today than yesterday. And Vanessa will no doubt send in more singers."

"I don't understand how Vanessa came to power," I said to Elise while we waited.

"Well, you have to understand what was going on in India," Elise began. She almost had to shout, because the Frescurans were getting louder. "The ashram there had been very popular for a long time, and many Westerners came to Guru B in the sixties and early seventies because he was the most willing to take them in. So naturally, the guru was looked upon with a certain esteem, since he helped raise a little tourist revenue." Elise was honest. "But then the government changed, and they weren't too keen on all these Westerners coming in."

"The new government wasn't too keen on the guru's financial stronghold," Madeleine inserted.

"Well, no," Elise said. "And then there was his health." She tried to whisper as much as she could. "That's one reason why the United States was a nice place to go. He was popular already, there was a following, there was land, inexpensive land, and there was a dry climate where anyone could breathe freely."

Jeeps of pilgrims, maybe twenty-five people in all, now pulled into the area around the tree. They kept their distance from the

Frescurans, but they grouped into a noticeable pack. I heard an obi lead the men and women in vocal exercises. Vanessa apparently insisted on giving all pilgrims a chance to sing, but according to Elise, Vanessa simply wanted to overwhelm the town with a battery of new faces each day. All to say, we outnumber you, we will win whatever we want.

"Vanessa orchestrated the move," Elise explained. "She convinced the guru that she could find the best place to go, and well, she did more or less. She also convinced the guru to make a quick exit. He just got on a jet one day and flew to Washington. No one back in the ashram understood, but finally word got out that the Buddhafield was being shifted, and so that's what happened."

"The guru trusted Vanessa?" I asked.

"Sure, she was there for a long time before the need to move even came up. Almost as long as me. We're both from Britain, you know. I used to believe in her, too. Then she started doing all these things." Elise waved at the chorus now poised and ready to sing. "Vanessa earned her way into the guru's heart a long, long time ago." Elise looked bitter. "She donated her family fortune to the ashram."

"What did the money come from?" I wondered.

"Oh, her family had a construction company. They had started with munitions factories and then after the war, expanded into building. Demolition, then construction." Elise laughed.

In the distant desert, we saw the silver spark of a limousine and the escort jeeps that followed. It was only a matter of minutes before the guru would zoom past. The Frescurans chanted, "B is bad! B is bad!" Meanwhile, the small but ample chorus of pilgrims started singing Handel's *Messiah*. The obi shouted, "And he shall reign," and the chorus exuberantly cheered, "Forever, and ever!" They started singing when the first glimmer of the limousine could be caught in the distance, and they sang triumphantly, indeed louder than the townspeople, even after the guru tore past the tree. He whipped by in an instant. Although the Frescurans never stopped chanting, the pilgrims rested, waited for the guru to return.

Madeleine was uncharacteristically silent. Elise looked wistfully into the open desert. She turned around and said to me, "I wish you'd seen the old ashram, the first one. Life was simple, the rituals were simple, the goal was pure and white. You could see so clearly how smart and aware and supersensitive Guru B is, and you imitated his model. I don't know where it got messed up. I don't think we should have left. . . ."

I heard Elise, but I stared at the back of Madeleine's head, and then out at the barren turf. United in spirit, the pilgrims all came to the ashram to escape—some literally escaping failed romances or marriages, some fed up with the world, but everyone trying to elude the universal loneliness that had enshrouded their lives and cast each day in fatiguing despair. For the first time I understood what it was that had attracted Madeleine to Rancho Flora, why she really wanted to cover it. Sure, she was interested in the politics, things coming to a head—sure, she wanted to break the mystery, get the scoop, be the first to really report from inside the cult. But most of all, she was drawn to Rancho Flora in the same way the average pilgrim was pulled in—there was an aching, lonely spirit in Madeleine herself. Madeleine was less lonely within the cult of lonely hearts. The pilgrim to the ashram in the desert was a person who perpetually grappled with a tenacious, hurting, nagging, preserving memory. What was spiritual enlightenment beyond an attempt to pass beyond that memory? She came disguised as a reporter, but Madeleine was a pilgrim. I could be so sure of this because I realized that I was also a pilgrim.

*T*orches combined to form a river of fire wending its way through the desert from the ashram to the Great Tree. The cult was out this evening in full force, and every chanting, marching pilgrim carried a torch. The parade was led by Vanessa and all the key obis—the only one missing was Elise, who was in all likelihood spending a quiet night at home with the guru. I was up near the front of the parade, with Madeleine, who behaved as if it were her birthday and this picture-perfect event had been staged just for her.

Meanwhile, the town of Frescura was staging a rally at the Great Tree. From the desert, the rally loomed like a bonfire on the horizon. The rally had begun at eight tonight and would continue until dawn. People came from all over the county to send a single message: The cult should go somewhere else. At some point, the cult was going to march up alongside the town and wage its counter-demonstration, and when the two crowds converged, I was sure there would be some yelling.

When the cult had come fairly close to the town at the tree, I ran ahead. I could hear the voice of the padre amplified over the whole landscape. The muffled priest declared, "We will protect our way of life, we who have endured this climate for over four hundred years, and for centuries before that...."

I climbed the ridge and suddenly was among the town, the county mumbling supportive hoots at the padre. The Frescurans formed a circle around the Great Tree, as if to protect it, claim it, make a stand. I could see Sam Burns standing by the padre on the platform, looking worried. And suddenly the flames of the torches held by town members bent away from the desert. A gust of wind seemed to come out of nowhere. But it was the cult. People were concerned: what had been a low-hanging star had evolved into a snake, and what had been a snake had clearly become a mob marching on this assembly. They became louder and louder.

In the back of the crowd, strange as it seemed, I thought I saw Frog. Yes, it was Frog—here, with all these people, standing with his arms folded and a cigarette dangling from his mouth. He was the last person I would have thought to get involved with this. Frog told me once that as a nuclear physicist, he thought he should have taken some kind of political stance, but he never did beyond signing the occasional petition. He said it was a source of guilt, his passivity, yet he remained distanced. He wore a twisted smirk of puzzlement—as if he were having some kind of out-of-body experience.

Frescurans now looked out at the desert more than they looked at the speaker. They were distracted by what Vanessa wanted them to see—an army of light moving toward them. Faster, louder. I thought that the town might jump down the slope and charge the intruders, but collectively they froze.

I dashed back down the ridge and ran back to the approaching cult. Now the cult was singing louder, singing anything that came to mind (not necessarily the same tune). Vanessa smiled with nonchalance, as if she were just out for her nocturnal constitutional—and well, sure, a few friends had come along. She looked so glib, I hated her.

At the same time, I could hear Virginia Martinez trying to regain momentum, I could hear her voice shouting into the microphone. "I have cooked my burritos here all my life. . . ."

I found Madeleine again. "They're about to run into each other."

"I know," she yelled.

". . . And I will the rest of my life," Virginia bellowed, "spicing each tortilla with the jalapeño from this soil. . . ."

"It's getting messy," I said to Madeleine, but she couldn't hear me. She looked back, studied the crowd.

I ran ahead again, over to the side of the march, up over the ridge. I could see Vanessa leading the pack. I felt the townspeople shuffling about, anxious, getting ready to defend their ceremony of anger. I saw Frog, not too far from me on the fringe of the battle. He looked out over the ridge in horror. The cult's torches almost touched the town's torches.

Then what happened happened fast. A disaster is like a great feast: it takes a long time to build up, but once it begins, it unfolds quickly. A fraction of time, but so much destruction. Just as the two bodies met, the angry rally and the mob of pilgrims shouting louder and louder, the Great Tree shivered with a minor boom, and then the entire tree erupted into flames.

Initially some people were injured, but not by the flames so much, even though blazing limbs came crashing down, but by the crowd's panicking and dispersing. I would have expected a lot of screaming, yet everyone was silent. The fire loomed large and mas-

155

sive, bright orange and violent. The ring of people, hundreds, mauve and Frescuran intermixed, moved back and into the desert and down the highway, back from the burning tree. The tree was on fire, what could be done? Nothing. There was no water, no rain, no other trees to burn, nothing to be done other than endure the quick and sad slaughter. No one would ever know exactly how the blaze began. With all the torches it could have been anyone's fault. I always believed it was Vanessa. At the moment the fire erupted, she was the closest to the tree. In fact, I could almost see her throw her torch javelinlike into the air to hit the lowest limb. I couldn't ever be sure.

The tree burned, the hush persisted, and all you could hear was the roar of the fire. I was able to see Frog again, standing fairly far away from the fire, letting the retreating pilgrims and Frescurans run by him. I managed to approach him without getting trampled as I cut across the crowd. "This is sad, Frog," I said.

"Sad, indeed."

A branch crashed and orange twigs dove toward the crowd, which stumbled backward. The silence that had lasted for a while now gave way to a general kind of chaos and mayhem, loud cries of disbelief. Some people ran back toward town, and many pilgrims withdrew into the desert night. All fled from the sad and powerful bonfire, throbbing with heat, abundantly fueled.

"Poor Arbol," I heard someone say, "there's no peace for him."

Most of the townspeople and pilgrims had retreated within fifteen minutes. Vanessa was gone. Some people tried to put out the fire.

"If everyone blows at once . . ."

"No, no, no, that'll really do it in."

Some people tried to shovel dirt onto the tree, but that was futile. The blaze was too tall. The tree was engulfed in fire, and it took on the appearance of an orange mushroom. Branches crashed down. The roar of the fire was loud, a subtle cracking melody rising above the bass rumble.

"If the tree branches as much as rustle, it's supposed to be a dark omen," I said to Frog. "What do you think this means?"

Frog didn't hear me. He was peering through the thinning crowd. Focusing on something, someone. Then I could see that he was staring at Madeleine on the other side of the fire, standing among some pilgrims.

"I don't believe it," Frog muttered under his breath.

"What?"

"There she is."

"Who?"

"To think," Frog muttered, "she's one of them."

"Her?"

Then Frog turned to me and shook my shoulders. He was a half foot taller and could weigh down on me. "You shouldn't have gone to that place."

"No, you don't know what it's like. . . ." I started to say. Now, all around, those who remained were beginning to fight over whose fault this was. A brawl started up, fistfights lit by the continuing fire.

Frog let go of me and ran the gauntlet. He came very close to the fire. Just then, the tree exploded in its most meteoric final splendor. Like a grand finale to an evening of fireworks. Frog emerged from the apocalypse and walked toward me. I hadn't moved. I knew to wait for him. It was darker, but there were many miniature fires all around, the big bonfire having been exhausted to some degree, and people wrestling at my boots. It was darker, and I couldn't be sure, but I thought I saw Madeleine being tugged at the elbow by Frog. They were moving toward me. Madeleine wasn't exactly going against her will, but she was making it hard for Frog to lead her.

They reached me and Frog said nothing. He simply pulled my arm, and Madeleine was shouting, "What the hell do you think you're doing?"

I wanted to say, it's okay, it's Frog. But then I realized, of course, she already knew him.

Frog finally said, as it became apparent that he was hurling us into his jeep, "I'm taking you somewhere safe."

Madeleine tried to get out of the jeep but Frog started driving, and I was too overwhelmed to move or say anything. We zoomed away.

Then the burning tree was a dull light behind us and we were on the road to the Rancho Fantasy Eccle. No one said anything. Madeleine looked mad, surprised. Frog looked tired. Madeleine didn't need an introduction to the man who had pulled her out of the crowd. She was not one to be pushed around, but she had gone with him because this was Frog. She looked baffled, astonished, as did he. For me, the dawning clarity of the moment was powerful, uplifting. I was full of things to say, none of which was appropriate to the mood. They had no way of knowing that their reunion for me was a glorious coming together of all things in my own life, the past crashing into present. The connection I had never pursued was a celebration of how things can come full circle.

The coincidence as it coalesced from my perspective was as much of a shock as the Great Tree's burning. Nothing was as chilling as riding in the backseat of a jeep, two people up front, each waiting for the other to say something. She was probably amazed that she was with him. He looked amazed that he had pulled her out of the crowd. He could have left her there. Maybe at the scene of a disaster, against our wits we cling to anyone we have ever loved. I was left to look back at the tree until it was out of view, then to endure the most haunting of all silences, that of two people deliberately not speaking, two people who thirty years earlier had been lovers and had had a son, who five years ago was struck dead by a meteor.

*T*ycho galloped around the ranch house, his short legs stomping like a thoroughbred's, because he was so excited to have guests at Rancho Fantasy Eccle. It was such a rare occasion that he raced around most of the night, hopping from the couch I lay on to the one Madeleine was on, and bolting in and out of the bedroom where Frog lay awake, unable to sleep. No one slept, we all pretended. At first we lay awake mourning the Great Tree, and then we were lost in anxious speculation about the next day.

The following morning, I woke up from what would finally have been a nice nap if the sun had not risen with noisy brightness. Madeleine seemed to get up at the same time. Frog was not in the house, but we saw him right away, outside, painting window frames. Madeleine went into the kitchen and made coffee for herself. She wore her sunglasses, of course, and the place was silent. If Tycho hadn't meowed at one point, I would have thought that I was trapped in a world inhabited by mimes.

The house consisted of only three rooms, yet these chambers were cavernous. The living room and bedroom were filled with competing patterns of faded and worn rugs, tattered blankets draped over cracked leather furniture and bulky Spanish wooden chairs, and little vases collected over the years, most of these vessels with chipped brims. Beams across the ceiling were notched, and some of these notches were painted in pale colors according to no particular master design. Broad floorboards were warped and unpolished. There were bookshelves everywhere with thousands of multiply read volumes, the books I had borrowed at one time or another. The place had acquired timeless antiquity: it was never dusty or dingy, just weathered.

The vast kitchen was the most interesting room in the house, with its tall cabinets, old fixtures, a basin that could be converted into a darkroom sink, if Frog wanted to pull out a developer and print some cosmic photographs. But the room, despite cast iron crockery hung up on the walls, seemed more like a craftsman's workshop than a kitchen. In one corner were equipment and tools with which Frog could grind his own lenses. He had a spinning wheel with which he was skilled enough to fabricate his own telescope parts, deft enough to assemble his own spectacles. I used to watch him spin a circle of glass against sandpaper and molds and then polish it with a series of lotions and powders. I preserved an image of Frog kicking a potter's-wheel-like contraption, his glasses balanced on his forehead, ever so delicately holding the fine sandpaper against the rotating crystal. He had to keep the wheel rotating at a steady pace, and he had to hold the future lens against the mold with a firm hand. This way he could secure precise concavity.

All morning Madeleine sat in the kitchen and looked over some notes, while Frog walked through his chores outside. He painted one window frame twice. Madeleine and Frog prolonged a ban on speech as long as possible. It was funny though, because somehow each person had a sense of what the other one was doing. Without looking up, Madeleine moved into the living room when Frog started painting the wood around the exterior of the kitchen. They were like planets aware of each other's orbit and determined not to collide.

Toward lunch, Frog had painted his way inside the kitchen, and Madeleine wanted to find a typewriter. Frog made himself his daily burrito and found a bottle of tequila in a cabinet full of translucent liquor. Madeleine looked behind every piece of furniture in the living room. Finally, they converged.

"Do you still have that little typewriter?" Madeleine asked.

"How the hell can you stand to participate in all that?" Frog had thought about these words all morning.

"All what?"

"You know perfectly well what. In that meteorite-worshiping cult polluting the desert."

"They hardly pollute the desert," Madeleine said. "Where's the typewriter?"

"I don't know."

"Look," Madeleine said, "I have to type out some notes."

"Propaganda," Frog inserted.

"Whatever it is, I have to get it written up. And I didn't ask to be brought here in the first place, Frog." He looked at her. "I didn't want to come here," she insisted. But she *had* climbed into the jeep. And she was still here. She could have left when she got up.

"You can leave anytime you want." Frog shook his head and took a swig of tequila from the bottle.

"I plan to," Madeleine assured him. "But I've got to get these notes organized before we go back." I knew this wasn't entirely true. Madeleine could have waited until we were back at Rancho Flora.

"We?" Frog said.

"Coyote." Madeleine looked at me. "I assume you're coming back with me?"

I nodded, Of course. I was anxious to get back to Matthew and Amy.

"Oh, Coyote," Frog moaned, "what's wrong with you?"

"It's weird up there, Frog," I said, "kind of an adventure. I've actually met some interesting mauve people." A look at his face told me I was off the hook for a while because the word "adventure" sounded healthy to Frog's ear.

"Do what you like," Frog muttered. But he turned to Madeleine and said, "The mauve people stole my meteorite, and I think they're crazy."

Madeleine did not respond to the latter part of the comment, since the first bit was news to her. "It was *your* meteorite?"

"You got it." Frog rubbed his eyes. "Coyote can tell you all about it."

"You can?" Madeleine looked at me.

"It's a long story." I didn't want to get into what I knew when.

"Frog, I'm not one of them." Madeleine took off her sunglasses, which did not help her to seem convincing. "I'm reporting for *The Friscan.*"

"I'm sure you are."

"And now I have to work on this piece."

"I always hated the word *piece*," Frog said.

"Look," Madeleine sighed, "I haven't seen you in a long time. You could at least be nice and tell me where the typewriter is."

"I just don't understand how intelligent people"—Frog sounded nastier than I'd ever heard him be, frighteningly like someone I didn't know—"can fall for that mauve crap."

"Well, if you let me write my article, you can read all about why intelligent people fall—no, they don't fall for anything. . . ." Madeleine seemed uncharacteristically exasperated.

"Why did you go off and become a mauve person?" Frog was persistent.

"I'm not wearing a jumpsuit, I'm not a pilgrim, so get off that kick."

"I don't believe you," Frog said flatly.

"Fine, don't believe me, I don't care. Just tell me where the god-damned typewriter is. I know that you know that I am not a pilgrim."

"It's a strange world," was all Frog was willing to concede. "One thing is simple," he asserted, "and that's that no matter how you cut it up, they stole my meteorite, and now they burned the tree—"

"I'm not going to defend Rancho Flora, but they didn't necessarily burn the tree."

"They burned the tree," Frog said quietly, "and they are ruining this desert. And you should not help them ruin it."

"I'm not, and who are you, Mr. Frog Reading, to say that the ashram is ruining the desert? Have you ever been up there? You haven't."

Frog threw up his hands, grabbed his bottle of tequila, and stormed out of the house. Tycho followed him down to the observatory. Madeleine stood silently for a minute, and I tried to find something to say.

"Shit," Madeleine burst out. "I've got to find that typewriter." She dashed toward the bedroom.

I listened to Madeleine go through closets and open drawers and I wondered how she could so casually peruse the contents of Frog's life. Maybe she wasn't looking for a typewriter at all but simply wanted to reacquaint herself with this man's accoutrements, make sure she still knew him. After a while, the noises in the bedroom subsided. When Frog had moved into the ranch house, he had found a daguerreotype of the lonesome cowboy Eccles, who died at the turn of the century. Eccles wore a sombrero that dropped to his ears, and he maintained a straight, intimidating smile. Frog framed the sepia picture and hung it over his fireplace, beneath a calf skull. I could stand at the daguerreotype of Ecclesiastes Eccle and pretend to look at his austere stupor while actually watching Madeleine go through a cedar chest at the foot of Frog's bed.

Madeleine had found the typewriter there early in her probe. I had forgotten it was in the trunk, and possibly Frog honestly hadn't remembered where he had put it, as well. Madeleine continued, sunglasses again hiding wide eyes, to go through all the papers packed into the chest. She lifted out the textbooks Frog had written, the folders containing the original manuscripts, and she proceeded to remove other things. Certificates and diplomas, award medallions, a folded-up lab coat, a black ceramic mug that I think must have sat on Frog's desk, a silver pen, lots of papers, articles, and monographs. Madeleine emptied out the entire chest, until she was surrounded by piles of tanned paper and the few objects lost in the mess. A brass magnifying glass. A slide rule. And several wads of letters, each tied together with a red ribbon.

She quickly returned the contents to the chest as she had found them, a determined look about her to avoid getting caught snooping. She didn't put the typewriter back, and she retained one wad of letters.

I looked at the lonesome cowboy, his straight smile, and it seemed to match Madeleine's placid gaze as she pulled the delicate letters from the packet. Careful not to crunch the paper in her hand, she skimmed each one. I couldn't tell, but I thought I saw a single and rare tear emerge from beneath one green plastic lens and run down her cheek. Maybe I just wanted one to appear. I think I must have watched her for an hour. These had to be letters written by her, if Frog had kept them and tied them with a red ribbon.

At last Madeleine put the letters on top of the trunk and in a daze carried the typewriter into the kitchen, not even noticing me standing and staring at the framed sepia face over the mantel. She found some paper and began typing on the kitchen table almost as soon as she sat down, typing out her notes as fast as she could, fast as if she didn't want to think about what she had just read. Maybe it was not the content of the letters that had rattled her. Maybe it was the mere fact that they were there, preserved.

I crept into the bedroom, and with the typewriter clapping away, I knew I was unobserved. I read one of the letters from beginning to end. The postmarks were from Paris. The handwriting was Madeleine's, alien in that it was smaller and steadier. The letters were addressed "Dear Frog," signed "Love, M." These were love letters from a time when Madeleine was covering some moment in French history and Frog was back at a lab in the States. I sat there and read the letters as if they were chapters in a novel. Madeleine's prose sounded like the way she talked. Add to that, however, a teaspoon of frivolity, a tablespoon of pure, hard-packed romanticism.

I took the wad Madeleine had pulled and shoved them into one boot. I wanted to reread them all later.

I skipped past Madeleine in the kitchen and walked outside and down to the squat white dome of the observatory, the mud igloo with its spyglass to distant galaxies. Inside, I saw Tycho on his back sleeping by the telescope. The dry-mounted photographs of the heavens tacked up along the low part of the smooth-walled dome looked like windows at night. Frog sat in the adjacent, rectangular lab between two parallel counters over which there were shelves and shelves of dark, sparkling meteorite fragments. The counters were littered with logbooks and texts, with various chemicals and tools, and a special instrument that assayed mineral content.

"The problem is," Frog said, "that I know if you, Coyote, are hanging out at that place, there must be something there worth seeing. Right?" Frog sounded much more like his old self, casual and clever, and I was relieved.

"There is," I was quick to reply. "I've been there a month, and I still think it's an incredible place."

The bottle of tequila was almost empty on the counter. Frog was polishing a lens. He was engaged in the arduous and plodding process of cleaning his telescope.

"It's like a pueblo, like another planet just dropped in the middle of nowhere," I added.

"Like an egg in the skillet," Frog hummed.

"Sure."

"I don't have anything against anyone," Frog said, "you know that. They stole the meteorite right out from under us, and well, as ugly as that was, I've lived with it. But now they burned the tree."

"I know," I said. "It's horrible. But if you're inside, and you really see what's going on, it's wonderful and sad at the same time." I was groping, putting together things I hadn't thought about before.

"How?"

"The pilgrims could have a good thing. A utopia, and a neat one at that, as far as utopias go."

"Not that you know so much about utopias." Frog wrinkled his brow.

"No," I admitted, "but this place has a queer cool breeze blowing constantly. They've built a little city there. They're all bright, lonely people trying not to be lonely. They listen to this guru, but his influence is more psychiatric than religious." That occurred to me for the first time. "People are happy, you have to realize that. But there are some rather vexing mysteries. There's something beneath the surface. A whole other city." I almost told him about Amy's ruins embedded somewhere.

"It's curious," Frog murmured. "But did they have to invade my desert?"

"Sorry." I shrugged. I found myself apologizing for Rancho Flora. "They had to land somewhere."

"She's writing her *piece* now?"

I nodded.

"She and I . . . ," he started to say, and stopped. "She was the one." A slow nod on my part made it seem as if I were just now putting together what I had figured out in the jeep ride away from the fire.

"She'll get quite a book out of all this," I said.

Frog was wiping pieces of glass and mirrors with a special cloth drenched in a creamy lotion that wouldn't leave any scratches. "You better believe it." Frog sounded bitter.

"She's discovered a lot."

"Has she?"

"She says she's happy to be back in the desert." I made up anything I thought Frog wanted to hear. "Exploring."

"She said that? 'Exploring'?" Frog murmured. "Is she happy?"

"Happy? I think Madeleine's the sort of person who's happy if she's working."

"Same old Madeleine," Frog muttered with faint fondness. He swaddled the telescope lenses. I think he cleaned his telescope as often as he painted doorframes turquoise. "She there with anyone?" Frog was abrupt, uncomfortable asking me this.

"No," I replied simply, when what I thought was, I can't even imagine her with you way back when, let alone with anyone now.

"Does Madeleine seem okay?" Frog asked the lens.

"Yes," I said. "We've become friends sort of by accident. She's hard to get to know, but I like her. She wears her sunglasses a lot of the time."

Frog nodded. "They filter light." He thought that was a logical explanation and was clearly used to this quirk. Then out of the hot, thin air he uttered softly, almost hoping I wouldn't hear him, "I missed her." And that was the one and only time I heard Frog express any kind of regret or any sort of admission that his hermitage had a price.

"Well, you didn't show it." I smiled.

"I guess not." Frog studied his telescope. "She irks me sometimes."

I sat on a stool next to Frog and sipped his glass of sharp alcohol. It burned my throat, but I drank it anyway. Frog opened a drawer in a counter and pulled out a pad of paper and a pencil. Often when I visited him and he wanted to explain a principle of science or to map out a constellation, he'd reach into the drawer and pull out a pad. Today he drew a bunch of squiggles and arrows, which I didn't understand. Frog's diagram looked like a simple explanation for some very complex phenomenon of physics, vectored lines demarcating forces and photons. Frog had drawn two points, and from the first extended an arrow coming down toward the other. The straight line stopped before the second point. Then Frog had marked an X where the arrow stopped. And from the X, he penciled several squiggles in different directions, all deviant from the straight path. He put arrowheads on the ends of the squiggles. The second point remained isolated in space, untouched by the line or directed squiggles. I couldn't imagine what I was going to be taught, and then it dawned on me. I shivered.

Frog had never really talked about his son's death with me. But then again, he had never talked much about his son. I didn't even know his name. A lot of rumors had wound up in local lore. Some people said that Frog had had some kind of argument with his son and actually killed him, buried him, a sordid affair flushed into the timeless, memoryless desert. However, for each person who offered a tale of atrocity, there was someone who said that Frog had discovered the body, and to protect someone somewhere, he had completely concocted the fiction about this being his son. There were those who said the corpse was actually Arbol Magnifico's age-old remains, which wandered through subterranean channels to appear where the next tree would sprout up. Some people simply claimed Frog had hallucinated the whole story, a result of either heat or tequila. Nevertheless, all of these exaggerations were long ago dropped. No one talked much about this ordeal anymore.

"It was five years ago," Frog started slowly. "Madeleine and I didn't talk much. I didn't visit my son that often, mostly just when Madeleine was away interviewing a foreign dictator. I'd go and see James"—the name carried a caustic sizzle when Frog pronounced it—"in that awful wet, smoggy city where Madeleine was living . . . probably still lives. James never visited me."

Frog told me he had sent his son books in the mail, but never talked to him over the phone (Frog didn't own a phone for a long time). I gathered that James, as a teenager, had grown increasingly fascinated by the man who sent him science books in brown-paper wrapping, whom he saw so infrequently, once a year maybe. I had not seen a picture of James, but I couldn't help but feel a certain fraternity now—we had received books from the same man.

"Madeleine had gone to Asia somewhere to report on some catastrophe of democracy"—Frog was cynical—"and the plan was that James would come live here."

"How old was he?" I interrupted timidly.

"He would be a couple years younger than you," Frog said. "So he was going to come here." Frog held his pencil to the second point on his diagram. "Madeleine gave him the car keys and said good-bye. The thing was, well, he was old enough to drive in the state he started out in." Frog pointed to the first dot. "But not the one he was going into." Frog pointed at the second dot again. "He never showed up. I called the police. I couldn't get in touch with Madeleine because as usual she was somewhere where the phone lines had been clipped." Frog's pencil now went over and over the solid line of the drawing. "At first I just thought James was using this chance to run away from home."

I thought, this would be a tendency he'd have inherited from Frog.

"But finally, I heard from some state police that his car, Madeleine's car, had been found north of here, quite far north." Frog's X marked the spot. "The car did not seem to have failed mechanically, and there was gas in the tank. The engine turned over after a few gags. But all four doors were flung open. No James anywhere in sight. I was so mad at her for not calling to see that he got here all right, for sending her son, our son, into a state where he wasn't old enough to drive." Frog pointed to the various squiggles radiating from the X, squiggles falling short of the dot that was Rancho Fantasy Eccle. "I assumed that he had gotten out and walked."

Like his father, a son had been drawn into the hot clay. This was the point at which I had become familiar with the story, not through Frog, but from Frescurans who had heard police reports.

"I left messages on Madeleine's answering machine, that's all I could do. It took me a while to blame myself at all," Frog softly admitted. "Anyway, I'd drive all around in my jeep, starting north where the car was found, and continuing south. I scanned the whole desert at night, too, but then went over the area by day convinced I might have missed something. I hadn't been in my observatory, and I missed what I later found out was a rather spectacular shower, specimens of which fell near here. Near the place where we found the meteorite and the mauve people stole it. So that's where I found James finally. The stupid thing was that he was closer to me than I had realized. Ten miles or so from here. It took two weeks, and I found him in a meteorite crater."

"Struck dead by a meteorite." I repeated the one lasting line from all local accounts.

"Sort of," Frog said. "There were crows there, so I knew."

Frog leaped into the soft pit and cried and cried. James had for some never-to-be-explained reason wandered into the desert, and then he became weak. He happened to wander to a meteoric hot spot, and he was knocked down by the massive stone that whizzed by him. He wasn't knocked down literally, not even pushed over by the wind. Knocked over in surprise, perhaps. It fell at his feet, and he fell in the crater. Frog found him after the scavenger birds had feasted, the rummaging birds that came out of nowhere and from far away.

"I told Madeleine that he was struck dead by a meteorite," Frog said, "because that's how I wanted to think of it. Quick, spectacular, painless. No one understood," Frog grumbled. "He was so young." The arrowed squiggles reaching in all directions, the final vision, the heavy piece of a star plunging into the earth. I patted Frog on the shoulder. "It's okay," he said.

"I wish you'd told me before," I said. Not that I would have known how to console him, not that I had time back then for anyone but my ever-emerging self.

"It's taken this long"—Frog breathed in—"to talk about it at all."

"Why didn't you tell Madeleine what had happened when she returned to the country?" Madeleine must have heard the frantic messages on her machine and gone wild. She apparently came straight to Frog's.

"I couldn't." Frog shrugged. "I was mad at her."

It must have been cruel for Madeleine. Her son was dead, and Frog wouldn't tell her where he'd buried him. He blamed her for letting the boy wander off alone, then not checking to see if he'd made it all right. She could blame him—where the hell had he been all the boy's life? They suffered, and the saddest thing was, they suffered apart. They left each other, Frog hoarding the details of the death.

"She threw a bowl at me," Frog said. He touched a tiny scar over his right eyebrow. "And she got some men from town, and she must have spent two weeks finding the crater. She exhumed the body, took it back to her smoggy city. I watched her dig, I watched from a distance, but I couldn't, I just couldn't help," Frog said. "That was the last time we saw each other before last night."

Maybe in the queer span of time apart, they had begun to cope with their loss, the last thing that bound them together. The last image she had of him would have been Frog's holding his sleeve to his head to stop a bleeding wound. And he of her: Madeleine bent over hot soil with a shovel, digging relentlessly for a rotten body. Maybe now they would reach back farther into the past, before this episode, before all the sadness had set in, back to a carefree, un-complicated time when lovers started out. Maybe I was just dreaming.

Frog crumpled up his drawing. He cleared his throat. "Madeleine is brilliant." A wry grin. "But she has this bad habit of going places where things are falling apart, and she has some odd notion that if she reports things as they are, she can save what was good and toss out the evil."

"That's rather noble."

"I think she's a jinx," Frog said quite seriously. "I mean, consider all the scenes she's covered, how she always arrives at a place just before it collapses, before most people even realize the revolution is dawning. She has impeccable timing."

"Does she?"

"Oh, yes. But with her exclusive interviews and her tireless, thorough reporting, she always ends up destroying what she set out to save."

"I don't see that at all in this case." Despite its problems, I was sure the cult would last.

"You will," Frog said. "It's a rule of history: if Madeleine Nash is

171

there to cover something, it will fall apart. Madeleine Nash is always, inexplicably at the scene of a disaster—as if she designed the whole collapse."

I knew that Madeleine liked to cover places in turmoil, people in trouble, but this notion of impending doom and upheaval was new to me. I thought about what I knew of her reports, what she'd told me, and a pattern did emerge. Madeleine investigated a scene because she journeyed to where it was dangerous, volatile, where a leader was as precarious as a kite, where the sky might remain azure but where the wind in that sky might change abruptly, smashing to bits everything paper and balsa. Madeleine had arrived in the desert: what did that mean?

I was left to ponder all this when Frog decided to go on a quick run. This was when usually he napped, but he couldn't go back into his house, he didn't really want to deal with Madeleine. At first Frog had been horrified to see her again. But he was softening, becoming curious, allowing care to surface. A certain resentment emerged, too, a flake of a broken heart.

I watched Frog walk out to the ridge overlooking the desert. Then he pulled off his shirt and pants and boots and stood for a while. A slender man, still in shape. In his boxer shorts, barefoot, attractive, he proceeded to drop over the ridge and run in the desert. It was a strange thing to see, Frog, nearly naked, running among the cacti and brush, the heat of the baked ground seemingly unnoticeable to his seasoned feet. He didn't run anywhere in particular, but rather in circles, jerkily changing direction now and then. This must have gone on for a half hour before he climbed up the ridge and picked up his clothes and walked into the observatory. He collapsed into the chair by the telescope. "Still young," he mumbled. His body shimmered in sweat.

"I thought you were going to run until I had to come down there and scoop you up."

"Hot." Frog was a little out of breath. He remained mostly naked and continued to clean the long cylinders of his delicate instrument. We talked about the ashram again.

At one point Frog said, "But you'd agree, no one has any place building up the desert like that."

"Why?" Though I knew what he wanted, for me to allay his worst fears of intrusion, for me to assure him that his world had not really been invaded. But I knew there was nothing sincere to say to convince him of what he wanted to hear.

"Why? You know why," Frog grunted. "There has to be a place," he insisted, "where people can go and hunt meteorites, and be by themselves, and not have their meteorites stolen out from under them."

"Frog," I said, "it's an island, with its own breeze and pair of palm trees."

"Is it safe?"

"What?"

"What Madeleine's doing, her snooping around."

"Oh, I think she knows what she's doing."

"I just don't know what she's doing here," Frog complained.

Then it occurred to me to lie. "You know," I told Frog, "Madeleine mentioned you a couple of times." I was as vague as possible.

"She did?"

"She said if she knows anything about stars," I improvised, "it's because of you."

Frog chuckled briefly, and I felt as if my fib was worth it.

Toward the end of the afternoon, Frog picked up his clothes and boots and walked toward the house, the cat at his heels. Tycho stopped briefly to bray at a lizard, and then he scampered ahead. It didn't occur to Frog to put his shirt or pants back on, he was used to living alone. I lingered behind him and watched the gray hair go through the shiny turquoise frame. Frog was only wearing his boxer shorts. Madeleine was still typing, and I thought she didn't notice this. But she said, "Frog, you're not wearing anything."

Frog replied flatly, "I know, Madeleine, I'm not wearing a thing." He disappeared into the bedroom, and I heard the shower moments later. The well was not too far from the house, and you always heard it clunk when the water was pumped. A familiar clunk, soothing to me, like an old song.

"You were talking to Frog for a long time," Madeleine said to me.

"Yes. I told him all about your work." I was becoming an ambassador.

"I'm sure he didn't care. Why'd you bore him with that?"

"Oh, quite the contrary. He asked lots of questions."

"It never occurred to me"—Madeleine shook her head—"that

you might even know him." She took off her sunglasses, which meant we could talk.

"Small world."

"But it's so spread out around here." Pause. "We used to have a good time." Madeleine smiled. "But that was a long, long time ago," she sighed. "He showed me the Great Tree, told me about Arbol—" She cut herself off. She remembered that I knew all this already. "Frog has a nice setup here," she said to me.

"Yeah, when I was so unhappy I couldn't stand it, I'd come here and just hang out, feel at home."

"Home." Madeleine nodded. "Frog was quite a physicist in his day."

"I know."

"There's a Reading theory for something I've never understood," Madeleine said.

I had seen it in a book, and when I asked Frog about it, he said that it was nothing.

"Frog and I had fun," Madeleine whispered softly. "He could be very funny, very tender, very romantic—with grand notions about how to do things right: the right wine, the right setting, vast open spaces to carry on a romance."

"He came here." I thought that was a measure of Frog's romanticism.

"That was impulse." And just as Frog's mood had swung from misty reminiscence to terse bitterness, so moved Madeleine. "Frog can be a jerk."

"Oh, we all can." I shook my head.

"But he's so impatient. So arrogant. So impulsive. You probably haven't seen that," Madeleine said.

I had just watched him disrobe and dive into the desert and run around in circles. But I answered her, "No, I guess not."

"He just up and does things, thinking whatever he's decided must be right, because he's right about everything in his mind. He never considers the consequences others pay. Selfish jerk."

I decided to stretch the truth again. "Well, actually, I never made the connection before last night—I mean I never knew your name when I was growing up—but Frog would tell me about all sorts of adventures, and he always spoke rather kindly of you."

"I don't believe you." Madeleine shook her head. She could not be lied to, but I could tell she wanted to believe my fib. So maybe she did.

Frog emerged from the shower and cooked dinner for us all. Madeleine told him that she would get out of his way, if he took her into Frescura.

"You're not in my way." Frog tried to be nice. He was unused to having everyone at his house—I could tell because he was so fidgety—but he seemed genuinely pleased to whip up this concoction of spicy vegetables and beans.

The first part of the meal was quiet. Compliments were bestowed upon Frog for his mixture of every type of thing I knew grew in this area and was in stock in Frog's pantry, and for the soft bread he had rather quickly baked. It was blue, as Frog used blue cornmeal in everything. Tycho sat on the table like a centerpiece, watching everyone eat, making sure all were content with their meal. Now and then he was offered a piece of food, which he declined. He licked his chops though and dashed to his own bowl of food on the floor, then returned again to preside over the three of us. Frog never cooked for anyone, and he hadn't cooked for me for a long time, so he seemed nervous about what we thought.

"It's marvelous," Madeleine said first.

"Yes," I voted.

About halfway through the meal, Frog turned to Madeleine abruptly and asked, "Remember when the jeep broke down that time?"

She smiled yes. And they continued eating quietly. The sound of forks against plates was louder than conversation.

Tycho cleaned himself while sitting in the center of the dinner table. He could nap anywhere and he bathed himself at the oddest moments. While Madeleine and I ate the food Frog kept doling onto our plates from a cast iron skillet, Tycho balanced himself on his rump, his legs fell into a V, and with perfect extension, he proceeded to clean his lower half. He swung his head back to get generous sweep, and then he licked his belly and his tail.

I speared a carrot and a red bean and a piece of tomato that must been soaked with every hot spice known to man. Madeleine ate slowly, arranging a series of morsels on a fork tine. Frog dropped a slice of the blue corn bread onto his plate and mushed it into the vegetables—so I followed suit. Anyone would have thought that these peculiar styles of eating, Madeleine's skewering and Frog's bread mushing, might be unusual, but I was used to both of them, and it occurred to me that they were used to each other.

"So you find it challenging to investigate this cult?" Frog asked.

"Yes," Madeleine said. "It is."

"You've been there awhile," Frog noted.

Madeleine nodded. "I want to follow the election."

"You like elections." Frog reached over to the counter to grab another basket of bread.

"They're a queer thing," Madeleine admitted.

"There's also this Vanessa woman," I inserted.

"Don't tell him about Vanessa," Madeleine muttered to me.

"Who's Vanessa?" Frog asked innocently.

"Why?" I said to Madeleine.

"He'll become fixated on her." Madeleine speared an onion. "He'll try to figure her out. He sees a problem, he has to solve it."

"Figure who out?" Frog asked.

I didn't dare answer, and Madeleine looked at her plate.

"Madeleine, why won't you tell me who Vanessa is?"

"Because you have a bad habit of hearing about strange people and then inevitably psychoanalyzing them."

"So do you," Frog protested.

"It's my job," Madeleine said.

"Okay, okay. Drop it." Frog waved his hand toward the wine bottle.

I poured more wine. Frog never drank wine, and I think this bottle must have been fifteen years old. It was slightly acrid, musty. A drop spilled on the table and Tycho plunged his silver nose into it, only to lift his head and show me a lockjaw grimace, openmouthed, his lower fangs exposed.

"Did Vanessa set the tree on fire?" Frog was persistent.

"No." Madeleine glared at me.

I stared back. "No," I backed Madeleine up.

"Who did?" Frog wondered.

"Who knows?" Madeleine snapped.

I decanted the rest of the wine. There was a long silence during which the three of us took long sips.

"Remember," Madeleine said to Frog out of the blue, "the time we were at the Mexican border coming back to the States—"

Frog laughed. "And the patrol cut open my string of chili peppers because they thought we were smuggling drugs?"

Five years was a long time, and Frog and Madeleine had dealt with each other as infrequently as possible for a while before that. I found it strange that these two people came together finally so peacefully. They started to tell stories to each other, not filling in the details for me, almost as if I weren't there.

"How about the time we were locked in the cyclotron?" Frog said while he brewed thick and potent coffee.

"There are a lot of places to go to in this country," Frog announced when we had finished our coffee.

"So?" I said. For some reason I thought he was directing this at me and not Madeleine.

"What are you saying?" Madeleine asked with a suspicious tone, as if she knew exactly what he meant and had been waiting for this comment all day.

"There are plenty of other places to explore in this country," Frog said. "You didn't exactly have to come here to do a book."

"What are you saying?" Now, sadly, Madeleine was angered.

I didn't want them to be hostile to each other. I thought about all the times when I was getting to know Madeleine when I had also thought of Frog, without even realizing a connection existed.

"What you are saying," Madeleine answered herself, "is that I shouldn't have come back here. Right?"

"Maybe." Frog didn't seem to want an argument. But he had started it.

"It's not just your desert," Madeleine said. "People build ashrams now."

"So it seems."

"And you can't hide forever."

"I know that. But you didn't necessarily have to. . . ." He stopped.

"Yes, I did," Madeleine said. "I wanted to."

"Right," Frog mumbled under his breath.

"What are you afraid of?" she snapped back.

"Nothing, Maddy, nothing you would understand."

"Uh?" I intervened. "Guys?"

"What?" Madeleine cracked her whip at me.

"Oh." I didn't really have anything to say. "I just was wondering what did happen when you got locked in the cyclotron together." This had to be left up to my imagination. I saw naked bodies and cold, shiny metal.

Now I was worried that after Frog and Madeleine had come together, they were thrust apart. It occurred to me that if they spent enough time together, maybe they could work things out. But Frog was about to take us back to town. While Madeleine was in the bathroom, while Frog was revving up the jeep, I decided to tell him something, some lie that might just get him to come to Rancho Flora.

"I guess I should tell you"—I pretended to hesitate—"that there has been an ugly rumor floating around the ashram. Concerning our meteorite."

"What?" Frog was of course concerned.

"Well, there's talk of breaking it up."

"What does that mean?"

"I'm not sure you want to hear all this." I frowned.

"No, no. Tell me," Frog begged.

"There's talk," I improvised, "of sawing it into hundreds of pieces so that everyone can share in the stone, so every pilgrim could have a chunk."

"You're kidding?" Frog was suitably horrified. "That's just awful. It's immoral. How could they chop up a meteorite?"

I didn't answer him. Oh, this was farfetched. This wasn't going to get Frog to Rancho Flora. All I did was worry him needlessly.

Frog drove us to Frescura. He dropped us off at the Sunflower Café, which was conspicuously bright and fortified with a series of stern-looking mauve people protecting their parlor from angry Frescurans. We later rode back with some pilgrims and passed the heap of ashes that was what remained of the Great Tree. Some townsfolk shouted obscenities at us as we passed and then continued with what they were doing. The Frescuran Coalition overnight became the Coalition to Replant the Great Tree: already men and women were shoveling away the ashes to make room for a sapling.

En route to town in Frog's jeep, there had been no conversation. Neither Frog nor Madeleine had anything to say, and in the darkness, I felt the same unbearable pressure I had endured as we drove away from the fire. Now I thought that I had witnessed an isolated incident, Madeleine and Frog's meeting up again. But maybe more had been mended than I realized. I sniffed a cedar scent, which now and then wafted up from the letters stuffed into my boot.

jeep whizzed past us, and Madeleine and I waved away the pilgrims offering a ride down the hill. There was a particularly frivolous, cool morning breeze rolling over the ashram, and so we opted to stroll along Walt Whitman Way. We were headed for the temporary housing being set up for the imported bums. There the look of the ashram had become notably altered. However, the rest of the hill seemed as magnificent and splendid as it had appeared on day one. We looked all around us in our downward walk, and we saw pilgrims hoeing square plots of bean plants, in the refectory stirring vats of carrot soup. We saw our neighbor David, who was experimenting with a new tabbouleh recipe, chopping leaves of fresh mint. We saw Sandra, proudly sporting a new blue obi, orchestrating the piping for the new hotel. Other pilgrims spackled walls with mud and concrete, positioned talus beams to support a roof. Someone was patching a hole in the road. Everywhere people built things: expert craftsmen carved designs into a new ponderosa pine armchair, and someone was hammering a desk together.

A cool breeze, a nice walk. Major mysteries about the ashram lingered and loomed—Madeleine had become preoccupied with them—yet this morning at least, I wanted to pretend that nothing in the world was wrong. I wanted to pretend that the Great Tree had not burned—and at the ashram, it was easy enough to dismiss the fire. No one talked about it or seemed to mourn its loss. The sight of Elise driving a jeep uphill bothered me. I knew she'd deposit some bit of information with Madeleine, which would then send her into some consideration of current events, which would give her reason to cast some dark shadow on something.

"Nice day." Elise zoomed closer. When she was a yard away, she whispered, "Okay, thank me later."

"For what?" Madeleine asked.

"I've arranged an audience with the guru," Elise said, first making sure no one was nearby and listening. But some pilgrims were descending the hill behind us, and Elise's round face scrunched up. "I'll tell you later."

"Great." Madeleine waved good-bye as Elise chugged up the road. "Well, that's good news."

"Yeah." I tried impossibly to match her enthusiasm.

"This is perfect," Madeleine said, nodding. The interview, after all, would mark whatever she put in print as exclusive, important, significant, a scoop.

I felt uneasy, though. I'd been thinking about what Frog had said about Madeleine's interviews. At a bend in the road, a beam of sunlight rendered me blind for an instant. In the flash of green afterimages, I blurted out something without really thinking about what I was suggesting.

"Frog says," I started, "that you go in interviewing a leader with the intent to highlight the ruler's benevolence. And that you try to bring out what's good, get rid of the bad."

"Frog said that?"

"He said," I continued, "that you end up destroying the people you meant to help out." I exaggerated. "You destroy whatever you touch, he said."

"And so, after I interview the guru, I'll just end up destroying Rancho Flora?" I detected a small bit of anger in her voice. She made it seem as if this were a joke.

"Well, I mean you are always in a place right before it falls apart. You are always at the scene of a disaster." I was matter-of-fact. "You have impeccable timing," I quoted Frog.

"So what?" Madeleine took off her glasses. "You believe that crap? That I single-handedly destroy places? That my reports bring down the king? Frog's been throwing this shit around for decades. You believe him?"

"Well, not really." I was sorry I'd said anything. I knew that Frog's words were laced with a bitterness I didn't understand.

"It's occurred to you, I hope, that I explore places exactly because I feel that some major, historical change is about to occur."

"I know." I backed off. I didn't know what I was doubting. Maybe I was just trying to be Frog, to defend Frog's point of view, whatever that was.

"Coyote, seriously. Do you believe that crap?" She stopped walking.

I had had no idea that this issue would ruffle her feathers. "No." I didn't. "I don't know why I . . ."

"I'm hurt," Madeleine said. Her eyes became very crystalline in the sunlight. She combed back her gray-blond bang with thin fingers. "We've been through a lot, and I trust you and like you, we'll go through a lot more—things are getting messy, after all." Madeleine was being honest. "And I need you on my side."

"You do?"

"Well, yeah. I wouldn't know half as much if you weren't around." She continued walking. "We have a lot to do."

I stood in place, amazed. I had to jog to catch up with her. "I'm really sorry," I said. I meant, I'm the one who is thankful. I felt cruel, and I was a little mad at Frog for putting these thoughts in my head. What a trick: not to get caught in the middle between ex-lovers. By way of further apology I told Madeleine, "I've been a mess lately." I had.

"Matthew still?" Madeleine asked.

I nodded. "I haven't talked to him since we went to his studio." I had not really avoided him, but I had not seen him around. Amy had advised me to give him time. She told me that he went through some rough stuff before he came here last year, he was not here just for her. Matthew was a pilgrim at this spa in the lonely desert, too. I had to find out why.

"Well, you can talk to him now." Madeleine pointed ahead of us.

We had approached the camp for the bums, the shantytown, and among the pilgrims who were busily putting up new shelters and attending to the disoriented poor souls was Matthew, glowing, working hard.

"Hi," I said.

Matthew was digging a narrow trench with a shovel. He was shirtless, and his chest glistened. He looked up and was as surprised as I was. I turned around to explain that Madeleine was going to interview some of the bums, but she had already slipped into the little village.

"Well, I missed seeing you," Matthew said slowly. A little uncomfortable, but at once alleviating the awkwardness.

"Me, too."

"I got worried when you didn't come back right after the fire."

"Oh, you didn't need to worry. What are you doing?" I asked.

"I've volunteered down here." He whispered so that the pilgrims working all around couldn't really hear him. But he didn't whisper quite softly enough, and I know that our conversation was overheard in part. "I think the whole thing sucks," Matthew said. "These poor people."

Everywhere there were confused men and women, mostly older. Older than the average pilgrim—that contrast was immediately evident. Most of them slept, some were drunk. I wondered if they were even aware that there was an entire mud-brick city beyond this stretch of metal shacks. They were obviously pumped with alcohol and kept at a level just below functioning sobriety. If they appeared content, well, maybe they were to some degree. They were, in an odd way, being taken care of.

"There's a woman here," Matthew said, "who used to make corn kernel bracelets on my porch."

"It's horrible, the whole idea."

"So, I'm helping out." Matthew dug up a shovelful of clay. "There's not a whole lot we can do to stop this disaster, they're here already, so I want to make them as comfortable as possible."

"That's sweet," I said.

"It's not sweet." Matthew began shoveling again. "It's got to be done."

"Well, I'll be back," I said. "I'm just going to go find Madeleine."

"Coyote, I hope you're not mad at me."

"I'm not." I wasn't at all. I walked behind a metal shanty and Matthew was out of view. I saw Madeleine at the other end of the project.

Now, when you passed through the rainbow arch of Rancho Flora, you were almost blinded by the reflection of the sun off the metal huts. You were no longer greeted by the splash of mauve running by beige adobes, as we had been. The first pristine look at El Dorado was absent until you moved up the road a quarter-mile. These metal houses, prefabs bought in some northern state, were too hot to sit in during the day, so the new members of the ashram would sit in groups along the road, like refuges waiting to be shipped to the next country that might accept them.

According to Madeleine, the first thing that happened when you arrived here, if you were one of these refugees, was that you were greeted by an obi and taken to the administration building, which the cult-run town council had designated as an official site for voter registration. Then you were outfitted with a bottle of liquor, a blanket, and directed to one of the dozens of metal huts. The bums didn't wander uphill: some obis and guards monitored the traffic. The bums were definitely segregated, consigned to their ghetto. Maybe they were drunk, some of them, but they were lucid. I had trouble with some of the twangy dialects (my Spanish had to be pulled out in some instances), but Madeleine was able to understand anyone. She found a man who called himself Charlie, and she talked to him for much of the morning. Charlie had shoulder-length hair and glassy brown eyes, a deep complexion. He looked tired, but oddly unconcerned with what was happening. He seemed to believe that he was dreaming.

Madeleine asked, "Where did they pick you up, Charlie?"

"In Piedras Negras." Charlie's accent was thick.

"Where's that?" Madeleine said.

"Guatemala, you know," Charlie said. He made it seem as if we should have known. "Near the border."

"With Mexico?"

"Right."

"That's where the women with the blue belts found you?" Madeleine pointed to an obi in the distance.

"Oh, no, no, no. That's where I was born. I've"—Charlie hesitated—"still got some kids there, maybe a wife, too."

"Well, then where did the women with the blue sashes find you? I want to know where you were right before you came here."

"In Agua Prieta," Charlie said. "That's where they got me."

"That's over the Mexican border," I told Madeleine. This man was probably an illegal alien. But if Jakarta and other obis were overseeing the voter registration, such an infraction would not matter.

"What happened?" Madeleine asked.

Charlie grumbled, sipped from a bottle. "It was awful. Like being dragged off by the police. Worse. First they said they had a job up north."

"Who said this?"

"Two of those women. A job up north."

This was the pattern that emerged: first the hobos and homeless denizens of border towns were bribed with the prospect of work.

"One said, 'Don't worry 'bout passports, visas, we take care of all that.' Well, I don't like being told to do anything. So, I said, 'No thank you, ma'am.'"

"Then what?"

"They said I was too sick to know a good thing when I saw it, and so they lifted me up."

"Did you fight back?"

Charlie laughed. "I don't know, maybe. But the next thing I remember, I was in this bus, with lots of other people I'd never seen before. They gave me a bottle, I shut up." Charlie waved all around. "Now here I am. Not so bad, huh?"

"You like it here?" Madeleine asked.

"Why not? It's a pretty good job, this voting thing."

I wondered what would happen to these people once they cast their ballots. Vanessa was clearly not investing in permanent fixtures for them to live in.

"It is a little creepy here," Charlie told us. He crossed himself. "Did you see those trees they got out front?"

Madeleine continued to talk to Charlie and others. While many seemed to be legitimate U.S. citizens—we found maybe ten people who were probably not—they all had been bribed, told of a more prosperous life, and promised a chance for a roof over their heads. So they came.

I wandered off to find Matthew again. I passed a woman who was lying on her back on the ground, arms and legs completely stretched out. She wore a raincoat. I tried to see if she was okay, and she told me that she would kill me if I continued to block her sunlight, so I stepped back.

There were thirty or so of these prefabricated metal houses, I guessed. Once you were within the network of metal homes, you had no idea that this was Rancho Flora. It was like some downtrodden, tornado-stricken pueblo, barely alive. The breeze was the only clue of what lay beyond.

Matthew and another pilgrim named Jared had dug a trench for a metal wall, and then they propped the walls up and hooked them together into a roofless square. Now they lifted on a rippled plastic roof. Matthew's gray T-shirt was tied around his neck, and his sideburns and hair were soaked with sweat.

"So is that it?" I asked when they had lifted on the roof.

"Pretty much," Jared said.

"No way," Matthew contradicted him. "We're just supposed to move in the cot now, some blankets, a bottle of rum. But I found some linoleum in a supply closet up where they're building some new houses."

"You'll put down a floor."

"Yeah, I mean otherwise they'd have to walk around on the dirt." Matthew shook his head in disgust.

A blue van drove up Walt Whitman Way. Lulu and another blue obi hopped out of the front, and after they opened the back doors, two or three women stepped out. They looked rather mundane, and they all wore the same blue polyester supermarket jacket. You had to wonder where the obis were finding the new recruits.

"There just aren't enough houses for them," Matthew complained. "Vanessa comes down here. She treats them like we're doing *them* a favor. I wish she'd be more thankful."

We watched the new women stumble over to one of the huts. They looked as if they hadn't slept in a while.

"Nothing like voter registration." Madeleine appeared behind us. She was uncharacteristically cynical. "Nothing like free elections," she added. "Anyone for lunch?"

"Lunch," Matthew sighed.

The three of us caught a ride on a jeep traveling uphill. We hopped off by the school to pick up Amy. Ever since she'd started planning the dig, she was cheery. I saw her notice Matthew and me sitting together in the backseat and then smile to herself.

"How's school?" Madeleine asked.

"Fine. The lizard in the ecosystem died," Amy reported.

"That's sad," Matthew said.

"Well, the kids caught another." Amy shrugged. "Easy come, easy go."

"That's what I've always said about lizards," I said.

We marched into the refectory, where lunch was under way, where the ebullient chatter of mauve people filled the long hall of long tables with shiplike buoyancy. The whole galley gently rocked. On the food line, we passed Chuck, the museum curator. He smiled. "Come by and see the guru's new car." He was proud.

"Sure," I said.

"And twelve new watches." Chuck gleamed. I could picture him carefully synchronizing the sparkling, shiny gold pieces with the rest of the collection.

"Have the soup." Illyanna crept up beside Matthew and me. "It's turnip and squash."

"Mmm," Madeleine hummed, but she stuck to salad, toast, and coffee.

Arlene, who once ran a chain of Texan Laundromats and now was in charge of ashram landscaping, and Rosco, a onetime investment banker, now a sign painter, were sitting at a table near the one the four of us elected. They looked rather dreamy-eyed. Rosco tugged Madeleine's sleeve and whispered, "Arlene just found out she's expecting."

"That's wonderful," Madeleine said. "Is it?"

"Oh, yes." Arlene beamed. In a way, I suppose the whole ashram was pregnant, since a child belonged to every parent.

Sandra passed by us. "I fixed your shower," she said.

"Thanks," I said.

We had all opted for the hot dish, the eggplant chili, except Madeleine. We didn't talk much at first because the four of us, without realizing we were indeed watching the same thing, were staring at a conspicuous table of women off to the side, all obis. The blue obis usually made it a practice to disperse themselves among the pilgrims at lunch. But today many gathered at one table because Vanessa had shown up. She didn't normally appear at meals, and even now she wasn't eating. It seemed as if she were convening an impromptu meeting. She could probably just talk about anything and the obis would remain glued to her, fascinated and engaged.

"They can't do anything but listen to her, they're enthralled," Madeleine said. Madeleine was on the verge of saying something else about Vanessa, when Vanessa rose from the group of obis and excused herself to walk over to our table. It was as if Madeleine's voice were a magnet. We waited silently until Vanessa had taken a seat next to Amy.

"Hello, everyone," Vanessa said coolly. "Amy, I am so sorry about the little lizard."

"News travels fast." Amy smirked.

"Bad news travels fast," Vanessa corrected her. Vanessa picked up a salt shaker and spilled some of the white powder on the table. "I don't know about you, but I don't think small children on a Buddhafield need to witness firsthand the impurity of death so early on, do you?"

"Lizards die," Amy said. "It's just one in a series of sad facts."

"Well, I think if you see that one is sick, you should do something, like replace it with another, and that way the children don't have to watch it die." With her pinky, Vanessa brushed out patterns in the salt she'd spilled.

"Actually, Vanessa," Amy said, "the kids wanted to dissect the little bugger."

Vanessa cringed. "Did you perform an autopsy?"

"Not yet." Amy smiled. I guessed that the dead lizard had probably been tossed into the trash.

"Well, Madeleine." Vanessa turned toward our side of the table. "I've been busy, and we haven't had a chance to talk much." Vanessa continued to play with the spilled salt. She was forming streets, patterns of city blocks, rapidly pushing the salt over a larger and larger part of the table.

"I guess not." Madeleine raised an eyebrow.

"How long do you think it will be before an article comes out?" Vanessa asked this politely, with seemingly mild interest. However, the fact that she had nothing else to say, no small talk, rendered her impatience transparent.

"I can't be certain." Madeleine was honest.

"No?" Vanessa was anxious. More streets lined with salt.

"There's so much to write about."

"Well, you might want some feedback, no?"

"Sure." Madeleine smiled.

"I'd be happy to look over your drafts." Vanessa nodded as she said this, and when she looked at all of us, we all seemed to nod with her. "Show me what you've written," Vanessa said, "and maybe I can offer some advice."

"Sure," Madeleine lied.

"I'm sorry if I seem pushy," Vanessa persisted, "it's just that— well, I said it, didn't I? No need to be redundant. I'm just hoping you'll get something out soon." Vanessa repeated herself anyway. Then with one hand, she brushed the complex system of roads and alleys she'd designed off the table, stood up, and swiftly departed the long hall.

When Vanessa was out of earshot, Madeleine whispered, "I'm telling you, she's got something in the oven."

"What?" Matthew wanted to know.

"I'm not sure." Madeleine seemed frustrated.

"She's in the way," I blurted out.

"What does that mean?" Madeleine found this amusing.

I didn't answer because I wasn't sure what I meant. I just felt this: Vanessa was in the way, holding back progress, complicating something elegantly simple. She talked, you nodded, you didn't want to seem contrary. Yet you knew deep down that you didn't trust her, believe her at all.

Amy had seen Vanessa in India, when Amy visited the guru that one time in a different decade. "You know if you saw her back then, you'd know that while she seems steady and sure now, she used to be bonkers. I mean she made everything up as she went along."

"How so?" Madeleine was intrigued.

"Well, once I saw her pitching rocks out of a window. She was throwing these rocks the size of baseballs out the window, and we all ducked because we thought this crazy lady was trying to hit us." Amy found the shock of gray in her hair, and as she told the story, she wound the long tuft into a braid. "Okay, then the rock-throwing stopped, and out of the building rushes the guru. Suddenly, our beloved guru was frantically collecting the stones which Vanessa had thrown out. It was weird, as if Vanessa had been trying to get the guru to leave his stone collection behind and get on with watches and cars, and as if the guru had said no, what are you doing, and ran out to clean up her mess, to gather together his precious stones. So the guru's there, and all of the pilgrims of course were helping him, and everyone, including myself, was trying to help the guru gather his stones together. It was wild."

"What did Vanessa do?" Madeleine wondered.

"Well, soon enough, she realized her gaffe, and she hopped into the fray and she collected more stones than anyone else. In fact, I remember being elbowed by her as she tried to get a stone before I did so that she could give it back to the guru. And in a strange way, the whole scene became this kind of purging session, a group dynamic of a new order. The guru finally delivered this improvised lecture, which was really just a thanks for helping him pick up his stones. And Vanessa stood there proudly, as if she had planned the whole event."

Much of the dining hall had cleared out now. The four of us and some slow eaters remained. The rest had shuffled up to the temple.

"Fascinating," Madeleine answered Amy's story.

"You know," Amy said, "the guru used to be a really sweet guy."

"He probably still is," Matthew suggested.

Amy reminisced, "He just had a way of listening, making you figure out your own problems."

"Like a good shrink." Madeleine nodded.

"It's too bad no one gets to see much of him anymore," Amy lamented.

There was a lull as we finished our lunches. I noticed that Amy was daydreaming, now winding her hair into a ponytail. "Earth to Amy," I said sweetly.

"Oh." Amy giggled and looked at the table. "I was just thinking about the dig, and I thought we could start tonight."

"What dig?" Madeleine was quick.

"Oh, dear." Amy had forgotten that Madeleine was sitting there.

"Time for the lecture," I said quietly.

"What dig?" Madeleine could not be lured away so easily.

"Well, I wasn't going to tell you," Amy said, "but I've kind of got this dig in mind."

"Where?"

"Here," Amy said. "Near the solar panels."

"This is fascinating," Madeleine said.

"Amy is afraid that you'll put something in an article too soon," I said.

"Before you've actually found anything?" Madeleine asked. She was thinking in terms of professional reputations.

"Not exactly," Amy explained. "I'm afraid that Vanessa will try to block my work. She wouldn't like me to find the Lost City."

"The Lost City?" Madeleine smiled. She loved being able to pry something loose from someone's grasp.

Now all pilgrims had left the refectory, left all the dirty dishes for later in the afternoon, and we were alone in the hall. Nevertheless, Amy whispered. This vast chamber might be bugged. She hesitated. She really did not want to let Madeleine in on the secret.

Madeleine, expert at everything, but most expert at making someone feel comfortable with her, rattled off some tale that proved that she was sensitive to Amy's concerns. "You know I did some work in Peru once. . . ." Amy's policy changed. She told Madeleine the scant myth of the Lost City and the tribe of outcasts married across forbidden boundaries.

"Fascinating," Madeleine chimed.

Amy picked up momentum. "And we don't know much about this group, because all record of them has been left to oral legend.

We think that they survived by trading turquoise, and we think that they mined the stuff somewhere around here. Many people discount the whole myth. There's no proof. Oh, it's probably not here—I've been wrong about it before."

"We won't know until we dig," I asserted.

"When will you excavate," Madeleine wondered, "and not be noticed?"

"At night." Romantic Matthew smiled.

"Fabulous." Madeleine tapped the table. "I'll help."

"Okay." Amy was reluctant but then enthusiastic. "Okay, great."

"Folks," Madeleine said, "it's time for the sermon." She stood up and walked toward the door.

Amy shook her head. "She's persistent, isn't she?" she whispered.

"She finds out what she wants to find out," I said.

"I guess. I admire her." Amy sighed. "But my God, she's *persistent*." She turned to me. "I hope she doesn't tell anyone about the dig."

"She won't." I was confident.

But Amy wasn't sure, so she decided to catch up with Madeleine. Matthew and I walked up the hill together. "You don't understand something," he said to me.

"What?"

"Well, Amy has never shared anything with anyone remotely like what she's sharing with us."

"But you visited her on all those digs way back when."

"I wasn't invited, though. I just went. Amy didn't turn me away."

"So why the sudden change?"

"Because of you, my dear."

"Me?" I liked the way Matthew said "my dear." "Me?"

"You make her feel good about herself, about her work."

"I do?" I did? "When? How?" I liked Amy, I really did. She could be petulant and insecure, but she was also so blatantly honest, open. I'd had lovers before, mentors, people I looked up to and wanted to be with—but never a friend whom I affected in any way. This was odd. "How?" I repeated.

Matthew wouldn't say, and we walked into the temple and sat in the rear, against the wall directly facing the podium. I stared at the meteorite—just seeing it up there on the altar made me furious. Don't worry, I'll rescue you yet, I thought.

"You look annoyed about something," Matthew said to me.

"I do? Well, it's just that I was in the desert when the pilgrims found the meteorite," I whispered.

"You were?" Matthew whispered back. "Really?" He seemed impressed.

"Yeah, with Frog. It was Frog's find. I'll tell you about it later."

The lecture today was nothing unusual. I spent most of the time in a daze, examining Matthew's hands in his lap. Vanessa managed to mention the election with every other sentence. But before the lecture, something unusual did happen, which I think only Matthew and I saw, no one else seemed to notice. Just before Vanessa and the guru emerged from the tunnel entrance to the dais, it appeared as if Vanessa was putting out a cigarette. Now, no one smoked around the guru. It was common courtesy converted into religious custom. The result was that the guru, having suffered Vanessa's company through the tunnel passage, looked particularly ill, more ashen than usual, pale. At one point in the lecture, he even coughed an awful, loud cough, which Vanessa ignored. The guru looked old and fragile. He looked old and fragile anyway, but Vanessa's rude smoking may have prompted this more visible sickliness. Also, Vanessa had been alone with the guru—usually two other women helped the old man shuffle along. So the guru had entered at a rather slow pace, which only accented his age (and for me, having heard Elise's health reports, the fact of his disease).

After the lecture, Matthew and I exited the temple. "I have to get back down to the shacks," he said.

"I'll help you." I had no idea what I was doing. I had not lifted a finger at Rancho Flora. I'd thought about it, but I had done nothing. But I had this need to prove myself charitable to Matthew, as kind as he was. And so I followed him down the hill, and I stripped my T-shirt, like he did, and tied it around my waist.

I labored, and I supposed I would have stopped if Matthew had stopped. We worked during the time when, in the hot world, laborers took a siesta, when pilgrims ritualistically frolicked, and we worked all afternoon. We shoveled out narrow trenches in hard soil, and we lifted the flimsy aluminum walls into the ditches. Matthew and I piled dirt around the walls, then hooked them together. One swift wind would knock them over—even a mild dust storm could knock things awry. It was Matthew's idea to fortify the prefabs with extra pieces of wood. We had to sneak over to other construction sites to snag some scraps of lumber. Then we lifted on the plastic roofs and tried to nail them in place without shattering the cheap material. I suggested that we line the ground with plastic before positioning linoleum into a makeshift floor. Finally, we carried in the cots, found blankets, and made the beds. Matthew wanted to sneak up to Vanessa's hothouse and steal some of the tulips I'd told him about, but I suggested that this was not a wise idea. Luckily he agreed.

I toiled for the sake of the bums, and for Matthew, until I was so fatigued I operated like a machine. We would finish a house and pause. I would lick the inside of my wrist, wipe my brow, yawn, and then we would move on to the next hovel, which, by the time we finished, was still pathetic, but was a little more homey than designed. As we worked, something dropped out of Matthew's trouser pocket, and I picked it up. He was unaware that it had fallen out. It was a piece of string, two pieces actually, braided, but not really braided: they were tied into a series of strange, tiny knots. I had noticed the belt he wore was tied on in an unusual way, and once when I asked him about it, he admitted that his mother had taught him how to twist and fold rope into every kind of nautical number. I saved the piece of string from his pocket. Later in the afternoon, another one fell out. The knots were tightly juxtaposed, and each knot was tied differently from the one next to it. The braids were like his abstract totem poles in a way. Matthew most likely would never know they were missing—there was probably a whole wad of them buried in his baggy trousers. I was actually able to pickpocket another one, a third, when he bent over to pick something up. I decided to keep the knotted strings and in the tradition of the guru, begin a small collection.

Working next to Matthew, I was a mess. I was alternately gleeful and angry (though I didn't dare exhibit any frustration). I had to know him, I had to know every square inch of him, I was burning up with impatience. On the surface, he seemed easygoing, accessible. Yet there was a mystery running through him like an underground spring, and I was so thirsty for that sparkling water—I could breathe bubbles floating up. He wasn't being intentionally coy. I knew that. He wasn't vain like other people I'd known, interested in maintaining an attraction, drawing you in, nothing more. Something fearful was stirring at his molten core. So I had to voyage inside and prepare myself for a long passage.

We labored until just before dusk. I was exhausted. As tired as we both were, Matthew and I climbed up the hill, walking all the way up Walt Whitman Way to watch the sunset. Moving toward the equinox, the sunset was pinker, less peachy. The bottoms of the clouds absorbed the soft light and for a brief moment were entirely consumed in the refracting passion. This was a pastime throughout the region: at dusk, people gathered from all over to watch the sun dip into the horizon. It was the most usual, mundane thing that could happen, but it was so magnificent in this part of the world that we made a point of stopping what we were doing and collecting each other to see it. And even if you were alone and absolutely happy to be by yourself, this was the one time when you missed the company of other people staring silently at the sky.

Dusk had mostly fallen when we saw a man in a crisp new jumpsuit and with hair pulled back into a small ponytail, a man wearing gold-rimmed glasses and carrying a cat over his shoulder like a baby, walk up toward the temple. I was too surprised to call his name, and he was too determined to get to the temple to notice us, though I think the cat, eyes translucent in the settling night, meowed a hello.

"That's Frog," I whispered to Matthew. I was astonished.

"Your Frog?"

"My Frog, Madeleine's Frog. I think he's going to check out his meteorite. I can't believe he's here."

"What's he doing?"

"I have no idea."

"He seems to be wearing a jumpsuit," Matthew pointed out.

"He would never become a pilgrim. Not in a thousand years."

"Then why is he here?"

"I'm not sure." Maybe for the meteorite. Maybe for Madeleine. Frog became a dim figure, his hair the last image to fade, and soon he and Tycho were inside the temple, reunited with the piece of a star.

*A*t night my cat eyes could see so well that I didn't really need a flashlight, but Amy insisted that I carry one. She handed me a backpack, too. It was awkwardly balanced, full of trowels and brushes. Amy herself carried a map and a special twine grid she had woven to lay over the site. Matthew lifted three large shovels over his shoulder. And Madeleine carried a backpack similar to mine. From Amy's house, we stepped into the deep blue evening.

"I'm always amazed by how quiet it can get here at night," Madeleine said.

"The quieter the better," Amy answered.

We headed toward the base of the hill beneath the massive solar panels, chatting quietly. Amy had sneaked back here to make some preliminary surveys, but it felt as if we were going over for the first time. Soon the four of us arrived at the fence separating the two sides of the hill. We were safe: no one had spotted us, no one would see us. I peered beyond the fence. The secret side of the hill seemed watered by a magnificent fountain of mystery.

"I think we should just cut a hole through the wire," Amy said.

"Too suspicious," I said.

"All right," Amy commanded, "over we go."

Madeleine, more than twice my age, was the first to scale the fence and climb down the other side. Amy and I tossed our gear over. Matthew pitched the shovels like javelins, and then he hopped over in two impressive, athletic leaps. Then Amy and I pulled ourselves over, like reluctant recruits at boot camp. We trotted over to the expanse beneath the solar panels, which were impotent without the day star. We had to wait while Amy prepared her twine grid.

During the day, the archaeologist had surveyed the geography of the area to find the place where the excavation might be most fruitful. Amy had known that she could find maps of the area in Lulu's office, and sure enough in her desk, she found an important tool in her investigation. If questioned, she would have said something about a school project, but no one saw her sneak in and steal the folded paper. The map detailed the contours of the oasis, showing specifically where the land had been built up. It was possible that if indeed ruins lay beneath the ashram, they might be hidden under the modified terrain, the hill, and therefore be virtually impossible to get to, at least covertly. On the other hand, while much of the dirt was brought in from elsewhere in the desert, some of the land that contained the ruins might have been bulldozed and moved about, wrecking ancient structures. The early soil sampling to Amy's naked eye seemed to show that the piece of property underneath the solar panels had been undisturbed, and indeed Lulu's plot confirmed this. There still remained unpleasant possibilities for disappointment: the wind could have blown the shards of pottery here and nothing lay beneath them; or perhaps only a small camp of nomads had lived here for a brief time, not establishing anything of consequence. My job was to make Amy forget the notion that she might dig and dig and find nothing.

Now the archaeologist laid the twine grid over the area of exploration, a neat net, a large graph of five-by-five-foot squares. It was tied in such a way that it could be lifted and folded up when we ended our research, and unfurled and opened in the dark hours of our hunt. This afternoon, Amy had hammered a few small pegs into the earth to which the net could easily be attached and dismantled in a minute. We would be assigned different squares of the grid and would begin to carve out what Amy referred to as test pits.

"So Coyote says you two are interviewing the guru soon," Matthew said while we waited.

"We two?" Madeleine shot me a mean look.

"Aren't you?" Matthew asked.

"Don't you need help with that?" I called to Amy. She had attached the grid to half of the pegs.

"I'm fine," she said.

"*I* am interviewing the guru." Madeleine said this to me and not to Matthew.

"You should ask him what the B stands for," Matthew said.

"Will do," Madeleine promised.

Amy pulled the last bit of the grid into place. It covered a large area. She gave us a quick lecture in technique. Now we were set to dive into the soil.

"Amy," Matthew pointed out, "we only have three shovels. So maybe Coyote and I could share a test pit."

I liked this plan.

"No fair," Madeleine protested. "They can't team up. They'll win."

"Win?" I laughed. Was she serious? She was.

"Amy, if they team up, they will find something first."

Amy was a little annoyed. This was important business to her. More bodies meant more test pits going at once.

"Okay." Amy donned her schoolteacher voice, splitting up the class into ecosystems. "Let's try two groups and see how it goes."

"Well," Madeleine resolved, "let them work together, but I'll dig alone, thank you."

"Fine," Amy huffed.

"It's too bad Frog isn't here," I said. "He'd really be into this thing."

"Well, maybe we can find him and—" Matthew started to say.

"I'm telling you," Madeleine interrupted, repeating the same thing she'd insisted to me all through dinner, "you didn't see Frog. It's just very unlikely. Why would he come here? You don't know Frog," Madeleine said to Matthew, "but he doesn't like people much, and he wouldn't go to a place where there are a lot of people."

"Maybe he wanted to see his meteorite," I suggested.

"It wasn't Frog," Madeleine insisted.

"Okay. Maybe it was someone else," I conceded. I was beginning to agree with her.

"Folks," Amy said, "I've never met this Frog fellow, and I've no idea whether he's here, but—"

"Okay, yes," I cut her off. "It's time to dig." After all, we only had so many dark hours in which we could excavate. We were assigned pits, Matthew and I sharing space at the bottommost quadrant, Madeleine and Amy each at opposite corners, out of sight, mostly out of earshot.

I had worried that we would turn over a lot of dirt and create a questionable mound of earth, which might possibly be seen by a pilgrim working on a broken solar panel. Amy said it was a chance we had to take. She decided that if someone saw the trenches, they would write them off as part of some new project. For five years, new construction had been the norm at this oasis.

So we began. The best thing to do with the flashlights was to set them on the ground in such a way that they lit the immediate area you probed. From our corner I could hear Madeleine and Amy chatting across a wide space, but soon Matthew and I created our own banter. Matthew seemed tall, since he was standing up and carefully ploughing the dirt with the large shovel—lifting a thin layer of sandy soil onto the blade, and examining it for shards of clay or mud. I crouched low to the ground and strained my eyes to examine the earth I held in my hand and in the shiny trowel. Pieces of innocent clay could glisten, at times, suspicious ore present in minute flakes.

"Amy always feels them," Matthew said.

"The ruins." I nodded.

"Can't you just envision people underneath us, all walking around? I mean, I could picture a whole city, but I don't feel anything. Not yet anyway."

I had a different image. I saw empty rooms, abandoned and uninhabited. A ghost town. Amy knew something of the geology of this area, and she knew that this strip of the desert had not always been so barren. At one time, it would have been at least as wet as the savanna beyond where the Great Tree once stood. In fact, the tree itself had been some kind of symbol of the green that might once have thrived here.

"You know," Matthew said while he shoveled, "I think Madeleine's wrong."

"About what?"

"Our seeing Frog," he said. "I mean sure, I don't know who he is, but I think if you said it was Frog, it was Frog."

"Well, Madeleine's probably right—"

"Perhaps Madeleine," Matthew suggested, "does not *want* Frog to be here. So as far as she's concerned, he is not here. Look." Matthew held a piece of fired clay in his shovel. The difference between this piece and the lumps of ruddy clay one often unearthed was that this material had been in an oven of some kind, or more likely baked in the sun. It had a delicate glaze to it that kept it from crumbling completely. "Look," Matthew said again. He was thrilled with his discovery. "It was a whole six inches underneath."

Matthew brought the piece to Amy, who collected them.

"Swell." She kissed her brother on the cheek. "Madeleine found a shard already, too."

Madeleine's was smaller, but an ever-so-faint red quality suggested that it had once been painted with a pigment. Tomorrow, Amy would test the fragments and try to date them. She would use chemicals she kept in the tiny vials we had fetched for her. So far, she estimated that the shards thus collected were pieces of pottery fabricated from A.D. 300 to A.D. 1000, the earlier date the more likely.

Matthew returned to his—our—test pit a little less ebullient. "Not that I want to compete with Madeleine," he confessed, "but she seems to want to compete with me. With you."

"She's like that," I said.

The small bit of pottery was all we found for a long time. I did not get bored at all, however. The slow, meticulous ploughing, the delving into the cool soil with bare hands, engaged me. Matthew and I didn't talk for long stretches because this concentrated, monotonous pursuit became an act committed almost hypnotically. For Matthew, I imagined, this was nothing new. He'd been on digs with Amy before, and the careful chiseling away at the earth had to be like sculpting in hard stone. Or maybe the sensation was fresh for him, in the way that each new block of marble was exciting.

Madeleine, who worked tirelessly all day to report the continuing saga of Rancho Flora, had surprised me by joining the three of us in an all-night effort which only meant that she would get little sleep. But she was the sort of person who couldn't stop working, and she was intrigued by the possibilities of what Amy hoped to find—and she simply liked the fatigue. She enjoyed wiping herself out, she had to prove that she was inexhaustible. She was happiest running marathons. And running marathons, perhaps, was a way of avoiding any thoughts about Frog.

Hours passed. Parts of our dig went a few feet down, but still we found nothing.

"Is this what it was like when you visited Amy?" I asked.

"More people were there," Matthew said, "and they worked by daylight. At night, they played cards."

"We could play cards," I said.

I thought I saw a fragment, but it was a lump of clay. I dug deeper, a little carelessly, and I thought I hit something. I kept sifting the dirt and removing clumps of earth and throwing them into the mound beside the pit—all without telling Matthew what I saw. I wanted to be sure I had found something before saying anything.

"So you want to play cards without cards?" Matthew asked.

"Sure."

"We can play strip poker."

"You're a tease," I said. This was a tender issue, but I was barely aware of what I said—I was too busy trying to figure out what I might have found.

"Poker, five cards, deuces are wild."

"And one-eyed jacks," I said.

"Fine."

"Okay, deal."

"One for you, one for me. . . ." Matthew dealt the invisible hand. It was all talk.

"Oops," I said.

"Oops?"

I had now realized that I was on the verge of a large object. Matthew, standing at the other end of our pit with the long shovel, was too preoccupied with playing the game to notice what I was doing. I had nearly chiseled whatever this was with my trowel. Increasingly I used my hands—gingerly but tenderly. I crouched low to the ground.

"Oops, you gave me one card too many," I said.

"Did you see it?" Matthew sounded serious.

"No."

"Put it under the deck," Matthew said.

I complied in mime.

"Okay, how many do you want?" the dealer asked.

I could feel a curved surface. "Two," I said.

"Dealer takes four," Matthew said.

"Four? You have to have an ace or a wild card to take four."

"I know the rules," Matthew grunted. "Okay, what do you have?"

"A pair of threes," I said, "using a one-eyed jack. And three tens," I improvised.

"Silly," Matthew said. "That's a full house."

"I know. What do you have?" And it occurred to me that he had to remember exactly what I had, because this invisible game wouldn't work, if he duplicated any card I held.

"Just a pair of fives." Matthew made it easy. In a quick gesture, he pulled off his T-shirt. I gulped. I had wrongly assumed that invisible strip poker involved invisible stripping. The dim light of our flashlights cast shadows on the contours of his chest.

As I dealt the next hand, I realized that whatever I was uncovering might not be all in one piece. What was it? It felt too solid to be pottery. But it wasn't just a rock, I could tell, because there was something distinctly fragile about it. A little more probing, and I could tell that the object seemed to taper off, and then I thought I felt the edge of another object.

I lost the next hand. Matthew came up with a straight, ace through five, and I only had a pair of nines. I've always had trouble remembering what beats what, but I knew I'd lost, and I took off my shirt.

The clay around the object was redder, shinier, and more compact than the soil we had been digging through. I had exposed a curved surface no larger than the size of my hand, and then a round corner of something else. But I could dig no further, because this harder soil was impenetrable. I was afraid of damaging something if I chipped too hard with a metal tool.

Matthew won the next two hands and I was without boots. The soil felt cool underneath my feet, softer on the gouged-out parts of our pit. There wasn't a lot of noise coming from Madeleine and Amy. They might have been playing their own version of invisible cards, invisible gin rummy maybe.

Soon Matthew leaned on his shovel with only one booted foot planted in the ground. If you wanted to lose, you just had to deal. With invisible cards, the person who laid his hand down last had no problem gaining control, assuming he didn't use cards already spent.

"What do you have?" I asked. I had now found yet another object lodged firmly in the red clay next to the first one—it, too, seemed round, slowly tapering out. The first object was taking on an oval shape.

"A pair of kings, and three aces."

I thought, I could do this, I could win. . . . "I have the other ace. I have a royal flush," I said.

"Damn," he teased. He stepped out of his pants.

He dealt the cards, and he won, and we were standing in an archaeological pit in our jockey shorts. I held my flashlight over what I had been uncovering. I had scooped out an area about twelve inches long, three inches in depth. But I couldn't seem to find the bottom of the first curved artifact. I needed help.

"I have something weird here," I said.

"What?"

"Look."

Matthew was amazed. "I'm quite surprised at you. You're very talented."

"Why?" I said.

"Because you can find things like this and play poker at the same time."

Matthew bent down beside me. Whatever I had uncovered was sturdy, but nevertheless ancient and fragile. Matthew felt the piece and was able to remove some more clay underneath it. He smiled. He took my hand and ran it underneath the egg-shaped thing.

"This is the bottom, but feel," Matthew said. A fourth curved object was embedded underneath.

I pawed the cool earth. "A whole pile of whatever they are," I said.

More slowly, and with more patience than I had ever displayed, I spooned the clay and sand from one edge of the first piece. Matthew couldn't contain his glee. I wasn't sure if he lost his balance or if he meant to do this, but he fell against me, and in pushing himself back into a kneeling position, he kissed my hunched-over back. A cool, wet kiss. He cleaned out the other side of the object, and we were able to lift out, finally, that first oddly shaped thing. It was not pottery. And we looked into the pit we were gouging out, and we saw what seemed to be an endless trove of these . . . these clay-covered . . . what?

"What are they?" I wondered.

It was the size of my hand, but egg-shaped, heavy. Matthew held it in his palm, and with his free pinky, he brushed off the layer of silt. He carefully wiped the object against the hip of his jockey shorts. Slowly, he revealed a certain bluish luster. "Turquoise," he said.

"Turquoise? You mean it's not a cup or something?"

"Turquoise." Matthew was thrilled. "Amy said—"

"Turquoise!" I yelped. Of course.

Matthew polished the green-and-blue-veined gem of ancient mud with extraordinary delicacy.

"We really should get Amy. She'll know how to get all of these out. We probably shouldn't even be wiping them off. Amy? Madeleine?" Matthew called the others over to our pit.

Responding to what sounded like forboding urgency in Matthew's voice instead of the excitement he intended, Amy hurried over, Madeleine behind.

"What?"

"We found something," I reported.

"Why are you in your underwear?" Amy asked.

Madeleine and Amy were still clothed and they giggled between themselves about our near nakedness. I don't blush much, but now I was as red as clay.

"We were playing invisible strip poker." Matthew sounded completely reasonable. "It's impossible to get all of these out. But look."

He handed her the turquoise lump.

"Well, that's interesting." Amy was cautious. "It certainly is turquoise."

Amy was deft. She knew just how to dig out the remaining chunks, and with long fingers, she delicately and swiftly carved a foot-wide, foot-deep hole.

"It's beautiful," Madeleine said. She held a smaller piece and brushed it against her jeans. It smiled its green shine.

"In *our* test pit," Matthew muttered.

"This one's a little chipped at the top, but it's in great condition." Amy assessed the one she held. "Sometimes," she explained, "soil can aggregate around something and preserve it no matter how much the earth is moved." Indeed the packed clay seemed to surround and provide a womb just for the pile of turquoise chunks. The rest of the dirt was as sandy and gritty as ever.

In the end, there were maybe fifteen or so of these turquoise lumps, most the size of my fist, but a few no bigger than my thumbnail. These rocks definitely had been treated once upon a time. They had been carved and cut and polished by human hands. "This is a wonderful find," Amy stated soberly.

"More than wonderful," Matthew said. "Extraordinary," was his word.

"Well, it could be anything. Maybe we'll find something that can put this stuff in some sort of context," she said. Madeleine nodded.

"But turquoise." I was excited. I knew that Amy was a scientist, objective in the way Madeleine liked to be objective, but I also saw a person who as a rule held back from getting excited, who could be very defeatist. "You told us about how the legendary tribe traded turquoise. . . ."

"Yes." Amy nodded. "It's true." She breathed out a wide smile.

"Such splendid rocks," Matthew added. He hugged his sister. "Amy, they're all polished—I can just see the ancient people chipping them out of the mine."

"Yes," Amy conceded, her voice higher, "this is exciting."

Madeleine was the only one who remained cautiously quiet, but she beamed a smile of approval.

Amy finally burst out and cheered, "It really could be down there!" Amy lay on the ground and shushed the three of us. For a minute, she put her ear to the soil, as if it were a wall and on the other side she heard a conversation. She eavesdropped through history. "I definitely feel them kicking." She finally stood up. A verdict: "This is it." The ancient ruins of the outcast tribe and their turquoise mine.

"It's cause for celebration," Matthew declared.

Madeleine and Amy returned to gather their materials and something to put the turquoise in. Matthew lingered for a long time over the pile of blue stones. I looked at the glint in his deep-set eyes. He squatted low and threw all his weight on his toes. His near-naked pose was sculpture itself. He teetered, polished the turquoise with his pinky.

Dawn crept into the horizon and we had to return home. I had pulled on my pants, and I handed Matthew his, but he just held them against his waist. He seemed lost. Finally he said, "We found it, Coyote."

"Yes, we certainly did."

Back at Amy's, we dusted off the stones (although some had to be tested with chemicals before being cleaned). We revealed round and polished specimens, each veined wonder a little model of the landscape back when ample rivers rushed through it. The streams of darker lines cut through the smooth terrain. No one went to sleep that night, because we drank beer and lemonade to celebrate our discovery. We had uncovered glorious proof that something lay beneath us, that obscure myths might have an origin. Amy was happier than I'd ever seen her, and in her mind, Matthew and I had found the lumps of stone just for her. Maybe we had. However, after Madeleine went home, after Matthew wandered into the next room, shut the door, and went to bed, Amy's smile slipped into a frown. Maybe it was the beer. She pouted.

"What's wrong?" I said.

"I don't know."

"Well, something's wrong."

"Coyote, a bunch of stones doesn't mean shit."

A tear slipped down her cheek. I dried it with my finger.

"Why?" But I knew why. We had found something strange, and because dubious myths were in place, we had jumped to conclusions. It had been our game, Matthew's and mine, and we were guilty of infecting Amy with our hysteria.

"It's not like we found a *wall* or anything, or a lousy piece of a *bowl*, or some *bones* or mud bricks or . . ." Amy flapped her hands.

"We will," I asserted. She was right though, the find could have been nothing more than a strange cache of southwestern jewels, an anomaly pressed into aggregate clay. Although an explanation was warranted, because the stones had been prepared, as if they were ready to be traded. . . .

"Maybe someone buried them there," Amy said.

"You felt them kicking, didn't you?"

"I did." Amy nodded. "How scientific," she gasped sarcastically.

The turquoise might have been a tease, a fluke of nature or a forgotten treasure trove. But now, after the first foray, I had to take whatever doubts I had myself and bury them. Amy gave up too easily. I had to help her. Her head slipped onto my shoulder, she closed her eyes. I felt the pulse in her temple against my skin.

She fell asleep, her head pressed against my chest, and I was left to stare at the closed door to Matthew's bedroom. I tried to replay our poker game, hand by hand. We had found these ridiculous, splendid turquoise eggs together, and there was a moment when I was certain that we could find anything if we tried hard enough. I replayed the game again, but it became increasingly difficult to remember the turns. Now the long season of the summer seemed short, its inevitable denouement all too near. Seasons in the desert might go undetected by foreigners—it was windier at some times, significantly hotter in other months, and the remote prospect of rain existed for a brief spell—but these clues were subtle. Summer, however, was the most defined season of all, it had boundaries drawn by shifting light. And when summer ended, you had the feeling that whatever it contained also came to a close. Outside, the ashram began to stir with another day. Pilgrims scurried to their jobs. I was anxious: time was slithering away, a crazed Gila monster dashing off, and I tried to grab its tail, I had to capture it now.

*Y*ou can't be serious," Madeleine said. She picked up her tape recorder, found a spare cassette and a pad, and left our house.

I ran after her. "Of course, I'm serious, why wouldn't I be serious?"

"Mr. Coyote Gato"—Madeleine stopped—"this is perhaps the most important part of my whole investigation, and you cannot, will not, blow it for me."

"But we do everything together, and you yourself said—"

"I don't care what I said." Madeleine continued walking up the hill toward the temple.

"Madeleine, I want to interview Guru B with you, and I won't say a thing."

"Right," Madeleine puffed. I was a pace behind her, and when I moved more quickly to catch up, she moved faster. We would have been a silly sight, me shouting at her to let me in on her audience, admittedly a ludicrous request on my part, and her not knowing what to do with me—then Madeleine skipping ahead as fast as she could, until we moved at a rapid jog. But no one did see us, because Elise had arranged for Madeleine's audience during the time of the dynamic meditation. She had taken care of everything, even made sure Vanessa was out of the way, occupied. Vanessa was not even on the ashram—after the lecture, she had gone to Chiaroscuro on business.

"No," Madeleine said. She turned around, but I was now next to her. We passed the school. "Get lost," she muttered.

"Madeleine, stop. Why not?"

"Because you simply cannot come with me."

"I want to see you in action," I said.

"You've seen me in action already. Good-bye."

"No, just let me operate the tape recorder or something."

Madeleine ignored me until finally we passed the empty temple. Finally she turned and was going to once and for all, physically if she had to, get me off her tail. This was a crucial passage, this interview, and she had to do it the way she had interviewed countless other very important people. "Look, I don't know what Frog used to let you do, but—"

"Madeleine," I interrupted, "if I don't go with you now, the whole thing will be incomplete—What? Are you okay?" She was looking over the ashram in a removed daze. She seemed to survey Rancho Flora with a certain sadness. "Are you okay?" I asked again.

"Fine." She paused. "It's funny the way I said, 'I don't know what Frog used to let you do,' isn't it?"

I sighed yes. Parents, parents who operated with different sets of rules. Madeleine, rough explorer, with rough cheeks and bony hands, lean Madeleine, fit enough to climb a mountain, Madeleine about to do what she did best, was frozen in time present and freely drifted, ventured, into years past and lost. I knew that she was feeling maternal for the first time in a long while. Madeleine Nash: she'd grown up in a small town, gone to college, met Frog, become a famous journalist, traveled the globe, lost Frog, lost her son, traveled some more, been alone, come back to the desert—and now, after having journeyed so far and for so long, found Frog again and run into me. She was sent reeling back into the dizzying past, and when she awoke and saw me standing there, I became the lucky recipient of pent-up, rediscovered motherhood. Over a week had passed since the Great Tree had burned, and there was a wispy cloud strung up in the sky, a sentiment now in the air, a sentiment that anything could happen. Don't be surprised by surprises. Frog had appeared at the ashram (though Madeleine still dismissed this as a mirage). And now Madeleine, unexpectedly, surprised me.

"You can come with me," she said almost inaudibly.

"I can?" I was shocked. I hugged her.

"I must have lost my mind," Madeleine said to herself.

"Are you sure I should join you?"

"I don't know. Why are you giving me time to change my mind?"

We approached the gate to the other side, and a mauve person confronted us. Elise drove up in a jeep an instant later and motioned to the guard to let Madeleine and me come through. The guard dutifully complied with the obi's order. Elise took us directly to the guru's palace. She raised an eyebrow at me.

"I can't get rid of him," Madeleine said. "I adopted him."

"Well, I told Guru B to expect just you," Elise grumbled in low tones. "Maybe he won't notice. He's not been feeling well today," she confided. "A bad headache this morning. He says he's all right now." Elise displayed the skepticism of a concerned mother. She led us into the palace, through one of the enormous, empty rooms with a red tiled floor, into another room and yet another. Our boot heels made the only conversation. Finally we entered an empty room with some chairs in the middle, the guru in one, his back to us.

"Guru B," Elise said, and the old man woke up from a nap.

"Hello." Madeleine shook the guru's hand. "This is Coyote."

I reached for the guru's hand as well, but the guru just waved vaguely at me.

"I brought him along to work the tape recorder, so I wouldn't have to be bothered changing tapes and so on," Madeleine explained. The guru didn't seem to care at all. If anything, he looked delighted to have a larger crowd gather around him. Elise brought over another chair, and the three of us sat facing the guru. Guru B sat up (his chair, unlike ours, had arms). He wore his usual white, gold-trimmed gown. Silence. I had never heard his voice. Madeleine was setting everything up when the guru blurted out a cough. I pressed record just in time.

"It is a horrible thing"—Guru B exploded with sound—"that such a beautiful tree burned so suddenly."

We slid our chairs back an inch in response. The man had a voice of enormous, bass volume. Without shouting, he boomed out whatever he said with amazing thunder. And in this empty room, the sound rippled in a rapid wave to the wall and then bounced all over in deafening echoes. The man who had gone into silence had the most overpowering speech.

"Did you look at the tree often?" Madeleine asked. This was an inert question, but she was probably too astonished by the guru's voice to come up with a more significant reply.

"Yes, every day we waved to it as we drove by. Very pretty. Horrible thing. But it will be back and grow again." Maybe he was partially deaf and could not tell how loudly he spoke.

"How can you be sure a new tree will survive?" Madeleine asked.

"'Ever returning spring.'" Guru B smiled a grin of crooked teeth as he alluded to Saint Walt. His white beard was feathery, combed of any gnarls. He wore eight wristwatches for the interview, a kind of formal gesture. After all, this was the first time since he was in India that the guru had spoken officially with a member of the press.

"When you drive to Frescura, do you sense the anger of the Frescurans—the protests, the shouting?"

"Outside the Buddhafield"—the guru slid his words together in a liquid slur, which had the effect of softening how loudly he projected—"one has to expect hostilities to rain." The guru clearly liked the way he sounded so he added, "Rain in a world where there is little rain."

"What do you and your disciples gain," Madeleine asked, "by disrupting the town, by threatening their way of life?" A loaded question, but she couldn't afford any indirectness: a religious leader might moor his answers in a haven of exegesis. "Why is it necessary for Rancho Flora to absorb the rest of the area? You have your oasis in the desert, why expand?"

"Well, it's complicated," the guru said—his accent tended to swallow *L*'s and make all vowels either longer or shorter than necessary. "But every man is essentially the same man inside, and it is only a matter of time until this spiritual harmony spreads to the outside of all these men."

"But in effect"—Madeleine tapped her pen—"your movement comes across as a jihad."

"A jihad? We do not force anyone to do anything."

"Can you idealistically expect every man to transcend in the way you prescribe?"

"Yes." The guru flashed an arrogant smile.

"Everyone in Frescura, then, could become enlightened?"

"Yes."

"You're a man of wisdom," Madeleine threw in, "and you're very well read. I know you taught philosophy before you founded your first ashram. Surely you've encountered philosophies and religions quite different from the teachings you espouse."

"Yes, yes." The guru waved the arm without watches.

"Well, how can you reconcile these forces and the ways of the overwhelming majority of this state, this country, the world."

"Let me state it simply." Guru B looked at the ceiling. "The world is made up of good and evil," he improvised, "and we can't expect the dominant harmony to be accepted by those who are inherently evil."

"And maybe these forces of evil are among the constituency of Frescura and the vicinity?"

"Of course."

"But"—Madeleine was cautious—"you did *just* say that the proper spirituality was contained inside everyone and that it could ultimately spread to the exterior, as well." The guru smiled and nodded. "But now you're saying that some people are evil and impenetrable."

The guru was no fool. "Do I contradict myself? Very well, then, I contain—"

"Guru B"—Madeleine caught the old man before he retreated into a Whitman poem—"let's leave questions of spirituality aside and talk in terms of the real world here."

"The spiritual world is the real world."

"Yes, but you are a man who has traveled all over the globe and you are certainly aware of social trends and politics."

"Okay, yes," the guru admitted loudly.

"Let's say that Rancho Flora wins whatever it wants to win with the public question on the ballot."

"Which is the lawful entitlement to the Chiaroscuro County seat." Guru B apparently was not entirely asleep to the temporal progress of his vision.

"How will you finance the expansion?"

Guru B shrugged. "I am not involved with finance."

I don't think Madeleine bought that response. "Well, you're aware that you seem to reap a profit, what with the cars and jewelry."

"I am sure you are familiar with the administrative core of the ashram," the guru said as he nodded toward Elise, "the ones in blue obis. They deal with the money. I can't ask questions."

"Why not?"

"I have reached a plane you cannot imagine."

"Are you saying—for the record—that you have no sense of the ashram's financial status? That Vanessa and the obis don't show you the books?"

"I am simply above it, my child." The guru raised both hands to his head and twisted his braided white cap once to rid an itch.

"Do you ever fear that Vanessa is doing anything behind your back?"

"Vanessa will be canonized someday." Guru B's eyes twinkled. He looked at Elise. Clearly this was an issue they had discussed. If he knew anything negative about Vanessa, he would not implicate her. The old man, as white as snow, except for dark hands, a dark wrinkled face, and a dark shape beneath the flowing robes, guarded whatever suspicions he had.

"Guru B," Madeleine said cautiously, diplomatically, "sometimes, it seems to me that the whole project at Rancho Flora has gone beyond you, beyond your control, possibly your vision, and beyond the original intent of your program toward transcendence." I was amazed Madeleine could get away with this. But brutal honesty might bring out brutal truths.

The guru looked momentarily pensive. "Sometimes," he said, "we don't know how large a Buddhafield is." He knew what the question implied, but he didn't want to discuss it.

The tape stopped and I quickly flipped the cassette. The guru watched me and smiled approvingly, as if I'd fetched his slippers.

"I want to go back to the time in your life"—Madeleine looked sternly into the guru's eyes—"before you were world famous"—a little flattery to oil the question—"not too long after your celebrated epiphany."

"That's a long, long time ago," the guru sighed.

"Yes." Madeleine smiled. "But try to remember what you thought and felt in those days. Describe what it was you hoped to do for the world."

"I wanted, plain and simply, to help my pilgrims see that there was no reason for loneliness in the world. I wanted them also to see that there was good hidden beneath the evil in the acts men commit. Ah"—the guru wagged a finger—"you are thinking that I must be an idealistic fool to think I can change the world. Right?"

"I'm wondering," Madeleine admitted, "why you thought your ashram would matter."

The guru wheezed a bit, to which Elise sat up straight, concerned, but it was a false alarm. "I don't know, to be very honest. There are so many things one can't explain, many things one knows, once one has transcended." The guru spoke as softly as he was capable. "May I tell you a story?"

"Please," Madeleine said.

"A personal story?"

"Please," I echoed Madeleine by mistake and blushed. The guru had baited me and now reeled me in.

"When I was a boy in Benares and made daily excursions to the river to gather stones, I saw something once which both frightened me and woke me up to how completely cruel one man is to another, if these men are unenlightened, but how enlightenment can lead to harmony. I saw two men. One man was traveling the world without any possessions, except a bowl."

"Just a normal bowl?" Madeleine asked.

"Your average bowl, you know? He used to have a spoon, too, but he realized that the spoon was unnecessary, because he could put whatever he needed to eat in the bowl with his hands or he could just dip the bowl into the river to pick up water. He had pared his life down to the most essential thing, and he felt purged. He used this bowl to gather water from the river, he drank from the bowl, and then he washed himself. Enter the second man. Well, the second man owned nothing at all. He was totally impoverished, and he spotted the first man, who looked wealthy by comparison. He saw the first man's bowl, and he decided he wanted to take a drink, and so he clubbed the first man, stole his bowl, and ran away." The guru paused to clear his throat. "The first man woke up from his concussion, he realized that now he had nothing. But he battled this emptiness with a celebratory act." Guru B grinned. "He could use his hands to cup the water, he didn't need a bowl at all. He put his hands together"—the guru's hands formed a vessel—"and he drank water from the river and washed himself and so on. And he was even purer after the theft of his bowl." The guru clapped. "He was better off."

"I'm not sure I see how this relates to what we were talking about," Madeleine confessed.

"Ah, yes. What was that?"

"About the first ashram. Why you began—"

"Oh, yes. So you see how vicious the act of terrorism was, but you also see how the evil was converted into absolute transcendence."

Madeleine nodded.

"You see that the epiphanic moment is stronger than anything else. It dominates all struggle and crisis of the spirit."

Madeleine nodded again. I nodded, too.

"The thing which happens, the stealing of the bowl and subsequent realization that a bowl wasn't needed in the first place"—the guru wheezed—"is different in each person. But we all can attain that moment. A long, long road, but we can get there. And once we're there, we are not alone anymore, because we are with all the other people who use only their cupped hands and have forgotten about their bowl." The guru paused. "Nobody needs to be lonely," he proclaimed. "What good is that?"

"None, I guess." Madeleine smiled.

"None indeed. We don't have time in a short earthly life."

Nobody needs to be lonely, but the desert is the breeding ground for loneliness: how could the guru's vision survive? His story, quite frankly, hadn't moved me much—yet I was convinced that this guru could help someone in trouble: he could listen, say something that might make you think of something else immediate to you, help get you out of a rut. He could do all this, but did he even talk to pilgrims anymore? No, and it made me mad. It seemed to me as if this white-bearded sage had given up, as if he had let something fragile and precious slip away. Did he know it?

"Will the world really end in a great explosion," Madeleine asked, "as you've predicted?"

"If I said so, yes." Guru B nodded.

"That's not just a scare tactic? To enroll more pilgrims?"

"To live in this world is to live in constant fear of one thing or another," the old man professed. "There will be an ugly explosion."

"I want to ask you about your meteorite," Madeleine said. "I heard a rumor that it was stolen from someone in the desert."

"Stolen?" The notion was absurd to the guru. "No, it was a gift from my children," he stated proudly. Guru B glanced at the many faces crying the time on his wrist, and then looked at Elise.

Elise cleared her throat and said, "Uh, Madeleine? The guru has to get on with his day, so we have to wrap it up."

Then the guru coughed a loud and ferocious storm of phlegm. A tornado of wheezing followed. Elise got up to fetch an oxygen tank, but the guru signaled her to sit. The guru was ill, there was no hiding it. Guru B seemed to me, and I'm sure to Madeleine, suddenly dispensable. The obvious fact was that someday the guru would just die. Vanessa would probably then rule alone, she was already in control. And then it occurred to me that if the guru died today, Vanessa could take over now, she and her loyal following of obis. The guru was already sequestered in his palace, in his cars, treated like an aging monarch who long ago had abdicated power.

The guru rested for a minute, and then, as if he hadn't been short of breath at all, he stood up, his back somewhat stiff. He put his hand on Madeleine's shoulder, to pat her as his daughter, to lean on her while he straightened himself against arthritic nagging.

"Guru B, what does the B stand for?" Madeleine asked.

Elise blushed, as if to say, What are you trying to do, make him fall down? "Now that's enough," she said. How could someone be so *brash*?

The guru ripped a thunderous, scary laugh. "I can't say." He grinned. "It's a secret. But if you like"—and he directed Madeleine and me out the door to the hallway leading to the road—"you two can come with us for a little drive before my nap."

Elise said, "Guru B, are you sure you're up to all of this entertaining?" One moment he looked as if he might collapse, the next he was spry and eager to show off a sports car.

"I never get to see anyone," the guru protested. "You never let me see anyone anymore," he said to Elise. He could get cantankerous.

We walked out to the street, to the guru's smart red car, not really big enough for the four of us. "Madeleine," Elise whispered, "you don't know how unusual this is."

"Sure I do." Madeleine grinned. She'd snatched exactly what she'd gone after. The guru climbed into the driver's side, and Elise sat next to him. Madeleine and I had to fit into a narrow backseat not really made for passengers. We sat uncomfortably with our knees pressed together, my thigh smushed against hers. Elise, in the front seat, clutched an oxygen tank with her legs. In a flash, the guru pulled out onto the road. The car raced low to the ground. We zoomed up and down the road on the secret side of the hill, and out onto the desert highway—in and out, up and down the two roads that formed the guru's racetrack. Too fast to hear conversation, too fast to feel safe. The guru loved his red sports car, today's choice. He lived for every minute of this escapade. Guru B, a determined look about him, drove with one hand on the wheel, the other clutching his beard so that it did not fly in his face.

"He drives like a maniac," I told Matthew that night at the dig.

"Don't exaggerate," Madeleine said, "he was just showing off."

The dig that evening proved fruitless. Madeleine started a new test pit, and Matthew and I enlarged ours. Amy was in a hostile mood. The business of archaeology was a slow one, Amy kept telling us that, yet she was the most impatient of us all. After a while, Madeleine went to sleep, which left me with Amy (who at one point threw her shovel like a spear into the night, like a child losing a game—there was no approaching her during such petulance), and with Matthew. He seemed tonight eager and able to break my heart. I was willing to work hard, but he avoided conversation. We dug in silence, and when I said something, he would at most shrug a reply of indifference.

"Why don't you tell me what's wrong?" I tried to be nice.

"Nothing's wrong." Matthew was chilly. His mood made me so unhappy, and finally just angry—one day he could be so jovial, the next day somber and removed. There was a bit of the recluse in him. Sometimes I worried that the next day he might disappear, he might run away and hide in his studio and never be heard from or seen again. I was completely unprepared for his brooding. Every bit of discord seemed like a major setback. Then I became mad at myself, of course: I hated the way other people's moods, especially this moon-child's, could completely eclipse my own.

"Fine," I grumbled. I tried to dig for a while longer, but I couldn't stand the quiet, and finally I just left the excavation early. Amy's curt mood perturbed me, and Matthew's deliberate distance bothered me more. For days now we'd inched closer toward some common orbit, but tonight he pushed me away. Or he said, hold it right there. I was not sure how much of this back-and-forth, hot-cold nonsense I could take. I decided to become a cat, and as with each retreat into myself, I resolved to remain a cat.

A small ball of tumbleweed rolled by. You could chase it, go after it. Maybe it was camouflage for some form of desert vermin, some meaty lizard. You had to attack the ball of dust and weeds, attack it from every angle. Pull it apart, jump back, go at it again. Again. It was dark and quiet, and I thought I heard an intruder, an invader nearby. . . . No, I was just making it up. So I attacked the tumbleweed again. I became fatigued. Tired of the game. Bored. I let the ball of weeds roll away.

I stretched out on my back, no longer a cat, instead a frustrated fool staring at the fading night, the brightening morning. Becoming a cat was no fun, no longer a retreat. It used to be easier to be alone. As dawn dripped in, I watched the stars flicker and sputter like dying fireflies.

We did not see Frog anywhere. Time passed and I concluded that I had seen a mirage. Finally one morning when Madeleine and I were in our house during the morning prayers, we saw an envelope fly under the front door. I picked it up and immediately recognized the handwriting. "Frog?" I said, and bolted out the door. "Frog!" I shouted, but no one was in sight. I ran around to the back of the adobe, to the front again. There wasn't a single mauve person to be seen, and all I heard was the vague hum of sleepy meditations.

Madeleine thought it was someone else who had written the note to her. However, as she began to read the letter, she sighed, "Gee whiz." The note was indeed from Frog, and all he indicated was that we should meet him up in the temple after the lecture.

"My, my, my," Madeleine said, "I guess I was wrong, you did see him."

"What do you think he's up to?"

Madeleine was silent, afraid to know for sure. She disappeared into the shower. I thought I heard her banging her fist against the shower wall.

At the lecture, I sat with Madeleine. We surveyed all of the pilgrims' faces, expecting to find Frog, but he was not yet there. Vanessa delivered a rather flowery sermon, and the guru looked like a drugged zoo lion. The pilgrims descended from the temple after the lecture, and soon a familiar hush filled the siesta hour. Madeleine and I waited in the empty synagogue, but Frog didn't show up.

"See, it was a joke," Madeleine determined. "Someone else wrote that, and . . ." Her voice trailed off.

From the same entrance Vanessa, the guru, and attendant obis used, Frog appeared. He wore a jumpsuit, and his gray ponytail was neatly pulled back. A cigarette emerged from his fingers. His glasses frames glistened. "Can you believe it?" Frog grinned.

"Can I believe what?" Madeleine said suspiciously. We joined Frog on the stage by the meteorite.

"Well, this is one of the best specimens I've tracked. It's worth a mint—monetarily and scientifically—and it just sits here getting greasy with that old fool's sweat."

"Frog," Madeleine said brusquely, "what the hell are you doing here?"

"Well, I was teaching some women how to find meteorites, but now I'm carrying out a new assignment." Frog smiled. He was being deliberately evasive, just to tease.

"What women?" I asked. "Blue obis?"

"Yes. Vanessa made me teach them how to track a shower. Poor Tycho, though, he hates it when I give away secrets. I told him I wasn't really divulging anything too secret, but he didn't believe me. I left him back there." Frog pointed behind him, toward the secret side of the hill. "And he probably is very unhappy with me."

"Wait." Madeleine glared at him. "You haven't answered my question."

"How 'bout this place?" Frog waved his arms around the temple. He ignored the pressing question. He was behaving the way he did when some spectacular arrangement of stars draped the sky. "It's really quite an intriguing city. Not what I expected."

Madeleine lit a cigarette nervously. "Have you been brainwashed or something?" She exhaled.

Frog shrugged. "Not that I know of."

"Frog, how long have you been here?" I asked. "I thought I saw you over a week ago."

"Really? Yes, I've been here awhile," Frog admitted.

"Why haven't we seen you?" I asked.

"This was the first time that I could meet you. I've been slaving away, teaching physics to these women. I wanted to get to you guys earlier, but I was being tested, sort of. I have to prove something, though I'm not entirely sure what. I've been sequestered in a room with a blackboard, but now I can roam freely."

"You're leapfrogging a step," Madeleine complained. "How did you get here? I mean, how did you even perchance arrive at Rancho Flora?"

"Ah," Frog said, "I just came here. After the fire, after you all left, I became curious. I decided to check Rancho Flora out for myself, visit you, and then get my meteorite back."

"Then what?" Madeleine asked.

"Then I'll do what I always do, run tests, determine mineral content—"

"No, Frog, then what did you do after you decided to come here?" Madeleine could be patient with anyone except Frog.

"Oh, I drove in one afternoon—all these bums were coming in at the same time."

"They're here to vote," I explained.

"Well, this Vanessa person"—Frog raised an eyebrow—"was out there greeting people, and I guess she picked me out of the crowd."

"She often greets new pilgrims," Madeleine said.

"So Vanessa walked toward me with her hand extended, and this fake, fake smile, and she said, 'You're a famous physicist.' How did she know? 'I've heard so much about you.'" Frog mimicked Vanessa's crisp accent. He shook his head. "I wanted to run away."

"It's no surprise," Madeleine said, "that she'd know you. She knows a lot about the region, I'm sure."

"Well, it bothered me." Frog's paranoia no doubt flared up. "I was having enough trouble just standing there, all those . . . people there . . . Tycho was complaining, and I . . . I was going to leave."

"But you didn't," I said.

"No, because the next thing Vanessa said was, 'You're here to claim that meteorite.' I froze."

"I'm telling you," Madeleine insisted, "she's on top of everything."

"What did you say?" I asked.

"I said I'd like at least to be *with* my meteorite, maybe as a pilgrim."

"She bought that?" I doubted that Vanessa did.

"I guess so," Frog said, nodding. "Though she said, 'I'm surprised that a recluse like you would make the transition from isolation to population.' That's how she phrased it. I got nervous again, I was worried about . . . I don't know what. Tycho was meowing. I decided to leave. But then Vanessa said, get this, 'If you ever want to see your meteorite again, you'd best meet me up in the temple after sundown.'"

"A ransom," I suggested.

"Well, I confessed to her," Frog went on, "that I had heard a rumor, in fact, that she was planning on chopping up the stone into hundreds of bits and dispensing the fragments."

"Where'd you pick that up?" Madeleine laughed.

"Coyote told me." Frog looked at me.

Madeleine glared at me and mumbled under her breath, "Coyote makes things up sometimes."

"And Vanessa answered me. She said, 'There's a thought, chop it up, I like that.' She made some memo into a tape recorder she had in her pocket. 'Chop up the meteorite.' Needless to say," Frog sighed, "I met her later that day." Frog lit another cigarette. He and Madeleine were creating a smoky aura around the meteorite. "This time she was more pleasant, actually quite kind. She's a weird person. . . ." He was probably going to offer some bit of insight, but he must have remembered Madeleine's aversion to his psychoanalyzing. "Vanessa spent a good half hour babbling about my work. She knew all of it, from Reading's law to all the other garbage I ever got involved with. All of it. Technical stuff, too."

"I didn't know Vanessa knew physics," I said.

"We don't know what Vanessa knows about anything," Madeleine muttered.

"Vanessa explained," Frog said, "that her husband was an engineer. That's how she knows all this stuff."

"I didn't know Vanessa had a husband," I said. This was news.

"Elise never mentioned him," Madeleine added.

"He died a while ago," Frog explained. "That's what she told me. Before she met up with Guru B. But before he died, he had some vision of a city in the desert—because that's what he did, he built cities in the desert, the Middle East actually, for oil-drilling nations."

"You're telling me that Rancho Flora is in part a vision of Vanessa's late husband?" Madeleine was astonished.

"His dying dream?" I couldn't believe it.

"You're telling me that Vanessa has a soul?" Madeleine chuckled.

"She's a complex particle," Frog said. He hopped off the bema and proceeded to weave his way among the concentric benches. Frog described how Vanessa asked if he truly was interested in a pilgrimage, and he tried to convince her of his spiritual convictions. "She said that the ashram had a real need for scientists, that I could rise quickly if I wanted. All I had to do was prove myself."

"What proof?" Madeleine asked. She climbed off the bema and approached Frog. She mimed a request for a cigarette. Frog lit a new one from his, then handed it to Madeleine, a cinematic gesture.

"I've been teaching the obis how to find meteorites in the desert," Frog explained. "All day and night. There was a lot to teach."

Madeleine just shook her head. "I'm surprised that you're giving away trade secrets." I was surprised, too.

"Well," Frog said, "Vanessa said that if I led this seminar, that would be proof of my dedication. Sure there are trade secrets, but it's not all about formulae and calculations, you know? I'm not too worried about competition." Frog laughed at the notion. "You have to realize that they found this meteorite purely by luck. Anyway, I'm on my new assignment now," Frog announced.

"Right now?" Madeleine looked around.

"You're with us," I said.

"That's part of it." Frog smiled, evasive again. "Maddy, you are."

"Oh, wait a minute," I said. "Do you think that Vanessa knows about you two?" I found this hard to accept.

"Unbelievable." Madeleine seemed amazed. "She does her research."

"What's your assignment?" I asked.

"It's very simple. Vanessa keeps saying, do this, and then I'll tell you a little secret. That little secret is beside the point as far as I'm concerned, but I figure that if I just stay on Vanessa's good side, I might be able to get my meteorite out. I've taught the women how to find meteorites, they think they can find their own, so maybe Vanessa will give this one back to me. I think that's what will happen."

"I wouldn't be so sure," Madeleine said.

I was doubtful, too, but Frog was convinced that if he committed a few more good deeds, he'd be rewarded.

"What do *I* have to do with all of this?" Madeleine asked reluctantly.

"Well," Frog stated matter-of-factly, "Vanessa wants to know what your article is going to be about. What angle you're taking."

"Fascinating." Madeleine looked annoyed.

Frog didn't seem to pick up on Madeleine's obvious displeasure. He said rather glibly, "So what's it all about, Maddy?"

"Oh, terrific"—Madeleine puffed—"you think this is swell. Spy on the press—"

I pathetically tried to change the subject. "It really is an incredible meteorite."

Madeleine was mad. "—and then Vanessa will say, 'See if you can't get her to adjust her article a bit.' And you'll be all for it."

Frog was easily nudged into talking about our catch. "It's got a lot of magnesium in it. See all the sparkles?"

"You must have said something to her," Madeleine said more loudly, "to make her think that you could influence me."

"These specks here"—Frog went up to the bema and touched the rock with his pinky—"indicate silicon deposits normally found in chondrites, but which are appearing in this rock, even though we're in the Iron Belt."

"You probably said, 'No problem, I can handle her,'" Madeleine snorted, "and you would if you could, just to get your goddamned rock back."

"Did we talk about how pronounced the grooves are?" Frog asked me. "The meteorite must have encountered an extraordinary amount of friction during its descent, and we're lucky it survived the plunge without breaking up." Frog noticed I was looking at Madeleine. "What?" He feigned innocence.

"Why are you here?" Madeleine said. "That's my one question."

"To get this." Frog tapped his meteorite.

Madeleine rolled her eyes. "All you're doing is giving Vanessa an edge."

"I don't think," Frog said, "that what you necessarily say has to be what you end up writing."

"Frog, I shouldn't have to say anything at all." Madeleine seemed not to have heard Frog. Or she did, and the issue was actually unrelated to Vanessa. Madeleine simply did not want Frog here. She could visit him on his ranch, but she wanted him off hers.

I desperately tried to come up with something to say, but before I could utter a word, Madeleine said, "I know your stone is important, Frog, but I don't understand what made you come here. What made you take your cat and leave the seclusion of your ranch?" What did she want him to say?

He paused, lit yet another cigarette. "I came here because I wanted to see you," Frog said to her, "and you." He turned to me.

Madeleine's frown evolved into a sigh, and then a faint smile. Softly she said, "It's nice to see you, too." But Madeleine was not one to linger in sentimental sunlight. "I don't know, Frog," she said, "I don't think you can just waltz out of here with that rock. Vanessa, for God knows what reason, has got something else in mind for you. She wouldn't be throwing out these assignments if she didn't have some kind of larger role for you to play," Madeleine speculated. "Something big. In any event, I'm dying to know this little secret. What are you smiling about?" Madeleine looked at me.

"Nothing." I realized I probably looked like an idiot and I tried to check my grin. I was just happy to see Madeleine and Frog united again. Frog had come to the ashram, now he was here with her. Maybe they'd have time to talk. . . . I noticed that Madeleine was looking irritated again, as if she wanted to pick a fight.

"Well, I'm not going to tell you what I'm writing about." She frowned.

"Why not?" Frog asked. "What's the big deal?"

"No one has *ever* censored me."

"This isn't about censorship." Frog was annoyed now, too. "Just make up something and I'll have something to say to Vanessa, and I'll have done a good deed, and I can get my meteorite back—"

"See, you're not here for me."

"Yes, he is," I whispered. No one heard me.

"You're here for that goddamned boulder." Madeleine almost sounded jealous. "I wish you'd just roll it away and go."

"Great." Frog polished his glasses on his jumpsuit. "Look, if I'm in your way, I'll just leave."

"No," I said.

"Oh, it's okay," Frog said to me, "in all likelihood I've done enough good deeds to ask for the stone back. I mean, we did find it first, Coyote."

"Never in a thousand years"—Madeleine was cold—"could you, Mr. Frog Reading, understand anyone. Least of all Vanessa, queen of Rancho Flora."

"Watch me," Frog shot back.

"Watch you?" I was confused.

Frog walked outside to a jeep and indicated we should follow him. "I know for a fact that as we speak Vanessa is dealing with immigration officials in her office."

"Immigration officials?" Madeleine was more interested in this than anything else. "I'm surprised Elise didn't mention their visit to me."

"She probably didn't know about it," I said.

"I'll just go there now, ask for my meteorite back," Frog said, "and Vanessa will say sure, take it."

"Never," Madeleine insisted. "This I'd love to see."

"I'll get it and leave the ashram, and I'll get out of your way." Frog started driving downhill. Suddenly I was terrified that Madeleine was wrong, that Frog would pull off some trick, leave with his meteorite in tow.

As soon as we walked into the administration building, we could hear Vanessa's voice bouncing off the walls of her commodious office. She and Jakarta sat at their chairs at the glass table (Elise was noticeably absent from hers), and two men dressed alike in short-sleeve blue shirts and gray slacks, both with crew cuts and square jaws, were arranging folders in their laps. "I'm sure, gentlemen," Vanessa was saying, "you'll find nothing unusual. Every procedure was followed to the letter of the law."

The two officials stood up from their chairs. Jakarta said nothing. She just watched and looked tense. One official said, "But as I said, we simply can't say anything until we conclude our investigation."

Vanessa tried to be polite. "I realize that, of course. I'm simply reiterating my point that I don't see the need for the continued questioning. You have the papers, the visas for all of us, including the guru."

"But how can we say these haven't been falsified?" the other official asked. "It's simply the next step in the investigation." He packed files into an already overstuffed briefcase. Vanessa escorted the two men out the door. As she breezed by us, I noticed a rather plastic smile, clenched fists.

"What's going on?" Madeleine asked Jakarta.

Jakarta looked rather wan, but she managed to say, "Oh, we're just clearing up some documentation."

In a flash, Vanessa was back, muttering to herself, "I don't know who the hell they think they're—" But when she stepped back into the office and saw us, she pretended to be calm.

"I'm sorry to disturb you," Frog said politely.

"What can I do for you?" Vanessa smiled insincerely. To Jakarta in a barely audible whisper: "Find Lulu. We have to talk about where she filed the you-know-what. The real you-know-what." Jakarta slipped out of the office quickly.

"I have a question about the meteorite," Frog said.

"Oh, well, perhaps it can wait until another time. I'm swamped, absolutely swamped." Vanessa sank into her tall chair. "Paperwork." Vanessa waved her arms over her desk. She began to organize the pile of folders in front of her.

"Well . . ." Frog was fishing in his pockets for something to say.

"How are you doing, Madeleine?" Vanessa lit a cigarette and flipped back her hair. She nodded at me to say hello. I wanted to say to her, "By the way, I loathe you"—but no occasion arose for such an outburst.

"Fine," Madeleine said sweetly. "Sorry you're having trouble with the immigration bureau." She eased her way into a sensitive topic.

"What trouble?" Vanessa was quick to reply. "No trouble at all." She shuffled folders she'd already neatened.

"There's an investigation into the guru's visa?" Madeleine persisted.

Vanessa breathed out a long and contrived laugh, long enough for her to come up with a lame defense. "Oh, it's nothing, nothing at all. Just some confusion," she improvised, "about something rather unimportant. Nothing at all, just a little paperwork. But what"—she laughed again, inhaled—"would the world be without a little paperwork now and then, why, it would be . . ." She looked at something on her desk and didn't finish the thought. She looked up. I tried to imagine what the little secret she promised to tell Frog might be, but it was impossible to pick out one thread in what was most likely a three-piece suit of mystery.

"Well, I'll come back another time and talk to you about the meteorite," Frog said as the three of us left. Vanessa waved good-bye in our direction, and by the time we had passed into the hallway, Vanessa was already on the phone, smoothly ranting.

Outside, Frog immediately blurted out to Madeleine, "I know what you're thinking, that I have some kind of fantasy of—"

"Shut up, Frog," Madeleine cut him off. "That was marvelous."

"What was?" Frog was puzzled. I could see that Madeleine had slipped into a kinder mood.

"Thank you," Madeleine said to Frog.

"Thank you?" Frog was baffled.

"I've never seen Vanessa like that," Madeleine said to me. To Frog: "You helped us uncover a bit of information."

"I did?" He shrugged.

"She was completely caught up in this immigration business," Madeleine said. "Preoccupied. Nearly lost her cool, you saw that, right? Thanks for getting us in there for that." Madeleine patted Frog on the back.

"So what's the deal?" I asked Madeleine.

"The immigration people must have something on the guru.

Maybe his papers were fudged ... Who knows? It's wonderful stuff. Hey, Frog," Madeleine said, "let me buy you an ice cream cone."

"Okay." Frog was still baffled by Madeleine's enthusiasm for what from his perspective was a failed attempt to regain his meteorite.

"Wanna come?" Madeleine asked me as she hopped into the driver's seat.

"No, thanks. You two go on ahead." I waved them off. It was wonderful, the afternoon was fading, and I could watch Madeleine and Frog drive into the desert, to town to get ice cream. There was hope, hope in the form of a double scoop and sugar cone. Friends could find each other, work things out, reach back for lost love. I watched them drive off, and I swear the scene made me dizzy.

In the next few days, Madeleine and Frog behaved like teenagers in summer, courting, venturing into town to devour more ice cream, talking late at night. I wasn't sure what Frog did all day long, I didn't see him. But he always came to the dig early in the evening, and he would escort Madeleine someplace to chat. At the same time, Frog openly plotted to retrieve the meteorite. The plots included me. I was to be an accomplice in the theft of the stone—which would not really be theft, since we were reclaiming what was ours. He saw himself hauling the meteorite out to the desert somehow, and I would meet him out there with a trailer and jeep, and we'd transport the boulder to safety. Frog would ask me if I thought any of this was possible, and I was quick to tell him no. I knew that once Frog had captured the meteorite back, he would leave the ashram for good, retreat into his hermitage and no longer linger over ice cream with Madeleine. I didn't want Frog to get the meteorite—I didn't want him to walk away, not now.

To make matters worse, Vanessa had plans for the meteorite. Since the Great Tree burned down, many pilgrims had grown scared of leaving the ashram. They feared (rightly) Frescuran hostility and bitterness, and they believed all the local lore predicting some horrible event if the tree was disturbed. Superstition mixed with fear, brewed and bubbled each day, so that the prevailing sentiment was that the desert was not the pilgrim's home, only the ashram was. All of this ran counter to Vanessa's vision of seizing county control, possibly building ashrams elsewhere, expanding.

The election was coming up and the tree burning had dented morale at a bad time. Vanessa saw a need to do something symbolic, and so she seized upon a notion Frog had planted in her head (which I unfortunately had instilled in Frog's paranoid mind).

Madeleine heard from Elise that Vanessa indeed planned to chop up the meteorite into a thousand pieces and dispense them to all pilgrims. The fruit of the desert would be shared. Everyone would have a little chunk of cosmic ore. What these fragments were supposed to be, according to Elise, were gifts from the guru to his disciples. Vanessa had manipulated the meteorite and molded it into a symbol of gloom, apocalypse, the universe falling apart. When the guru cut up the stone and doled out the gifts, he was symbolically conquering the fate of the world, saving those on the Buddhafield, telling them all they were safe, protected, above the chaos that would rain down. That was the theory in all of this anyway.

I had to do something; I'd never done anything in my life, and now I knew that I had to *do* something. I had to act now, before Frog stole back the meteorite, before Vanessa smashed it into a thousand shards. But what? And then it occurred to me—Tycho told me what to do, how to do it.

When Frog would visit the dig (which Amy was not big on—she was afraid he'd blab), he would bring Tycho with him. The cat would jump into the ruins and help us excavate. Little white paws whacked the soil in question with suspicious intrigue, as if some ancient vermin roamed beneath the surface among the ancient ruins. Sometimes Tycho just liked to play with the twine grid—he seemed to think it had been set up just for him—but most of the time he actually managed to do some work. One night, however, Tycho was accidentally reversing the process. He was playing with the mound of unearthed clay, shoveling it back into the pit with one paw, as if this were a game. He would tentatively paw the mound of clay, and then with great glee swat the dirt. He was burying what we'd uncovered, and that's when I said to him, Tycho, that's it. Tycho cocked his head at me, What's it? I said, Thank you, you've given me an idea. Anytime, the cat purred back.

I could bury the meteorite in the desert. I could steal it from the temple, take it to a spot only I would know about, and bury it. I mentioned the idea in abstract terms to Matthew. I said, "What do you think would happen if one day the meteorite were to disappear?"

Matthew instantly grinned. "Oh, that would be wonderful. It would be like throwing ten cream pies right at Vanessa's nose." Matthew was possibly the only person who liked Vanessa less than I did.

"Promise me you won't mention this to anyone."

"Mention what?" Matthew looked puzzled.

"That I was talking about the meteorite's disappearing. Promise?"

"Sure," Matthew said.

And so, over the next two days, without even thinking about what exactly I was doing or what might happen as a result, I devised a plot and carried it out. One day, I snuck out through a hole in the ashram fence and walked up to the highway. I found a spot off the road that I knew I'd be able to find again. There was a rather large cactus on one side of the road, about ten paces away, and on the other side of the road, there was this dried-out mesquite shrub, barely alive. Alongside it, I shoveled out a hole in the clay deep enough to entomb the meteorite. The ground was hard, and the task was time-consuming.

The next day at dusk, I made sure that a forklift was left by the temple. That was easy enough to arrange: I just drove one over from one of the construction sites. And that night, I left the dig early, pleading fatigue. Dawn wasn't too far away, but it was a time when I was sure I'd run into no one. I drove the forklift into the temple, right up a main aisle through the octagonally arranged pews, up to the bema, and I raised the two forklift tines up to the level of the meteorite. Then I used two sturdy beams of wood as levers and with all my weight was able to nudge the meteorite toward the forklift. I practically had to hang on the levers just to move the boulder an inch. I felt as if I were completely ripping my shoulder muscles in the process. I never could have lifted the meteorite, but I could maneuver it bit by bit toward the machinery. Luckily, there was a slight rake to the edge of the dais. All physics were in my favor. The last couple of inches were the most difficult—I was exhausted. But finally, I was able to nudge the stone onto the tines. I strapped the meteorite to the forklift, covered it with a canvas drop cloth, lowered the metal arms, and as fast as I could get the three-gear vehicle to go, I sped out of the temple and down Walt Whitman Way. I could barely see around the rock—I was afraid of crashing into something. I had a terrible time figuring out how to steer, but if I sat on the edge of my seat, I could see just enough of the road ahead.

The meteorite questioned me. It hummed, This is a nice gesture, saving me from becoming souvenirs, but do you know what you're doing? Do you know what might happen?

The fact that I didn't have an answer sent a chill up my spine. So much adrenaline was flowing through my body, into my forearms, the back of my neck, I thought I might explode. I drove downhill, and at one point I was worried that the load and the slope of the hill would cause the forklift to topple over, somersault. But that didn't happen. Then, with only the flat part of the hill to go, I thought I heard a jeep approaching me, but it was actually passing along some distant cross street. I was safe. A woman standing outside a metal shack in the shantytown watched me drive by, but she didn't seem to care what I was doing.

The one thing I was afraid of was that I might encounter a sentry at the rainbow gate, or that I wouldn't be able to pass through it for some reason. But no one was there at four-thirty in the morning. From the inside, opening the gate was a snap. I drove past the pair of palm trees. I made it to the clay crypt I'd carved out. I lowered the stone carefully—unloading was certainly easier than loading—and then I methodically combed the soil back over the pit. I looked over my work, and it occurred to me that burying a treasure might be an act more dog than cat, more of the coyote in me. I liked that notion. I'd brought with me a piece of metal I had found, a strip a few feet wide, which I attached to the back of the forklift. When I drove back to the highway over the same path I'd driven out on, I was able to drag the metal strip behind me, erase whatever tracks I'd made, and remove all trace of my having been to the desert before dawn.

That morning at the ashram, I smiled like a maniac at everyone I passed. I possessed a powerful secret. I felt spent but strong—the way you feel the morning after you've made love the first time, or rafted solo down a river gushing with rapids, or even hiked in and out of the fiery desert. I felt larger than the morning sun, as if I could do anything.

*R*ancho Flora and Frescura were similar in that when some event occurred, a different interpretation was launched by each constituent or pilgrim as to what it all meant. I remember once that in Frescura, it rained for two straight days after a season of drought. The café was full of town members who attributed the downpour to everything from pure meteorological machinations to some obscure facet of the Arbol Magnifico myth. I remember that Virginia Martinez said she saw a three-legged dog racing down the street with a red chili pepper in its mouth, and that always meant rain. At the ashram, the rumor of the missing meteorite tripped up and down the hill at a casual pace, and once rumor was verified as fact, the place was abuzz with speculation. Some said that the guru had taken the rock and moved it to the museum or brought it to his palace. Some said it had been stolen by angry town members eager to pick a fight. I heard a few pilgrims actually claim that it was possible that the stone had spontaneously combusted, then evaporated, and more meteorites would now plunge down to replace it—this was the onset of doomsday. In any event, a genuine scandal had broken out, and pilgrims anxiously awaited the lecture today, where some kind of explanation might set everything straight. I had not expected this reaction, not so quickly. I was thrilled to measure the effects of my caper, but at the same time, I wondered what I'd set in motion.

The first thing Matthew did when he saw me this morning was to pat me on the back and whisper, "I don't know how you pulled it off."

"Pulled what off?" I played dumb.

"Oh, go on." Matthew giggled. "I know, I know."

"Know what?" I was pathetic at putting on an act like this. Actually, I was eager to share my adventure with Matthew and had hoped he would figure it all out. "Okay," I whispered back to Matthew, "you can't tell a soul, you absolutely can't tell a soul. Not Madeleine or Frog or Amy. No one."

"No problem," Matthew said. "You can trust me," he added, and I did. My trust seemed to matter to him. "You're very clever." The way he said the word "clever" was somewhat erotic and made me feel attractive.

Vanessa, as it happened, had spent the morning off the ashram.

She was in Frescura checking up on election details, making sure lists bore the right number of registered names, insuring her victory. She subsequently missed the morning's revelations. She also barely made it to the lecture on time, or so it seemed. I saw her zip up to the temple in a jeep at the last minute. She looked frazzled, out of breath, when she and the guru appeared on the stage together. Apparently no one had time to brief her.

The guru walked into the temple and I could tell he missed the meteorite right away. I was sure that Elise had learned of its absence but chose not to worry the old man. He entered the synagogue unprepared and he kept looking behind him as if he might be in the wrong place. Vanessa, on the other hand, noticed nothing different. I got the impression that she had written today's sermon during the jeep ride back from town, and she was preoccupied with its clever delivery. So she began to speak what was supposedly the guru's text.

"Sometimes in our city"—Vanessa flipped back her hair—"we become preoccupied with fear, fear of what people outside our Buddhafield think and say."

All eyes were on her. People shifted in their seats. Why wasn't there any acknowledgment of the absent treasure? Maybe it would be worked into the lecture.

"But we must realize that our way of life—" Vanessa came to an abrupt halt in midsentence. She must have looked out of the corner of her eye and seen that things were not as they were the day before. "... is a way of life ... to live." Vanessa smoothly rolled into the sermon a little further, ignoring for the moment the issue on everyone's mind. But no matter how hard she tried to continue, the blush rose in her skin. She kept glancing over where the meteorite had been. I sat with Madeleine in the last row, and we could see her turn into a human tomato.

"This is great," Madeleine said to me. She was enjoying every minute of the afternoon drama. "I get the impression she doesn't know where it is either."

Vanessa continued to talk about the importance of standing tall and combating fears of what townspeople thought about pilgrims, but her voice kept trailing off. Finally she did something she'd never done before. Usually, the guru's lectures were delivered by Vanessa at the podium, and the stance was always one of we. Now we must do this or that to reach a higher plane. But she interrupted her reading and stepped aside from the podium, so that she could speak for herself, not for the guru. She looked out at the audience, and for a minute, I thought she might demand to know who stole the meteorite. But instead she calmly said, "And now I must tell you all of a magnificent gift the guru is making to each and every citizen of our ashram."

Madeleine was craning her neck, measuring the response of the pilgrims. She murmured in my ear, "Look, they don't know what's going on."

"Many of you have noticed that the meteorite is not here in the temple this afternoon, and that, my friends, is because it is being polished." Vanessa clapped her hands.

"Polished?" Matthew giggled. A few pilgrims looked at him, and I had to nudge him to keep quiet.

"And after it is polished, it is going to be carved up. Yes, it will be divided into a thousand chunks and each pilgrim will receive a piece."

The guru was listening. He seemed to be scanning the audience for someone who might explain why anyone would want to chop up his wondrous gem.

"That is the guru's wish. He wants us all to partake in the glorious harvest of the cosmos." Vanessa had found a poetic tag-on. "The guru wants you to know that we on the Buddhafield command that cosmos, we are safe from, larger than the disasters that will someday destroy everything beyond our haven." Then Vanessa stepped back up to the podium, no longer flustered, and she delivered the rest of the sermon. She wore a smug, self-satisfied expression that masked what must have been a hellfire inside her.

With one look around, I could detect some uneasy movement of crossed legs and folded arms. Why had she stepped aside from the podium, and why had she interrupted the sermon? Why did the guru look vaguely confused? I knew that they were asking these questions, and for the first time I saw flickers of doubt in the faces of pilgrims. Just flickers, but wrinkled brows of puzzlement nonetheless. I think that many of the men and women forming mauve petals at Rancho Flora knew that this was all a bluff, a hastily concocted promise. No, they probably didn't know that much— but they did have an inkling that something was wrong in their ideal world.

At the dig that night, all Madeleine could do was talk about the day. Vanessa, apparently, had lost her cool at a special blue-obi meeting. According to Elise, Vanessa never actually admitted that she did not know the meteorite's whereabouts, but she ordered a full-scale investigation into its removal from the temple. She said she wanted it returned immediately.

"The pilgrims saw the way Vanessa scrambled around looking for an excuse," Madeleine said. She had walked over to my test pit.

"Maybe the stone really is being chopped up and all that," I suggested to Madeleine. I thought about telling her the truth, but then I thought she might get mad at me for meddling in ashram affairs—and her story.

"No way." Madeleine smiled. "It's been stolen." She was sure. "At first, I actually tried to believe her, that the meteorite was under the knife. But it's especially clear from the way she spoke to the obis. Elise believes that Vanessa's done something evil with it, sold it maybe. I convinced her that Vanessa is in a complete fog. Oh, she'll chop it up as soon as she finds the stone, but she does not have a clue to where it is now."

It was late when Frog finally made his way down to the dig. I couldn't see his face too clearly, but when I did shine my flashlight toward him, he looked rather pallid, unusually grim. Tycho was in his arms, the cat sniffing the air with his silver nose. "I've just come from a talk with Vanessa." Frog squatted down to release the cat and didn't stand up, instead sitting on the ground. "She told me that little secret."

Madeleine was thrilled. "Great." She dropped her shovel.

Frog shook his head to say, Not great at all.

"Did she talk about the meteorite?" Madeleine wanted to know.

"That's how it all started," Frog explained. "She called me into her house to discuss it. I thought she was going to ask me what to use to cut it up—can you believe that? But get this, she said, 'I am hoping you will be able to find another meteorite of a similar size as soon as possible.' When I asked why, she said because she just wanted one on hand."

"So she didn't admit that it's lost?" Madeleine said.

"Lost? It's lost? She didn't say that." Frog sighed. "I told her first of all how rare the one find was, expressing my regrets, of course, that she would choose to break it apart. But all she did was get me to promise her to track another one, and she wants it next week, as if I control the asteroid belt or something. It's lost? That's awful. I was napping all day. I didn't know. I'm worried, Maddy, worried about the health of my meteorite."

"I wouldn't lose sleep," I said. "Vanessa really doesn't know what happened to it."

Frog didn't seem to hear me. He lit a cigarette and continued, "Then she started talking politics. She told me that once Proposition Eight was won, control of the county zoning board would be firmly held, and the cult would follow a program of expansion."

"That's nothing new." Madeleine shrugged.

"Oh, right, I know," Frog said, "just wait. Then she said the most horrifying thing, she said, and I'm quoting her"—Frog raised his finger—"'Soon the whole desert will be covered with ashrams. Rancho-this, Rancho-that.'" Frog was speechless. He saw that Madeleine was going to shrug again, This is nothing new, so he held up his hand. "It gets worse."

"Oh, no." I was sympathetic.

"She told me that the ashrams would be connected by a nuclear power plant, and by television hookups so that the guru could appear all over the desert at once."

I saw the horror that Frog saw, the desert littered with buildings. I knew why he was so upset, so bothered. Madeleine did, too, but as she kept indicating, this was information she had more or less already gathered.

"I asked her first of all how big can the Buddhafield get," Frog said. "'As big as it needs to be,' according to Vanessa. I asked how she thought all of this would be financed, and she said, 'Don't you worry about that.' Then she dropped the bomb." To a physicist, this was a rarely used expression. "Vanessa told me that she wanted me to be in charge of the expansion. Her husband had planned Rancho Flora, and she wanted me to build the nuclear power plant, TV station, and satellite ashrams all over the desert. I said, 'Why me?'"

"And she said something to the effect of, you're the first great scientist to make a pilgrimage," Madeleine answered. "Right?"

"Yes." Frog was unimpressed by Madeleine's accurate guess. He took off his glasses to clean them on his sleeve. "That's what she said." Faint semicircles remained where the lower rim of the glasses touched his cheek. "She said, also, that I knew the desert well."

"That you do," I agreed.

"Yeah, so I can ruin it," Frog croaked. "She's crazy."

"I told you," Madeleine said, "that she had some master design the moment she set eyes on you. Probably before. Maybe she even kidnapped your meteorite to get you here. Maybe she even invited *me* here to get you here." She laughed. "Anything's possible. Or you just waltzed in and she just saw the opportunity, seized the moment."

"And I haven't even told you the little secret yet," Frog moaned.

"Vanessa wants you to redesign the desert," Matthew said. I also thought that was the little secret.

"No," Frog said. "The little secret is quite big. Vanessa claims that she's already purchased the tract of land for the new ashram." Frog gasped at the horror he revealed. "She wouldn't tell me where, but it's somewhere in the desert."

"A new tract of land." Madeleine perked up. "Now that's good, Frog. That's news. She's already got her next chunk of the desert." She digested the revelation. "Great."

"It's not great," Frog said. "It's the worst thing I've ever heard."

"No," Madeleine said, "I meant it's great that you found that out."

"She says it's sizable," Frog whispered.

"Anything else?" Madeleine was taking mental notes.

"No." Frog looked defeated, saddened. Tycho meowed.

"I'd love another chance to prowl around her house," Madeleine confessed. "We're missing something about her. Something." Madeleine grabbed a fistful of air. She did not like for anything to elude her.

"Well, why don't we go exploring?" I asked. Maybe we could find a deed, a map, find out where the next ashram would be built.

"When did you become a spy?" Frog glared at me.

Soon Madeleine and Frog had shuffled away to talk. Amy was particularly frustrated tonight because she could barely get any work done. She had to stand guard. The obis were scouring the ashram, looking everywhere for the prize, and Amy had a hunch they might come over to the solar panels. She was right. At one point, Cassandra showed up, and Amy greeted her. Before Cassandra had a chance to say anything, Amy explained.

"I'm looking for the meteorite, too," Amy said. "I'm using all of my archaeological skills, and I'll find it."

"Good work." Cassandra was satisfied and left us alone.

After Cassandra was out of earshot, Amy, in one of the worst moods I'd seen her in, said, "Idiot," and began shoveling clay once again.

Matthew and I were alone. He had become warmer again in the last day or so, returning inexplicably to his friendly self, and I resolved not to study his every shift in mood so carefully, with such anxiety.

"I have to say," he stopped digging to say to me, "I'm proud of you."

"That's sweet."

"No, really, I'm proud. I thought you were just the kind of cat who rubbed up against people's legs. But you can do more, you can do tricks."

"I can do tricks that you don't even know about."

"I'm sure," Matthew hummed.

Later on Matthew said, "I know we haven't found anything new, but in a way I don't mind. I just like digging."

I agreed, there was a certain languor to these evenings. We continued to lift off layers of dirt and clay, and I had the feeling that we weren't just trying to find some ancient city buried beneath the new citadel. I had the feeling that we were looking for a place to live ourselves, for our own spill of adobes along a cliff where our own haphazardly connected, wayward, newly assembled family along with all of the other lonely souls of the desert could congregate and thrive.

I could picture the city beneath us, I could see myself running up and down the slope of dwellings. Moccasin feet followed worn foot ladders, steps the previous generation had carved into the hillside to climb from one level of homes to the next. Here someone wove a basket, there someone mashed red pigment against a stone. People sat in circles talking. Someone baked mud bricks for a new house to be added on to the ever-sprawling village. Nearby, a group of men and women polished turquoise until the dazzling luster glowed in their palms. I could look down the hill and see the mines in the distance, where patches of green were pressed moss-like against dank stone walls.

We had to uncover our own lost city to become lost in. A city, however, that would only last for a while, because someday wind and dust and clay would sweep over it, weather and time would render it extinct. For now, we had to find this one ancient place.

The desert sometimes seemed like an endless afghan, a beige blanket knobbed with a few tufts of green. You could take an end of the desert afghan and lift it in the air, shake out the wrinkles of hills only to watch the blanket settle again, this time with new rifts. So we had to lift the desert with a tug and before it settled, discover what it covered.

*A*ll attempts to replant the Great Tree failed. For three weeks the town of Frescura had attempted with sapling after sapling to nurture a new arboreal wonder, hoping for a miracle despite the widespread belief that miracles occur only once in any one place. Whenever you passed the spot where the tree had presided, you immediately saw a circle of townspeople. They swept rakes and hoes over what seemed to be an endless pile of black ash. Not a single flake of bark had been spared. The embers had expended themselves for an entire day following the fire, kept warm by the sun, and after the embers were spent, there was this ash. Not just normal ash like that resulting from a typical wood fire, the typical pinyon in the hearth, but instead a fine powder, black sand almost, as if a volcano on the other side of the globe had dripped its dregs through the core and strata to emerge here. And this powdery ash was impossible to clean up. When you tried to comb the ashes into a pile, the disturbance whisked up the dust into a small tornado and colored you black. If you tried to sweep the ashes into a bag and quickly distill the energy possessed by the ghost tree, the bag only ripped open and spilled a black tidal wave.

When a new hole was dug, a skinny, healthy tree was dipped into the earth, watered at great expense, and delivered the best possible care a sapling could get. But the ashes swaddled the baby in a dark, choking shroud. Tree after tree died almost immediately after planting. The abutting area was vast, and so after a while Frescurans tried to nurture a new tree in a nearby spot. But a curious thing happened each time a trench was carved out for new roots. They encountered the black ash—as much as one hundred yards away from the site of the original tree—a wellspring lying below the surface of the earth, but not liquid, just dusty, insidious, parasitic powder. Not only had the tree burned, but so had its massive roots, and not only the roots, but the entire network of underground nutrients. Ultimately the town would give up, renaming the Great Tree the Only Tree. All desert dwellers now lived in fear. No one could fathom what portent was signified in the total demolition of the tree. It was cruel that the desert wouldn't give back the regal wonder, unfair that the desert kept another one from growing. Increasingly, this desert seemed to me like an indifferent despot entertaining his whims at any price.

The special election day was a week away, and tension mounted at the ashram. Tension that could be measured in the way pilgrims often seemed to rush about for no reason, assigning themselves more tasks than they'd been given, working with frenzied zeal. Tension due to the fact that progress toward enlightenment had been inextricably tied to the positive outcome of Proposition Eight. Each day, Vanessa hectically read the lecture, which harped upon the spiritual necessity of victory. Vanessa went out on a limb—she said the guru had delivered a prophecy that the utopia would advance on September first. Usually, the guru's predictions and forecasts were about the far-off future, nothing so near, nothing so readily judgeable. But the guru had said that Proposition Eight would be answered yes, and yes would simply have to happen. The imported homeless people waited to make this happen, they waited with nothing to do, and when you drove past the shanties you could see them sprawled out, leaning against the hot metal, bored, longing to roam past the guards who made sure they stayed put.

Vanessa could be seen driving a jeep up and down Walt Whitman Way, whereas she used to spend most of the day on the phone. A few reporters were now invading Frescura to cover the burning of the Great Tree. That made for a nice article, and normally shy townspeople were eager to cast blame on the cult. A local television news helicopter even passed over the ashram, hovering briefly above the little citadel. However, no one was interested in covering the cult's point of view. Articles that appeared were about the destroyed tree with little space devoted to the expanding cult. Vanessa was increasingly frustrated and every day asked when Madeleine's article would appear, and Madeleine finally lied and named some arbitrary date. But Vanessa, it seemed, had too much on her mind, and she only pestered Madeleine if she ran into her by accident. Madeleine avoided Vanessa to some degree but nonetheless had become obsessed with her. Madeleine's time at Rancho Flora was now completely devoted to following Vanessa about. And Vanessa pestered Frog, too. Whenever she saw him, she asked if there were any meteorites on the horizon, and Frog would make up something, anything just to make her go away.

Vanessa was desperate, I knew, to retrieve the meteorite. Part of the reason she spent more time driving around Rancho Flora than working in her office, I think, was because she herself was looking for the stolen rock. The scandal flourished. Something I never thought would transpire was happening—a group of dissenting pilgrims quietly grew in number. Pilgrims who could see through Vanessa, who had opened their eyes the day she appeared to be flustered during the lecture, the day she promised asteroid bits for one and all. Not many pilgrims, but enough for everyone to notice. Elise didn't help matters. When some of the doubt-stricken mauve people asked her about the meteorite to see what she would say, she told them bluntly, "Vanessa knows as much as you do about the stone." Elise said she relished these moments when she could strike back at Vanessa. A few pilgrims, formerly exemplary members of the ashram, even challenged Vanessa when they saw her driving around. I heard David, for example, say, "When are we getting our meteorite chunk?" But taunting Vanessa was the least of it.

One night, a group of pilgrims went on a mild rampage: they tore down the CHERISHED, DO NOT GO BEYOND THIS POINT sign at the secret side of the hill. They invaded the private homes and according to some reports went swimming—skinny-dipping, in fact—in the pools of the elite donors. Another night, a group of pilgrims took a tour of the obis' dormitory and the next day wore tulips in their jumpsuit lapels. (Vanessa delivered reprimands during the lecture, but that was all she could really do—expulsion from the ashram was not an option until after votes had been cast.) These pilgrims saw Vanessa as someone who kept them from direct contact with the guru—they were right—and they wanted someone else to run the ashram. In their minds, the guru was being held hostage in a way, they wanted to release him. But these pilgrims formed a small minority, and all their defiant acts really did was feed the paranoia of the majority. I wasn't sure what I had hoped would happen when I buried the meteorite—I wasn't sure what would occur next—but I suppose I wanted each desert dweller to find a well and splash a little fresh water in his face. I wanted him to stretch, wake up, find the road again and continue on his journey to wherever. If nothing else, people were looking for the hot spring.

Paradise in the desert sometimes seemed possible—I couldn't imagine living anywhere else. And then, more frequently now, I found the desert suffocating, and I wanted to abandon it. Matthew and I talked about this.

"Somehow," he said, "I can't see myself leaving. I feel like there are things I still haven't done here."

"Look at it from my perspective," I reasoned. "You've been outside, I haven't."

"I'm much happier with the sculpture I've done here," Matthew said.

"I feel choked sometimes," I confessed. Matthew and I weren't really in disagreement, yet I worried that the desert in some vague way was carrying us toward discord.

Not too long after Madeleine announced her intent and desire to get back into Vanessa's rooms, we set out on our reconnaissance mission. The plan was simple, executed swiftly. We waited, as before, until the lecture was underway. The guard stuck his head in the basement tunnel to hear the sermon, and Matthew, Madeleine, and I sneaked over to the secret side. Matthew jumped into some shrubs right in front of the power station. From this vantage, he would be able to determine when the lecture ended, when the guard returned to his post, so he could run and warn us to flee to safety. Madeleine and I plunged into the fantastic landscape of the ashram's secret side. The cooler breeze, bluer sky, and plots of green and water seemed at once more miraculous than it did during previous visits and more like a mirage, a vision of something far off and impossible. But any mirage is a fresco of hope gessoed on to a wall of deceit.

We made our way, as before, past the guru's palace, the obis' dormitory, and entered Vanessa's portion of the house. Frog was already there, with Tycho over his shoulder, having slipped in on his own. Soon we snooped in Vanessa's rooms, aware that we had little time to find whatever it was we were looking for. First we checked the closet thoroughly and then moved on to a desk full of nothing but stationery and envelopes. A few pens, a dictionary. A calculator. Nothing else, not even any of the financial records, or what Frog was eager to find, the deed to the new tract of desert land. We covered every inch of the floor, we lifted couch cushions in the next room, and we inspected the cupboards of a small kitchen curiously outfitted only with netted bags of grapefruit.

Nothing. We searched the closets a second time. We went into the greenhouse, and there we were overwhelmed by the hyper-oxygenated air, air almost wet with plant warmth. We went over everything we had searched a second time.

Madeleine and Frog continued to search the greenhouse, but I noticed that Tycho had remained in the bedroom. I knew him well, and I knew how he only became fixated on something if there was good reason. A peculiar smell, for example. Tycho was scratching at the base of Vanessa's broad bed. It was a platform bed, and he could not get underneath it. There were drawers on the side of the platform, but they were empty.

What? I asked the cat.

Tycho looked up at me and meowed longingly, Please, tell me what I smell.

I don't know. I petted him.

There's something weird here, the cat meowed. I won't shut up until you tell me what smells so weird.

I scratched his jowls and tried to soothe him. And then, to stand up, I happened to lean with extra weight on the bed. It moved slightly. But not like a normal bed moves—this bed moved with a certain mechanical ease, as if it were on casters. But not casters. I looked down and saw tracks inlaid in the floor. I pushed the heavy bed another inch, and it moved more on its little wheels. Tycho scratched more ardently. He meowed. I smelled something, too, maybe. But what? "Frog, Madeleine," I called to them. "I think there's something under the bed."

Without saying a word, the three of us pushed the bed on one side, and with a little force, it slid almost completely away, sort of like a trundle bed, until it ended up against a wall. Under the bed, sure enough, was something—metal doors, like cellar doors. Tycho leapt on them, and Frog lifted him off. "Good boy," he commended the cat.

Madeleine and I lifted open the doors. They were heavy, but I could have managed them by myself, if I had to. The doors flung back to reveal a pit probably four feet deep. Nearly the entire space was filled with similar square white sacks containing the same thing. They were clearly marked DANGEROUS and EXPLOSIVE SUBSTANCE. And KEEP AWAY FROM FIRE. Each sack was boldly printed TRINITROTOLUENE, and in some places just TNT.

"What the hell is all this?" Frog said. He restrained his cat from diving into the sacks of gunpowder.

"Why does she have a stockpile of TNT?" I looked at Madeleine. What sort of terrorism did Vanessa plan to wage?

"I have no idea," Madeleine said. "Maybe she's planning a small-scale war."

Frog pointed out a laundry basket on one side of the pit. In it were packs of surgical masks and surgical gloves, and a series of mortars and pestles. There were some other chemistry accoutrements, test tubes and syringes, materials for handling the dangerous substance. "The thing I don't see," Frog said, "are any devices for detonation. No wires, electrical devices. Maybe that stuff is in there somewhere."

That was all we had time for, however, because Matthew flew into the room. The lecture had ended. We had to escape, even though Vanessa was not necessarily coming back here right away. We closed the floor-closet doors, we moved the bed back into place, and then the four of us, Tycho, too, ran outside to a jeep, a getaway jeep that Frog had positioned earlier. In an instant we were gone, Frog up front with the cat on his lap, Madeleine driving, and Matthew and I holding on in the backseat. We zoomed down the winding road, down through the secret side of the hill, our little foray having created more questions than answers. We drove off, in minutes out of the ashram, out to the highway. Madeleine sped more quickly than she had to, but we were all, I think, fueled with adrenaline, on an adventure. Back through the desert we drove, back toward where the Great Tree once stood. At some inconspicuous point, we'd turn around and head home.

The wind in the open jeep flung back Matthew's hair, mine, too. Then I started to stare at Frog clutching the cat, and Madeleine up in the front seat. They looked handsome together. Just as when we tore away from the fire at the Great Tree, I was struck not by the moment at hand, then one of terror and now one of excitement, but rather by the coupling of two independent souls. Each was a beautiful person in his or her own right, but I saw that together, on this adventure in the desert, they looked even more handsome, more rugged, wiser, more worldly, complete with each other. Gray hair flowed in the breeze. Madeleine sturdy behind the wheel, Frog pushing back with one hand against the dashboard. An undeniable purpose and energy united them now. I was transported to a dream world where we weren't racing away into the desert after having just discovered a trove of explosives, a dream where Matthew and I weren't hanging on in the backseat. I removed myself, Matthew, even the cat, and for a moment Madeleine and Frog were young lovers racing alone through the desert over thirty years ago, faster and faster, ripping through the salmon reefs.

I heard Madeleine's voice, the narrator of the passionate letters I had stolen from Frog's ranch. I'd reread them all in secrecy now, read them several times and kept them hidden behind some books. *Dear Frog, I was thinking the other day about all the times we got lost together. Remember? One day we just drove nowhere, down a highway, desperately lost, and we stumbled upon an abandoned property. You wanted to stay there. But you had to go back to your lab, and I had to cover the French elections. You wanted to go back, and someday we will. I can't wait to drive on the open road with you again, it's so cathartic, and I don't care if we get lost. . . . Dear Frog, I was sitting in a café today and I thought about that ranch again. We stood on that broken-down porch, me complaining that the roof would collapse if we as much as uttered a word, and you trying to clean the windowpanes to look inside the house. Remember? We went inside. . . .*

I saw young lovers break into the abandoned ranch house, and I saw them plunge into the dusty, empty main room. I watched him undo her blouse, with each button a long kiss, while she removed his belt, trousers. He centered himself along the line parting her chest from breast to navel, and she pushed his shoulders down. Passion in an abandoned ranch house, but contrary to Madeleine's letter, only Frog would return.

I came back to the present, saw Madeleine and Frog, saw Matthew next to me, the cat looking back with a curious twinkle as if he had read my mind or as if he understood my penchant for nostalgia. My dream made me certain of one thing, and that was that while Madeleine and Frog now rode in the jeep thirty-plus years later, somewhere they also existed simultaneously as young lovers, frozen in time, still on a voyage through the desert.

That night, Amy had a headache and did not want to go out on the dig. Matthew and I volunteered to go alone, but Amy insisted that we simply let a night pass without excavation. So we complied. We thought about bothering Madeleine, but she was off somewhere with Frog, no doubt speculating about what Vanessa might blow up with the TNT. We sat in Amy's house, growing bored, unable to move about, because Amy said our motion bothered her head.

"I know." Matthew's face lit up. "Let's go on a hike."

"At this hour?" It was close to midnight. He could have said, let's go on a *walk*, but he had said *hike*, as if he had something longer and more significant in mind. I was suddenly wide-awake.

"Sure." He pulled a blanket from his bed and found a canteen.

Tycho had been with with us since we got back to the ashram. We had asked if we could entertain the cat, feeling as if he should be rewarded in some way for the day's discovery, and Frog was happy to let us borrow him. Now the cat, too, was bored. He hopped up to Amy's lap only to nag her pain. "You going out?" Amy said with her eyes shut.

Matthew filled the canteen with lemonade and picked up a six-pack. He threw the blanket at me to carry. "We're going on a hike," he announced.

"Take the cat," Amy groaned.

We marched into the drowsy, moonless night and aimed ourselves for the desert beyond the fence. I couldn't remember a night in which the stars populated the sky more densely. The sequins seemed like people talking out of turn, but once we walked a few yards they became a respectful and silent audience who watched us saunter out of the ashram, cross the road, and continue for a mile until we found a stretch of desert that was purely flat, with nothing in sight, with rather soft ground.

On the way, I pointed out where the meteorite was buried—standing over the spot gave me goose bumps. "Maybe I should check and make sure it's there," I said.

"You know it's there," Matthew told me. "It's safe. Who's going to find it? You and I are the only people in the world who know it's here."

"I guess you're right. Well, I'm glad you know where it is, so if I drop dead or something, you can retrieve it."

"Don't talk that way," Matthew said.

The cat at times was at our heels, sometimes dashing off into the darkness out of the range of our flashlights so that we could only see two glowing ovals of eyes, but always returning to brush against our legs and ask for a belly rub. We spread the blanket on the ground and lay on our backs and looked up at the spectacle. Now we were the audience and the night was the performance.

"There are more stars than usual out tonight," Matthew said.

"They're so resonant," I said. "Resonance" was a word Frog would use, a scientific term for astronomers. But I meant that the backdrop was black and smooth, that the stars went from their two-dimensional crispness to a three-dimensional fullness. You could almost feel the vibrations of these burning bodies.

"There's the Milky Way." I pointed to the cluster of smaller white points low on the horizon, a creamy wave of stars of varying size. It looked like a pane of shattered glass.

"Where?"

I took Matthew's hand and folded his fingers into a gun. I tried to position my eyes where his looked, and I aimed his gun at the galactic bedspread. "Nebulous," I said. But I didn't mean like nebulae, the various blotches that could be white dwarves or other galaxies or things astronomical. I meant that the spurious cluster, truly milky, had an absorbing quality.

We spilled beer and lemonade into mugs Matthew had brought and concocted the standard blend. Tycho went to sleep on the edge of the blanket. Not really asleep, because without any notice, he would stand up, stretch briefly, and bolt out of sight, only to return moments later, settle down into a nice furry ball, with his head tucked into his stomach, and then nap again.

"Everything is luminescent," I said. Here again, I didn't mean anything scientific. Luminescent: you looked at the sky and you felt that the sparkle burned a permanent image on your retinas. "Watch," I said. With my forefinger, I traced the stars in the constellations we could see. With so many stars to choose from, I was lucky to find what Frog had made me memorize. "That's Perseus." I pointed out one Y-shaped formation. "He's a hero." Then I found, with some difficulty, the scant diagram of Pisces Austrilinus. "The southern fish," I said.

"They never look like what they're supposed to look like," Matthew said. Lingering disappointment from a childhood revelation. "They're a little abstract."

"Well," I said, "how about this one, the whale." This constellation took a while to sketch. Two rhombuses connected by a waist and sporting a tail.

"It's going to eat the southern fish," Matthew said.

"Look," I said. A flash of a star dove between the whale and the fish.

"What?"

"You missed it. A meteor."

"Shit." Matthew was mad he had been looking in the wrong place at the wrong time.

"Another one will come. They're rarely alone."

"Shit," Matthew said again. He wanted badly to see a shooting star, not that you didn't find them all the time in the desert night, but I think he wanted to see one at the same time I did.

"Look." Five minutes later in the same spot, another meteor swam by. An instant, and the speck was gone, its trail blue for a split second.

"I saw it." Matthew grinned. It was as if I had given it to him.

"Look at Vega." I pointed to what looked like the brightest star in the sky. It hung lower than I remembered it did. "In Japanese and Chinese lore both, Vega is on the western side of the celestial river, depicted by the Milky Way."

"Over there." Matthew proved that he knew where to find it.

"And on the other side of the river is Altair, Vega's lover." I had to point randomly, because I couldn't remember exactly where Altair was. "And according to the myth, once a year, on the seventh night of the seventh moon, a bridge of magpies reaches across the river so the lovers can unite."

"They walk on the magpies?"

"Sure."

"So maybe that's tonight?" Matthew suggested.

"Sure," I said. We didn't stop to ponder that the seventh night of the seventh moon was probably a while back. "And if you look ever so close to it," I said as I wiggled my finger around the bright white star, "you can see a distant galaxy."

"That haze?"

"Yes," I said. Actually you were supposed to need a telescope to see the nebula in the direction of Vega. But the night was so completely clear and perfect for stargazing, we couldn't rule out that this patch of white haze, a hint of a star, might be another solar system. We looked at Vega for a long while, and then I said, "It's a sultry star, isn't it?" It seemed so much more torrid and intense than any other star in the night, so illustrious that it drew other stars toward it like a magnet. It sucked you up, too, if you stared at it too long. It sweltered, and I grew hot thinking about it.

"Sultry, huh?" Matthew raised an eyebrow. "I have never known anyone who made the stars seem so exotic and sexy." Matthew pulled me toward him.

"I like words." I tried to take his compliment humbly.

"I like—" Matthew started to say. "Hey." He noticed something in my pocket.

"What?" I saw what he was looking at.

"I was wondering what was happening to my strings," Matthew said. He reached over to my pocket and pulled out the tangle of his knotted strings and threads I had been collecting. Each day when I was with him, I tried to pickpocket them. Now I had a whole bunch.

"I was saving them," I said. "You can have them back, if you want."

Matthew inspected his linear doodles. He blushed, a little embarrassed that I had been picking them up. "It's a habit I have—"

"I like them, they're original."

"Just knots." Matthew shrugged. He shoved the tangle back into my pocket. "You can keep them, I guess. But you know who would really like them?"

Of course: art for the cat. I pulled out one string, which I think in a former life had been a sneaker lace, and I dangled it in front of Tycho. He woke up, saw the string, and in a moment of disbelief watched it wiggle above his nose. Then, as if the cat thought I weren't watching him, Tycho leaped up on his hind legs and surrounded the string in a strange dance. He jumped in the air as I dropped the string. One end was in his mouth, and the rest dragged between his short legs. With his head low, he dashed away with the prize as if it were captured prey. He disappeared into the darkness. He would play in privacy and in a matter of minutes return, having abandoned the string, which would never be retrieved.

"Glad we found a use for them." Matthew smiled.

Now the constellations seemed to be talking once again, and our blanket seemed to hover, rotate. I reached for him, and to my surprise and delight I found him pulling me toward him at the same time. Our cautious caresses lapsed into epic embraces. I lifted his shirt over his head, he followed suit. There was a single moment, a first meeting of unexplored warm flesh, when I was sure that somewhere in some far-off galaxy, a star exploded. His body warmed mine, mine warmed his, back and forth, until our separate climates evened out. I'd studied the lines and contours of his body before, but now the moment dictated a closeness beyond inspection. Beyond vision altogether, when the rest of our clothes and boots flew every which way like signal flags. The cat seemed to dance, too (later I realized that he had discovered the wad of strings in my shed trousers).

I found myself flying through a new and fabulous landscape, and I had to explore the whole map of clay canyons and lush grassy hills and ebullient trout-flowing rivers and serene poplar forests. I would have driven off a cliff if he hadn't pinned me. And then, by landslide, earthquake, tidal wave, by some natural feat, we splashed into one scene, one beige desert plain, one strip of distant purple mountains, one backdrop of azure sky, one landscape.

The cat curled up against my naked thigh. I think we all fell asleep. I don't remember who reached over for the unoccupied end of the blanket and folded us into a cozy roll. After a while, still night, the stars as bright as ever, we rolled onto our backs again, drank some more beer and lemonade. I lay on my stomach and won a back massage, which was truly one of the more splendid things a sculptor's hands could do.

"Matthew?" I said. "You told me that I had to ask you questions."

"Yes."

"Did I?"

"Oh, yes," he answered.

I was not exactly sure what I had in fact asked him—but I had collected a curious wad of knotted strings, and maybe that did the trick. I was still dizzy, in a state of pleasant bewilderment, surprised by Matthew tonight. I knew that there was much more I needed to learn. "Who have you loved in your life?" I tried (impossibly) to ask casually.

First I heard about the times he thought he was in love. Then someone was invoked, and Matthew stopped massaging me and he lay on his back, and I felt his body become cool, lose its heat, and shiver.

"What was his name?" I asked.

"That's the horrible thing." Matthew gagged. "I never knew."

After Matthew bought the movie-set ranch, he met a Native at least fifteen to twenty years older, who had been squatting on Matthew's new property. The man survived by selling the corn-kernel jewelry he made. The nameless man had worked at a turquoise mine, but he lost his job when the mine was completely stripped, and so he made these necklaces and sold them on the road. Then Matthew jumped ahead. The man died tragically young, and when relatives and family friends arrived at a funeral reception at Matthew's house and saw the dead man's unfinished work, they set out themselves to complete the necklaces and bracelets. They would dry and sew corn-kernel jewelry until they took care of all of their relative's leftover earthly tasks—they believed that then his spirit could freely roam the land in peace knowing that everything was tended to. So they worked the afternoon of the funeral out on the interior porch of Matthew's house, and after a while, Matthew suggested that they stay the night, since he had plenty of room, and they did. The relatives worked through the next day, some of their friends coming to help out. Then they never left, and that was how the atelier was inaugurated, and that was how Matthew came to share his studio with fifteen or so old men and women. They continued in the spirit of the dead man, and their invitation to work and live at Matthew's house was open and never discussed.

Whenever Matthew had asked the man what his name was, the man hushed him. After a while, Matthew allowed himself to stop pursuing this question. The man was strong and handsome, but what Matthew liked most were what he referred to as their balloon sprees. The man knew about a place where hot-air balloons were launched. He could get work helping people cast off. Over time he got to know some of the voyagers, and then they would invite him up on their lofty excursions. Matthew went to the launch ground with the man, and the two of them got to soar above the desert in the slow-floating baskets—Matthew even learned how to pilot the balloons. He said there was nothing more thrilling than when the loud fire lifted the brightly colored globe of canvas over a valley and the desert was spread out beneath him like an endless bowl of fine grain.

The nameless man had been a restless person. He was often bored and drank to combat a terrible ennui. He inflicted violence upon himself rather than on the "beautiful lodestone" (as he referred to Matthew), who had wandered into his life one hot afternoon with a silly deed in his hand. And Matthew failed to detect the man's increasing unhappiness. One day when the two of them were at the airfield, the man was horribly drunk. He was working with Matthew on one balloon, but suddenly he disappeared. Then Matthew heard a lot of shouting and saw that the man had stolen another balloon and was going up in the air by himself. The man was lifted away, and he didn't go very far before something went wrong and he flew the vessel into the wall of a butte and was killed on impact, the balloon bursting into flames. Matthew was devastated—he felt tricked. He had never penetrated his loneliness, and now he was mad at himself for being so self-absorbed. One had to ask questions of people, Matthew learned, otherwise terrible things might occur. He ran away from everything, and he joined his sister at Rancho Flora. He pretended that he was there to keep her company, but like everyone else who pretended to come to the ashram for some special, unique reason, he was a pilgrim like the rest of us.

I tried to warm Matthew up. He was filled with storms and clouds, dark weather he needed to tell someone about—I could be that someone. We slept and woke again, as if this long night contained many days. Sleepy dreams and waking moments blurred together, became indistinguishable.

"I can turn into a cat," I said at one point.

"You already told me."

"Well, what can you do?" I asked, not really expecting an answer.

"What can I do?" He stood up in front of me and smiled. He was completely naked and he glowed like the absent moon. "You can find the cat inside you, while I"—Matthew picked up Tycho and balanced the groggy animal on his shoulder—"can find the person inside the cat." I remembered that dream Frog had once. Something about these two men, Frog and Matthew—they could unzip fur suits and let the little people out.

Matthew set Tycho down on the blanket, and the cat cocked his head and stared up at the man who was wiggling his fingers at him as if he sprinkled holy water. Then it happened in a flash: the cat no longer was there, but the famed sixteenth-century namesake, Tycho Brahe, stood on the blanket in miniature—the man occupied the same volume the cat had. It was a man nonetheless who appeared almost as a hologram, a fuzzy illusion. There was his silver nose to replace the one he had lost during the duel over something mathematical. Tycho stood on the blanket, less than a foot tall—nevertheless, this was the master astronomer who had reigned over the world's largest and last naked-eye observatory on an island near Copenhagen. The little man pointed toward the sky, at a star dying on the horizon, a supernova. He smiled at a discovery that proved a theory—the universe was a changing thing, mutable, not stable.

"You see?" Matthew whispered.

"Yes," I said back, but I spoke too loudly, I guess, and the little person stepped into his fur suit again and in a flash became Tycho the cat—assuming the same squatting position, looking with a cocked head at the waving fingers. He shook his head clear of some strange dream. He stretched his back into a dome. Then the cat bolted into the darkness and returned seconds later hoping to find one of those fabulous strings again. I fell asleep. Or maybe I woke up again.

Later the stars left the sky. I woke up first—I knew finally that I was awake, not dreaming. Matthew smiled as he slept. What next? I asked the sleeping beauty. What happens next with us? But today the question lingered only as long as the first red fringe of the sun on the horizon. I was too happy to worry. I picked away the tumbleweed that had in the last hours silently amassed around our blanket. The canteen was empty, there was no beer, and I was thirsty, groggy. We were out in a plain with nothing but the dry elements. The cat slept, too. But the sun was rising and I had to wake Matthew with a nudge. He pretended to still be asleep. "What?" he moaned.

"It'll be hot soon," I said. "Tycho will want to go back to Frog." In the best interest of the cat Matthew got up on his feet. He combed his hair with his hands and looked for his clothes spread out all around us. Silently, we hiked back to the ashram. I looked at Matthew, at the cat leading the way. I closed my eyes and pretended we were in a car. Matthew drove.

* * *

252

When we returned from our desert sojourn, Matthew went back to his house and I headed toward mine. The pilgrims were just beginning their morning prayer, the faint hum echoing over the waking hill. I carried Tycho over my shoulder, and when I was still ten yards from the place Madeleine and I called home, the cat dove toward the door and pushed himself through the mauve-painted frame. When I entered the house, I, too, could sniff the air and smell the familiar odor that Tycho was drawn to. He was busy inspecting the clothes that lay all over the couch: a jumpsuit, some boots, and then the all-telling pair of gold-rimmed glasses unfolded on the coffee table. Then I heard a murmur, voices in the next room. The bedroom door opened a crack, then all the way. I froze.

A naked Frog, winding his hair into its stubby ponytail, stepped out, but because I didn't move, and because he was blinded by nearsightedness, he didn't see me. What struck me as odd was how freckled his body seemed. I watched him find a pair of underwear on the floor, and I watched him step into his jumpsuit with a certain awkwardness, as if he weren't yet used to this apparatus of clothing. Then he donned his glasses and eyed me.

"Coyote?"

"Yes?" I said, embarrassed for both of us.

In typical Frog fashion, he was not surprised at all. He simply said, "Well, you could sure use a shower. What did you do, roll around outside all night or something?"

I looked at my bare arms. "More or less."

"I know that we keep discussing it," Madeleine said from the bedroom. She didn't know I had returned. "But I just can't understand why—" she entered the living room and saw me. She was wearing a kimono that I didn't even know she owned. It was green, with golden lapels and a golden tiger crawling up the back. She'd never worn it before.

"Oh, hello, Coyote." She smiled, as unfazed as Frog that I had stumbled in. She found a cigarette and sat down next to her groggy partner. "My, you're filthy."

"He was rolling around in the desert," Frog explained.

"That would do it." Madeleine nodded.

Tycho jumped up on the couch and positioned himself between Madeleine and Frog. A family portrait. There was a kind of comfortable warmth in the room, a domestic dew, and I was disoriented. It was a dream. No, it was real, and I felt dumb. I had thought that when Frog and Madeleine met up at night, they were just chatting. I thought that Frog crept home like a teenager each night—he certainly was not here when I would return. I did come home late, as it was getting light outside, but it had not occurred to me that he spent most of the night *spending the night*.

"Maybe I should take a shower if you guys think I'm so dirty." I was looking for an exit.

So I floated into the bedroom and shed my clothes. I stepped into the shower, slumped against the stall, and thought about Frog and Madeleine. A rush of cold happiness poured out of the shower nozzle, and I woke up to the fact that this was what I had hoped for all along. But how long could any remarriage between these two last? A rare moment, an eclipse, parallax. When would they drift apart again? However, as I looked at the clay washing off my arms and legs, I was in a romantic mood, fatigued by bliss, and so romance blurred reason. I chose not to think about the past or the future, the past replaying its plot in the future. I scrubbed my dusty body and considered only what was happening here and now.

When I stepped out of the shower and began to dry myself off, I overheard the conversation in the next room.

"But even then, even then why couldn't you tell me what had happened?" Madeleine was saying.

"I couldn't say it," I heard Frog utter. "I hated you, I blamed and despised you."

"I never hated you, Frog, not even when I threw the pot at you."

Silence. I didn't dare move.

"I missed him," Frog whispered.

"You could have come and visited more, you know. Was that so hard?"

"Yes."

"Why?" Madeleine asked.

"You've never understood why I came back here," Frog muttered.

"Of course I did," Madeleine replied.

More conversation I couldn't hear. I caught only fragments.

"It was too hard to say good-bye each time," Frog said. "James seemed so mad."

"You were probably mad at yourself more than anything."

"Don't analyze me."

"Don't pretend," Madeleine said.

"I just wanted him *here*, and he would have liked it."

"I thought so, too," Madeleine said. "I sent him."

Then an unbearable stillness. My heart pounded so loudly, I was sure they heard it in the next room. There was nothing more that they could say. They could go over and over their failed affair, the way they were each to blame for their son's unhappiness, for his demise, but the final moment, his death, his absurd and inexplicable death, had to be left for cruel speculation. They would never know why and precisely how he died, whether it was suicide or freak accident, whether they were to blame. They could hack away at residual bitterness over how they acted toward each other, sure, but bang, they would come up against the same maddening, uncertain ending every time. That was why they had to talk it out again and again, and that was why Madeleine and Frog would never be able to reach any point of resolution or absolution, a way out, a way to go on beyond their son's death. They arrived at this point each time with fuel and determination, but they collapsed before the denouement, they were left in the world of grief, one more time losing a battle to the hot desert that kept answers from them.

I emerged from the bathroom wrapped in terry cloth just in time for Madeleine to say, "Well, I've got things to check up on," and leave. Already dressed, she was off like a doctor to make her rounds.

"You're clean now." Frog leaned against the bedroom door while I changed. I plopped down on the bed, just a fresh T-shirt pulled on. "I've got to be going, too," Frog said, and then disappeared. Tycho meowed good-bye. The door shut. But as I sat on the bed, I saw Frog still standing there, and then I heard a mirage of Frog speak. He told me something I'd heard about before, about his return to the desert. I fell backward down a spiral to a day years ago.

Frog was working at an accelerator in a mountainous part of the coast, and he calculated how long it would take him to reach the desert. Meteorite hunting, that was the new frontier, something he had wanted to do for a long while. Staying away from the desert each year made the yearning more painful. Stars fall in the desert—that had been the rationale. With this notion, he could return.

It was the middle of a chilly night, and he was running an experiment, waiting for a computer printout. The numbers began to take on nightmarish insignificance. He had stopped caring about pinpoints bouncing around within pinpoints, about elusive bundles of energy. So with his white lab coat still on, he left. He did not think about Madeleine during his long getaway, but he did think about little James. James would come and find him one day, and he would wait. For now, matters could be explained with a diagram. He saw himself as a line and Madeleine as a line with an opposite charge, and they weren't connected, they didn't collide anymore. What was left was James, the squiggle between them, an exchange of energy. The child would find him, this was what he had to tell himself. Explain it with a diagram, in a letter. (A letter never sent.)

He had told the technician at the computer that he was going out for a smoke, and he would look at the fresh data when he returned. By midmorning, he was lost. The highways in the part of the world he entered were sparsely punctuated with gas stations, much less so than now. Frog finally found a gas station, a one-pump job with a small house and ICE sign. So Frog was offered an ice cube to suck on while the attendant filled his car with fuel and discussed the various highways old and new. The attendant was oracular. He said, "You're not from around here."

"No," Frog said. "I was. Then I wasn't, and now I am."

"So you are now? Where you headed?" the man asked.

"I'm not exactly sure."

The attendant unfolded a map on the roof of the car. "Well, are you going over here?" the attendant suggested. "Or over here?"

"I can't really say." Frog was puzzled.

"Wait a minute. Do you know where it is you're driving to, or are you just going nowhere in particular?" The attendant held his hand in the air, palm up, waiting for a response.

"That," Frog admitted. "The second thing you said."

"Well," the attendant chuckled, "if you don't know where you're going, you can't be lost, because you can't get lost if you're not going anywhere."

By the end of the next day, Frog stood over the desert, on a ridge, and looked at the barren plain. He felt joy, and then that moment of pure bliss wafted away. He became sad, lonely, and this mood passed quickly, too. He was in an energetic mood, then lethargic. The desert is an immense place, and compared to its vastness, sentiments are small. Once they surface to the blush in your skin, they float away in the open air. Your emotions become the wind when the atmosphere is otherwise still. Frog ripped off his clothes, looked out over the desert, and then he ran. He bolted down the ridge and dropped down to the floor of the desert, and he circled and popped back up the ridge to the low cliff. Then he dropped down into the hotter plain, and backed out. He wove his way along the ridge. The rite of running along the hot tundra was purging. Each day, he resolved, he'd run in the desert, then have a drink, take a shower, get on with life.

I opened my eyes, and I was sitting mostly naked on a rumpled bed, staring at an empty doorframe. I knew that there was something to learn from the story of Frog's return here. If I left this world, I, too, might be driven back to this love-hate landscape. There was no avoiding the desert, a secret lover. The best way to prevent this lover from interfering with your life was to include it, make it feel like a partner in the grand scheme. If you tried to jilt it, you'd end up as crazy as Frog had, and ultimately drawn back anyway. The world is strange, and the desert is the strangest place. It is the capital of strangers. Stars fall here—this is where they stray. I will always carry an image of Frog with me, like a wallet snapshot: Frog after dusk looking into the sky. Anticipating constellations, expecting meteors. I had the sense that he could see very far with his naked eye, and that he probably considered the heavens to be not too different from the desert.

*E*lection day arrived. I woke up early, but Matthew was already awake. When my eyes focused, I saw his naked back as he stood at his bedroom window and gazed out at a murky dawn. His slender wrists supported him as he leaned against the window frame. I tried to breathe slowly, as if I were still asleep—I just wanted to watch him standing there, brooding about whatever. His nudity was still a new and marvelous phenomenon. Yet without turning around, he somehow knew when my eyes had opened.

Matthew said, his back still to me, "So many people came here, but for what?"

"Where?" I cleared my throat.

"The desert. Rancho Flora."

"Oh." I yawned. "I don't know. They came to find a higher plane of being."

"The desert has a lot to offer"—Matthew sighed—"but I'm not sure this higher-plane thing is one of them."

"Maybe they found something else," I suggested.

"I suppose." Matthew turned around. "I was just thinking about what we were talking about last night." We had stayed up late talking once again about travel, now more than before a tender topic. "See, I haven't found that something else yet, and I need to."

I really did not want to reenter the circuitous conversation so early in the morning. "But we can come back," I said quietly.

"*You* could go away, come back, and find me later," Matthew suggested.

"I don't want to leave without you."

"Me, neither."

Matthew detected my frustration and changed the subject. "I was also just thinking about all the homeless people Vanessa dragged out here. The really unfair thing is that after they vote today, they'll be of no use to her. And after all this time in a place to live with things to eat and drink, she'll just toss them into the desert." The residents of the metal-shack shantytown were going to be bused into Frescura, and it was quite unlikely that Vanessa would let them back in Rancho Flora once she had milked their votes.

"Why wouldn't Vanessa want them for the next election?"

"Because I'm sure she can scrape up new bums whenever she

wants, so why keep on these people? She's not interested in becoming a welfare agency. She's a monster." Matthew stood up and pulled my ankles until I was halfway off the bed.

"C'mon where?" The morning was so peaceful, a fan was pointed at the bed, the sheets were cool, I could linger here awhile. . . .

"We should bring them something."

"Okay," I conceded, and tried to find my clothes on the floor. I deliberately pulled on one of Matthew's gray T-shirts, which was too big for me.

Suddenly, we heard a crash in the living room, glass being smashed. When we bolted through the door, we found a tearful Amy holding one of the polished green stones in her palm. There was glass all over the floor. She'd broken a window, apparently with a piece of turquoise.

"Amy," I said, "are you all right?"

"Don't!" Matthew yelled, but it was too late. Amy aimed her arm at one surviving pane of glass and pitched another turquoise chunk through the window. Glass flew everywhere. Matthew and I ducked. She threw three more pieces outside before Matthew was able to wrap his arms around his sister and before we could calm her down enough to stop. If Amy had her way, she would have thrown out all of the stones. I looked at the innocent pile. Some of the magic had worn off, and they were just shiny green rocks without promise of something more magnificent.

"Why are you doing this?" I tried not to sound angry.

Amy grinned bitterly. "Because it feels great." She plopped down into a couch. "I'm officially calling off the dig," she announced.

"You can't do that," I said.

"Watch me," Amy sneered.

"Why?" Matthew rolled his eyes, weary of sibling petulance.

"You know, it's not just your excavation," I protested.

"Fine, go ahead, be my guest, leave me out." Amy threw up her hands, exasperated. "I give up."

She gave up so easily, without a real fight. She lived with the delusion of having tried. "Amy, I'm so bored with all of this."

"So am I." She pointed to the window. "Which is why I'm getting rid of those insidious stones."

"I mean I'm bored with the way you whine." A pause. "I suppose you've failed," I said sarcastically.

"Yes." Amy looked glum.

"But you haven't earned the right to give up," I improvised. I looked at Matthew for support but he just nodded, Say more.

"I haven't?" Amy looked confused. "Yes, I have, and it's not something that has to be earned anyway. My mistake was in letting myself for one minute leave a scientific perspective to get swept up in the whirlwind you and my brother created."

Whenever Frog brought a new specimen into the lab, Tycho was always the first to smell the rock—not because the meteorite emitted a peculiar odor, but because the cat smelled this new thing, this new being, a new presence, and he was curious. And when I helped lift layer after layer of soil, I smelled . . . something different, ancient ruins new to the world again, like the new boulder in the lab. Surely I found all this digging at night exotic, romantic, but so what? I had this scent to go on. So I pushed Amy.

"Regardless of whirlwinds," I said, "you still haven't earned the right to give up."

"I'm telling you, I don't know what that means."

"It means you go out at night to one spot, big deal. Maybe you could try to wage a full-time, full-scale probe. Maybe you could exhaust all the possible stretches of untouched soil, and if after all that you don't find anything, fine, you failed, and fine, I got carried away."

Amy glared at me, then stood up, and stepped toward the pile of rocks. Matthew stood in front of the turquoise to protect it. But Amy passed him and walked outside. She picked up the pieces she'd discarded. Matthew had told me that by dragging Amy out to the stretch beneath the solar panels each night, I made her trust herself again, something she'd long ago lost the ability to do. But I felt that I owed more to her than she to me—she was the one who introduced the idea of an excavation, the splendid, hopeless dig, and she was the one who shared it with me, with us. Amy returned a minute later and deposited the chunks with the rest of the pile. Without saying a word she walked out of the house again, without even looking me in the eye.

"Bye," I said shyly as she left. When she was gone, I moaned. "I don't think I helped matters much by being so mean."

"You did," he assured me. "Now we have other things to worry about."

When I stepped out into the day, I wanted to go back inside—my instinct to stay in bed was right. The mania that had spread over the ashram was frightening. The pilgrims could be seen hugging each other at every opportunity, talking a lot and loudly, and trying to pretend that the whole day, regardless of political significance, was a holiday. No one performed assigned chores, the school was closed for the first time (so there was the added, rare frenzy of children playing games), and forms of prayer, the lecture, and dynamic were unofficially suspended. The people of the cult at Rancho Flora sat outside in bunches and enthusiastically awaited the fate of Proposition Eight. A yes vote would destroy a dam holding back the river toward enlightenment. No one considered what a no vote would mean.

Madeleine and Frog both drove to Frescura early, to the post office polls and the main action. Vanessa was there, too, monitoring the voting, and her noticeable absence at Rancho Flora granted an unexpected liberty to those mauve people who had been waging their subversive protest against her since the meteorite disappeared. After Matthew and I had procured some fruit and bread from the refectory, we started to drive downhill. Now and then, we'd drive past a group of pilgrims who seemed to be quarreling. It seemed as if one pilgrim were trying to sell two or three others on something. We kept passing these groups and picking up only snippets of conversation, but finally when I saw David standing in the center of a circle of mauve people and slapping the back of one hand in the palm of the other, I made Matthew stop.

"Don't believe her for a minute," David was saying. "This vote is not about county charters, it's about her, and she's messing things up." *Her* had to be Vanessa.

"But who are you to say don't vote," said a pilgrim I didn't know.

"Don't vote?" I stepped in.

"We're encouraging pilgrims to skip going to the polls today," David told me.

"But all the lectures—" Arlene started to argue back.

"That was Vanessa's word, not the guru's," David said.

To Matthew I whispered, "They're conspiring, can you believe it?"

"There will never be enough to make a difference," Matthew muttered back. "Vanessa's probably taken a possibility of such a plot into account."

"No, Matthew, there is a chance"—David had heard him—"that

we *can* make a difference, if we cast the right ballot by not voting. Keep Rancho Flora pure."

"What makes Vanessa so evil?" Illyanna asked boldly. "What has she done to you, David?"

"She did something with the guru's meteorite," David said. "I think she lost it."

Matthew nudged me. I wanted to correct David, but I kept quiet.

"How can you lose a meteorite?" Rosco wanted to know.

"I don't know." David released a calculated chuckle. "Okay, so she didn't lose it. Worse: she sold it and has taken the profit for herself. Whatever she did, she lies to us. She always has. The guru isn't allowed to speak to us directly."

"Well, I think you're completely wrong," Rosco said. "The guru wants it cut up for us and so it's being cut up."

"Well, then where are our precious little chunks?" David demanded.

Just then Lulu and two other obis drove up in a jeep. They hopped out and started running toward us. As they neared, David shouted, "Remember, don't vote, keep Rancho Flora pure," and he then tore away. His flight caused Lulu and the obis to stop, turn around, and run back in their jeep. They zoomed away down a side street, presumably to chase David, neurosurgeon-turned-sous-chef-turned-infidel.

Matthew and I continued downhill and noticed obis chasing down other pilgrims. The obis were loyal to Vanessa, and they were desperately trying to quell the conspiracy.

"Wow," I said to Matthew.

"Not wow," he answered back. "There are only a handful of them. They won't add up to much."

Down at the metal shacks, the vans to transport the bums were lined up, and the tinny drone of megaphones operated by a handful of obis was waking up the makeshift pilgrims. The vans would take the bums first, in shifts, and then pilgrims, too, who also had their jeeps, so that over the course of the day, everyone would get a chance to vote. The megaphones were reminding the barely initiated pilgrims of their appointed task, of the right answer.

Matthew and I passed among the groggy people and inserted apples, pears, and bananas into their pockets, and we tore off pieces of bread for them to munch on. Soon vans and jeeps started driving past the pair of palm trees, out into the desert. A slow procession to town passed along the narrow highway. Someone had the idea to turn on headlights, perhaps mistaking the idiom for something other than a funeral rite. Vans and jeeps were returning from town, with fewer temporary pilgrims than seemed to be leaving. Matthew had unfortunately been right—they were probably not offered rides home.

Vanessa's absence also licensed Elise to do something Vanessa would never allow. At one point toward noon, the guru careened down Walt Whitman Way in his favorite green convertible, with Elise in the passenger seat looking nervous. Vanessa would have insisted he be chauffeured in his limo, but the guru behaved like a child whose parents had gone out for the evening. He spun down the winding road, his beard blowing in his face, waving his arm as he drove, a halo of gold spread around him, a magical sparkle created by the reflection of all the watches he had donned for the special day. He wore a dozen on each arm. Pilgrims lined the road and cheered him on, and even Matthew and I, nonbelievers, found ourselves rooting for the green sports car. After the guru was gone, a golden afterimage remained.

Matthew and I decided to check out the action in town, so we hitched a ride with some pilgrims. We arrived just after the guru did and watched from a distance as Elise helped the old man, looking spry today, walk up onto the long porch of the post office, bypass the long line of voters, and go inside. He wasn't actually a citizen, and he wasn't handing in a ballot—he was simply checking out the scene—but Padre Christopho thought that the guru was not waiting his turn to vote. The padre, who was keeping people in line, a very stoic assembly of mauve people and townies intermixed, jeered, "He should have to wait like everyone else!" But the guru seemed like royalty, and even though the Frescurans despised him, those on line were timid about joining the padre in his complaint. Some pilgrims heard the clergyman's protest and out of habit began singing the *Messiah* as they used to at the Great Tree. Soon Guru B emerged, and the pilgrims sang more loudly. Elise managed to get the waving guru into his convertible, and the two drove away, stopping briefly for some ice cream down the street.

Matthew and I saw Frog toward the front of the line of voters.

"It's just too close to call," he reported. He was watching the voting tables, keeping his own tally. You entered the post office, checked your name off with Isabelle Burns, checked your name off with Jakarta, and then were given a ballot that you ultimately dumped into a large, padlocked pine box.

"Where's Madeleine?" I asked.

Frog pointed to the other end of the porch. Madeleine was leaning against a post, standing deliberately in a shadow, listening to what appeared to be a conversation between a very angry Vanessa and a distressed obi. I crept over to Madeleine and she winked me a hello and raised her forefinger to her mouth.

Vanessa was saying, "You're telling me that they're going around and telling people not to vote at all?"

The obi nodded.

Vanessa threw her hands up in the air. "Why don't they come and vote no, if they want to ruin everything?"

The obi mimicked Vanessa and threw her hands up in the air. "Are you going to go back?" the obi managed to say.

"No." Vanessa turned around abruptly and scowling, oblivious to us, walked right by.

"Is there really a revolt?" Madeleine asked me.

"Not in any major way," I told her. "But it is surprising."

"I've seen it before on election day." Madeleine shrugged. "What's surprising is what Vanessa just said—that she's not going back to the ashram to attend to it. That doesn't seem like her, does it?"

The voting continued and the day passed quickly. Madeleine, Frog, Matthew, and I retreated to a corner table in the Sunflower Lives, where we waited with the rest of the town and tried to assay the vote count.

"I say the cult wins." Frog took a swig of tequila.

"I don't know," Madeleine argued. "A lot of pilgrims were no-shows."

Frescurans gathered in groups and waited patiently for the outcome they'd prayed for. When someone walked into the café after having voted, everyone inside clapped. Virginia Martinez greeted each no-voter with a handshake and free beer, which she had been advertising for a week now. The second beer, however, was not free. Nevertheless, it was as if each voter had just completed a marathon, and the beer was a prize for each person who finished. Finally the sun went down, the polls closed, and it didn't take long before the ballots were counted. The tension was unbearable.

Isabelle Burns, Sam and the padre behind her, burst into the café like gunslingers into a saloon, and the sheer glee on Isabelle's face answered the question. A loud cheer rushed through the café, pitchers of beer were instantly circulated, and out of nowhere, music and dancing erupted. "We won, we won!" people were chanting.

"I don't believe it," Frog said to a fresh glass of tequila.

"I can," Matthew said. He whispered to me, "I think you're to blame. It all started with the meteorite."

Maybe I was, maybe I wasn't. In any case, an unexpected hollowness crept into my arms and legs. Guilt, though I'm not sure why. In completely vivid terms, I remembered an incident I hadn't thought about in at least ten years. I was around seven or so and I went into the general store and shoplifted a key chain that had a charm on one end, a globe painted in light-blue oceans and dark-green, almost black, continents, the world with an inch diameter. I wasn't caught, I lost the key chain maybe a few months later, but there was a feeling then that went unmatched (not even when I was picked up for having a dime bag in my pocket), a cold rush of panic and desire and dishonesty all at once. I think I had wanted to be caught when I was seven. I don't know why. I had to laugh— was that what I wanted now, should I turn myself in?

Enough county residents had voted all over to keep the cult at bay, and Vanessa's elaborate program of imported pilgrims in the end was undone by the real and devoted pilgrims she had never questioned. The whole town rocked with excitement. Virginia do-si-doed around everyone in the café. Her great apron even brushed against me and she grabbed my hand and spun me into a turn. The padre became quite drunk and began shouting out the Gospel while the rest of the Frescurans cheered drinking songs louder. Proposition Eight was gloriously defeated. All around people danced and sang so that you couldn't help but be infected with happiness, no matter what you thought of the outcome. Except Madeleine, who wore a frown—not of anger, but of confusion.

"You yourself said the town would win," I said to her.

"Oh, I know." She tried to smile but couldn't. "I'm just perplexed."

"By what?" I asked.

"By Vanessa," she answered.

"Aren't we all?" Matthew tried to be cheery.

"Why didn't she go back to the ashram to try to stop all those pilgrims trampling her master plan?" Madeleine was stuck on this. "And now don't you see? She has to *do* something."

"How so?" Frog wondered.

"She blew the election, which she had practically made it impossible for the cult to lose." Madeleine lowered her voice even though the café was too noisy for anyone to eavesdrop. "Plus she's got the immigration people moving in on the guru. Plus there's a coup in the weather forecast."

"She has to do something," I agreed.

"I think that she has something planned, and that's what bothers me." Madeleine rapped the table with her knuckles. "Vanessa is simply not the sort of person who just lets things happen. She knew that she might lose the election. She didn't go back to the ashram. She has something planned."

"Then why'd she make the vote so important?" Frog said.

"I'm telling you, she has some scheme in place," Madeleine insisted.

We sat in the Sunflower Lives for hours, listening to the partying all around us, silent as we tried to imagine what Vanessa would possibly do to make up for her losses, for the cult's losses. Nothing came to mind. Frog looked bothered. He despised mystery and hated not knowing the solution to a formula, and even Matthew was quiet, now glum. We sat in the corner of the café for so long that we outlived the victory party. It was forced out onto the street when it became late and Virginia Martinez could not stay awake. Finally she threw us out, too, and we were left to pace the dusty street, unlit at night, except by the church. We ended up by the church gate (I thought I heard Padre Christopho inside the chapel belting out a show tune). We all would have been happy to go home, go to sleep, but Madeleine wanted us to stay in town—as if she were on the brink of some discovery, and moving now would jeopardize that revelation.

I had been considering the problem for a while, but I was almost afraid to say anything, afraid I would derail Madeleine's train of thought. But I saw her look at me and ask, What's Vanessa's game, as she had so often in the last weeks. So I answered, "Maybe Vanessa doesn't need a ploy. She's already in control of the cult, even with a few dissenters. The guru's not much more than a prop. I think she can pretty much do—"

"You're right and you're wrong," Madeleine cut in. She paced. "You're wrong in that as much as Vanessa runs Rancho Flora, she also depends upon the guru for her power. But then, hell, you're right, the guru is a prop. And he *has* been looking rather ill lately. We know he isn't well, he's sick, he could just die, and then what happens?" Madeleine spoke rapidly, barely breathing. "Worse, he's become a liability, what with the immigration investigation. I mean"—Madeleine walked the length of the churchyard—"deportation would be more damaging than death. His cult would have to follow him." She clapped her hands. "What if he *were* to die? It would be better for the ashram. There'd be no deportation. A death which could be capitalized upon might serve Vanessa well."

"A martyrdom?" Frog seemed astonished.

"A martyrdom, of course, I've seen it a dozen times." Madeleine nodded. "The guru would be more useful to his cult right now if he were lost in myth, if he were a symbol, immortalized as a god. Vanessa has to make this happen." Madeleine rubbed her hands together. She slapped me on the shoulder as if to reward me for steering her on the right track. "I think that this has always been an option for Vanessa, a last resort, something she could do. Now she has no choice, because this is the only way the ashram can recover and go forward."

"This is the way she can take over," Frog grumbled.

"Well, in many ways, she's acting in the interest of the ashram, carrying out the guru's vision, you see? She wants the ashram to expand and cover the desert, and perversely, this is a way of fulfilling that mission without interruption, without the setback of the lost election."

"*How* will she make the guru a martyr?" Matthew wanted to know.

"That's the next question." Madeleine paced more rapidly, with larger steps. "She's got to move quickly to contain today's damage. If Vanessa really wants to get some steam from the guru's death, he should die now."

"She has that stockpile of TNT," Matthew reminded us. "She's going to blow up the guru," he decided.

"She does have all that TNT for no reason," Madeleine agreed.

"She's going to blow him up." Matthew was certain. I closed my eyes and saw the guru's limousine rolling along the highway, and boom, the car exploded into flames. My heart thumped when I remembered what the guru had proclaimed during the interview: there will be an ugly explosion. Matthew and I now paced alongside each other, crisscrossing Madeleine's stride. Only Frog remained in one place, leaning against the white wall of the churchyard. In the distance, a pair of headlights appeared, and we watched a jeep speed toward us. It became apparent that it was an ashram jeep, and then when it was close enough, we saw Elise driving alone.

"Hi," I shouted.

Elise skidded to a halt. "Madeleine," she said, trembling, "I looked all over for you. I finally guessed you were still in town."

"What's wrong?" Madeleine climbed into the jeep's passenger seat.

"I just came from the emergency obi meeting." Elise tried to calm herself down.

Before Madeleine had a chance to say anything, I asked, "What was Vanessa like? Was she upset?"

"Not really," Elise said. "In fact, I was surprised that she was not particularly concerned. She was cool and ran the meeting as usual. She even cracked a joke at one point."

"What's going to happen?" Madeleine asked.

"Vanessa insisted that we can't make it appear as if the ashram is in any way defeated. So tomorrow, everything has to happen as it always does." Now Elise was no longer shaky, just mad. "I think it's ludicrous. The pilgrims will want answers. But Vanessa says an uplifting lecture will be all the guru needs to do to make everyone happy."

"No deviations in schedule?" Madeleine wondered.

"No," Elise said, "and the thing that bothers me, the reason I wanted to find you, is that Vanessa insists that the guru must go to town and get his ice cream like he does every day. I know that it's a public gesture, aimed at the town, but it might be embarrassing for the guru. I don't think he should go."

"Did you say that in the meeting?" Madeleine asked.

"Yes, and Vanessa insisted on it. She was weird. She must have said at least three times that the guru has to get his ice cream cone.

And then she kept using it as an example of how things have to appear normal."

"She's just being persistent," Madeleine said, though I knew she was thinking something else. "You're worried about the guru and that's fine, but from what little I know of him"—Madeleine patted Elise gently on the leg—"the guru is not one to let anyone embarrass him."

"I guess not," Elise said.

"You look tired," Madeleine said. "Drive home, get some sleep. Tomorrow, let the guru get his ice cream. It's a small pleasure." Elise nodded. After Madeleine climbed out of the jeep, Elise drifted into a U-turn and headed back into the desert. I was amazed at how easily Madeleine at once consoled Elise, garnered necessary information, and manipulated the woman so that she could get her out of the way.

"I didn't want to worry her," Madeleine said after Elise was gone, "but you know what I think?"

Frog laughed. "What? Vanessa's going to poison the man's ice cream?"

"Vanessa did insist on the whole ice cream routine," I said.

"All Vanessa needs is a dead guru," Madeleine said. "Dead, as if the election itself killed him."

"The guru is going to get his ice cream," I said, "and he's not going to make it back to Rancho Flora alive. . . ."

Matthew seemed reluctant to go along with our theory. "I still think she's going to blow up his limo."

I thought it was cute the way Matthew still pushed his scenario, but Madeleine had no time for farfetched notions. She shook her head. "Too overt. Not Vanessa's style. Poison is," she said. "C'mon, let's get some ice cream."

We walked over to the Sunflower Café. It was late now, Frescura was asleep, and the one pilgrim who was working at the parlor was about to close up for the night. The four of us walked in, looking deliberately hungry. "I'm sorry, I was just about to lock up," the pilgrim apologized.

"Oh, okay." Madeleine was polite. "You're really about to leave?"

The parlor attendant looked at the ice cream tubs all closed up. "I'm actually just about done here," she said.

Madeleine noticed a space where one tub should fit in. "It looks like you have one left open."

I peered over the counter and saw that Madeleine was about to repeat my gaffe. "That's where the banana mint goes," I whispered, trying to save Madeleine from embarrassment, and then I remembered our mission.

"I was just putting in a new tub of the guru's flavor," the parlor worker explained politely.

Matthew and I noticed two tubs sitting at the far end of the counter. We could see the new tub of the yellowish ice cream, but we could also see the old one next it. Matthew said, "The old tub isn't finished yet."

The parlor worker looked at the tubs, "Oh, I know. But the new one was sent over and so I have to replace the old one."

"Vanessa sends over the ice cream." Madeleine confirmed what she already knew. I thought I heard her whisper to herself, "Perfect."

"Yeah." The pilgrim saw nothing unusual in what was going on. "Normally she waits until the guru finishes a gallon and she sends over another one—about once a week. But she sent instructions: change the tubs tonight. So that's what I'm doing." We let her finish her task and then walked out of the store with her. She locked the door, waved good-bye, and then drove away toward the ashram.

"I suppose," Frog said to Madeleine, "you want to break in."

"You better believe it. I'm sure the ice cream's laced."

Breaking in was easy. We simply snuck around back to an alley, and with a few hard kicks, we pushed open the rather flimsy mauve-painted door. Inside the parlor, we grabbed the new tub of banana mint that had been fitted in place in the refrigerated counter for the guru's next visit. "Let's go to the Sunflower Lives," Madeleine decided. "We need to test the stuff."

"Amy has all sorts of chemicals and equipment," Matthew reminded us, "for figuring out what minerals are in something and how old they are." So Matthew was dispatched back to the ashram.

Frog, Madeleine, and I went down the street to the Sunflower Lives and banged on the closed and locked door until Virginia Martinez stuck her head out from the second-floor window. "What do you want?" she barked.

"We need to get inside," Madeleine said.

Virginia disappeared, lights came on in the café, and a few minutes later she appeared at the door. The ice cream had melted somewhat. "What?" Virginia looked at it. "You came here to have a party?" she growled. She had put on her blue apron over her nightgown. "Party's over."

"Virginia," Frog said, "we're sorry to bother you, but we need to test the guru's ice cream to see if it's been poisoned."

Virginia wrinkled her nose. "Who would do such a thing to that old man? He's gonna die someday anyway."

"Not soon enough," Madeleine quipped.

"Well, well, well. Should I phone the sheriff?" Virginia moved toward the kitchen.

"Not yet," I said.

"I'll call Sam," Virginia decided.

While we waited for Matthew, Frog, the scientist among us who seemed to understand best what to expect in a tub of poisoned ice cream, made empirical observations. He sniffed the ice cream. "It doesn't look like there's anything wrong with it." We smelled it, too, and we waited.

Matthew came back with great speed. He entered the café carrying two shoe boxes of vials and a square metal case. "I found this stuff, but I couldn't find Amy anywhere."

Frog looked at Amy's machinery and vials of chemicals. "I can handle this stuff," he said. "I use similar equipment to test my meteorites," he assured Madeleine. Frog set up shop on a table and began testing the ice cream in a variety of ways. He would spoon some ice cream into a petri dish and then pour some chemicals over it. He would mix ice cream and one of Amy's compounds in a test tube. He kept shaking his head.

Sam Burns walked in looking unshaven and tired. He nodded and sat down, puffing. "Someone poisoned the guru," Virginia announced.

"No." Sam frowned.

"Yeah, they put cyanide in his ice cream," she told him.

"He hasn't been poisoned yet," I corrected Virginia. She glared at me—I was ruining her story.

"And it's not cyanide," Frog said. "I looked for that first."

"Arsenic?" Madeleine wondered.

"No," Frog determined a short time later. The ice cream was melting and getting soupy. The room grew sickeningly minty. Virginia, perhaps bothered by the notion that ice cream might affect the refried aroma of her café, decided to cook up some burritos for us. Matthew and I helped Frog prepare samples and test them with other chemicals to see how they interacted, to see if the ice cream turned certain colors. With the machine Matthew had procured, Frog could take a minuscule bit of ice cream and search for traces of certain compounds—analyses were spewed out in the form of numbers on a roll of adding-machine paper.

Over the course of the next hour, longer perhaps, Frog tested and retested the banana mint ice cream for every poison he could think of. Madeleine had seen a few attempted poisonings of dictators in her day, and she would suggest things like "Chlorine," to which Frog would answer, "Nope," a short while later. "Mercury?" "Nope." "Hydrochloric acid?" "Nope." "Potassium cyanide?" "Just potassium, from the bananas." "Curare?" "Nope." "Strychnine?" "Nope." Finally, Frog looked at all of us, dug his finger into the gloppy ice cream and flung a dollop of banana mint into his mouth.

"Frog!" Virginia was horrified. Sam gasped.

"Delicious." Frog licked his lips. "The guru knows his ice cream."

"It's poisonous." Virginia was worried.

"I hate to disappoint you all," Frog said, "but there isn't anything wrong with this ice cream."

"Shoot." Madeleine slapped the table. She wasn't willing to give up. "I was so sure it was the ice cream."

Matthew seemed pleased. "I still say that Vanessa is going to blow up the guru's limo."

"Will you get off that kick?" Madeleine snapped. It was late, she was tired and short fused. I squeezed Matthew's hand to let him know she didn't bite.

Frog backed Madeleine up. "Besides, I told you I didn't see any wires or electrical equipment for detonation. They could have been stored somewhere else, but it just doesn't seem likely, we made a thorough search. We only found that basket with surgical masks and gloves."

"But why does she have all that TNT?" Matthew was still mad that his bomb theory was shot down. "Why does she have masks and gloves?"

"Oh, TNT is dangerous to handle," Frog said. He had become

well versed in explosives during his physics days. He explained matter-of-factly, "TNT is an addictive substance, and anyone who handles the stuff has to be careful not to get much powder on his skin or to breathe in too much dust."

"TNT is addictive?" I asked.

"I didn't know that," Madeleine said.

A plot started to fall into place in my mind. I was a liar. This summer I started to lie less, but I could still pick out a fellow liar. Schemers can identify fellow schemers. Frog talked, and puzzle pieces locked together.

"Oh, sure." Frog was happy to elaborate (listening to him, I was transported back to his observatory). "There are some famous case studies of dynamite-factory workers who were overexposed to TNT and who subsequently became addicted. One man went on vacation, he was gone from the plant for a week. He was young, healthy, except unbeknownst to him, he was dependent on the TNT. He dropped dead of heart attack. He suffered withdrawal while he was away from work."

"Withdrawal from the TNT causes you to have a heart attack?" Madeleine digested the facts.

Frog nodded. "Not in every case, but if you're dependent upon it, and it's taken away, your coronary artery might burst." To which Virginia and Sam both cringed. "That's what happens," Frog apologized for being graphic.

"But it would look like a massive heart attack," I said. Frog nodded. "And it would result from the TNT's being taken away?" Frog nodded again. I launched my hypothesis: "What if Vanessa had been putting the TNT into the guru's ice cream?" It was perfect—demented, but perfect.

"Yuck," Virginia groaned.

"And all Vanessa had to do was get the guru secretly addicted. He wouldn't be aware of his dependency, no one would. She could maintain his addiction. And then whenever Vanessa wanted to pull the trigger"—I folded my hand into a gun—"she just had to take the TNT *out* of his ice cream. He would suffer withdrawal and in a week or so die from what would appear to be a normal heart attack. Vanessa could control when the guru dies."

"No wires necessary," Matthew conceded.

"Vanessa could control when the guru dies," I repeated myself, "and she can make him a martyr at her convenience."

"Wonderful." Madeleine was thrilled. "Plus," she'd gathered, "the trace of what caused the murder would have been removed at the time of the murder—Vanessa would take the poison *out* of the guru's diet. The crime wouldn't be traced."

"You got it." I smiled. Madeleine looked at me as if I had given her a present. This scheme fit into her portrait of Vanessa. A secret plan, something she'd been plotting and carrying out for a long time.

"Did the guru complain of any troubling symptoms?" Frog asked.

"Nothing that couldn't be blamed on his asthma," Madeleine said.

"No, remember," I interrupted, "Elise said that the guru used to get headaches?"

"That might be a side effect," Frog said. "That and a destroyed liver, but the liver would take a while to go."

"Don't forget"—Madeleine was excited—"the guru was old and sick anyway—these symptoms and a heart attack wouldn't be too extraordinary. There would probably be no investigation, no autopsy performed on a holy man. Vanessa could simply claim that the election sent the guru to his grave. Vanessa would then rally her forces. . . . Brilliant," she tagged on.

"Yuck." Virginia issued her pronouncement a second time.

"You figured it out." Madeleine beamed proudly at me. Matthew squeezed my shoulder.

I did feel proud. "We still have to prove it," I said modestly. If there was TNT in the old tub of ice cream, it would mean that Vanessa was indeed drugging the guru, maintaining an addiction. Frog determined that there was no TNT in the new tub, which meant that if Vanessa planned to assassinate the guru, she had hoped to initiate the withdrawal phase with his next ice cream cone. Matthew and I were sent back to the Sunflower Café to fetch the old tub of banana mint ice cream. We found the discarded tub in the trash in back, and we took turns carrying the still-cold, fat cardboard-and-aluminum cylinder down the street.

"More ice cream!" Virginia winced when we carried it in. She ran into her kitchen and threw something on the grill to combat the minty odor. Frog started to make his tests. Madeleine looked on anxiously.

"Where was she getting TNT?" Sam asked.

"Oh, she's been running construction operations for years," Madeleine said. "She'd have no trouble getting explosives for building purposes, to clear away an unwanted obstacle."

At one point, Frog tasted the allegedly tainted tub, just a small morsel, not enough to harm him, and he decided, "There's no taste—it shouldn't take much to do the trick—and the banana and mint probably overpower what gunpowdery taste there is."

"Not to mention the fact that the guru's tastebuds may not be as sharp as they once were," Madeleine added. "No one else ate the stuff."

"Two questions," Frog sighed. "Number one, why TNT? It's not a foolproof method. Not like a barbiturate. And number two, how the hell did Vanessa know about it?"

Madeleine said, "Well, barbiturates would have made the guru noticeably sleepy, sleepier than he already is."

Just then, Frog pulled a thin printout through his fingers. "Bingo," he reported, "it's spiked with TNT."

It was not common knowledge, this TNT poisoning. Not even Madeleine had heard of it. But I remembered another bit of information to answer Frog's second question. "Elise said that Vanessa's family was involved in munitions and construction, right? Her family probably had to deal with some worker dying on vacation. And when Vanessa wanted to do away with the guru, she probably didn't think twice, she probably just remembered this bit of trivia, family lore, some mishap she'd overheard when she was a child."

Madeleine punched me lightly in the arm, proudly. "Good memory."

Vanessa had to be arrested as soon as possible. The evidence of her conspiracy was in the form of a melting tub of banana mint ice cream. We woke up the sheriff, who hurried north from Chiaroscuro, and it was around four in the morning by the time he and Sam Burns and another officer drove up to Rancho Flora. Oddly enough, the police were in effect saving Vanessa from a group of pilgrims who maybe a few hours later were planning on staging a clumsy coup—they were simply going to demand to know the whereabouts of the meteorite. But Vanessa was apprehended before she was called upon to make up any more excuses, the bandit saved from the lynch mob.

Somehow Vanessa must have found out that the cops were coming after her. What she did was almost like an admission of guilt, because were she innocent, she would have faced the sheriff and smoothly denied allegations and called down an obi who was also a lawyer. But she retreated into her greenhouse, to the closet where her rifle was stashed. What followed was a scene in which the sheriff tried to lure Vanessa out first by shouting nicely, and then by threatening to use force if he had to. Vanessa had just the one rifle, but she also had a lot of TNT on hand. Luckily, the TNT was under her bed, and the police and Sam Burns were in her bedroom, aiming their weapons at the greenhouse. After a half hour of intense waiting, Vanessa fired her rifle three times—each time, a smashing sound occurred. She had knocked off a trio of tulip pots. Then, she walked through the greenhouse door, her hands in the air, and surrendered herself. The police handcuffed her, took just one sack of TNT with them as evidence for now, and left the rest under the bed.

All my adrenaline had been poured into solving the TNT plot, and I was completely exhausted. All I could do was think about Vanessa. Who was she? A powermonger who had built this city, who wanted to build a whole desert of ashrams, and who probably had the interest of her cult somewhere prominent in her heart. Sure she was ruthless, oily, manipulative, but I felt sorry for her when I thought about her handcuffed, in the backseat of a police car, zooming downhill with pilgrims looking on, driving away from Rancho Flora. Vanessa was a lonely person like everyone else, and she had executed her plot all alone. Through these manipulations and plottings, she had probably thrown herself further into her own solitude. She was a pilgrim who had made her pilgrimage all the more impossible.

Madeleine said to me on the ride back into the desert, "That's that," as if now she could write her articles. "Now the ashram just needs to find where the meteorite was hidden."

I was going to ask why she was so sure the stone had been hidden, but I didn't.

"What's wrong, Coyote?"

"Nothing," I shot back quickly. "Why?"

"You look like something's bothering you," she said.

"Nothing," I lied, though I was sure Madeleine didn't buy it.

I wandered the hill as the sun rose. The adobes were washed this morning with brighter light, a yellower warmth that cast the cornerless mud walls in an uneasy jaundice, separating them from the soil and slope with which they had blended so smoothly until now. The houses seemed as fragile as plant life, as temporary as tumbleweed. I was fatigued, plagued by the insomnia you get when you find yourself waiting and you're too weary to identify what it is you're waiting for. I was mad at a place—it was frustrating to be mad at geography—maddened by an unpredictable person who one day might embrace you, lavish you with praise, adore you, and the next day treat you with caustic indifference, relish your vulnerability, arrogantly make you feel as if you would never be quite compatible, always just a little inadequate. If a place could be a person like this, and I knew the desert was, I had to find the strength somewhere to tell him off. Matthew did not want to leave, but I had to convince him to come with me. All my life this world had been where I played, learned, loved, and despaired, and now I knew that I should move on, take Matthew, venture to another planet.

I had wanted to be alone as I wandered around, but I kept bumping into troubled, baffled pilgrims. Each person looked blankly at the desert beyond the fence, as if some kind of explanation might be spotted like a mirage, and as long as enough distance was maintained, that puddle of a picture would remain intact. The sun had risen and revealed a troop of reporters camped out at the rainbow gate. They hoped to get inside, but for now, all they could do was tackle disenchanted mauve people who were leaving Rancho Flora. Inside the ashram, the spirit was low, the air filled with dusty rumors. Many people were packing their bags, abandoning the cult for good. For those who still believed that when Vanessa spoke, she spoke for the guru, the guru's prophecy of a successful election outcome had failed to come true—the infallible guru had erred in his prediction. For those who had at any time trusted Vanessa, revelations about her corruption, indeed her savage plot, were painful. Things that weren't supposed to happen on a Buddhafield had occurred. Perhaps that explained why the climate was changing, why it was warmer today than yesterday, the cool breeze vanished, the charm of the oasis gone.

Matthew was sleeping, and since I couldn't be alone now, I decided to join Madeleine in the administration building. After Vanessa was arrested, the guru and various obis had been alerted (if they hadn't already heard Vanessa's rifle shots). They began to congregate around the glass table to figure out what was going on. Madeleine sat with them—that was where I found her, with Elise, key obis such as Jakarta and Lulu, and the guru. Frog was there, too. He sat in a corner, as if he were waiting to give Madeleine a ride home, but I joined everyone else at the table. As soon as Vanessa was ushered away, the obis who learned of the debacle had ransacked the greenhouse. For the blue obis, the discovery that Vanessa had been poisoning the guru was twice as shocking as it was for the average pilgrim, for not only had their spiritual leader been attacked, but also their own subcult had been blown apart. Their devotion to Vanessa became instantly humiliating: they had been betrayed. People such as Elise and Jakarta knew that Vanessa had to be hiding the account books somewhere, and slowly they found the thin volumes of ledgers stashed into secret compartments Vanessa had constructed under the counters of tulip plants. One by one, account books arrived at the glass table. Each obi and Madeleine took turns perusing the columns of ink. The ledgers carried an awful scent of tulips, which made everyone nauseated and uneasy. This morning no one mentioned the TNT because the guru insisted that there was really nothing wrong with him—he felt fine—and the accounts should be examined before he was attended to medically. Almost as a courtesy, Vanessa's name was not mentioned.

The account books told a horrible tale. As the morning progressed, we learned that Vanessa had financed expansion and livelihood at the ashram by borrowing heavily. The cult was in debt, the cash flow problem acute. The guru, seated between Elise and Lulu, across from Madeleine, had been reading the ledgers as they came in, but he said nothing. He just coughed once, grumbled a little. Finally, however, he rested both hands on the table, shakily pressing his palms to the glass and leaving bony prints, and he said in his booming voice, "We're broke."

No one could respond. Vanessa had steered the ashram to the edge of a cliff. "Yes." Madeleine was the only one to concur.

"We must do something," the guru shouted. "Can't we do something?"

Elise looked as if she wanted to say something, to come up with the answer, but when she opened her mouth, only "What?" came out. Lulu started to cry.

The guru then pronounced one word, which sounded like "Mars." The room was large, and it was hard to understand him because the echo of his voice muffled whatever he pronounced.

"Mars?" Elise asked politely.

"Cars, my child." The guru smiled and tugged on his long white beard.

"What about cars?" Elise said.

"You'd be willing to sell off some cars for a little cash?" Madeleine caught on.

"Yes." The guru took a deep breath. "For cash flow." He was apparently not entirely above material and financial concerns.

"Excuse me, Guru B." Jakarta put her hand in the air. "But your collections in the museum—"

The guru cut her off with a half-raised arm. His wristwatches sparkled. "Yes, they have served as vehicles toward my own transcendence, but I no longer require them. How much are they worth, all totaled?" The guru stared at Elise with his liquid eyes.

"Oh, but, but—" Elise protested.

"Millions." Madeleine was encouraging.

"Okay, then, we're fine for a while." Guru B smiled. "Fine. We survive." He folded his hands on his lap.

A few minutes later, the obi Cassandra waltzed in waving a document in her hand. "We finally found it," she said to Madeleine. "Just like you said we would."

"Great," Madeleine said. "I knew it had to be wherever she was hiding the account books."

"Found what?" I asked.

"The deed to the new tract of land." Cassandra handed the guru the papers. "Vanessa had already purchased ten square miles south of here."

"Ten?" Frog stood up. He looked pale. He stepped over to the table and stood behind the guru.

The guru slowly unfolded the piece of thick paper, and now Madeleine stood next to him, as well. Everyone looked at the page, and those of us who couldn't see it watched the guru's face light up. The guru clapped with excitement. "Ten square miles of gorgeous desert," he said (shouted).

"Desert," Frog muttered. And then Frog looked at a page of vellum that accompanied the deed, a surveyor's map. He realized where this property lay in the desert. "Oh, my God." He looked even more ashen. "Oh, no," he groaned.

"What?" I asked. "What?"

"That new tract of land is practically next door to my ranch!" He couldn't believe it, and I tried to lay a calming hand on his shoulder. A thought instantly occurred to me: when Vanessa introduced herself to Frog, she surely knew that the cult and Frog would someday be neighbors.

Cassandra misread Frog's reaction and thought he was excited. "Howdy, neighbor." She slapped his back.

"We don't have the funds for expansion," Elise said to the guru.

"We will grow someday," Guru B announced with confidence.

"But of course for cash," Frog stepped in, "you'll have to sell it. For the money. Right?"

"No, no, no, child." the guru said, everyone his child. "You can sell cars, but you must never sell land. Land is holy. Cars now, never land."

Then Madeleine spoke. "Actually, Guru B," she counseled, "I've had an idea all morning." It was Madeleine after all who had told Cassandra to look for the deed, Vanessa's little secret that Frog had uncovered. "I'm not sure you realize it, but the pilgrims are a bit edgy. They're quite upset."

"Naturally," the guru admitted.

"The best thing would be if we could find the meteorite. That might restore order."

"It would?" I swallowed. Did I want order to be restored?

"That's silly," Frog grumbled.

"And the press," Madeleine continued, "is pounding on the gate. They're going to write their stories whether you like it or not, and they might as well know the truth." Madeleine was direct. "So why not take control of the situation and hold a press conference?"

The room was still. Frog looked at his rediscovered lover with a wrinkled brow. The journalist was getting involved.

Elise broke in. "The guru has gone into silence. He can't—"

"The time has come to pull Rancho Flora together." Madeleine dramatically argued her case. "Or it will fall apart forever."

"You are wise," the guru decided quickly. "You are saying that I can have a press conference and speak directly to my pilgrims, as well."

"Right." Madeleine folded her arms to wait for a response.

"I like it." The guru smiled.

"I can speak for you," Elise said.

"With all due respect," Madeleine said, "half the point is to have the guru speak himself."

"She is right." The guru nodded. "Very good, very good. The re-porters—they will ask questions?"

"It might get messy," Madeleine admitted, "and you'll have to be prepared to talk about Vanessa."

"Yes," the guru sighed. "But what else will I talk about?"

"The future," Madeleine said. She made it seem like a simple enough assignment. "And when everyone, reporters and pilgrims, want to know what will happen next, you just wave this." Madeleine picked up the deed.

Frog sank into a chair. "No," he muttered, but only I heard him. "The light from an ashram would ruin my sightings."

"Very well, it's done." The guru moved to stand up. He took the deed from Madeleine. Elise and Jakarta helped him stand. "The lecture today will be a press conference. Now we should get some rest." The guru patted Madeleine on the shoulder as he left, two hard and solid pats, and then he was escorted out of the building. The obis all left, too. They felt relieved, relaxed somewhat, because at least a plan of action was in place. A natural order would return in time.

Only Frog, Madeleine, and I were left in the large room. The desk was littered with the flower-scented account books. As soon as the obis had gone, Frog whispered, "Are you crazy?" Madeleine didn't answer him. "I never realized that the tract of land was—was—"

"Oh, c'mon." Madeleine lit a cigarette. "You know that deed is just a symbol. You don't have anything to worry about. The cult has no money. They'll never expand, and people are already leav-ing. The best they could hope for is that the guru opens up the other side of the hill and things become a little more honest around here. And if the guru starts talking to his disciples again, then there's a chance." Madeleine puffed calmly. She had only de-signed the press conference to help the guru boost morale, keep the ashram spiritually afloat. "I wouldn't get worked up about it."

"Worked up?" Frog waved both hands in the air. "How could you have even suggested what you did?"

"I just told you. It's not a big deal."

"Oh, Maddy," Frog groaned. He heard only what he wanted to hear.

I sat in Vanessa's chair and tried now and then to fit in a comment—a "But" or a "Look, guys"—but Madeleine and Frog shot barbs at each other too rapidly.

"What are you doing here anyway?" Frog harpooned her: "I didn't know that journalists helped make up the stories they reported."

"Get off it," Madeleine speared back, "you know that I can't just sit here and not say something."

"You're more than *saying* something, you're taking over."

"What I'm trying to do is inject a little common sense. Lives are at stake. Look, Mr. Frog Reading, you're not mad at me for getting involved, you're mad at yourself."

"Oh, right."

"You're mad at yourself because Vanessa was using you."

"I never fell for her game," Frog protested.

"So what? You're still pissed."

I thought to myself, I don't have to be here—I don't have to listen to this. But I couldn't move.

Frog squinted. "Madeleine, I think you really want to see the goddamned cult take over the desert."

"Right. Maybe I do." Madeleine rolled her eyes.

Frog refused to detect her sarcasm. "And destroy it. You have never understood what was important to me," and the argument tripped down the stairs to a personal level. "You don't care about the desert."

"Selfish, as usual." Madeleine launched a missile. "Just thinking about yourself."

"Yeah, well, you get a kick out of messing things up," Frog fired back. And with this, he remembered I was in the room. He looked at me with a longing face that said in one tearful shake of his head: Why did I come here?—why did she come here, to torture me?—why doesn't anyone appreciate the barren desert?

"I do, other people do," I said out loud. I was mad at him. Why did he always assume that no one else cared about what he cared about?

"What?" Madeleine said angrily.

"Nothing." I shook my head.

"You know, Frog," Madeleine said slowly, "I'm not so sure it wasn't you who stole the meteorite."

"Well, you got me there." Frog smiled. "You're right, Maddy. It was me. I stole the meteorite and I drove it back to my ranch."

"You did?" I was stunned.

"Yes," Frog lied to me. "I took it back to my ranch, which is where I should go now."

Madeleine simply shook her head. She thought of a last word maybe, but puffed out a long and thick stream of cigarette smoke instead.

"Right now," Frog said, "I have a cat to feed." And with that he nodded good-bye to me and left the room.

"I can't believe him sometimes," Madeleine said, frustrated.

"Maybe he didn't steal the meteorite."

"Oh, that's beside the point," Madeleine muttered. She looked at the mess of account books on the glass table. She started to make notes, and I wasn't sure if these were notes to feed into the maw of her article, her book, or if these were notes that would be of use to the guru and the obis in their reconstruction of the ashram. I watched her work, a curl of cigarette smoke delicately, steadily rising from her fingers.

What a dilemma: I had to tell Madeleine the truth, I couldn't stand pretending anymore. I wanted her to know Frog didn't mean what he said—how could he, it was false. But then I knew that if Madeleine discovered that Frog had lied, her anger would only be fueled further. Futility overwhelmed me, but I saw that in a vague way, there was a certain serenity ahead, at least in my mind, if I confessed all that I had hidden.

"You know when I found the meteorite on the secret side of the hill, before it was presented to the guru?" I started.

"Yes, why?"

"Well, it wasn't the first time I'd seen it. I found it with Frog."

Madeleine shrugged. "Great."

"Madeleine, I've been afraid you'd be mad at me and so I didn't tell you this, but . . . I stole the meteorite from the temple. 'Stole' is the wrong word, it was stolen from me—and Frog. But I hid it," I said.

Madeleine was silent, I was sure she was going to lambaste me.

"Sweetheart, I figured that out a while ago," Madeleine said matter-of-factly.

"You did?" It seemed to me that one spent one's life coming out about things people already knew to be true.

"You've talked about everything we've seen and heard and observed here," Madeleine said. "But you were conspicuously quiet about the meteorite disappearance."

"I thought you'd be mad," I said.

"Well, I didn't like the idea at first." Madeleine lit a cigarette from a dying one. She offered me one. As a rule, I didn't smoke, but I felt the need to take one, light it, not really puff, but just hold it between my fingers and let it burn. "I thought you were getting involved in a way you didn't mean to."

"But you're not mad now?" I was confused.

"No," Madeleine said. "It occurred to me that you did know what you were doing."

"I did? Oh, yes, I mean, I guess I did. What was I doing?"

Madeleine didn't answer me at first. Then she said, "Making the world turn. Making people think. You make me think."

I wasn't entirely sure what she meant, but what she said sounded glamorous in a way, so I felt vaguely proud. And then I remembered why I'd finally brought all this out. "Frog lied," I said.

Madeleine just nodded.

"Why?"

"That's Frog," was all she said. I could tell she was injured, though she didn't want to show it.

"Sorry." I tried to match her nonchalance. "Very sorry," I added on.

"Whatever." Madeleine glanced down at the account books.

"But wait." Something occurred to me. "If you knew that I had taken the meteorite, why did you challenge Frog?"

Madeleine didn't look up. In a barely audible whisper, as if this were the most secret truth she'd ever revealed to me, she said, "I wanted to see what he'd say."

A fist hit my stomach. A test had been offered, and Frog had failed. This had probably not been the first time Madeleine set Frog up to see what he'd say.

"Do you think I should return the meteorite to the temple?"

"I can't tell you what to do," she said.

"Why not?"

"Because you hid the fucking thing." Madeleine scratched her brow with the middle finger of the hand holding her cigarette. "And only you know whether to bring it back."

he press conference took the place of a lecture. At the guru's request, the reporters had been allowed inside the ashram hours earlier. Some curious Frescurans joined them. The newcomers wandered openmouthed, awed by the little city even though the pilgrims weren't working this morning and the normal industrious buzz and bustle was absent. Some pilgrims had continued an exodus from Rancho Flora, but the vast majority hung on. Pilgrims, obis, reporters, the handful of Frescurans, the media with their omnipresent cameras, filled the gold-domed temple. Madeleine sat with Matthew and me in the audience. Frog was nowhere to be seen. The mere breath of subdued chatter caused the great hanging panel sporting the guru's outdated portrait to quiver. The petals of benches radiating from the altar at Rancho Flora were in fullest bloom.

The guru played out the drama perfectly. First, a few obis emerged from the rear entrance to the stage, Elise among them. Then, in anticipation of his entrance, flashbulbs went off. Seconds later the guru strolled ever so slowly up to the stage. TV cameras hummed, and I thought all the light would make the guru fall over, but he was steady as he assumed his throne. Vanessa's podium had been removed. Elise stood up to make an introduction, and another obi took the guru's pulse while he surveyed the audience. "Today's lecture," Elise said, "will actually be an opportunity for dialogue, a chance for you to ask Guru B questions, and for him to offer us his wisdom in direct response."

The guru was looking at Madeleine, I could tell. He had located her in the crowd. "Hello," he said, his voice booming.

The crowd stirred. This was the first time almost everyone in the room had heard the guru talk. The shock of immense volume caused all of us to wiggle back in our seats. Even with all the people in the sanctuary to soak up sound, the echo was deafening. I could even feel the wood seat beneath me vibrate. The media's boom mikes propped up over the edge of the stage had to be withdrawn a good foot.

"Due to the extraordinary events of the last day, I will break my silence," the guru projected. "I would like to clear up this unholy mess, so that we can move on with our precious journey. I will say this: as many of you know, Vanessa was my right arm at Rancho Flora, a blue obi, a leader. Yesterday she drifted off the road toward enlightenment. She has left a mismanaged bankbook"—the guru was frank—"and she tried to poison me." Now he bluffed, "She is someone who tried so hard, so desperately to achieve the highest plane, and my children, I tell you from my heart, she came close. Her fall," he thundered, "should be a lesson to us all. The closer one comes to arriving at the golden plane of enlightenment, the farther one will fall if one strays from the single path." There was silence. The guru looked as if he were about to add something. Instead he smiled. "Would anyone like to ask some questions at this point?"

"Is it true, sir, that the ashram faces bankruptcy?" one reporter asked.

The guru responded emphatically, "No, not at all." He was sharp. "The ashram has been wounded, if you will, but with the proper care can be nursed back to health. We still have considerable assets at our disposal. Next. Yes?" I got the feeling that the guru liked this format.

"Are you, sir, on your deathbed as a result of Vanessa's alleged poisoning?"

"I can tell you that I feel quite fit." The guru raised his arms. "And my spiritual vision is pure and clear." He put his arms down. "Next."

A man with a microphone asked, "You had made it a prophecy that Proposition Eight would be answered yes, and it was voted down. How do you explain your forecast not proving true?" A tender issue.

The guru smiled. "I say many things, and they are all true, because I don't know anything but truth. You see, I said"—the guru defended speeches he had not even written—"that our pilgrimages would be advanced by the election, but I did not necessarily mean that the particular worldly outcome would matter. We advance down the narrow path when we overcome challenges and are strengthened. And that was what was won yesterday, a challenge which today we continue to overcome." An evasive answer that was tangled enough to suffice for the moment.

"Do you think"—a man stood up—"that Vanessa could have been controlled if you had intervened in any way? I think so."

The crowd rustled. I turned to see who asked and answered this bold question. It was David. He didn't look as if he expected an answer.

The guru wheezed in response (Elise lurched toward him, another obi tried to measure his pulse, but he brushed them both away). Finally he said, "One pothole can really wreak havoc with your alignment, sending you into the garage for repairs. But the car can be realigned, and the car can be tuned up, a tire change, an overhaul, a nice lube job. The car can be fixed and it can run better than before. Better than before!"

I looked at David, his face grim. Bloated metaphors were a weak deterrent against disillusionment.

A woman, a reporter, took the floor again. "What kind of future do you see for Rancho Flora?"

That was the question the guru had been waiting for. His eyes twinkled. "The future will be magnificent. I can announce today that despite temporary setbacks, we will build a new ashram very soon." He looked out over the audience in such a way that his face matched the wistful but all-knowing gaze of the large portrait above him. "The future will be brilliantly lit by a brilliant sun," the guru boomed, "and I leave you with one last word about survival. We survive, my children"—the guru was in command—"because we know how to build a city in the desert. And we survive because we can destroy the city and rebuild that city at any time. We survive because we *destroy* what is bad and start anew. We survive"— the guru teetered, his words becoming fuzzier and circuitous— "precisely because we can destroy and start all over again." He seemed to be looking for something grander to pronounce, but he fell back onto the same ambiguous proclamation. "We will . . ." The guru's voice trailed off while he searched for something to say. "We will . . ." He looked over to where the meteorite had once sat next to his throne. "We will build a new altar around a meteorite," he pronounced, happy to have landed on something. "So I tell you, my children," he concluded, "we must find the meteorite and build a new altar around it. That's how we will survive."

The hall was silent, the reporters and pilgrims puzzled. Elise allowed a few more questions to be asked, and soon about half of the temple had cleared out. Guru B left the stage. As he was climbing into the backseat of his limousine in back of the temple, a fleet of police cars came rushing up the hill. The sheriff, only entering the ashram for the second time in his life, the second time in less than twelve hours, yelled, "Hold it right there."

The crowd outside stood still, hushed. The crowd still inside the temple tried to figure out what was going on. Madeleine pushed her way through the pilgrims, and other members of the press followed. Cameras recorded everything.

"What's going on?" Elise asked the sheriff, now supported by a team of other policemen and a few familiar immigration officials.

"We have to arrest Guru B," the sheriff said. "I'm sorry."

Arrest? I was shocked. The pilgrims and even the Frescurans and reporters on hand seemed to stagger. No one could utter a word of protest. The guru looked rather amused, however, almost as if he had expected this, almost as if he enjoyed the attention. He simply sat down in the backseat of his limousine and waited while obis battled the police with words. I saw one officer kneel beside Guru B to read him his rights, and it looked more like the holy man was hearing a confession.

"What are the charges?" Madeleine demanded.

"Immigration fraud," the sheriff said. On cue, the immigration bureaucrats formed a line and answered a battery of reporters' questions about the crimes allegedly committed.

"The guru is not a well man." Elise started shouting at the sheriff. "You can't take him away—he needs to be weaned off of the poison."

"We can see to that at the jail." The sheriff tried to calm Elise.

"Can't you just put him under house arrest?" Lulu suggested.

"We don't do that around here, ma'am," an officer said. "Not with felons."

The guru was charged with falsifying visa documents and every other immigration crime imaginable. And after five minutes, the guru stepped out of his limousine and looked downhill at the pilgrims watching and crying, the reporters waving tape recorders, the policemen forming a semicircular barricade. He was on the verge of saying something, but he was suddenly speechless. Finally, he said, "Well, let's go."

"You can't take him away! You can't take him away!" Elise became hysterical. An officer had to hold her back. The crowd started to tangle with the line of officers as the guru was gently and swiftly escorted toward a squad car.

Shuffling unsteadily from his limousine toward the police car, the guru looked as if he might fall. Madeleine and I were up front, and we lurched forward and grabbed the guru's elbows. He was fine. I looked at the guru in the face, and I felt as if someone had died. I could sense his grief, grief he didn't want to let slip out. He hated to appear weak. All I said to Guru B was, "I'm so sorry."

"Sorry?" the guru chuckled. "Don't be sorry," he said to me at one elbow. "Don't be sorry," he said to Madeleine at the other elbow, even though she hadn't expressed this regret. "The traffic of life passes me by," he said to us both. "It has always passed me by, really. From the sidewalk, I'm nothing more than a bystander, you see." And with that the guru was fitted into the backseat of the police car, which parted the crowd of sobbing pilgrims and raced out of Rancho Flora, transporting the guru away from the Buddha-field.

I looked at Madeleine. "*Bystander?*"

An afternoon of confusion followed the guru's arrest. The guru had been taken to the jail in Chiaroscuro, where he would be held without bail (for fear that he'd flee into the countryside), and where he was attended to by a series of doctors who would begin weaning him of any dependencies. However, if he were ever needed at the ashram, if he could ever have been of any use to the pilgrims of Rancho Flora, that time was now. Although in all likelihood there was nothing he or anyone could do to keep the ashram from crumbling. The pilgrims' lives had been torn apart, and many were leaving. Angry, jaded, bitter men and women, some dragging children, each person clutching his few belongings, rushed into the desert, some in jeeps, some on foot. Film crews and reporters were on hand to eat all this up. Their relentless presence in a place once so closed off and private angered many pilgrims. I saw a mauve person try to break one photographer's lens.

Matthew and I wandered the ashram, in our own way trying to sort out the mess. Matthew wanted to find Amy. He thought the atmosphere was getting dangerous, but Amy was nowhere to be found. We hadn't seen her since she walked out of her house yesterday, and now Matthew was worried.

Down by the area where metal huts still stood, a group of maybe twenty pilgrims had gathered. They were about to embark on a trek to Chiaroscuro, where they would hold a vigil outside the jail, get arrested if they had to. They wanted to be where the guru was, because wherever he went had to be safe, holy. They figured that the Buddhafield traveled with the old man. Matthew and I strolled over on the other side of the hill (there were no laws now, anyone could go anywhere), and we saw the once-privileged pilgrims also leaving the ashram, apparently for good. People were stuffing cars with luggage, pottery, whatever they'd brought with them. They escaped fast. And as soon as a house on the once-secret side of the hill had been evacuated, pilgrims who had never dared to go beyond the temple now descended, trying to find anything of value. Pilgrims were acting irrationally, many of them, but those who were leaving were astonishingly pragmatic after years of living in an unreal world. They needed money to survive beyond the palm trees and rainbow gate, so they looted. At the museum, a bunch of pilgrims had to lock arms around the guru's automobile collection. Most of the pilgrims who protected the museum were obis, but elsewhere on the ashram, obis had stripped themselves of their blue sashes. Die-hard obis such as Lulu looked demoted, lost.

As the afternoon turned into evening, as more people fled, it became apparent that confusion would soon give way to chaos. Matthew and I ran into Madeleine, who was wide-eyed, almost child-like about the dissolution of the utopia all around us. She was driving around madly, interviewing, covering the front line. She wouldn't even stop the jeep: we had to jog alongside and jump in. In touring the scene with her, I could see that the majority of pilgrims had not yet left the ashram. Madeleine had observed, and it was not hard to see, that the pilgrims had divided themselves into two camps. We passed circles of arguing pilgrims—not so much a circle, but two opposing lines shouting at one another. The two groups each had apparently interpreted differently the guru's blurry words of wisdom, his concluding speech at the press conference, which now sadly seemed to be his last speech, and which now lingered in the heat of midday with more import than the guru had probably intended. He had encouraged destroying the city and starting all over again, and that vague, metaphorical decree became a mandate for turbulence. He had said that a new altar should be built around the meteorite, and so pilgrims were going to tear the ashram apart until they found it.

The first group of pilgrims had quickly formulated a literal reading and was now carrying out the guru's last order. They acted out of devotion, out of a belief that they fulfilled the guru's wish. These pilgrims set out to destroy Rancho Flora, literally destroy the place, so that they could rebuild, start again. . . . The second group remained levelheaded. They wanted to stop the destruction from getting under way, but they weren't succeeding, because I saw one house in the distance already set on fire, and Madeleine spotted another. But everyone, despite their differences, seemed united in one pursuit. Everyone wanted to find the meteorite—the stone for a new altar—because whoever held it on their side, it seemed, would win whatever it was that was supposed to be won.

Matthew had been riding around with Madeleine and me, but he hopped out of the jeep to try to find Amy again. As he ran away, I suddenly felt vulnerable, and I almost called after him to wait for me. But Madeleine drove off in another direction.

Pilgrims who had been shouting at each other were getting physical. We passed some brawling mauve people, drunk with anger, awkwardly wrestling. It was dark now, and everyone wielded torches or candles, and the pilgrims searching every inch of the ashram for the meteorite were in a hurry, clumsy with the fire. Some pilgrims were breaking windows in their frenzy and accidentally (or maybe intentionally) setting buildings ablaze. The path of destruction was moving uphill toward the temple.

Bedlam erupted, and Madeleine and I found ourselves in the middle. As we drove up the hill, pilgrims came at us, too, swinging pieces of wood. One pilgrim slammed her fist down on our hood so hard I was sure she must have broken a bone. No one seemed to recognize anyone anymore—we were traveling through a zoo of irrational animals. We had to abandon our vehicle and run for cover. Pilgrims fleeing, torching, fighting, digging—there was no end to the chaos, not even the blanket of night could drop down over the desert to dampen the upheaval.

Madeleine and I ran into an empty adobe that seemed safe for the time being. Outside, we saw a brigade of jumpsuits and shovels run by. "The stone, the stone," they were chanting.

"Maybe I should go and get it," I said to Madeleine.

"What? The meteorite? No, don't, Coyote," Madeleine warned. "You'll get ripped apart if you show up with that thing."

"I feel like I caused this mess."

"Oh, please. Please don't be so conceited and self-important."

"What?"

"We all made this happen," she said.

Outside, I saw Frog run by. I yelled out for him, and he managed to hear me above the din. He ran into the house carrying a shovel in one arm, Tycho in the other. Frog eyed Madeleine, and maybe she was infected by the insanity all around us, but she glared at him with the most savage gaze. I could feel her tear him apart.

"I'm going to see what it looks like from the top of the hill." Madeleine excused herself and brushed by Frog without speaking.

"Careful," I shouted after her. I looked at Frog's shovel. "You looking for our meteorite?"

"Yes," he said, "as a matter of fact. Know where I might find it?" he joked. "I'd love to get my hands on it before any of them do."

"Actually, I do know where it is," I confessed. "I hid it."

"You what?" Frog shook his head fiercely. "You?" Then he chortled, "Well, that was a neat trick. Except when most magicians make a lady in the audience disappear, they bring her back so she can watch the rest of the show."

"I was thinking of going and getting it," I admitted.

"I have a jeep and trailer all ready," Frog said. "I want to take it home finally."

Tycho meowed, It's time to go home.

"Madeleine knows that I hid the meteorite," I said.

"Oh," Frog answered quietly.

"She knows you lied to her about taking it from the temple."

"Yes, I suppose she does."

I heard the chorus of pilgrims outside. The stone, the stone. I might as well just let them tear the place apart—who knew what they'd do with the boulder once they got their hands on it? I decided that Frog should carry the meteorite to safety. "Let's go," I said to him.

As we drove out of the ashram, I could see that the riot of pilgrims, armed with shovels and torches, had moved farther uphill toward the temple. We descended through the ashram and crossed the path of destruction. Burning adobes were left behind, signs were overturned, and plots of soil were chopped up everywhere. They just didn't get it. The pilgrims infuriated me—they just didn't get it. The desert was beating them, the desert heat had infiltrated their minds and it was tricking them into self-destruction. Didn't they see? The hot world was cruel and there was only one way to defeat it, and that was to prove yourself larger than the landscape. . . .

"Which way, Coyote?" Frog said loudly. I pointed right, down the highway. I touched his arm when I wanted him to turn off the road. I pointed to the mesquite and cactus and hopped out of the jeep before Frog brought it to a halt.

I looked back at the ashram. Out here the air was serene, you couldn't hear a thing. The desert was playing tricks, pretending that the violence elsewhere was imagined, that the chaos was a figment. The only signs of any trouble were a few bright spots where houses were on fire. Frog and I dug and revealed the meteorite. Frog did most of the work. Tycho pawed the earth, too, eager to do some more excavating.

"Frog, why did you lie to Madeleine about this?" I pointed at the meteorite. I helped Frog lever it up slowly from the pit.

He said, "One, two, three!" And with all our strength we heaved the stone out of the ground.

"Why, Frog?" I persisted. Frog was busy now backing the jeep up to the meteorite. Then we lifted the stone into the trailer. My arms were sore when I released my grip. My whole back ached.

"Frog, you've got to tell me why—" I was insisting.

"Coyote," Frog cut me off, "I just have to get away from here. From her." He was apologetic. He couldn't look me in the eye. "I felt . . . too . . . crushed," he explained, "and she was waving that deed. . . . She knew I was lying. She wanted me to say something to really annoy her." Frog didn't say anything for a minute. Then, softly, "I need to go home now."

My heart skipped a beat. I had nothing to say, I just nodded. Frog and Madeleine were planets, in brief alignment now and then, but still steadfast in their own orbits. Frog claimed to be happiest all alone—that was a myth to put alongside all the other desert myths. I wanted, tried to believe him, but my heart was filled with so much disappointment, more than I could cope with. Not just about him or Madeleine, but about a whole solar system of lonely souls, disparate pilgrims doomed never to come together. Matthew, I thought, we have got to get to another galaxy and fast.

Slowly, pulses of sound, drumming chants, finally reached the desert from the ashram. They grew louder and more frequent. A dust storm was brewing. I couldn't think—my vision was blurry as if I'd overdosed on hot peppers. Suddenly I was sitting on a low branch of the Great Tree and I was counting the cactus plants in the dry basin below me. I had counted them all, an impossible task. I knew the number.

Drifting back to the here and now, I saw Frog about to climb behind the steering wheel. I ran up to him and pulled his elbow. I pushed him gently out of the way, and I didn't answer his confused look. I didn't hear him, if he said anything. Tycho stepped back from the jeep, (he knew what I had to do), and he ran a few yards away from us. When Frog jumped after him, I was able to make a getaway.

There was only one thing to do now. When the sun sets, or for that matter when it rises, anyone who is alone and has stopped to watch is not at all alone. All over the desert the sun's pageant is observed, the hot star melting into the uneven pink hills, and everyone, despite varying views, varying altitudes or varying eyesights, sees the same thing, and perhaps for a split second even thinks the same thought. The moment passes, we all retreat into ourselves. But at least there was a tranquil moment when no one was alone, when anything was possible. There was just one thing to do: I wanted everyone to look at me as if I were the setting sun.

I hopped behind the steering wheel and pressed my boot hard against the gas pedal. I left Frog in a cloud of dust and I zoomed back to the highway, swerved onto the road, and as fast as the jeep with the meteorite in tow could go, I raced, tore back to the ashram.

I flew past the palm trees, through the rainbow gate, and I steered myself straight up Walt Whitman Way. I was going so fast I had no time to scan the burning adobes, though I could see that more of the ashram was on fire now. I sped past the refectory, glass broken, debris everywhere. And I reached the top of the hill where the pilgrims were fighting each other and destroying what was left of the city. Straight ahead I saw the temple, where people with torches were running out. And on either side of me, I saw pilgrims, who cleared out of the road as I sped past.

As I pulled the meteorite uphill, the pilgrims all saw me and the stone. They ceased whatever it was they were doing, and a hush fell as I passed. The pilgrims parted, the armies split off left and right, and they looked at the glorious cosmic chunk of iron, a little dusty having been underground, but a spectacular orb nonetheless, sparkling green in the light of the fires. I ploughed the mob apart, and they looked.

I was practically standing up in the jeep as I drove. I wanted to get all the way to the temple, which as I drew closer, looked gray and about to crumble. Somebody's careless torch had set the great structure on fire. Fists of orange flames shook angrily out of the high clerestory windows.

"Coyote!" I heard a voice. "Coyote!"

I looked over my right shoulder and there was Matthew, running after me, his hand outstretched. He wasn't looking at me, he was looking at what the jeep was headed for, the temple wall. I wanted to reach back to him, and I did, I think—and as I reached, standing up in the jeep, I saw the meteorite bounce out of the trailer and roll backward. I reached back farther, toward Matthew and the boulder, but I, too, fell back. I fell into the backseat, then slipped onto the trailer, and then I tumbled back again out of the trailer. The car continued to roll forward with great speed and momentum. It smashed squarely into one face of the now sooty octagon, and the jeep burst into flames.

I was somersaulting backward when I heard a loud boom, a vibrating spasm of the most devastating seismic order. A massive tremor hurtled through the ashram. A tidal wave of thunder had to travel all the way to distant hills before it could find something large enough to bounce off and echo back. The earth quivered, it seemed, broke apart. I had taken a meteoric dive, and then I lapsed into the dreamy darkness of space.

When I woke up, a gray haze of smoke drenched the hill. I felt someone's hand holding my cheek, Matthew's hand, familiar and soothing, and when I opened my eyes, he pressed a canteen to my lips. "You're insane," he said. "Completely insane. Now you're down to eight lives."

"What happened?" I managed to cough out.

"You tried to drive the jeep into the temple. Which you did, actually." It was Madeleine who said this. Now she crouched down over me.

I lay on my back and looked at my feet. My boots were next to me. I touched a bandage on the back of my head.

"Wiggle your toes," I heard Frog say from behind me, and so I complied. "Oh, you're fine," he decided.

Slowly I sat up, Matthew's arm around me. Frog was sitting on the trailer I had towed, guarding the meteorite, which now straddled the axles. Tycho came over to my side, brushed up against my bare foot, and then sat down.

"There was an explosion." I was trying to recall what I thought had happened only moments ago. The night seemed lighter, though—morning wasn't too far off. I had been out for a while.

"Very unpleasant," Matthew said. "Very loud."

"The temple was on fire," Madeleine explained, "and then it spread downhill all the way to Vanessa's—"

"The TNT?" I guessed.

"The TNT," Matthew said.

Orange, tent-shaped flames had galloped down the other side of the hill, first to the power station, where the fire picked up considerable energy and momentum, enough to move downhill and gut the guru's house and obi dormitory. The house of cards that was the seraglio collapsed. And when the fire tumbled downhill and entered Vanessa's place, when the fire entered her bedroom and crept under her bed with the massive amount of TNT stashed beneath, the explosion broke everything apart.

The once-secret side of the hill was now rubble. The temple fortunately contained much of the fire. It became an enormous oven, a dragon that occasionally breathed out shoots of flames that would run down to and destroy a compound of homes. Structures like the refectory and schoolhouse were gutted. Adobes did not burn, but rather they became kilns, melted somewhat, and swallowed their contents with the blaze. The miracle of the night was that no one was killed, no one was trampled. Many were injured, ill from smoke inhalation, but everyone survived. There was simply no water to extinguish the fire—the planners of Rancho Flora had not considered such widespread destruction. The only building still burning now was the museum, thanks to the gas-filled cars.

"You scared me," Matthew said. I ached all over. I looked all around and I saw pilgrims still trickling out of Rancho Flora. No one was fighting or shouting, everyone just looked dazed. "I still haven't found my sister," Matthew said. "I don't know where she is, so I'm going to go look for her." He had waited for me to wake up, and he was worried.

"I'll come with you." I tried to get up.

Matthew pressed down on my shoulder lightly as he stood up. "You stay here," he ordered. "Don't move. I'm going to find Amy. And then I want you and me to get out of this goddamned desert." I could count on Matthew to surprise me at the oddest moments. "Okay?" He didn't wait for a response and went off.

Now Frog and Madeleine were sitting on either side of me, Tycho still at my feet.

"Sad, when paradise burns." Madeleine was poetic. She must have seen all this before, yet she seemed genuinely moved. I noticed some Frescurans were on hand to help clean up the mess and to help pilgrims move off the ashram. Reporters passed by, and film crews recorded the hazy aftermath. A minor bonfire continued here and there. As the sun rose, a thick haze of smoke consumed the dawn.

We sat for a long time without saying anything. I knew that Madeleine was mad, upset with Frog, but just as she had climbed into his jeep during the fire at the Great Tree, she simply sat next to him now. No one said anything, yet I had the sense that the disaster and loss were so immense that the fight the lovers had endured earlier seemed small by comparison.

Frog went off to find an intact jeep at one point, and he returned with one he could hitch the trailer to. Madeleine paced. She had to conduct interviews, record impressions. Frog announced that he had the trailer all rigged, the meteorite securely strapped down. He was going to take the cat, head home. "I guess this is good-bye," Frog said.

Madeleine searched her pockets for a cigarette. "I don't know, Frog," she sighed. She pointed to the meteorite. "I don't know why you lied about that fucker."

"I don't know either," he replied. "I'm sorry."

Tycho and I looked up at their faces.

"Me, too." Madeleine tried to smile. "I'm glad we got to spend some time together."

"You could visit me before you leave town." Frog shrugged. He found that he had a cigarette in his left pocket, so he handed it to Madeleine.

"Sure," she said. Though we all knew she would not visit him. "I'll be kind of busy, but—" She lit the cigarette instead of finishing the sentence.

"You have a book to write." Frog looked around at the burned-out ashram.

Madeleine hesitated, then nodded. She reached over to give Frog a quick hug, a kiss on the cheek. She looked down at me and said with a nod, I'll see you later on. Then she turned around, put on her sunglasses (though the world was filled with smoke), and disappeared uphill into the rubble. Madeleine was the one to wander away first, off to wrap up her investigation. Frog sat down on the ground next to me and watched her walk away. I saw Madeleine look into an adobe house with a missing roof. I heard her issue a cheerful hello to whoever was inside, and then she stepped in. She drifted away from Frog like an astronaut in a white suit and anonymous helmet cast from a spaceship, first falling slowly into the blackness, then with great speed flying away, until finally only a small dot twinkled in the distance, a star perhaps.

I looked at Frog's wan face. It seemed speckled with black dust. A rain of black ash, like black snow, was filling the air. The sky became populated by an infinite number of tiny flakes that floated over the entire stretch of desert as far as you could see. The fallout drizzled, even sparkled, yet it did not settle on the ground, nor did it linger on us. Instead it remained suspended in the web of thick, suffocating air—it hung just above the ground and our bodies. Everywhere I looked, black flakes bombarded and flattened the already flat desert—here and there a bit of green cactus or red tumbleweed shone through the grayness. The desert seemed to me a lonelier place than ever before. The haze slowly thinned, and the sun blasted forth with unbearable heat. Everything I thought I knew had been covered in an opaque gauze, and when that shroud was slipped away, I wasn't sure where I was—though the place looked familiar, I felt like a foreigner, and for the first time in my life, as if I didn't belong here.

Frog looked lost in his own universe. He was gazing out at the desert as if he expected it might rain ash again soon, as if there would be further fallout, despite skies turning blue, despite a hostile white sun. I could only guess at what he was thinking: the desert was changing—he was growing older—but those weren't the issues. He was not pondering the future. What made Frog straight-lipped, listless, pallid now, was an overwhelming barrage of dizzying black snowflakes, a storm he continued to endure, a rain of silent but unsubtle, unwelcome yet invited, pangs of nostalgia. Fear not of what will be, but rather fear of what was and what might have been.

Matthew appeared out of nowhere, running toward us. "Can you come with me?" he asked when he was close enough. "I found Amy." Breathless, he pulled me up. I wobbled and steadied myself against him.

I said good-bye to Frog and Tycho, but only the cat seemed to notice that I was walking away. Matthew led me down the hill away from the road. I looked back a few moments later, and Frog's jeep with the meteorite in the trailer and his cat in the front seat was snaking its way out of the desert city.

Matthew took me all the way to the edge of the ashram, to the bottom of the hill, to the mystery-filled other side, and as we rounded a corner in the property, he grabbed my arm, as if to prepare me for a ghastly sight. I tensed. He pointed in the air. "Look," he said quietly.

I looked too high, toward the solar panels. The panes of the giant apparatus were smashed into jagged triangles of useless silicon. My eyes started at the top and drifted down—I didn't know what exactly Matthew was pointing at. Then I saw what he looked at, and I gasped.

I followed the shattered panels down until I hit the excavation site, except there was no longer a grid of twine and the few holes of displaced soil where we'd dug out test pits. The explosion last night had performed far greater archaeological feats than we had accomplished with our trowels and picks. The Lost City had been revealed.

At the top of the slope where we'd been digging, I could see walls, fragile and thin mud-brick walls reaching out like bookends, and between arms of walls were a series of separate avalanches, deeper slopes of softer dirt and clay, which the ruins surrounded. We had chiseled away and loosened just enough soil so that when the explosives were ignited, a massive sheet of hard, weathered clay could be broken, and so that the earth could cave in and pour away from the ruins, then tumble down the rest of the hill. Walls and walls stretched for a hundred feet or so along the space where we'd chopped away and beyond the area of our exploration. They were a dark color, but yellow enough to contrast with the brown ground. The sun lit them at a peculiar angle. Beams of light were defined by dust in the air. At first glance, there were the sides of as many as ten to fifteen rooms across. In one spot, a sheer flat surface of wall faced us, indicating a third side, a front. I hugged Matthew. But where was Amy?

We walked closer to the exposed ruins. The adobe dwellings had been built along a cliff, using the natural surface as a back, and they were stacked just as the guru's palace and obis' chambers had been. These homes had been abandoned a thousand years ago maybe, and then centuries of weather shifted the landscape and buried them. Then unknowingly, the ashram used these mounds as the basis for the greater oasis ploughed on top. Closer, you could see the lines of the bricks, the long rectangular bricks of clay and mud. Some special mortar must have been concocted to create walls so firm and so solid that they could survive such a battery of attacks, natural and manmade. Excavation now would determine how much of a city was actually here. Houses conceivably could be wedged along a slope continuing down from where we stood now, beneath us.

"Amy!" Matthew yelled. A faint echo helped. "Ay-mee!"

"Hi," Amy said behind us. She was completely covered in dirt, the same hue as the newly turned-up clay—so I didn't see her at first. "Neat trick." She smiled white teeth.

"Amy? What happened?" I asked.

"The Lost City is now the Found City," she said. An explosion had unabashedly turned Rancho Flora into ruins, and now the ancient ruins didn't have to be so shy, they could surface, they had company. Ruins everywhere.

"After you yelled at me, I ran away. I actually got in a car and started driving away from here," Amy explained. "But I realized I was being silly. I turned around and came back, and I worked all through the night. At one point, I happened to whack the ground with my pick, and then boom! I thought I had hit a mine, but I realized that if I had, I wouldn't be thinking about it. I found myself falling over backwards, totally swallowed up in dirt." Amy pointed to the bottom of the hill where she had fallen.

"You're lucky you weren't hurt," I said.

"I actually was a bit out of it for a while." I pictured her somersaulting into unconsciousness. "There was too much dust and smoke to tell what had happened right away. But then I could look up and see this marvelous place. I'm so excited." Amy hugged me and then her brother. Then we, too, were covered in the beige dirt that had been trapped amid ancient city walls. "Now I've been digging out one room." Amy had wasted no time. She pointed to the farthest reach of the ruins. I could see a more defined house where she pointed. "Come look."

Amy led Matthew and me through the ruins to reach the area where she had been working. As we walked in her path, we fell down, and at one point, I stepped into a spot and sank into soft dirt that reached up to my knees. Matthew slipped somewhere else, and falling, he grabbed on to me, but I fell, too. Amy wove through the various rooms, and for a minute, I felt as if she were a realtor. After all, this was our city, the place I'd imagined as our future home. Finally, we reached the most renovated of all the apartments in the Lost City, and Amy lectured about the space. She ran her long fingers along a wall and said something about the way the ancient settlers had spaced adobe bricks far enough apart to allow for flexibility and shock absorption. Amy talked about all the work ahead.

I no longer imagined living here. It was a place of the past. Over here, an outcast tribe had mined and polished turquoise. Over there, around the hill, another outcast tribe had mined for something else. Silently I stared at the array of ancient dwellings, the rough, reddish surfaces of mud bricks that seemed to possess a mystery far beyond my grasp right now. All I could do for the moment was ponder the haphazard course of things in the desert. Cities rose, cities fell. Cities were swept over in clay, cities were reborn.

rom a distance, the ancient ruins looked like a city being constructed, not one being uncovered. The maize-colored walls slowly emerged as Amy and an army of novice archaeologists each day revealed one more room until a vast expanse of cliff dwellings rose from obscurity. Squat and roofless apartments were piled on top of each other to form a V-shaped complex that lay like a quilt over the carved-out slope. Some of these adobe cabins even had holes for windows and doors. In the two weeks following the explosion, fifty mauve people joined Amy's project. Amy found herself consoling disillusioned pilgrims by handing out picks and shovels. Everyone was on alert for more than just walls, and the excavation had to proceed at a careful pace. Indeed, some pottery and a few bone fragments (possibly human, possibly bovine) had been discovered. A few more caches of turquoise were turned up. When you walked closer to the Lost City, you heard a peculiar sound, a chink, like someone patting the back of a spoon against a stone. And that was how I envisioned Amy when Matthew and I left her at the dig, tapping a spoon against a rock.

One afternoon we came to talk to her, but she could not be interrupted now, and our vague good-byes (we weren't sure when we were leaving), had to be conducted while Amy worked. She was using a refectory serving spoon to dig away at a tapered urn lodged in the corner of an exposed room. In the back of this room was a beehive-shaped crawl space dug into the side of the hill, the walls of which were fortified with mud plaster and painted black. Faint etchings of deers and rabbits could be traced with a flashlight.

"I have to be careful," Amy explained, "because if I just pull this piece out"—she pointed to the half-submerged, zigzag-painted vessel—"I not only might break the clay, I might cause this wall to cave in on us."

Matthew and I leaned against the four-foot-high wall that the urn was pressed against. Slowly, to the tune of the spoon chinking against the clay, Amy was able to remove the urn. Though it was already cracked into three pieces, it stood ten inches high. It lacked a bit of the brim, but according to Amy was valuable because of the ruddy pigment preserved on its exterior. Amy stood up, dirt smudged all over her cheeks and elbows. She rewound her amber ponytail, scratched her wrist against her cheek, and inspected the urn. "Not bad," she said, proud of her find. With what looked to be a pastry brush, she delicately moved away some excess dirt. "Not bad."

So that was how we left her. Amy, aided by dozens of helpers, woke a thousand-year-old city out of hibernation. She delved into the past, and when she trained pilgrims looking for something to do and something to believe in, she unwittingly let a cult form around her—a new cult that fashioned its rituals around the digging. A cult of men and women whose immediate desire was that this dig last forever, because if it ended, they would be forced to confront more vacant despair than they could manage. At night everyone sat around a bonfire and played cards (with a visible deck) and speculated about the ancient tribe that had inhabited this city. History embellished by interpolation formed a new religion. People made up stories, but no one dared answer the one obvious question about the Lost City, how it came to be lost, in the same way that discussion of the completely disbanded ashram was also taboo.

Two weeks passed and most of the pilgrims left Rancho Flora. Only looters and squatters resided on the secret side of the hill. Some of the imported temporary pilgrims who had made it back after the election moved from their metal huts uphill to the burned-out adobes. A group of seventy or so mauve people lingered a little longer, then set out for various points in the globe, many to Greece, some to Indonesia, where for no particular reason they expected the guru would arrive someday to found a new ashram.

The guru was charged with immigration fraud, and the prosecutors wanted to try to deport him as soon as possible. The widespread belief among immigration people was that you had to get rid of a cult leader swiftly to avoid a riot among disciples—and actually, a group of twenty pilgrims was arrested when they stormed the jail to rescue Guru B. Elise was among them. But the guru stayed in jail and received medical treatment and would in all likelihood be booted from the United States before the end of the month.

As for Vanessa—she was discussed often by Frescurans in the Sunflower Lives (renamed the Sunflower Café when the ice cream parlor folded), who were eager to find a place for her next to the dark-haired bandit in an expanding mythology. There were so many stories to tell now. Vanessa was blamed for the burning of the Great Tree as well as the destruction of the ashram (though neither could directly be ascribed to her). Vanessa herself was also in jail, awaiting trial on charges of conspiracy to commit murder. Each week she was arraigned for something new, one fraud or another, election or immigration, and she was destined for a long sojourn through the justice system. I heard a report that she had angered the police one day when her jail door was accidentally left unlocked. Vanessa wandered into the office area, sized up the filing system, and decided to shuffle all the folders in file cabinets according to her own design. She probably thought her organizational talent would be appreciated, but it was not. After a short while, the newspapers and television lost interest in the legal maze. They waited to report on some future verdict months, probably years, away.

Frog had retreated back into his hermitage, and he never returned to what was left of Rancho Flora. He didn't see Madeleine again before she left the desert. He did what he was practiced at doing—he made a complete break with everyone and everything and dashed away in an abrupt getaway. I went to visit him once before we left. I drove out in Matthew's car (an act as satisfying as wearing one of his shirts). When I arrived at Rancho Fantasy Eccle, no one was in the house. I strolled through the palatial rooms, but I couldn't find Frog anywhere. I wandered down to the observatory, and at the foot of the telescope, Tycho was on his back, breathing lightly, extending a paw aimlessly toward some dream of a lizard. He woke up and rolled onto his stomach, but I soon had him purring back into a late-afternoon siesta. Cats led a pleasant life, and cat-dom would always provide me a nice haven from the exhausting world of fires and explosions, but lately I had less of a need to escape. I knew the cat lurked inside, that was enough.

The new meteorite dominated the lab. The monolith looked as grim and austere as ever, but now it seemed more alien than when it decorated the dais of the temple. Frog had apparently exposed a tiny cross section, and so a fragment lay on a table, green flecks glimmering in the diminishing light of the afternoon.

I looked outside and I made the mistake of putting my hand on a doorframe, which had just been painted, and so my palm was instantly coated in a turquoise gloss. I walked over to the ridge, surveyed the desert, and saw Frog running toward me. He jogged his way into the end of a run, finishing with a large circle. A shadow of his body cast a second hand, and as he moved, the shadow swept the mesquite shrubs like a giant clock. Frog bolted up the hill to greet me. "Hello," he panted. He pulled back his hair and wiped the sweat from his brow. "Matthew with you?"

"No. But we're heading out soon," I said.

"Where?"

"Not sure," I said. "Out of the desert anyway."

Frog indicated that I should follow him back into his house. We had never spent much time in his living room—it was like a sanctuary for silent thought, not for conversation—but Frog seemed eager to play host. He even shared a pitcher of lemonade and beer with me, skipping his tequila for the old concoction. We sank back into the cracked leather couches and drank from mugs with worn brims.

"You'll be back?" Frog asked.

"Of course."

"Okay." Frog nodded approvingly. "Matthew, too?"

"Of course."

We discussed the events of the past months, Frog doing all the talking. Not once, however, did he mention Madeleine. Nevertheless, I brought her up. "Will you ever see Madeleine again?"

Frog shrugged. "Sure."

"Anytime soon?" I asked.

Frog ignored me. "I had an odd dream last night."

Almost on cue, since the dream concerned him, Tycho appeared in the living room. He lumbered in, stretched, and collapsed to the floor. Frog had dreamed that he had woken up out of deep sleep to get a drink of water, and as he stepped out of bed, his foot hit something soft and furry. The cat, of course. But not exactly. It was just the fur suit.

"And I thought, this is sweet," Frog chuckled, "the little person is wandering around in the night. He got out of his little fur suit. So I walked around the house, looking for the little person minus the fur. I couldn't find him, and I worried that maybe he would walk into the desert and maybe he would get lost." Frog's hand was clenched. The story mattered. "I decided I would not go back to sleep, and I opened all the doors and windows just in case the little person needed to find his way back inside." All doors and windows at Frog's were still open. "I fell asleep here, on the couch, and then I woke up when Tycho crawled over my leg."

"The little person got back into his fur suit okay," I suggested.

"I expect so." Frog picked the cat up off the floor. Tycho was groggy, and he blinked slowly, like an old man. Then he thought of a place he'd rather be, and he hopped into the bedroom. I don't think Frog really ever wanted to meet the little person, know who he was—he just wanted to know that he was there, safe but not trapped.

"The meteorite looks good," I said.

Frog nodded. "I want you to take it with you."

"You're kidding."

"You should sell it, get some cash for your travels."

"That's quite generous, but I could never sell it," I said. I never could. "Besides, don't you need to make your tests—"

"I've got what I need," Frog said. He paused, hesitated, then admitted, "I just don't want it around, not even for a day. I just don't."

"Okay," I said. If the rock made him sad, I could take it away for him.

Frog went on doing what Frog had done for years. All alone, he hunted meteorites. I imagined visiting him years from now, and I was sure I'd find him here, unchanged, hunched over his telescope. But somehow, this was not a lofty, pleasant daydream. Seeing him again, catching up, sure, that would be fun—but there was something blue about the scene. He had made his return to his ranch seem easy, but I couldn't help but think that his life would never be quite the same simple routine—now a taunting memory of this summer would at times unexpectedly invade. Probably that's how it always had been, and now I just understood his struggle.

Back at Rancho Flora, Madeleine wrote her articles. She worked steadily in the place where we had lived, which hadn't burned, and at night, since there was no longer any electricity, she wrote by candlelight. Her plan was to finish a first installment, mail it to *The Friscan*, and then write two more. Then she'd return to the city where she had a house. She would spend the winter months high up in the mountains and write a book.

"What will you call it?" I asked.

"I'm lousy at titles," Madeleine said.

"What will it be about?"

"What does that mean?" Madeleine laughed. "You were here, you know perfectly well what it's about." In the candlelight, shadows made her cheekbones stand out more, and her eyes were smaller and more deeply set.

"What I'm asking, I guess, is how you will depict the pilgrims."

"What are you really asking?"

"Are you going to say that these were people who took some ill-spent vacation from life, who journeyed to the middle of nowhere only to come to their senses and return to civilization?"

"Oh, be real."

"I guess you won't say that, then." I felt a little silly.

"A utopia cracked," Madeleine said.

"Frog gave me the meteorite." I changed the subject.

"That was nice."

"You can tell him it was nice when you see him next," I said.

"Well, that probably won't be for a while."

I knew that was what she would say, but I must have looked a little misty eyed. Madeleine let her chin rest between her thumb and forefinger. She looked at me for a while without saying anything. Then she said, sighing, "I told you that even when you're with someone in the desert, you're still lonely. And that can make you crazy." She was right, she was always right, and that was why Matthew and I were abandoning this world for a while.

I flipped through finished pages of Madeleine's manuscript. "Where will you go next?"

"There are a number of possibilities." Madeleine started to rattle off exotic and distant places, all foreign, mostly South American.

"I thought you were going to cover the domestic scene," I said.

"Well, I'm itching to go abroad." Madeleine laughed at herself. "Can't stay here too long, I guess."

I tried to be happy for Madeleine the way I tried to be happy for Frog. He was a hermit, and she was a nomad. In the way that Frog had to hide out on his dusty ranch, Madeleine could not stay in one place. In the way that Frog's exile was not a choice but rather a life-style of survival, Madeleine knew that if she stayed somewhere too long she would inevitably meet up with all the pain she successfully eluded. She had to keep going and except for the purposes of historical comparison, avoid retrospect.

Madeleine and I shared a common, tangled story. I could already look back on this time spent with her with a peculiar fondness and know that it was in Madeleine's company that I started to see the desert, the world differently. It was as if before our odyssey I was able to see things, but if I had to describe what I saw to anyone, I would have failed horribly. Before, I only possessed vision, but now I could add voice.

Tired blue eyes focused on me, and late at night, one candle fueled only by a last puddle of liquid wax, one a little taller, Madeleine said, "I hope you'll come and visit me."

"Of course."

"Maybe tag along with me somewhere."

"Definitely." The thought of venturing to some covert cove of the globe with Madeleine excited me.

"Matthew, too. You guys will have to come up for a holiday."

"That would be fun," I agreed.

We watched the smaller candle gag and burn out. In the dim light of the remaining flame, Madeleine squinted and broke the serene moment with, "Now get out."

"What?" I was startled.

"I have work to do." Madeleine turned to her typewriter and started to tap away.

"Yes, you do." I looked at the candle still going. She had two inches of wax left before she could go to sleep.

So one day Matthew and I left the desert, the meteorite in tow. We drove through Frescura. The town looked the same as it did before the cult had invaded: the wide and dusty streets of low adobes, the bold statement of the whitewashed cross higher than anything else, and the potent white sun, now descending one more time. At night, the infinite glitter of stars would provide entertainment. Then, another day. There were cities that came and went, like the ancient city now exhumed, like Rancho Flora. And then there were places like Frescura, which suffered slow mutation, but which went essentially unchanged as the time line grew longer. What was it that kept things the same? Some sweet ingredient, the lemonade in the beer.

We drove out of Frescura. Without letting Matthew see what I was doing, I tried to remove the wad of love letters that I had stuffed into my boot and then place them into the glove compartment of his car. When I opened the metal door, a tangled ball of knotted strings fell out, and I made a mess. "What are those?" Matthew had his eyes on the road but saw the letters peripherally.

"Love letters Madeleine wrote to Frog."

"How did you get them?"

"I prowled."

"Read one," Matthew said.

There seemed to be more in the stack than there had been when I first went through them. I shut the glove compartment and left the letters inside with the strings.

"You're not going to read one?" Matthew had his eyes on the road, but he kept glancing over at me. "No?"

"Maybe later," I decided. I hoped that all love sagas did not bounce around the way Madeleine and Frog's story did. I did not want to reread the letters because I was afraid of their contents. I was afraid, too, to look back at all that had happened this summer, afraid that if I retreated to the clarity and honesty of hindsight, I might lose trust in the extravagancies of my imagination. Right now, all I wanted to do was sink back and enjoy this mapless ride. I watched Matthew's dark eyes follow the road.

The sun set behind us, and when the evening had become black enough, I looked over my shoulder, back at the lonely desert. I spotted a momentary speck of bright light low in the sky. It traveled in a hurried arc and burned a blue, effervescent trail that vanished an instant later. I followed the falling star as long as I could, I tracked the meteor, at once so frivolous and so dire. And then I looked back at the meteorite we were carrying. I realized that there was a vital errand I had overlooked before leaving the desert, something that could not remain undone.

"Turn around," I ordered Matthew.

"What? To go where?"

"We have to run a vital errand. Okay?"

"Sure." Matthew steered the car into a U-turn. "How far?"

"I'll let you know," I said.

We drove back through Frescura, back along the route to the ashram. Matthew never questioned me, and by the time we reached the spot where the Great Tree had stood, I knew that he had read my mind. He stopped, parked the car on the edge of the highway, and I had not even told him that this was where I wanted to come.

Without conversation, we removed the straps securing the meteorite to the trailer. Slowly we lifted the fallen star and carried it to where a tree trunk had been replaced by a pile of ashes. The ashes swelled somewhat as we lowered the heavy sphere, but they did not engulf it, they ebbed back. The meteorite did not stand as tall as the Great Tree did when it had ruled, but stone was less vulnerable than wood, and the miniature planet glowed at night. We abandoned the meteorite there and flew away, resumed our journey. Tomorrow someone might pass by the new monument and maybe stop long enough to tell a story.

We drove up to once distant hills, over the haunches of the perpetually sleeping beasts, and then beyond.